D1454051

THESE TREACHEROUS TIDES

ODDER STILL

D.N. BRYN

ODDER STILL

Printed in the United States of America
First Printing, 2022

Print (paperback) 978-1-952667-76-3
Print (hardcover) 978-1-952667-75-6
Ebook 978-1-952667-74-9

For information about purchasing and permissions, contact D.N. Bryn at dnbryn@gmail.com

www.DNBryn.com

Edited by Chih Wang with CYW Editing.
Cover design by Laya Rose.
Published with The Kraken Collective.

This work is fictitious and any resemblance to real life persons or places is purely coincidental. If you or a loved one suffers from depression or alcoholism, please avoid mind-melding parasites and seek professional.

Kraken
Collective

THESE TREACHEROUS TIDES SERIES BOOKS

This book contains numerous instances of alcohol consumption and fantasy violence. For full *content notes*, please turn to the back of the book.

An appendix of names can also be found there.

To anyone who struggled with their mental health in silence,
and found the courage to reach out.
You are not alone.

And to my cats: past, present, and future.

CHAPTER ONE

the other voice

We are all a complement of things:
of wants, of needs, of memories.
Past and future built into a single moment.
We are many made one.

THE PARASITE FUSED TO my neck appears dormant.

Parasite.

That's the best word for the immortal, fungal creature my homeland calls ancients. When Lilias chained me here, she rattled off her own name for it—an aurora. The pretty term slips in and out of her conversation as she sits at the wall phone beside this little house's curtained window, absently tapping the knife at her hip. Her gaze bounces to me, eyes fixing on the parasite like she's imagining what it might look like severed from my neck. Or perhaps what my neck might look like severed from my body.

But I fear the mess of black that clings to me like a second skin more than I fear my old blackmailer turned kidnapper. She's mortal, predictable: all anger and impulse and ambition. This parasite, on the other hand, has already defied everything known of its kind. When Lilias first claimed it as her pet, weeks ago and hundreds of miles south, it should have done as every other aurora has and latched to a nonsentient host to quietly begin producing the ignits our societies use as fuel. Instead, it decided to cling to me: a human. And for now, it only clings, not trying to wind itself into my body and seize control of it the way the creatures do to their usual hosts. Not yet, anyway.

I just have to remove it before then.

Somehow.

I give my chain an experimental tug. The hearth it's locked to holds firm, and my cuffs slide across the raw spot where they've rubbed through my fishnet gloves. The red sores make the skin around them look a dustier brown by contrast, as though the warm undertones are being drawn out.

The sight of them makes me crave the pop of a cork and the slosh of wine drunk directly from the bottle. Everything about this situation does. After the nauseous, anxious hell that was my first week in Lilias's brig, maybe I should be glad to be rid of the built-up alcohol in my system, but right now I would eagerly trade my health for the joyous release of a long drink and a good buzz.

Lilias glances up from her lopsided stool. The frizz of her bright orange hair swirls a little, barely visible in the gloomy morning light. She twirls the telephone cord around one finger like she might yank it in frustration.

"I don't care if we have to kill him in order to remove it," she hisses into the box. "I did not spend a whole damn year traipsing across the South to abandon this just because you're squeamish. Besides, he's a worthless recluse I set up as a cartel figurehead in Manduka when I realized he knew the region well enough to find me an aurora, and even they didn't want him. You're the one who said a single decent life is nothing if the population suffers, and this fool's life was, at best, a wreck of his own making."

My own making, my ass.

My mother's early death was not my own making. The

way her homeland, the Murk, rejected me was not my own making. Neither was Lilias bursting in, making me work for her by threatening the humble, rural life I had scrounged for myself just beyond the Murk's edges, nor the chaos and betrayal that followed. The way I tore the parasite from its home as a bargaining chip to let me return to mine . . . that *was* my fault, even if it had been on Lilias's orders.

A lot of good it did, now that the very thing Lilias wanted from me is stuck to my neck.

The rap, rap, rap of her nails fills the quiet.

"Fine, I'll come to Maraheem," she snaps. "But I'm leaving him in Falcre for now—he's safer here at my brother's house. I'll return for him once everything's arranged." She slams the receiver down so hard the whole phone box creaks, her cheeks aflame beneath her freckles.

I give her a smile that's all teeth. "Trouble?"

Lilias curls her lip. "Fuck yourself, Rubem."

"This is your brother's house, then? Shame he'll never be coming back for it." It's a terrible sort of consolation, knowing that if I have no one, at least she's in a similar boat.

She storms toward me. Her fist rises. If I dodge, she'll throw two in its place. I take the punch across my cheekbone. Beneath the aching black and white stars, the door opens and shuts again.

I let my pain stoke the tiny fire in my chest, making it sharp and bright: get rid of the parasite, get home, never get mixed up in anything ever again. The thought seems to pulse through my face along with the throbbing. My neck twitches.

The parasite warms, its rock-hard exterior going soft as silk. My heart slams into my throat, and I twist my head, peeling back the dirty fabric of my collar. A rainbow gleams across the parasite's black form.

It brings a flicker of hope. If the creature is finally awake, then maybe, just maybe, I can nudge it free of my skin. Maybe what I've been calling a parasite has been as trapped as I, awaiting its chance to escape with no Lilias to claim it. I prod it gently, trying to push the lip of it up.

Its dark, rainbow-strewn body peels back. It feels weak beneath my touch, each action shaky. The colors dancing along its body flicker.

"Hold on there, little friend. You can do this," I mutter at the parasite, employing the offhanded tone I take with my pet crocodile, and apply more pressure, trying to tug it away by force.

It seizes up, and its temperature jumps between scorching and freezing, as though I've short-circuited it. I let it go. It calms, becoming a subtle warmth against my skin, its colors faded but not gone. I feel as worn as the creature looks, but I force my shoulders to relax, releasing the tension that has built in my collarbones.

"What do you need, hmm? How can I help?" I keep my voice composed, but my heart wants to scream until the windows of this small house shatter.

It brushes against my skin, a touch I feel all the way into my bones, as though it's prodding the place where my despondency lives. No words come from it, nothing I can discern as speech, but there's a twinge of desire I know from every creature I've saved, that aura of desperation, of hopeless, exhausted need. After everything I've been through, all the betrayal and abandonment, I should be skeptical of this creature, this *parasite*. It's no animal—I can't apply to it the simple laws of trust that my pets follow. But if there's a creature in need of my help, how can I say no?

As though the thought opens a chink in my defenses, the parasite leaps in. Its presence turns intimate, like a foreign tissue wrapping around my organs, a rock thrown into my river, an alien leaf in my canopy. My energy snaps and wanes. A rush of dizziness turns my vision blotchy, and the fever beneath the parasite rages again.

I scream.

The parasite unravels two tendrils from its body, long and flexible. They lunge for my wrist cuffs and take hold. I yank my hands toward my lap, but the parasite's touch is like a vise.

"Now, now see here, we don't even have a safe word." I give a faint laugh, but the crude cover-up for my despair holds no humor.

The parasite's tendril arms skulk along my cuffs, and it slides into the locks. A pulse runs through the creature's entire body. The lock clicks open.

I stare at it, caught in the pounding of my heart and the slow retreat of the parasite's tendrils back into its body. The flourish of color within it fades. My vision rights itself, my fatigue trickling away. The cuffs fall from my wrists and clatter on the floor. This time when I touch the parasite, there's awe in my fingertips—awe in the proper sense: the kind of fear that blooms bright and settles like a blanket.

"I feel as though I should thank you, but really, we're not at that point in our relationship yet," I mutter, releasing some of my dread into the brittle words.

The parasite hasn't left me. It hasn't left my skin, and it hasn't left my mind either. Its existence sits there like a shadow in my periphery.

An odd spark of frustration tickles my chest, followed by a memory three decades old, the voice of my mother whispering me away from danger: *Go, Ruby. Run.*

What the fuck.

But the recollection still springs me into motion. I set my chains to the side, pull my feet under me, and creep toward the door. My legs tingle from lack of use, but I move with the same uncanny silence that's plagued me all my life. The wood doesn't creak beneath me, and the beads ornamenting my braids slip soundlessly by each other. My dark clothes don't even rustle.

I snatch Lilias's discarded flask off the stool.

No hesitation: I down the whiskey in one go. It burns my mouth, and I cringe as it hits my throat, but it's better than nothing. For a few minutes, the world will look a bit brighter, my future a bit kinder. I need that right now, with my nerves turning my melancholy into anxiety and back again, like some terrible cycle that digs deeper into my chest with each round.

Another tinge of foreign frustration fires me up to the front door. I smack the parasite, resulting only in a flicker of pain that runs down my entire spinal column. But it's right: I have to get out of here. I have to get out of here and find someone who can pull the parasite out of *me*. Cautiously, I slip outside.

My hooded trek here in the early morning couldn't have prepared me for this. Lilias must have dragged me hundreds of miles north of the Murk—thousands, perhaps. This foreign sky stretches too wide and vacant and grey after my lifetime of thick, green canopies; of blazing sunlight and monsoon darkness. It stares down onto a tiered, cobblestoned town surrounded by green hills and a wide bay. The whole place looks entirely uninhabited. A sharp breeze blows a mud-matted flier past me and whips salt through my hair. The swish of the paper against the street devolves into a silence so deep I can taste it.

Four streets below, the steep hillside turns into a jetty. I spot Lilias there, far enough away that her body is a pale blur as she pulls off her clothing and dives into the bay. I stand, frozen. She fails to reappear. Maraheem, she'd said— she was going to a place called Maraheem. Maybe it's some kind of afterlife for the drowned. But the idea that she might be able to hold her breath long enough to swim to the pair of fishing boats just off the coast is far less preposterous. And far less funny.

I follow the downward curve of the road, each step as quiet as the abandoned town. My path twists and turns toward the sea; elegant, cobblestoned bridges and tight, tunneling underpasses sprouting between the grey-stone buildings. The sign for the inn hangs lopsided. Stacked furniture huddles beneath sheets, some making piles so human I flinch at the sight.

My fingers ache with tension, and I flip Lilias's empty flask into the air as I walk. It's not as light as a coin nor as finely weighted as a pocketknife. On the fifth toss it slips between my fishnet-gloved palms and clatters across the empty street. Nothing else moves. No signs of life whatsoever.

I retrieve the flask and slip it in my pocket. Tucking my hands into my thin vest for warmth, I turn down an underpass. Papers hang on one side—advertisements, notices, a few warnings—but two specific fliers dominate them. The first must have once had vibrant colors, with the phrase *Maraheem has never been brighter* bolded across the top. The same Maraheem where Lilias is heading. The second flier is a symbol of a skull and crossbones behind a single word: *contaminated.*

It makes my wind-chilled skin feel sweaty. I rub my hands on my shirt in a vain attempt to relieve the sensation. As I keep moving, I pick out other contamination signs on the open streets, along with more faded-out fliers in the shape of the Maraheem one. Three distinct versions arise, each more aggressive than the last: *Jobs with forward momentum for all,* and *Don't miss out on the power of an ignation-fueled society,* and finally, *Come while you still can.* That must have ended with the most hostile motivation for the townspeople to move—the threat of contamination. All of the fliers twist now on the ocean breeze, the only ghosts of this forgotten, corpseless town.

The parasite tingles eerily against my neck.

Deep in a stairwell, shielded from wind and rain, I find a brighter, cleaner version of the final Maraheem poster—one so fresh I can almost make out the full text. The word *aurora* catches my eye, paired with an indication of research and a business named Findlay Incorporated. Someone in Maraheem knows about the auroras on a deeper level than I do. If I can avoid Lilias and find this Findlay Inc.—if she isn't also looking for them—maybe they can help me.

I step out of the stairwell onto a boardwalk rimmed by abandoned shops and looking out at a little beach. A large seal bobs in the swallows, black spots pebbling its grey coat. It scuffles onto the sand. Its whiskers rustle and its head lifts, revealing a gleam of metal in the folds beneath its neck: a brooch like the one Lilias never takes off. A rainbow glow swirls through the brooch's silver curves, almost identical to the way the parasite shines.

The parasite stirs against my neck, focusing on that rainbow light so firmly that I can't look away. My body turns toward the seal. I fight the motion as soon as I make it, a twinge of panic coursing through me. But the parasite's interest in the brooch overwhelms my alarm, spilling into me, through me, until I'm just as intrigued as it is.

Without meaning to, I leap from the boardwalk.

I cross the beach, each stir of the sand beneath my feet making no sound. The animal seems not to notice my approach. Up close, I can see the differences in its brooch's design, a crown where Lilias's curls like flower petals. It continues to radiate an aurora-like glow, casting a shifting spectrum of color against the seal's fur.

I feel the parasite's confusion well. It burns against my neck, and its desire sweeps through me. I have to see that brooch up close. I have to hold it. I have to—

No, no I don't.

But before I can stop myself, I'm tackling the seal, snatching its brooch away. With the gleaming jewelry in my hands, the odd emotions fade. My arms shake and my stomach turns. Did I just—did *the parasite* just—

The seal releases a startled bark, and ripples of color shoot along the brooch like an electric shock, mirrored by a similar storm that rolls over the animal. Fur swirls off it, skin sinking inward and legs spilling out, until there's a chubby human in its place. Or, perhaps more accurately, the seal *is* a human. A stunned human staring vaguely toward me with cloud-grey eyes that don't quite focus. Freckles coat his face, and his red hair flares back from his forehead in waves that curl up around his ears.

"Well." I swallow. "That wasn't what I expected."

CHAPTER TWO

no-man's lander

Multitudes within us, multitudes at war.
Questions battling for answers
with consequences we can scarcely afford.
Bloody compromises beneath torn banners.
Only ever ourselves to settle the score.

NOTHING IN THIS DAMNED North makes sense.

The once-seal yelps, a human sound this time, and shuffles away from me, all bare skin over plump curves. The freckles smothering his neck and shoulders end there, leaving him a glowing white in all but the two small scars beneath his nipples. He jerks his legs up, blocking his chest from view.

"Who goes there? Speak up!" A tenacious sort of delicacy radiates from him, as though he will force the world to accommodate his fragility and not the other way around, a glass sharpened to a perfect point. He stares somewhere past my shoulder, his gaze so distant that his eyesight must be terribly poor. "My family is of the big seven! If you wish to retain your life, you'd best give me that coat back."

I grimace at the way he says it, as though I ought to have known that already and be kneeling at his feet. No person or household should have the power and wealth to wield their very existence like a weapon. Particularly when a simple *please* would have done the trick.

I flick his brooch back and forth as the stories of the North snap into place. "You're a selkie," I say. "I always thought they were a kind of mer."

"Do I look like a mer to you?" His blind stare goes straight through me, and his fine voice is a knife's edge compared to the whiskey tune of my own.

I do look at him, my attention catching on his defined, auburn eyebrows and soft lips and the curve of his heavyset shoulders. I hastily redirect my focus to other parts of the present moment, where a parasite slowly leaches deeper into my body. Where Lilias surely still hunts me down. Where the only thing I want is to return to my pets and my no-man's land and my heritage of none.

My fingers lift instinctively to the side of my neck. I slam them back down before they can graze the parasite.

"Sorry," I say. "As I just poorly demonstrated, I don't have much knowledge of this region. I have a few questions, actually, if you don't mind."

"And I have priorities, ones which include, in a very particular order, my coat, my clothes, and an important meeting with an equally important corporation head, and only *then* potentially answering the questions of random foreigners," he replies. "So, if you'd be so kind as to hand me back my coat now—the brooch, if you ken."

"It's how you shape-shift?" I look at the device a bit more warily as I transfer it between my fingers, the silver, in its almost liquid-like crown pattern, glowing against my dark skin. It taunts me with the option to leave my human life behind. To escape myself, and the repetitive, leeching emptiness that tries to steal away my time and energy. Or to realize that no matter how I change, that this cycle of depression will follow me.

"Transform, not shape-shift. Like certain small groups of

near-humans, selkies possess a secondary set of genetics that the energy emitted by the brooch can activate. Which is why I'll be needing it back."

"Maybe I don't want to hand it over until my questions have been answered."

"That sounds like a threat."

"A warning."

"Why, don't tease, you'll get my hopes up." The selkie's lips quirk. "Fine, then. But my clothes are in the watertight chest beneath the boardwalk stairs. I won't be answering anything without *them*." He tucks a stray lock of his red curls behind an ear before extending his arm to me.

The motion draws my attention along the line of his neck, my gaze landing on the dip between his collarbones. I have to swallow suddenly. As I help him stand, I avert my eyes to the endless grey sky, as though whatever deities living in its northern vastness might realize this is the worst possible time to dump a very handsome, very naked aristocrat into my lap. I should pray they provide me protection. Or course correction, perhaps.

The selkie holds on to me as we cross the beach, though the self-assured way he moves makes me think he could manage on his own despite his blindness. A small trunk of clothing sits out of view, beneath the stairs, a thin, silver cane resting atop it. While he changes, I stand on the beach, tossing his brooch and catching is again.

He reemerges in a short cape of steel grey over a deep-blue suit jacket, fluid as a waterfall and so fine the silver embroidery shimmers as he moves. His polished, black boots are pulled over his dark pants, and the top of his curls hide beneath a small, perched hat of blue-and-black plaid that matches the trim of his cape perfectly. Somehow, he looks even better with clothes on. Fuck me.

He holds his ornate, silver cane with the poise of royalty, and the gentle swinging motion he gives it as he steps looks nearly as flamboyant as it must be practical. The sand rustles beneath his weight the way no ground ever has beneath mine. Each time he lowers his foot, it thuds. Even his breath has a sound, the tiniest billow, barely recognizable.

I move to his side. With each of my silent motions, the alone and the lonely creep up over my shoulder, reminding me that I will never be more than a ghost, a thing to be kicked down and kicked out and forgotten, not permitted to find purchase.

"Now for my questions," I say.

He startles, then composes himself quickly. "May I pose one of my own first?"

"If you must."

He plants his cane ceremoniously in front of him, the breeze licking at the curls that dance beneath the edges of his cap. "Do you have a name?"

I don't know whether to be suspicious or flattered. "Rubem . . ." Two titles pull at me, the Veneno surname I'd chosen for the rivers and the Murk-given full name my mother helped me craft. But both places had spit me out. When I return, it'll be to the little strip of nothingness that sits between them. "Rubem of the no-man's land."

"Rubem. A delight to make your acquaintance." His soft smile rides on a knifepoint. "I am Tavish K. Findlay."

Findlay. His name makes the parasite warm against my neck. I can't tell which of us draws up my memory of the flier. "You're from Maraheem."

"Aye. What of it?"

"I need to get there, by road, if possible."

"Well, you might have a bit of trouble with that." He points his cane toward the wind and lapping waves. "Maraheem is a city of selkies, as this town once was, but unlike any of our more mundane residences, this one is an *undersea* pinnacle of wealth and technology. The most high-tech, airtight metropolis of metal and glass you'll find this side of, well, anything."

My chest feels raw with a mixture of hope and despair. An underwater city. Just reaching it seems such a big task; my fire nearly wavers. So much to do, so little energy.

As though in tune with my mood, the wind kicks up, brushing at the little braids around my face and slipping a few over my shoulder. The clouds release a splattering of rain, so light and useless it might as well be mist, with none of the gracious concealment a dense fog would provide.

I scowl, scooting back into the cleft of the boardwalk stairs, both for its shelter from the crying sky and the cover its shadows offer. But I can't hide from all my problems the way I can from the rain. The parasite's body still weaves into my neck muscles—still waits to inflict me with unwanted emotions, to force its own desires upon me.

I expect it to react to the thought, but it stays as dormant as before my escape. Somehow that's more eerie. It's waiting, and I don't know why.

"Findlay Inc. is in Maraheem, isn't it?" I try not to sound desperate, and the question comes out with a bit of a growl instead. "They do aurora research of some kind?"

Tavish joins me beneath the stairs. "Findlay Incorporated," he says, pronouncing the title with something so firmly between pride and sarcasm that I can't tell where one begins and the other ends, "is the largest and most shining corporation within Maraheem, run by my mother, Raghnaid Findlay. We've owned the northern auroras for generations. We're the only place conducting aurora research this side of Alkelu—with all the technological boons to show for it."

The parasite tingles to life in a burst of heat, its confusion and distaste so thick it overlaps into mine. "Wait, you're saying you *own* the auroras."

"Aye." Tavish's brow tightens. "Is that not how it works where you're from?"

"Never." The mere thought of it feels more foreign than the eternal grey sky.

He seems equally confounded. "Don't yours latch to stationary creatures? Can you not just uproot the entire host? Or buy the land beneath it?"

"If you want the Murk Council to wring you alive. All the auroras in Manduka live there, and they belong equally to the swamp as a whole, the same with any tree or beast."

"But *you* didn't live in this Murk, Rubem of no-man's land?"

It's not a barb, the way he says it, like that fact is one of a million and not the defining cog that's spun my entire life into this position. But even a caress hurts an open wound. I respond to the ache with a bitter laugh. "I suppose I could have snuck into the Murk and stolen one." Seeing how that's technically what I did. "But I never wanted one for myself." The irony of that isn't lost on me.

Now it's Tavish's turn for a humorless bark. "Pardon me, but that's shite. Everyone wants an aurora. They're symbols of wealth and power which actively *create* more wealth and power."

"When I was placed in a position of wealth and power for a short time, all it brought me were enemies. The only thing I want now is a quiet life with my pets lounging across the deck and a bottle of wine beside my rocking chair."

Tavish's features shift in a way that's just beyond my ability to read, something tender around the edges. "You're a wee bit odd, Rubem of No-Man's Land." His tone contains all the confusing softness of his expression.

I put on a wry smile for no one but myself. "I get odder the more you know of me."

"How intriguing." Tavish hums. "But if that was your last question, I really, genuinely must be—"

A shout interrupts him.

I freeze, tracking the sound to the edge of the jetty. Another call answers it as the fishing boats I noticed earlier careen around the side of the tall jetty to our left. They carry four people, all redheaded and freckled, but none of them

Lilias. A huge bundle of nets writhes between the boats, pulling them toward the shore. One look at their haul and I know they're not fishing for prey, but for predators.

Their captive orca's black tail crashes down, white underbelly visible for a moment as it twists in the netting, snapping ropes along the edges. Green, blue, purple, and orange gashes cut across the creature's body, outlining its ordinary black and white markings. As it tosses its head, its gums shimmer with rainbows between silver teeth. The same rainbows as the parasite's in my neck.

Tavish holds his cane tighter. "What is it?"

"Poachers." The word comes out as a hiss.

A wave pushes the orca's tangled body onto the beach, wedging it against the sand. It writhes ferociously. The boats follow, their crews abandoning them to splash through the shallow water. They seem barely able to stop the beast from crushing them as it thrashes. One poacher draws out something that shines like death, half a harpoon and half an executioner's blade. I tense. My ears ring with the squelch of Lilias's heel tearing into my darling Blossom's neck, crushing the life out of the pet caiman, the most loyal of my sweet triplets. My tension turns to pain. It pulses through me, making all my misery and worry smolder.

With a deep breath, I smother the feeling.

The orca is not my pet. This is not my world. I can't stop this creature's death, and the more time I spend mixing myself up in other people's business, the more likely it becomes that the rest of my monstrous family will share its fate. If I engage with these poachers at all, it needs to be to get the parasite out of my neck, and my neck back south where it belongs.

As they toss more ropes over the shored orca, though, the parasite goes taut within the muscles of my neck. A surge of dismay and anger spills from it, flaring in tremendous waves that turn my mind hazy and make my heart pound—pound to a different rhythm, one controlled by a new drummer.

By the parasite.

CHAPTER THREE

the difference between sinking and falling

Each answer builds
a slow transformation.
Do I become less of myself with each new addition,
no longer a reflection, but a vague substitution?

IN SOME DISTANT LIFETIME, I sat across from Lilias on a wide, flat deck, the ignit cartel's riverboat creaking as it drifted beneath the jungle canopy. Splotched, golden light filtered around us both. It was too lovely for the monster dubbed the Lily of the North, and she seemed to know it, drawing herself into the depths of her cowl.

Her loose, long-sleeved garments were river-made, but they looked out of place on her pale, freckled form. She picked at a hangnail with her favorite little knife, one whose blade I knew intimately. Her thin nose wrinkled.

"Pull apart the town until someone talks," she said. "If no one there can point us toward the ignit hoard, then we'll know by the end of tomorrow." She didn't so much as glance at the colorful, softly glowing, stonelike ignits cradled in the bowl at the table's center—a vibrational blue, a heat-forming red, a green that would make the body die cell by cell—all currently in their inactive state.

The endlessly rechargeable energy they created could fuel a city's infrastructure and a tyrant's rise to power in equal proportion. They should have been enough for Lilias. But her ambition is a wild beast, rash and irregular. She wanted more, or she wanted their source—the auroras—and nothing less would satisfy.

"I'd prefer not to subject those people to the cartel's brutality." I scooped out the poisonous ignit from the bowl, flipping it between my fingers. Quaint, how the presently harmless stone could blister my skin and start me heaving with a single spark of electricity. "Give our scouts time."

Lilias flipped her knife around, driving its blade into a crack in the wood. "Time is not a thing I have in surplus. Neither is patience."

"I won't trade your haste for bodies." I gave the ignit another toss and a catch, wishing desperately for the box of wine I stashed below deck this morning.

"We're in the business of bodies. Maybe you got to be a pacifist—" She snorted. "Or should I say an *apathist*, because you lived in the middle of gods-damned nowhere. But now you'll be whatever the hell I ask of you if you don't want me tearing apart your stick house and the barbaric swamp it sits beside."

At the mention of my home, something small and hot burned inside me, something so very far from apathy. "Three more days." I forced it out, the call of the wine pounding behind my ears. "You installed me here, let me do the job you gave me."

"Counteroffer." She leaned in. "I kill you and lead this cartel on a rampage through your Murk, pulling up every single aurora they possess."

"Even you wouldn't be so reckless. Maybe you can keep talking the river scum into helping you, but the Murk never will. They'll have your bones on necklaces before you even figure out where their auroras are hosted." I left the rest unspoken: that outside those living in the Murk, I'm the only one who can locate the auroras. No one else had a parent from both worlds, the knowledge of the Murk's fog-laden swamps without their residents' unwavering commitment to them. "Let me do my job," I repeated, rolling the ignit across my knuckles and swiping it into my fist before it could fall. "I can get you what you want, and we can all leave happy." And then I could escape Lilias's mess for the bliss of not having to deal with cartels or crazed northerners or anything that walked on two legs and talked like this life owed it something.

My desire for that simple, old existence holds firm.

It grips me square in the chest now as I stand on this northern beach with the four poachers ahead and Tavish somewhere behind, but the aurora Lilias wanted so badly hits me with its anguished seething, brighter and more devastating than any emotion I could conjure for these orca killers. It pushes me, not toward my home, my life, my tucked-away corner of the world, but straight into their mess. I storm across the sand, propelled by such ragged waves of the parasite's resentment that even my silence can't stop the poachers from spotting me.

Once they do, there's no going back. Their eyes fix on the parasite, locked there as though magnetized. The sight hits each poacher differently: a sharper quiver in the wrist, a deepened scowl, a retreating flinch, a slow nod. The man with the harpoon-blade steps toward me.

"What—what do you—are you from the Findlays?" His arms shake and his breath comes in pants, blood smeared across his forehead. "Did they send you to help? We lost half the crew already today. This one was a beast to drag up, but we've finally tired it. With an extra hand, we'd have its body returned to Maraheem by midday."

"You have to stop this." It's my voice and my words, but not my emotion or my decision, at least not fully.

"They're Alasdair's orders." He stares at me. "We're supposed to collect the ignation."

Ignation?

The orca's writhing knocks into one of the poachers on the ropes, and the other two hunker down, shouting, "Hurry it up," and "We can't hold it much longer!"

The harpoon-blade's bearer turns back toward the orca. The creature makes no sound as he raises the blade above its neck, but the animal's endless black eyes bear down on me like a starless night. In the boat beyond it, I glimpse flesh with its same rainbow streaks—the raggedly beheaded corpses of two small sharks and a dolphin.

The squelch of Lilias's boot against my dear Blossom returns. With it comes more of the parasite's strange, foreign anger that feels like I'm watching my own temper rise from a distance. I try to calm myself, but the parasite burns against me, grasping at the memory of Lilias's kick and the fall of flower petals over my mother's corpse and every other death I've witnessed. Like a tsunami, it takes me over.

Tavish approaches. "What is going on here?"

But he's too late. The parasite's desperate rage fills me straight to my bones. It crashes through every misgiving I've ever had, every self-proclaimed banner of pacifism, and it's me who feels like rampaging, me who wants it in a way that annihilates all else. It's me, and it's not, and it is.

My muscles tighten. And my body moves on its own, leaving my mind to drift an instant behind it as the parasite and I fly at the poacher with the harpoon.

My hands snatch the knife from his belt. His brow lifts, but he turns his larger weapon on me a moment too slowly. I plunge the blade through the side of his neck. My lungs catch at the feeling of the metal slipping through flesh, but my burst of horror is consumed by the parasite's fury. As I pull back the knife, blood sprays from the man's gash in torrents. His eyes roll back, and his body drops to the water, the executioner's axe beside it.

The woman behind him stares at me in shock before releasing a grating shriek that hurts even through the foreign anger. She launches at me. Beneath the parasite's emotions, I want to run or to apologize, but that burning desire to save the orca is too thick and suffocating not to yield to. Knife already raised, I dodge her swing and I cut across her throat as though my hands have done this a thousand times instead of never. She collapses.

The third poacher drops his rope to reach for his weapon. I spring through the shallows faster than should be possible and wedge my blade through his ribs, angling it into his heart. His blood drips down my hand, hot and slick. Nausea coils through my gut and up my throat, nearly piercing through my haze of unnatural fury.

The final living poacher dives for deeper water. Mid-leap, his body contorts. A torrent of the parasite-like rainbows spills over him as his arms meld into his sides. Brown fur springs along his body. His shirt grows tight, and his pants split around legs that aren't legs anymore, but fat, furry seal fins.

The orca lunges at him. Its teeth close around his lower half. He barks, the sound turning into a scream as all his human bits reappear in another wave of color, arms and skin and a pair of bloodied hips caught in the orca's teeth. It chomps down.

The parasite's hostile anger vanishes in a storm of bile that burns the back of my throat. I stumble. My arms shake, and the knife drops from my fingers, landing in the water with the corpse of the poacher I just killed. The *person* I just killed.

Killed.

All the other despicable things I've done in my life feel small and fragile compared to this. This monstrosity. I'd have liked them to let the orca free, sure. I absolutely didn't want them dead. But while that anger surged through me, I had felt as though I wanted that, the way I'd wanted Tavish's brooch, only a thousand times worse.

Tavish slings frazzled questions of "What's happening?"

and "Did they leave?" but the parasite is all I can think about, all I can fear.

"Oh, fuck. Fuck." I tug at my neck, leaving red smears along my skin as I drive my fingernails into the parasite.

Parasite.

The word closes around my lungs as though the creature is physically weaving itself through them. Maybe it already has, one of its black tendrils wrapping around my chest, through my heart, and the other sliding up my spinal cord. The thought makes me want to tear out my bones.

'That would be counterproductive.' The voice of my right-hand man from my month with the cartel rolls through my mind like lyrics sung to the wrong tune, regurgitated with force.

Get out of my fucking head. But it's a command I have no way to enforce.

In reply, the parasite warms my neck. 'That would be counterproductive,' it repeats.

Is that all you can say? I snap back.

My skull pounds like a vicious hangover, and the parasite's twisted tone comes again, this time dragging up a memory from a few years back: a wine bottle under one hand and beneath the other, a newborn jaguar cub with a twisted paw I'd rescued from a boa. 'Lie down or you'll hurt yourself.'

I can't tell if that's an answer to my question or a new rebuke. It doesn't matter, because Tavish interrupts us by storming down the beach, his cane waving like a commanding scepter. It just misses one of the poachers, but then his boot connects. He bends down, feeling the corpse. As his fingers move from fabric to blood, his expression changes.

Slowly, like the building of an avalanche, a shudder slips through him. A breathless "oh" spills from his lips, tight and tumbling. He rises. "I thought it couldn't possibly . . ." His diamond-edged voice falters as he transitions from a stoic mask to a disconnected wobble. "You killed my brother's crew? Oh. Oh, good fuck."

"No!" It comes as a shout, too caught in the fear still pounding through my chest. I lift my hand toward my mouth, stopping only when I smell the blood drenching it. My stomach turns. "No, I never meant to kill them," I whisper. "It was all an accident."

Tavish makes a sound that's almost a scoff if not for the little quaver at the end. His fingers tremble as he adjusts his coat, accidentally leaving the blood he picked up from the dead poacher smudged on one sleeve. "Please do explain how you *accidentally* kill multiple people on a beach?"

"I don't—" The words catch in my throat, rough and tight.

I can't tell him the parasite made me do it, not for a million tiny reasons. It sounds impossible, should be impossible—he can't even see the thing in my neck. I have no idea how he'll react to it, this man whose family has collected every aurora and brutally killed the animals affected by their rainbow glow. I need time to match his perfectly pointed language with shrewd explanations of my own, but right now, all I have are blood smears and panic. My red-stained hands shake. I shove them into the water.

The orca gives a series of angry, hissing clicks as it attempts to twist free of the remaining netting, nearly swinging its tail into Tavish in the process. A new memory hits me, this one of my raised hand stopping my crocodilian, Sheila, from turning a trespasser into a snack, and with the line between my own goals and the parasite's so blurred, I don't know which of us grabs hold of it first.

"Whoa, whoa!" I force myself to project a feeling of calm despite the tension still rattling through me as I place a palm on the whale's side.

It settles beneath my touch.

"That's it, friend," I coo, pulling back rope and net until it can roll itself freely into the shallows. The momentary distraction helps a little, but it can't give life back to the bodies around me. It can't fix the mistakes of this day, this month, this lifetime. There's one thing I can do though.

I trudge soundlessly onto the sand. As I pass Tavish, I slip my hand over his wrist. He jerks away, looking more panicked than the mere startles my silent presence has inflicted on him already. I press his brooch quickly into his palm, and I let him go. "I'm sorry."

Tavish's expression loosens, and though there's worry in the twitch of his lips and the shallow, tight way he draws breath, he almost smiles. "You are forgiven, this time." There's an edge to his words. His mercy is finite, breakable. He's wiped my slate clean only so he might judge me afresh. Or leave me behind.

"I have questions still, but I don't suspect you'll want to answer them now." I drop onto the sand.

"Because you're a murderer? Ah, my apologies, an accidental killer." With his cane tapping my legs, he steps around me with ease. Then he lowers himself, gracefully, to the ground at my side. His lips quirk. "Now I also ken you're either a fool or a schemer."

I can't quite contain my surprise. "I'm what? Why?"

"You just handed me the one thing you could have bargained answers for." He gives his brooch a small wiggle before pinning it to the collar of his shirt. "A schemer might give it in order to grant me a false sense of control, and a fool because they don't understand its importance. Though you . . . Perhaps you're a third option."

I've lived beneath the heel of a boot long enough to sense whatever miniscule power I had left slip away. Of Tavish's list, he is certainly the schemer, twisting every vulnerability into a shield. It's intoxicating in its genius and distressing in its triumph. "Tell me, then, what am I?"

"A man on the verge of collapse."

A schemer indeed, making me trust him more with every moment. "On the verge? I'm alone, very far from the only place I've ever known, with nothing to my name and no way to return." I stop myself short of mentioning the parasite in my neck. I'll have to tell someone about that, whether him or another member of Findlay Inc. But not yet. "I've seen death, particularly as of late, but I've never killed . . ."

The shudder that runs through me resonates between the parasite and myself. It snaps, *'You'll hurt yourself.'*

Impossible, silt-breathing creep.

Tavish stares out to sea, his fingers fiddling with his brooch. Finally, he lifts one hand and finds my shoulder, squeezing it once before dropping his arm. "Sounds to me like some real shite."

"You don't know the half of it."

After another pause, he laughs. "I highly doubt my meeting will take place, seeing as there are corpses strewn across the site. So, it seems I have more time for you after all." By his smirk, he must be having far too much fun with this. Damn scheming aristocrat.

Still, I grimace. "I'm sorry."

"It was a long shot to start with." He slaps his palms together and stands. "I'll have someone collect these bodies later. I should even be able to convince the right authorities to excuse away their very obvious murder wounds. I assume there are obvious murder wounds?" There's a tinge to his voice, and it takes me a moment to realize he's hoping not for that answer, but for the one I never gave him earlier. The one against my neck.

I can't bring myself to tell him yet, not with their bodies still floating in the surf. "I'll pull them onto the beach."

He makes a dismissive sound.

I lift the first body by the armpits, and his scarf slips from around his throat, revealing a clam-shaped brooch of precious metals. The symbol of wealth strikes me, such a contrast to the dull outfit he and the other poachers wear. I nudge it, and the silver inlay sparkles, a faint glow rising from it, remarkably like an ignit.

I glance back at the poachers' boats, their rainbow-gashed victims decomposing on one of their decks. Lilias's flask floats between the two burial grounds. Beyond the waves, the orca leaps and twists, a blur of color against the grey morning sky.

"The poachers said they were killing the creatures for something called ignation?" I ask as I drag the body onto the beach.

"Our local fuel source."

I pause. "Another term for ignits, then?"

"No, but we produce it by deconstructing the ignits into their ignetic strains—by 'we,' I mean Findlay Inc., of course," Tavish explains. "Unlike the short bursts of energy released by ignits, ignation has no regeneration period."

"It got into the sea life?" I guess, returning for the next corpse.

"A recent leakage. My damned family is ordering them hacked apart for the ignation without proper study first."

My gut twists. That could very easily be me, hacked apart for the parasite. "Didn't you claim to be the center of aurora research or some other pretentious thing?"

"Aye, but this is different." Tavish snorts. "Findlay Inc. won't even publicly acknowledge the mutants' existence, only the risk of what they're labeling 'toxic chemical exposure' in these regions. They had this entire town relocated when the beasts started swimming into its waters, and two of our nearest underwater sister cities are on controlled lockdowns."

That doesn't particularly quell my nerves. "Can't you do something about that? *You're* a Findlay."

"I was attempting to do just that with my meeting today. But I'm the youngest of my family and mostly ignored for my efforts." His statement matches his tone perfectly, poised yet sulky. A blush creeps over his skin, and a curl of loose hair springs around his nose, looking all the more orange for the scarlet in his cheeks. "They would rather I keep to my minor charities and leave the real company business to Alasdair."

I set the final body onto the sand and press her eyes

closed. "That sounds tough."

It's an awkward reply, a little too late, too rough. I leave it hanging there like a noose and turn from Tavish to sign a short death proclamation over the poachers' bodies, for the benefit of my own guilt as much as for them, making each hand motion count: "We mourn for a life unknown and equally for the loss it will bring others. May you find peace as full as the quiet of the womb, and may the tears of those who weep for you become one with . . ." *The mists* is the proper saying, but this far from the foggy swamps of the Murk, the word seems wrong. I decide on "become one with the salt of the sea."

I was never going to have anyone to put my spirit to rest, not even back home. But here, thousands of miles north, the knowledge hits anew. I have been lonely before, but for the first time in decades, I feel fully, thoroughly alone, like I've turned invisible, moved a step out of phase with the rest of the world.

As I finish, I strip the scarf off the first poacher. The fabric flops against my neck, chilling my already freezing skin, but it covers the parasite from any prying eyes. I take a pistol while I'm at it, forced to tip the corpse a bit to remove it from his belt.

Tavish waits for me, his expression lost in thought.

Continuing down this path will mean trusting him—a strong, powerful resident of Maraheem, the kind of person who has kicked me, violently, from every place I have ever sought help—to gain the only thing I want. The one thing I need. I breathe in. "You wanted to know how I accidentally killed the poachers?"

As I say it, though, the wind shifts, pummeling rain into our faces as the drizzle turns into a downpour. I turn away from the worst of the onslaught and catch motion from down the beach, so far away that I nearly miss her: a naked, redheaded woman emerging from the water.

Lilias has returned.

CHAPTER FOUR

perimeter breach

If I look behind, will I find the past me gone,

an imprint in the sand,

the echoed end of a song?

IT'S TOO SOON. I should have found shelter—I should have—

Better to act now, berate myself later.

"Let's get under a proper roof first," I say softly, as though all I have to fear is the now pounding rain.

"If you ken this is worth running from, then you truly are not from around here," he says with a laugh, but he lets me guide him up the stairs without question, holding down his hat with one hand.

A set of shops lines the boardwalk, but their wide windows won't offer much protection against Lilias's bullets. I move us through an alley to a courtyard with clusters of delicate brush and little, twisty trees, small and slight compared to the massive, wild jungles back home, as though these are made from the very sea breeze that rattles through them. Behind them rears a great stone building, stained-glass windows on its second story offering a glimpse of swooping columns.

"This way." I press Tavish into a jog, the rain pelting us like an unhappy deity. His feet skid on the slick stone, and I wrap an arm around his back to hold him up.

The large front door opens smoothly for me. We duck inside, and I close it after us. Through the windows, I catch glimpses of the road beyond the courtyard plants, half shielded by a veil of rain. Gods, I miss the Murk's impenetrable fog.

"We have to get down." I tug Tavish against the door, leaning my weight into it.

He makes a disgruntled sound in the back of his throat. "Rubem, what are you—"

"Quiet!"

"Is someone coming?"

I respond by wrapping my arm around his shoulder and pressing a finger to his lips. Something rustles beyond the door. The knob rattles. I hold it closed with my shoulder, quickly checking my stolen pistol for when I pull the trigger on Lilias. There's no hesitation in the thought, not anymore, nothing but that terrible sound of her kicking my bleeding caiman over and over and over again. The gun clicks as I cock it.

Tavish goes stiff. I scoot away from the door, letting go of him to reach for its handle. He whirls, his cane moving with him. My instincts jerk me back. His cane slams into the pistol. It drops, skittering across the stone.

Tavish flings the door open. "Oi, get lost, did you?"

I try to tackle him, but our stalker vaults through the doorway like a bullet, barreling past him. She launches into me. Her fist collides with my jawline in a crack of pain and a smash of blackness. Heat springs from the parasite, but no haze of anger comes with it, just the subtle sense of determination. Through my blotched vision, I elbow her back. She catches my arm. Twisting her knee beneath mine, she plants her hip to mine and throws me.

As my shoulder hits the stone floor, I roll—straight into

my fallen pistol. I grab it as I pop back to my feet and spin, the barrel already aimed. It comes up level to my attacker's chest. My finger grips the trigger.

I freeze.

Orange hair spills around my attacker's freckled face, well-muscled build, and fiery gaze; a striking resemblance to Lilias. But this woman—this selkie, her brooch clearly poking through her tight, black cloak—is a little shorter, her snarling lips painted a deep maroon, and her wide eyes curve delicately around fine wrinkles, hooded beneath sloping lids. Her flat nose looks nearly bridgeless as she scowls. Water drips from her hair.

Tavish's cane hits my side, knocking the wind from my lungs. I barely register the selkie woman as she snatches my pistol out of my hands and knocks me back with a heel to my gut. Suddenly I'm the one staring down a barrel.

My breath returns with an ache, stirring my heart into an uncomfortable rhythm.

"Some fine perimeter scouting that was," Tavish grumbles. "Did you check for every potential villain but the one right in front of me?"

The woman talks over him, her voice rough and loose compared to his. "Hands up," she yells at me. "On your knees."

I'm not even surprised somehow, as though a part of me always figured it would come to this—to me following orders, carried by the tide. I let myself sink, lifting my hands slowly. The movement shifts my shoulders. My loosened scarf slips.

The woman's brow hitches, and in a shadowy blur, she flips my stolen pistol. Its butt crashes into my temple, sending a wave of pain through me. The world transforms, starry black. My palms hit the stone floor, then my shoulder, and I groan as I lie there, cupping the aching knot with one hand while my place in existence pieces back together.

The woman lays her boot against my neck, just above the parasite's resting place. Her voice echoes a little in my head as she rambles off without pause. "What's happened here, Tavish? Who is this? Has he done something to you?"

"Of course not, Sheona, I'm fine." Tavish reaches for her, so solid and decisive, like he knows she could never hurt him, not even on accident. His fingers find her shoulder. "Look at me, I'm fine, you ken? Rubem means me no harm."

"This crook?" Sheona presses down with her boot as she says it, the edges of her soles biting uncomfortably into my skin. "Then why's he has one of your family's auroras on—in—his neck?"

Through the pressure, I wheeze, "It's not—"

Sheona's foot snaps back, landing between my ribs. A flicker of warmth comes off the parasite, so slight I could have imagined it, but it's my own instincts that make me curl in my knees and cover my face with my arms—reflexes well honed by bands of Murk teenagers shouting *river-born silt stink* at me and by river-born shopkeepers who gave one look at my warm-toned skin and decided the only way to remove it was to cover the shade in blood. Here I am again, somewhere I don't belong. Only this time, I can't simply limp back to no-man's land.

And with each new pain, the fire that's driven me this far shrinks a little, the effort needed to stoke it just a smidgeon too great. The parasite lies listless within my neck muscles. Not invested enough, or perhaps just as tired as I.

I am alone. Even surrounded and embedded, I am alone.

Sheona's foot returns to my neck.

Tavish's face pinches into something unreadable. "Please," he says, though it feels like a courtesy not a plea, "even if this is the case, my family is not worth hurting him over."

Sheona goes still. "Fine." With the gentleness of a cat awaiting the pounce, she nudges my shoulder. "Tell us, then, where *did* you get it?"

It's almost funny how perfectly this moment mirrors the one that started it all: the piercing gaze of a redheaded woman, the constant presence of a gun barrel, the will to protest slowly sinking out of me, leaving only fear and fatigue and the great need for a bottle of wine. Lilias had held the gun that time, still just a nameless phantom, someone I'd ignorantly assumed I could scare off with a few shots to the sky. Someone I hadn't anticipated would return with friends.

It was her friend's weapons that turned the tide. They'd already nicked poor Sheila's leg before I managed to send her into the water beneath our stilt-house, and they continued to track my jaguars—hulking old Diadem, whose back leg had never quite healed after something bigger and meaner tried to tear it off, and little Monsoon, whose mother had vanished the week he was born—like they might shoot both cats just to stop their pacing, the harmless cub alongside the limping elder. It hadn't been a choice then, not really. I would have done anything to protect my pets. Anything, including joining the people threatening them.

Sheona nudges me again, harder this time.

I cringe. "There was this woman, a selkie, I assume—she has a brooch too. I only know her as Lilias, or by her signed name, a Lily. She came to Manduka in search of ignits and auroras, kept threatening to bring more of her people, to tear apart the jungle, my home, if we didn't give her what she wanted."

I had to do it, a part of me cries, *I couldn't sit back and hope she was bluffing, hope she wouldn't manage it.* But Tavish and his companion won't care about that. They won't care how I had nothing else, nothing but that one little plot of no-man's land and the animals who found refuge on it. Or how in taking the aurora for Lilias, I'd betrayed the Murk to appease her. Or how the guilt of that had carved itself into me, yet to scar, much less to fade.

I grit my teeth. "An aurora seemed like the easiest way to be rid of her, but then the creature I collected decided for some dreadful reason that I looked like a viable host and clamped onto me. When Lilias failed to tear it off, she brought it here—scared, I think, that if she was the only other thing around when she killed me for it, that it would latch to her instead." The cold floor digs through my hips, my shoulder, my limbs, forcing its way into my bones, where it meets a completely different chill: my fear over why the parasite chose me, a sapient creature, so different from anything their kind ever latches onto, and what it means to do with my body if it can gain control of it. "I escaped her this morning and immediately ran into Tavish. I thought, if your people knew more about the auroras, then maybe they could remove it for me."

Sheona snorts. "I haven't seen any sign of this Lilias."

"She went to Maraheem," I reply.

"Did she now?"

Tavish glares. "Sheona, if he were lying—if that aurora came from my family—they'd have told me. I'm at least that involved in the company." He sounds as though he's trying to convince himself more than her. "Besides, he didn't even know where Maraheem was when he found me."

"I still don't like this."

The cold keeps coming, demanding my attention now that the pain is subsiding. "May I sit up now? I promise I'm only dangerous if you're hacking up animals for sport." I try to make it sound humorous, as though being able to joke about the poachers' deaths is somehow a reason to trust me. Against all odds, it works.

"Sheona, let the poor man be! If he attacks me, you may pummel him all you like then, and not before."

She bristles, but slowly she lowers the pistol and tucks it into her waistband.

No move of Tavish's head or shift of his eyes signals he's turned his attention back to me, but I feel the heat of his consideration blaze across my face like a blush. "I do apologize for her; she's always a wee bit high-strung. Fantastic bodyguard, though, when she's not trying to scout an entire town on her own."

"You're the one constantly shooing me away," she grumbles.

"Only because I love you, Nana." Cane tucked under one arm, he offers me both hands and pulls me to my feet, using his extra weight as a counterbalance to my height. His thumbs linger on my fishnet gloves, a little tighter than mere hesitation. He traces just below the raw line of my wrists where Lilias's cuffs sat. "Everything I've been taught says that auroras never attempt to latch to people—to any being with a complex nervous system."

"This seems to be a fun new exception." I wiggle my shoulders as the parasite warms. It fades back to cold, but I can't shake its lingering presence. If it's latching to me the way it did to its last host, then the thing will slowly sift deeper into my being until my emotions are no longer mine, my body controlled by foreign impulses and desires. It will take me over from the inside out. Without the energetic buzz of alcohol, what little energy and motivation I can scrape away from my depression is incredibly valuable—I can't allow this damn parasite to supplant that. No matter how lethargic I am, I won't let it replace me. "Already the aurora can influence me. It killed those poachers, using my body. Or it imbued me with its desire to kill them, at least."

Sheona scowls. "So, you might not be dangerous, but you've got a thing in your head that can make you kill for it?"

"I don't think I'm at risk of random murder sprees. It was the idea that they were going to slaughter another ignation mutant that enraged it." My gut twists, because if it hadn't been for my shared distaste for the orca's death, the parasite might not have managed to overwhelm me so thoroughly. "But I still can't risk something like that happening again. Happening *permanently*. I need it gone."

"I've got a knife." The forearm-length blade Sheona pulls from her hip sheath looks like a knife the way a jaguar looks like a cat.

I hold both hands in front of me. "If that worked, I'd

already have it gone. Somehow, it's integrating into my muscles, maybe even my brain. Anything short of surgery will probably kill me."

"There has to be another way." Tavish's diamond-edged voice is a weapon right now. "Someone in Maraheem must ken it."

"Your mother—" Sheona cuts in.

"We won't tell her," Tavish replies, defiant in a way that seems nearly factitious, but I can't tell what emotion he hides beneath it.

Hope and fear mingle in my throat, creating a lump I can't swallow. A flier comes billowing up from the tunnel where Tavish and I ascended, snaking its way through the courtyard. Its wet form smacks into the window. I can just make out the skull and crossbones. I suppress a tingle of panic. "Will I be safe there?"

"As long as you're with us." He certainly sounds genuine. "If you're hesitant, though, you're free to walk away, aurora and all."

Sheona glares at him. "Tavish."

He ignores her. "I won't force you to come with us. If you wish to leave, this is your chance."

"Is that a threat?" I ask.

He smiles. "It's a warning."

The way he says it gives it an entirely new spin, a new tone, a new life, reminding me that he is so much cleverer than I could ever have expected. Looking at him now, his wet hair half dried and his cloak still rain splattered, the auburn freckles on his nose standing out amidst a mass of faded, browner spots, I can appreciate that. It doesn't mean I can trust him. But perhaps that's not important when my other option is to return to the South, where our knowledge of the auroras is limited and the chance is low that anyone will figure out how to remove it in time.

Home will mean nothing if the parasite engulfs me before I can reach it.

"Then take me to Maraheem," I say. "Will it be a problem if Lilias sees me? She'll want me back."

Sheona slams her blade into its sheath. "I'll make sure it isn't."

I nearly point out that Lilias isn't someone to be trifled with, but I don't feel confident trifling with Sheona, either, especially while she holds all the weapons.

"She sounds like a lower-city sort, I doubt we'll see her," Tavish replies. Before I can finish properly swallowing what *lower-city sort* must mean to an aristocrat whose family owns all the auroras in the region, he taps his cane against the floor, his expression too bright for me to tear down. "Come, then, no time like the present!"

The rain returns to a heavy mist as we cross the courtyard, heading back toward the beach. Sheona stalks one step behind me. Every haunting wave of a flier and gust of the wind and rattle of a shutter feels twice as lonesome now that there are three of us, as though I went from being a ghost in a graveyard to an invading force, a thing that doesn't belong.

When we reach the beach, I leap from the boardwalk while Tavish and Sheona make their way down its stairs. Tavish's confident stride looks smaller and clumsier with Sheona at his side. She scoots around him, always one step ahead, one motion away from catching or stopping or redirecting. It slows him down. But he says nothing.

He steals beneath the stairs to strip.

"Damn towns. How did anyone form shift here? Out in the open?" Sheona snorts. "Where are the lockers, the showers, the fucking modesty? It's shite."

"I don't enjoy it any more than you do," Tavish shouts, then grunts when he bumps into something.

"You chose to come out here."

"I happen to believe a deal with Greer O'Cain is more important than a clean transformation."

Another snort leaves Sheona. She digs through her coat

and draws forth a little, rubbery half-moon device with a metal front. Silver ignation gleams inside it, pulsing through the workings in a thin stream that casts a faint rainbow glow. She shoves it my way, waggling her hand when I don't immediately take it. "Put the soft piece in your mouth. It'll let you breathe."

I accept the device, wondering if she means for me to do so now or once we're in the water.

"You still have it?" Tavish steps onto the beach. His toes sink into the sand as he moves slowly on the balls of his feet, a blanket bundled tightly around him.

"It's handy, isn't it?" With that, Sheona stalks beneath the stairs herself.

"It was a gift to her spouse," Tavish explains.

I bounce the thing cautiously along my numb knuckles. "And it's fine that I use it?"

"I doubt they're coming back for it." There's a second meaning there: I doubt they're coming back for *her*.

"Ah." Despite all I don't understand of the woman, my heart cracks for this part of Sheona. Perhaps certain people are made to be used and left behind. People like us.

My gaze lands on Lilias's empty flask still bobbing in the water, each subtle rise and fall a taunt.

A deep-grey seal emerges from under the stairs, her silver-and-gold brooch catching the pale-grey light. Tavish hands his blanket to me and contorts in on himself. The snap of bone and the scratch of skin form a symphony both grotesque and beautiful. He shakes himself as his fur settles. With a whisker wiggle, he heads for the water.

I tuck the blanket into the chest for him and follow the selkies into their sea, a faded Maraheem flier twisting along the beach in my wake.

CHAPTER FIVE

lose the lost

I am not only replaced, but also consumed.

Not a shiny, new person, but the old, hollowed through.

The longer I linger, the more I'm eaten away

by each denial and indifferent day.

BACK HOME, THE SEA is warm. On a good day, it calls like a siren song, promising to soak away all worries in gleaming waves of crystalline blue. On a bad one, it assaults the coast, dousing the mangroves in its salt and ravishing the land. But always, always, it's warm.

My numb feet should not be able to feel the cold any longer, yet the northern sea nips at my toes the moment it sinks through my boots. It bites up my ankles, then freezes into my thighs. By the time it hits my chest, I can barely breathe. Clenching Sheona's device between my teeth, I hope for the best. I dive.

Ice floods my veins. I shake from the inside out, then back in again, as though my shivering reverberates into something greater with each tremble. My chest burns. I stop myself from shooting to the surface and gasp into Sheona's device. Air floods my lungs. One breath at a time, I grow accustomed to the sensation.

I swim after Sheona's and Tavish's elegant seal forms, waiting for my body to acclimate to the chill, but the shivers only grow worse. For once, I wish for the parasite's warmth. *Gods, you could at least be a little bit useful while you're killing me.*

In response, the parasite heats back to life and yanks a memory to the forefront of my mind: me three years ago, maybe four, attempting to remove a pair of leeches from a jaguar's leg as it twists and snarls, snapping at them anxiously itself. *'Calm down, you fool. It's not killing you.'*

Very funny, I reply. There's no humor in the thought, only a fierce determination that drives my arms to pump faster.

The parasite replies with the same bitter laugh I've given on many occasions. Then, its warmth spreads. It feels like a single spark in a frozen pond, but little by little the heat runs through me, settling the shivers. Slowly, my arms feel real again, my skin a living thing instead of a quake of rubber and ice. The memory returns, this time with the leeches squashed and the jaguar whining on the front porch as it gives me sore looks. *'A thank you would be nice.'*

That was the least you could have done, I shoot back. It feels odd, my voice arguing back and forth in my head, my past and my present out of alignment. But the parasite isn't me. It's a thing that eats through my very being, taking away what little of me I have the energy to be. Perhaps it feels my resentment, because while its heat lingers, its presence recoils. I keep swimming.

Tavish slows for me, Sheona's smaller, darker form circling dizzyingly around him. Her knife belt still hangs around her shoulders, perhaps for the practicality of having it when she transforms back, or—a funnier thought— because she's trained herself to use it with her seal mouth. Below us, dull grey-and-brown fish flitter through mounded rocks and fields of sea grass. A gaunt mer-person with grey skin and flippers at the ends of two nearly human legs works their way along the sand, poking at empty shells and lunging after flatfish. They hide behind a boulder as we pass, tucking tightly out of view.

As the seafloor drops farther down, the horizon seems to stretch on forever, all-consuming, shifting the concept of distance until everything is either here or there, but never in between. Something akin to an undersea bus tuts southward on sets of propellers. A blur of color near the surface passes our horizon. It reappears in front of us, and when I look behind a few minutes later, I catch it again. The orca from the poachers' nets. It follows at a respectable distance, circling so far off it barely registers.

After nearly an hour, we reach a glowing metropolis, so bright and beautiful it masks the grey of the distant sky. It winds through the water, window-lined chambers connected by gilded towers and tunnels that arch and dip, creating a many-story labyrinth of airtight buildings with channels of seawater woven through it all. As we swim between the buildings, I catch sight of little ocean courtyards where platformed rock formations teem with pastel coral and darting fish. Dolphins twirl in pods through the city's majestic tunnels, and sharks dart from cavernous crevasses between their metal supports. A few seals with rainbow-lit brooches rush by us, chasing each other toward the surface, and another submersible rises slowly through a large gap in the city's center that seems cut out just for that purpose, but otherwise the waterways remain clear of all but the congregated sea life and pristine ornamentation.

Tavish was right: Maraheem truly is the jewel of the sea.

As we swim deeper through the city's waterways, though, I spot a new set of buildings below us: hulking, windowless things of green-tinged metal, where the channels look like maintenance shafts instead of decorative courtyards. Sheona stops us just before we reach this lower, internal section of the city and veers us toward a room hanging off the side of one of the larger buildings. We enter a compartment so tight that I brush against Tavish as the door closes behind us.

Slowly, the water drains away.

I cough out Sheona's breather. Circulating air greets me: mildly cool, mildly fresh, and mildly smelling of salt. My soaked shirt and pants stick to my skin. Water seeps out of my boots and into the porous mat beneath us. The opposite wall pulls back, revealing more matted flooring that stretches down a hall with a dozen small changing rooms and a row of curtained showers. At the far end sits some kind of reception desk, then a doorway.

The receptionist glances up from his book. "Right on time, Mr. Findlay. I have your clothes in room two already, and Sheona's in three. And for you, sir—*rrr.*" He blinks from beneath his mess of auburn bangs and wrinkles his wide, freckled nose. His gaze bounces between my dark skin and the ignation-fueled device in my hands. "Aye, um, ID card confirmation? You have an ID card?"

While he fumbles through whatever protocol this is, Sheona has already dove whiskers-first into her changing room, her human voice shouting out a moment later, "No ID yet, but he's with us, unfortunately. Leave him off the books for now."

The receptionist swallows uncomfortably, but he doesn't protest.

Sheona reappears in a black outfit identical to her old one, scowling as she tosses me a plush towel. I pat my hair, turning it from drenched to soggy. I'm nearly finished doing the same to my clothes when Tavish emerges from his changing room, still buttoning his silver suit jacket, his wet curls askew.

He taps his cane to the floor—a new one, with a deep-blue and black color scheme—and calls for me. "Come now, Rubem, wouldn't want you to get lost in this great big city."

He says it bright and relaxed, but it still hits my lingering fears. I tug my once more wet scarf a little tighter around the parasite. "Lead on."

Tavish heads for the exit. My blood curdles as I catch up

to him, because each step I take makes my feet slide soundlessly within my boots. I try setting down my toes first, try rolling forward from my heels, try moving slower or faster. Nothing helps with the sickly feeling, nor the complete silence of it. I'm about to grimace right out of my skin when Tavish pushes the door open.

City sounds rush in: the rumble of chatter, the hum and beep and hiss of machinery, children crying and adults shouting. In the wide room before us stretches a systematic checkpoint. To the right, a gleaming sign with the words *upper city* crowns a series of majestic, golden archways, while the stout brass ones to the left have *lower city* written in worn, green paint.

Very few people leave the upper city, but lines of tired workers wait to enter it. They wear a variety of grey uniforms, some I can pinpoint as cooks or maids, and others too vague to determine. As the workers reach the upper-city archway at the front of their line, they unlatch their brooches, handing them over to be scanned by a machine with ignation running through the tiny tubes in its sides. Tavish leads me to the empty arch beside them, where a queue for upper-city residents would be. The guard on duty straightens as we approach, fidgeting with the bold letters pinned to her grey uniform: a *B* and an *A*. She's another redhead with freckles.

The rest of the room's inhabitants bear a range of orange, red, auburn, and strawberry locks mixed in with a few who've gone grey, and freckles cover all the skin I can see. Features and heights seem to differ among them, the typical slightly knobby northern look giving way to a variety of other traits, but always the freckles and red hair remain. *Genetics*, Tavish had said. It's clear what human genetics the seal-shifting bloodlines are attached to.

Tavish doesn't bother drawing out any kind of identification. He taps his cane against the guard's boots. "Oi, burd, you sleeping on the job again?" His teasing tone matches the softness of his expression.

She clasps her hands behind her back, her chest puffed out. "Never, sir."

Tavish laughs. He leans in. "My friend here doesn't have a visa, but I'll watch out for him."

Her lips bunch together. "Boss isn't gonna like that."

"Does your boss bring scones every Tuesday?"

"We ken you're only taking them to those medical center meetings," she grumbles, but a hint of red colors her cheeks as she waves Tavish through. "Still gotta run him some basic paperwork, though."

Now it's Tavish's turn to grumble, but the corners of his lips quirk. "Quickly, then, get on with it! I'm going to grab us coffees from up the lane. Sheona, be nice to them both."

He waves as he passes through the archway.

The checkpoint guard leads me across the room, back to the lower entrance, where she pulls out forms from a rack behind one of the queues and starts filling them out, skipping more of the spaces than she actually writes in and bouncing me questions I answer as vaguely as possible. I keep my gaze on the entrance to the upper, so I spot Tavish when he rounds the corner beyond the gates, three mugs held precariously in one hand.

He barely makes it into view before a flurry of movement from the upper city cuts him short. The lights fade and flare. An alarm sounds in the gate's central chamber, echoed by other bells throughout the city, each a searing siren that panics the civilians and sets the guards on high alert. Five of them draw out sticks that spark with electricity, and usher people back to the lower city. The rest set to work on metal gates, sliding them down to cover the archways to the upper. They gleam, snapping shut one after another. The lights fade and flare again.

In the chaos, Sheona seems to forget everything but Tavish. She sprints across the room, darting past guards and through one of the last open archways to the upper districts.

"Sheona?" I call after her, but the din swallows my voice,

sweeping it away in the pound of feet and the thud of my own heart. "Tavish!" I make it barely three strides toward him before one of the armed guards blocks my path.

"Back to the lower," he barks, waving his electric stick at me.

"Tavish!" I call over the guard's shoulder.

Tavish turns in my direction, but his unfocused gaze slides right over me. In the blaring alarms and oscillating lights, the group that surrounds him seems to come out of nowhere: five soldiers wearing BA pins on their grey-and-white uniforms and a pair of suited officials. They wrap around Tavish like a shield, the soldiers with their weapons pointed out and the officials placing a hand on his back, another on his waist. He flinches and tucks his arms in, as though he might slide through their grips.

"Retreat to the lower districts *immediately,* foreigner, or you will be detained!" the guard repeats, stepping toward me, his chin level with mine.

"I'm with Tavish Findlay!"

The guard grunts. "And I'm personal friends with the head of the BA."

I could fight him. If I made it past his electric stick, I could shove through the guards and scream Tavish's name close enough for him to hear over the din. He is my best chance at removing the parasite. But everything this day— this week—this life—has brought seems to crash into me at once, like a metal blanket over my shoulders and a clamp around my lungs, and I can't. Or maybe I simply don't.

As the suited officials speak to Tavish—speak over him, by the looks of it—his expression goes wide. Then it empties, filling slowly, painfully, with the kind of grief born of shattered shock, like his anguish comes through a broken mirror, the pieces not quite fitting together. The drinks slip from his hand. No one heeds them as they crash into the floor, a mug cracking and coffee spilling across the marble. Tavish grabs onto one of the suits, steadying himself. They guide him hurriedly back up the path, away from me. He doesn't protest, whatever they've told him clearly more important than confirming whether Sheona's brought me with her.

My hand goes to the parasite. If I had done anything but give in with Lilias, then maybe I wouldn't have this damn creature stealing my existence. Maybe I'd be nothing but me, sitting on my porch with a bottle of wine and three living caimans at my feet, watching one of the Murk spiders spin a web the size of my house between the massive swamp mangroves. Maybe I'd be half-depressed and half-drunk instead of this mess of terrible emotions that feeds the exhaustion and turns it into a monster.

But when the guard smacks the back of his stick into my chest and two others grab my arms, dragging me toward the lower districts, I don't have the energy to protest, my goal already too far away. They toss me out the dull, low archways to the lower city. A gate closes behind me, its thick bars coated in spikes. I grasp one, pressing my thumb to the tip. A bead of blood wells around the metal. Between these lower-district bars and the ones they've pulled down over the gilded upper city, I can't make out Tavish's group any longer.

The shouts of the disgruntled lower-city populace burst to life as the alarm bells fade away, the lights returning to normal. The guards offer them an array of replies, from compassionate to hostile:

"I'm sorry, laddie, there's just naught I can do."

"Go about your business!"

"You can check your radios for the reopening, but it probably won't be till the morning, I'd wager."

"Get your damn arses lower, you fucking bampots." This one rattles their stick along the gates.

I yank my hand back as electricity sparks through it, a jolt running up my arm only to be cut short when the parasite warms. The other people touching the metal shudder and drop, groaning in puddles on the ground. But I still stand, barely a tingle lingering in my muscles.

The crowd disperses down the stairs away from the gate. No matter how much I need Tavish's aid, there's no getting through to him now. And at the moment, the thing I need far more desperately than his help is a drink. These lower districts better have alcohol. I draw a breath and follow the crowd. My still-wet feet slide in my boots with each step.

At the bottom of the stairs, the ceiling rises, turning into melded plates of green brown that loom over the windowless hallway. Shops built from the same off-colored metal line both sides, their garage fronts gaping and their keeps guarding and hawking in the heavy din of crowds and chaos. Every corner and crevasse hides twisting machines and rattling pipes that shoot steam into the already sultry air. It smells poorly filtered, of sweat and salt and the tang of mixed waste.

The whole affair is the opposite of the wide grey sky. I love it with a backward, upside-down kind of affection that burns. The way this place flows around me, dense and hot and oblivious, it feels just enough like home to tug at my wanting without satisfying it.

I take a few more sloshing steps. Fuck it.

Plopping down on a crate beside a trinket shop, I manage to yank off my boots before the owner shouts me away. I tie them together and wrap them over my shoulders, continuing down the road in my wet socks. They pick up a thick layer of grime and dust from the filthy metal floor. They don't make a sound.

The parasite flings up my earlier words to Tavish, pairing them with my dirty soles and silent feet: *'I get odder the more you know of me.'*

That wasn't meant for you, I shoot back.

It goes silent as I work my way through the crowd, keeping to the sides as best I can on the chance that Lilias might still be here. My now wrinkled and ragged clothing blends with the thin, dulled fabric of the bustling populace, and my damp state doesn't seem to draw much attention. A few people give my freckles-free skin and dark hair a second look, but down in these lower halls, I'm not the only nonselkie among them, and no one dodges my presence. No one seems to have the energy. I have none to spare them either.

Neither do I have a direction, a destination, just the need for a stiff drink and a place to wait out the gate's closure. I scan the tiny, cluttered shop fronts for the combination of alcohol and a distracted merchant. Between a garage of produce in O'Cain Fishery cartons and one of frostbitten meat whose ice chests bear the same brand name, I find a woman lounged across a barrel with her own wares on her lips. I snatch a bottle as I slip by her, my presence a fog in an already vapor-strewn world of disorder and clatter.

I dive past a clunking, steam-powered trolley with a massive Sails and Co. logo across its side and disappear down a tight metal tunnel before uncorking my prize and guzzling. The wine tastes of vinegar and brine, and each swallow tears a layer off the back of my throat. I down half of it in one go. With my last meal hours gone, it forms a gentle buzz in my head and forces my strained neck joints to finally relax around the parasite.

My next priority should involve food of the free variety or information on the gate's reopening, but both options feel detached, and without a heading, my best bet for either is to wander until something useful presents itself. I keep drinking as I walk, trying to ignore the Findlay Inc. poster nailed behind cracked glass. *Ignation is a privilege* screams thick text that might have once been a silvery iridescent, the edge of a few letters still glimmering in the bulbous, green light that swings above the tunnel exit. I poke at the light. Its insides swirl, almost ignit-like, but lumpier, more irregular. Some kind of bioluminescent algae, maybe.

I search the main street chaos with purpose as I reenter, looking for any of the popularly advertised ignation among the throngs. Brooches peek out of most coats, but otherwise I find only steam power marked by Sails and Co. logos, more of the uneven lighting, and another Findlay Inc. poster across the side of a building that reads, *Keep your cloak on you—lost ignation costs us all!* It displays the fee for its loss at the bottom, the number of zeros at the end so outrageous compared to even the highest prices I've seen listed around the shops that Findlay Inc. might as well be charging for a chest's worth of ignits.

It seems the jewel of the world only shines for those viewing it from the top.

The parasite draws up another of today's memories, *'That sounds tough.'*

At least there's one thing I can agree with the parasite on. Findlay Inc. seems less and less respectable by the minute.

But that turns my thoughts to Tavish and to the jolt of sorrow that overtook him in the face of those suits. What could have happened to stir that kind of reaction? I shake away the prickle of worry just in time for a woman on the corner of two conjoining streets and a descending stairwell to wave a pamphlet in my face.

"The ignation spills are planned! Don't let them cover up the truth," she shouts. I make the mistake of pausing to look at her, and she bares her crooked teeth, her eyes locking aggressively with mine, as though she can hook me right through my pupils. "Findlay Incorporated is creating a shortage of ignation on purpose, keeping the levels low to prevent us from getting ahold of it!"

I lift a hand defensively, ducking to the side. "If you say so."

A stocky man coming from the other direction counters, "Fuck off, Jean! We all ken the damn uppers are just hoarding it. If there really were leaks, they'd be breaking our backs to get their grubby hands on the fuel again."

"Still got some shite going down with them." The man's companion nudges him. "The Findlays are using a new kind of ignation to make enhanced soldiers so they can take the BA on. Been testing it on sea life. My uncle's a cleaner in the upper and saw one with him own eyes: a great huge orca'd gone all sorts of aurora colors."

The woman—Jean—seems to forget my presence, leaping after this new conspirator with a heckling of demands, and I slip away. I don't know what specifics to believe amidst their convoluted claims. None of them quite match what I know from the deserted selkie town. But one thing is clear: no one here holds any love for the Findlays.

I cross the street once more. Another Sails and Co. steam trolley chugs by behind me, turning the walkway into a hazy mask of vapor so thick I could be back on the edges of the Murk if not for the stink of unwashed bodies and the subtle tinge of oil. I down the rest of my bottle. It doesn't manage to take away the lag settling into my step or the gurgling hunger in my belly.

As I pass a rugged, little place called Reid's Bar with dim lights and dingy floors, I catch the slightly metallic voices of two radio hosts.

"Looks like the decision on the gate's coming in soon, you wee scunners."

"Aye, but why'd the gates close at all? That's the real query here."

"Ha, we already ken that, MacNair. They saw your mum's arse in line and had a panic!"

While the hosts dissolve into good-natured insults, I step just inside the garage-sized front entrance and lean on the wall. A bit of it crumbles against my back. I slip my hands into my vest to keep from rapping my thumbs along my fingers as they grow bored.

No one seems to notice me, half the meager occupants distracted by a game of cards at a rickety corner table and the other half setting up a cauldron and bowls on a line of O'Cain Fishery crates. A food-splattered flier pinned to the end crate reads, *Soup kitchen dinners, every Tuesday and*

Thursday, free to all. The shriek of a toddler announces the arrival of its first patrons, tired eyed and dirty.

The radio box sits at the end of the bar. A Callum & Callum logo fills its side, its distinctive swirly ampersand the same one that curled along the gate guard's radios and electric sticks. I frown, just in time for the tone of the radio hosts' conversation to lose its joviality.

"Aye, MacNair, looks like we're getting the final confirmation in now."

The bar goes quiet. The child whines and his mother shushes him. Both hosts swear.

"Sorry, folks, looks like tomorrow's reopening will only allow in upper-city workers with permit level eight or nine. Until further notice, only permits eight and nine, folks. Nothing seven or lower."

At least it'll be open. I'll deal with just how to get through it without a permit when the time comes. Right now, my brain feels about as hazy as the lower-city streets.

A collective groan rises from the bar's occupants. One of the cardplayers slams his hand on the table, and the woman beside him hollers for another beer.

"Like you can afford that now," her companion grumbles.

The bartender begins preparing the drink, but a stout man, with white peppering his deep-auburn curls and faded freckles so prosperous that they form dull blotches, takes the beer and adds another five to the lot, delivering them with a mutter of "It's on the house."

"Don't go nowhere, you scunners, there's more news coming in soon. Seems our dear old and ugly mum, Bubble Entertainment, has deigned to grace us with a press release."

I shift off the wall and brush the rust from the back of my shoulders. My hand lingers near my neck. *Guess we're stuck here for the night.* The warm presence of the parasite makes a sweltering mark against my already moist skin, but it doesn't reply.

The soup kitchen attendants serve me a bowl of

something watery and pale. Its fishy tang goes against my taste buds' every longing, but I sit myself at the bar and force some of the food down.

When the bartender comes by, I filter through my pockets. "Got any booze worth two spare buttons, a wet ball of lint, and a crushed leaf?"

I receive a half-assed eye roll in return.

The older, stouter man sets his last clean glass to the side and shoos the bartender away. He slides me the same beer as the cardplayer's. "You look like this might do you better than the soup."

"No offense, but I'll need about ten of those before they start to help." I give him my best grin with the jest, though right now my best is a pathetic grimace of a smile that catches in my jaw and makes my teeth feel wrong.

"You and me both, laddie." He wipes his palms on a rag and reaches across the counter. Like a small number of the other Maraheem selkies, his features resemble mine—broad nose and full lips, his unbraided, auburn version of my curls forming a cloud around his head—but beneath the freckles his skin barely holds a tan. "Name's Ivor. Ivor Reid. I only got in ten minutes ago; you been hanging in the front there long?"

"Just stopped by for the announcement." I tip my head toward the radio, where an upbeat tune now plays, and give his hand a firm shake. "Name's Rubem."

The song ends. MacNair hops back onto the mic with a shocked laugh. "You wee scunners aren't gonna believe this."

"Spit it out for us, MacNair."

"Yeah, spit it out!" one of the cardplayers shouts.

A static-like whisper comes over the radio; then MacNair's cohost curses. "You're talking mince!" With a disbelieving grunt, the host's voice evens out. "The word we got is the gates are closed because Alasdair Findlay is dead. *Dead*. The heir to Findlay Incorporated was found today at 13:09 with his throat slit. There's no comment yet from the BA detectives, but by the heightened security throughout the upper districts and the complete closure of all gates, it seems they've no clue who did it yet."

An eruption of chatter drowns out the radio hosts' conversation. One of the cardplayers shouts above the talk, "See, they can't step on us forever!"

Ivor whistles. "I'll pour us both another."

But I only half hear him. The shock on Tavish's face seems whittled into me now, as if this news has opened a vein of empathy between us. His brother is dead. His brother, the heir to a company who lets these people live in the muck at his gilded feet. His brother, whose death the cardplayers now celebrate. His brother, a piece of the family who may carry the secrets to removing the parasite. Someone killed Alasdair Findlay. My heart twists.

If someone has reason to kill one Findlay, they could just as soon kill another.

CHAPTER SIX

here or nowhere

I am a current running backward,
an expanse that shrinks,
a bud withering before bloom.
A being lost to the chinks.

I SHOULDN'T WORRY FOR him. Looking around the bar, tattered and worn as the rest of the lower city, I should be doubting every good thing I saw in the youngest Findlay. Maybe I should even be toasting and cheering with the people Findlay Incorporated has driven into the dirt.

My feverish parasite tosses me a spattering of memories as though it's rifling through them instead of truly trying to communicate. Images appear of my month as figurehead of a cartel, of the wealth and status I told Lilias I'd need if I were going to find her the ignits she so badly wanted. I'd filled one of the old cartel head's courtyard planters with uncut rubies as a joke.

I tried to use that power to save the Murk, I retaliate. But I don't need the parasite's help to refute that. Its own existence in my neck is enough. I had a drop of influence, and I still caused more harm than good.

Tavish's words from earlier resurface, and I don't know

which of us pulls them up, the parasite or me: *I'm the youngest of my family and mostly ignored for my efforts* and *They would rather I keep to my minor charities*. It proves nothing, but still, it gives me hope.

I lift the last of my soup to my lips, gulping it down despite the fishy tang, and watch the line of scraggly selkies forming behind the cauldron. I can't rightfully judge Tavish on what little I know of him, but whatever he has done, it clearly isn't enough.

Ivor returns from handing out another full tray of beers to the quickly filling bar and sits beside me with one of his own. He lifts it. Unlike the wild hollers and fanatic conversations around the room, his smile is small and distant.

I click my glass to his and drink. The heavy, rich beer leaves a dark flavor almost like coffee in its wake. I take a second large gulp before setting it down. "Alasdair's death won't be as kind to the lower-district folks as they think, will it?"

"You aren't wrong, laddie." Ivor sips from his own glass. "It's been too long since anyone made a real go at knocking the corps down. Most don't remember how much more work's to come if anything's gonna change."

"The corps?"

"The big seven. The corporations that own this city and the Mara Diplomatic Assembly, and through it, all of the Mara coast from the island village of Melfearn on the Tormid Sea to the most populous of our underwater sister cities in the Braenakirk Gulf. These days, they barely even bother to stay behind the scenes." He gives me a hard look. "You're real new, aren't you?"

There's no use denying it. I bob my head slowly, tapping my nails to the side of my glass. "I think I know what you're talking about, though. I've seen the same brands all over the lower. All your food comes from the O'Cain Fishery." I hold up one finger, then pop up a second. "And Sails and Co. runs the trolley system."

"All other transport, engineering, and plumbing, too," Ivor adds. "Got their own special tools we can't replicate."

"Callum and Callum must be some kind of tech producer." That's three fingers.

"Aye, but everything you'll see of theirs around the lower's rented."

I take another drink, trying to pluck four more logos from my memories. The parasite flashes me a helpful image of the gate. "Your guards have BA pins?"

Ivor nods. "Battery Arms. Provides the manpower for every kind of law enforcement here—only the head family's personal bodyguards aren't connected to them."

"Those two on the radio mentioned a Bubble Entertainment."

"They run all the media and art since buying out Falcre's publishing house five years back. Been a real battle just keeping a few lower-district announcers these days." He takes over for me, lifting six fingers. "Next you got Druiminn Health running our hospitals—or in the lower, you could say *not* running them, since most've been closed up for about a decade. And finally . . ." His seventh finger comes up, only for both his fists to curl.

"Findlay Incorporated?" I guess.

"Findlay fucking Incorporated. They've got all the auroras, all the fuel, everything we need to flourish under the sea." He stands enough to tap a fading algae light about us, and the gentle stir brings the bioluminescence back to life. "From us downtrodden in the lower to the heads of the other six companies, we all breathe the air they clean and shift with the ignation they rent us."

"Well, fuck. So they control *everything*?"

"Everything of value. Except my bar, of course." He tosses another wink over the edge of his glass, but it dwindles amidst his wrinkles.

Too many wrinkles for his age, I think. "There's no ignation production or aurora-related research or anything like that happening in the lower? Or in these other Mara cities?" My dwindling hope sinks out of me at the mixture of anger and pain that crosses Ivor's face.

"Nothing even close. Everything fancy like that's been moved to Maraheem's upper districts, to the corporation's main headquarters. Big seven gotta have it all right under their noses."

The upper. Where I'll be fighting to reach tomorrow. Only this time, the process will be harder than simply shoving past a few guards to shout in Tavish's face. Maybe this has all been one long mistake.

"Of course," Ivor continues, "some of the wealthier folks pretend to do their own thing—boutiques under the bigger conglomerates, brands in the underwater sister cities you don't ken are the big seven until you look closer, some stuff in the selkie-dominated coastal villages that comes from the humans. And the seven are so scared of each other getting the leg up, they still let the assembly make the occasional impartial decision, long as it benefits the upper city. Things like the gates—gotta keep us filthy lowers from sullying up their pearly streets."

I take another sip of my beer, trying to hide my grimace. "Maybe this is rude or ignorant, but why does no one just leave?"

"And abandon what little we got? We own nothing but our food and our clothes—everything of worth we gotta rent. You think Eyrr or Lindfel would be happy with a bunch of ragged selkies making slums outside their cities? Would that even be any better than what we've got here? At least here's family. Here's home." The anger drains from his voice, replaced by a fatigue so heavy it's almost endless. "Some *have* left though. About four generations ago, back when things were first getting bad, one of the Gayle kids—the family who owns Sails and Co.—they went off their head about the corruption, took three ships, and sailed south to the siren seas, let on anyone who wanted to come. Every now and again, that cycle repeats."

"How did it all get so bad?"

Ivor sighs, taking a gulp from his drink. "Most of the company heads were powerful families even before this land was turned from the old finfolk city into Maraheem proper. They've always tried to influence the assembly as much as they could, but it wasn't until my ma was a wee bairn that they started digging their claws in proper. Everyone knew it was happening, they'd say, or else no one did, but I think it was really that no one thought it'd get this bad, or that if it did, they'd have time to stop it. They'd closed their eyes, and suddenly their elected government weren't theirs anymore. Most realized it'd be damn hard to fix without help, so they gave up."

Without help. My mind jumps back to Tavish. "No one from the upper does anything for you? What about that youngest Findlay?" I try to speak around the dread clutching at my throat.

"Tavish?" Ivor snorts. "He provides some aid if that's what you're getting at. He and Dr. Keavy Druiminn—the new Druiminn head, since her sister died a few years back—they keep trying to reopen the lower-district hospitals Keavy's sister boarded up, but . . ." His gaze wanders to the soup kitchen line, and his voice caves with frustration. "They got no real clue what's going on down here. They use their charities to feel better about themselves, but they've never set a solid foot inside our world. When's the last time they ate at a soup kitchen? Waited in a gate line that would never move? Brought shite wine to a funeral for a wee bairn who could've been saved with the medical tech they've got three levels up? Never. They go home to their mansions and pat themselves on the back for not letting us all die out."

I don't know what to say to that—perhaps there is nothing I have the right to say. My memories flutter again, the parasite wiggling around in my mind. It finds my nights of hunger and scavenging, my mother's last words and my nine-year-old sobs, the Murk shouting me away for being too muddy, and the river towns flinging me right back for having mist in my blood.

That's not the same, I protest.

It returns my earlier line once more, '*I get odder the more you know of me,*' but this time I swear there's sarcasm in the way it speeds up my voice, my own words going squeaky. A bundle of emotions springs forth, mine and the parasite's mixed together, but I purge them, stuffing them away with all the other feelings that are too large and confusing to deal with. I need a lot more alcohol before I can evaluate any of them.

"I'm sorry," I finally say.

"Aye. You and me both." Ivor takes a much larger gulp from his beer this time. Before he can finish, the bartender waves for his help. He departs with a friendly slap on my shoulder, taking the rest of his drink with him.

I nurse mine, slower and slower as I near the bottom. As I do, I watch the way Ivor moves through the bar, track the easy manner in which he interacts with the customers and the places where it gives way to a sincerity far deeper and stronger. For all of Ivor's friendliness toward me, a dark lump still sits somewhere between my throat and my stomach. I am just a passing breeze here, a foreigner for a kind soul to take pity on; a day to be made, not a life to align with. And even if I could be that, me with my ghost feet, with my Murk-tinged skin and silty-river blood that means nothing to these people, so long as I still have the parasite in my neck, they could never see me without the taint of its presence.

The radio announces the gate's limited reopening and Alasdair Findlay's death again, but they have nothing new to add except for long descriptions of the upper city's advanced security measures and repeated bantering about how the other company heads must be handling the murder.

"Do you think Greer O'Cain will sleep with a fishhook next to their pillow now, MacNair?"

"I know I already do," MacNair replies. "How else am I supposed to reel you back into bed?" The laughter that follows is so fake it could be made of cardboard, but I can't tell if it's the joke they don't find funny or simply its existence in their current, otherwise harrowing program.

I take the last sips of my drink to the most shadowy part of the room, where I lounge in the noise of the cardplayers and try to forget that terrible look on Tavish's face. I can't make myself plan, much less move, as though some tiny, melancholic monster in my chest is stealing away my agency little by little. At some point I must've drifted off, because the lights are dim and the crowd has dwindled to a few ragged adults at the counter. Ivor progresses around the room with a step stool, dumping packets of powder into each light without moving them. Feeding the algae, maybe.

He bumps his boot against my leg as he passes. "There's a cot in the back room if you want it. One night only."

One night only. The story of my life.

But I take the cot, happy not to be sleeping on the Maraheem lower-city streets. I'm less afraid of Lilias, who must know I escaped but should assume I'm fleeing along the coast, and more daunted by the idea of my scarf falling while I sleep. In the undersized cot, I tuck my neck to the limp pillow, my feet against a bucket of red paint and a pair of stained brushes, and face the low shelf that blocks my view of the door.

I think of stealing the biggest bottle of whiskey in Ivor's liquor cabinet, but I don't. I think of taking the butcher knife to the thing in my neck and ending this chaos one way or the other, but I don't. I think, also, of Tavish. He drifts through my flighty dreams as a phantom, a laugh, a signpost at the bottom of an empty pit.

At some point in the night, the bar's gated front rattles. Someone passes behind the shelves. They ascend the stairs into Ivor's home compartments, their key jiggling in his lock a moment before it opens.

A deeper, darker sleep takes me then, surrounding me in a black fog that's not the shadowed grey of the Murk at midnight but a true void, rainbows flittering through it.

I jerk awake to the feverish scalding of the parasite against my skin, cords of its heat searing into my nerves until it feels like their sting and I are one and the same. I slap at the creature, and the burn flares before fading away. It leaves me panting and moist, trembling from my bones outward. I glance around, then slowly peel back my scarf and crane my neck. My own chin blocks most of my view of the parasite, but the skin along my shoulder looks wrong, where it meets the creature: rotten with rainbows.

Bile chuffs up my throat. I quickly rewrap the scarf to keep from heaving, but the image remains, those blisters and gashes of color creeping into my body, carving up my flesh. I have never felt so much like the mists from whence I came, as though a heavy breeze will blow me away. This parasite is a rising gale.

I can't stay here and let it disperse me.

My filthy socks come off, and I shove my bare feet into my mostly dried boots. I give a few hopeless tugs to my outfit. Ivor's bucket of cherry-red paint looks sharp and stunning compared to the dirty, faded reds on my vest. Without that contrast to put it out of focus, my skin holds a warm auburn beneath the brown. But there's no river people to hide my heritage from here, and the selkies' most common skin tone is nearly the same level of pink. I don the vest, tug up my collar, roll my sleeves, and head for the bar.

Ivor Reid chops onions behind the counter. The handle of his knife rattles with each slice. "Bridies'll be done in a bit, if you want one."

I have no idea what a bridie is, but nothing sounds palatable right now. "I'll pass, but thanks. And thank you for everything. You're doing good work here. If I could help . . ." I can feel the floor through the soles of my shoes, reminding me I'm not a part of this world.

Ivor's smile shines. "If I required anything in return, it wouldn't be good work, now would it, laddie?" He digs into his pocket and pulls out a bronze coin I recognize as a cheap piece of currency that covers street snacks and trolley rides. He tosses it to me.

My thumb and first finger catch it on instinct, flipping it across my knuckles before depositing it into my pocket. "I suppose not." My lips tug but fail to rise. I tap my fingers to the bar. "You don't happen to know a way into the upper city that doesn't involve going through a gate?" I keep my voice low, casual, but it seems to hit him like a scream.

He wipes the back of his hand along his cheek. "Those ways aren't worth the risk." There's a rumble beneath his words, not a storm but an earthquake. "Trust me. Stay in the lower districts, out of the way, or leave Maraheem entirely if you can, but don't sneak into the upper city, not with everything that's going down." His eyes gleam. He sets down his knife and leans across the counter, clasping my arm. "Get somewhere safe, while you've got the chance."

I grant him the best smile I can muster—a sharp, bitter thing that eats through my cheeks the way the parasite eats through my neck. "I wish I could."

As he lets go, my drooping scarf catches on one of his torn fingernails. It tugs a strand loose, ripping a gap in the fabric. The scarf slips. I pull it back up and tuck it beneath my chin, but Ivor still stares, his gaze wide and rigid.

"You're—" he starts.

"Nasty rash, isn't it?" I move away.

He steps toward me and bumps into the counter. That seems to finally yank him from his shock. Before he can ask more, I slip out of the bar and jog down the street. As the commuting masses engulf me, I try to throw off my anxiety. Ivor will never see me again. In this overcrowded maze, I'll be just as lost to him as I am to Lilias.

CHAPTER SEVEN

one very excessively bad plan

I am emotions echoing:
back and forth, back and forth.
Resurrecting darker, emptier—
cinders in the hearth.

MORNING IN THE LOWER districts is like evening in reverse. People flow with the ease of fish schools and the noise of a marketplace. The conspiracy theorist already sits on her corner, a pamphlet in one hand and a dingy, black coffee in the other. The trolley clatters by, people shifting out of the way and pouring back onto the street like waves on a beach. Some of them tap the algae-filled streetlights as they walk, making them burn a little brighter. The ceiling machinery sounds a bit squeakier, the air cooler but no less humid.

I head for the nearest gate, asking directions every few streets as the twisting tunnels and looping stairways throw off my sense of direction in a way that the convoluted interwoven branches of the swamps somehow never could. Down here, it's as if there's no north and south any longer. Everything exists in one disordered, twisting labyrinth built of hollers and laughs and sobs solidified into this rusting, half-green metal maze.

As I near the gate, the ceiling opens and the street widens, letting the trolley turn a circle in front of a listless fountain with a seal-tailed statue summoning a gurgle of green-tinged water, its bronze form exhausted by a buildup of grime. The stairs beyond are all but empty. At their base, three workers paint over a red symbol as a guard watches, the Battery Arms insignia of a *B* and an *A* boasted brightly on his grey-and-white uniform.

The trolley crawls to a stop behind me, releasing a wave of steam. As the vapor clears, my blood goes cold, and the parasite boils against it. Lilias stands there, a hat flopping against her back and one hand still on the trolley exit. She scans the square, eyes sharp, looking for something—for someone. Her gaze lands on me, and her lips curl in a triumphant snarl.

Someone knew I would be here. Someone must have told her.

Her expression sparks a montage: My boat drifting through the fog just after I'd sent for the aurora that now weaves itself into my body. My anxiety increasing with each half hour that lapsed, until it seemed to take physical form in Lilias shouting demands for more, faster, immediately, or else, more and more disbelieving each time I told her I was working on it. Her fury finally turning into her boot against Blossom's side, over and over, until the poor caiman couldn't hiss, then couldn't move, then couldn't breathe. And her final statement, the only one that managed to sear itself properly into my memory: *You have two more of these nuisances, I'm told?*

Both of Blossom's brothers are safe at home, but that doesn't stop the anger that tingles up my heels and through my knees, as though the caiman blood Lilias left smeared across my boat deck had sunk into me. The fear grows in time with it, locking me in place like cold, cruel manacles. I want to charge and I want to run, the way Blossom couldn't, the way I couldn't while watching her die. I want to, but I can't. I can do nothing at all.

The spell only breaks as Lilias lunges for me. I shove off her first punch with my forearm and slam a fist into her gut, but she catches hold of my tattered scarf and pulls. It rips up the middle, starting with the tear Ivor's accidental tug made and unraveling the worn threads. I grab for it as I stumble backward, but that just yanks it free entirely. It drops to the ground between us.

People still clamber around us, lost in another billow of vapor, but their sound doesn't reach through our shock.

"It's latching after all," Lilias whispers. She takes a step— one more than I can seem to—treading on my fallen scarf. "Wonder just how long you'll be sentient for? Well, we'll be locking your body away in a lab, anyway." As she talks, her hands run through motions that aren't quite Murk signs and aren't quite fidgets.

Her words repeat in my head. *Locking your body away in a lab. Just how long you'll be sentient for. Latching after all. How long you'll be sentient. How long.* Then the cycle jerks to a stop, the parasite panicking over a specific phrase: *'Locking away.'*

Terror douses all my other emotions, washing away my dread and fear in a haze of reactions not my own. It drives me away from Lilias, carrying me along the rim of the fountain, toward the stairs. I half expect a bullet in my back. Instead, Lilias bolts after me.

As I round the fountain, I run into the workers covering up the graffiti symbol, only the fishlike tail of it remaining. Their guard shouts as I leap between them. The wet paint slips beneath my feet. I catch myself and keep moving. Toward the gate.

This was not a good plan, I shout, but the thought feels distant, listless. The parasite's fear distorts my vision, and the closed archways on the lower side of the gate come up too fast, their spikes facing out. I scream. My mouth never opens, but the sound pounds through me, and with all my might, I throw myself away from the barbs before the parasite can run us both to our deaths.

I crash to the metal floor with a thunk that blurs the world. The parasite's heat snaps out, taking my energy with it. Groaning, I push off the steps. I have three seconds to think—three seconds in which Lilias runs up behind me, the slew of guards still turning toward me from their short line of permitted workers. My options: Fight past Lilias and vanish into the lower city, letting the parasite dig deeper. Or, fight into the upper city and hope that I can reach Tavish before anyone worse finds me.

Good plans are for people who value their continued existence, and mine is going to include a parasite slowly consuming my brain. Maybe a terrible plan is in order.

I scream and charge the open archway.

Unlike the smaller side gate Tavish brought me through, this entrance is expansive. Two platforms rise out of the floor on either side of the chamber, one holding a submersible, propeller-laden vehicle painted with a Sails and Co. logo of a crossed spyglass and hammer. The light-up board below it boasts a launch time of an hour and a destination I don't recognize. I steer around it, heading for the only currently open archway to the upper city.

Workers yelp and scoot to the side as I sprint past. The first guard lifts her weapon too slowly, and I dodge, the tails of my vest flaring as I leap and duck. The rest charge me. They approach on all sides, electricity crackling down their weapons, but they slow to a mixture of caution and violent alarm, their gazes locked on the parasite.

"Never seen an aurora up close before?" I ask.

A tremor runs through the guards. The one at the crux of the half circle speaks up. "You got a level eight or nine? Anyone attempting the gate without a level eight or nine gets a three-month sentence."

I lift my palms to my sides. "No, but I have something the Findlays will want very much to see, don't you think?" I pause, glancing back at the lower districts, to where Lilias stands in the shadows of the stairs, her face half-hidden in her broad hat. Her posture screams rage. "Unless you believe it'll make the Findlays *happy* to lose an aurora?"

Despite their visible BA allegiance, this statement seems to kick them all in the gut. They step forward as one.

"Give it to us, then," the same guard barks.

"If only it were so easy." It comes out more a grumble than I mean it to.

The guard's freckled cheeks go red. His weapon shakes, the electricity sparkling. "Hand it over!"

An armed attendant dressed in black pushes into the gate from the upper districts, their straight bangs flaring over eyes that could match Sheona's, lash for lash, as they strut into the space. Their polished boots squeak against the pristine floor. They bear no trace of the BA insignia. They wave the guards back. "If you touch that aurora and it dies, it's your arses on the line."

They snap to attention. "Aye, Mx. Malloch."

"At least someone's got sense around here," I mutter.

"You're not wrong, but you've no right to say it." Malloch stops in front of me. Their eyes narrow on the parasite. "Where's it from? How long's it been there?"

"South," I reply. "And a little while, but it only started properly digging in yesterday."

Malloch spins on their heels and strolls back toward the upper city, motioning for me to join them. Most of the guards return to their work, but the one who spoke earlier follows us with a second on their heels.

"Mx. Malloch!" he calls. "We'll escort you."

"That's unnecessary, Gillies," they snap. "The aurora, and by extension this one's host, are under the authority of my client, Raghnaid Findlay. The BA can stand down now."

Gillies holds his stick tighter. "We insist."

"Un-insist, then."

"That'd be a breach of protocol. The civilian came through

our gate. It would be irresponsible to leave them until we know they're in the Findlays' care."

Malloch's jawline pulses. For a moment, it looks like they might refuse. Their gaze flickers across the chamber, past the submersible vehicle platforms, and through the archways to the lower city. A slow breath leaves them. They nod curtly and march out of the gate with such controlled fire that I'm almost glad for the BA presence.

I have to jog to catch up. "Do you know if—"

"No," Malloch cuts me off, the sort of rebuff that's not aimed at a question, but at a person.

I shut up, half because of the edge in their voice and half because as we enter the upper districts' version of the main gate square, my concept of speech deteriorates.

The extensive wealth hits me in the chest with beauty so striking it becomes a kind of violence, each polished marble floor tile shining against my grimy leather boots. I'm too small to stand within it, to look up at the high, arched ceiling and pretend I came from anywhere but the dirt.

Here, the lights gleam with electricity. Ignation courses through the walls. The air smells of aristocracy, of elaborate spices and the fullest bloom in an endless rose garden. Gilding creeps like vines up the sides of their seal-tailed fountain, the statue's majestic face tipped skyward as it launches a rush of crystal clear water into a ring of hanging oyster shells that sprinkle it back down into the miniature lake below. A massive pane of glass makes up the wall to our right, granting a majestic view of an ocean courtyard, a pair of dolphins spinning above the colorful coral.

That's when I realize the biggest difference between this and lower—beside the hoarded wealth and the crisp, temperate air and the subtle, rainbow-infused shine of the ever-present ignation—is the lack of people. A few lower-district workers move swiftly around the edges of the wide pathways, their grey uniforms made for the shadows, while pairs or trios of the upper dwellers take their time, their elegant suits and cloaks and trailing dresses so silken and shining that one minute in the lower city would sully them. I count a dozen in all. A dozen people in the same amount of space that a thousand could have crowded.

I'm still watching the extravagance as though it might pounce, when Malloch leads us into an upper-city trolley car made of sleek lines and cushioned seats, ignation flowing through its center. They scowl at the BA guards and cast heavy glances at the back door while the carriage whips us higher into the city with none of the rickety chugging or steam spouting of the lower transportation. When we finally disembark, I'm brushing at my filthy outfit instinctively, as though I can wipe the stain of who I am clean if I just presented myself better. The impulse makes me flinch because I know it's not mine. It's not the parasite's either. It's this damn place scowling down at me, telling me to get out, like the rivers and the Murk both did all my life.

I keep my hands firmly at my sides, twisting my fingers in and out as Malloch marches me up a wide set of iridescent stairs and beneath a gleaming sign for Findlay Incorporated, moving at such speed they seem determined to leave the BA guards behind. Inside, tall glass walls reveal the endless ocean, water gently streaming down the ignation-laced pillars that support them. A message must have been sent ahead, because the door guard—still BA, even here—waves us along without comment, through pearl-studded gates, up an elevator of glass, and down a final, gleaming hallway.

I glimpse only a few people: a woman in a suit carrying binders across a courtyard, a man and his androgynous colleague talking in hushed tones beside a waterfall, and an open office with a chair so high backed only a gloved arm is visible around its side. A pair of black-clad individuals with pistols in their belts nod to Malloch as we move down a hallway to a set of double doors.

Inside, six wealthy selkies stand around a half-circle table with the chairs still tucked in, conducting what sounds like a shouting match after all the quiet. I spot the Findlay in the room immediately.

She takes the center space, bearing Tavish's stout build and his magnificent jawline and identical shark-fin eyebrows. Her silver hair wraps around her head, and her freckles are muted, her pale skin made pinker by the gleam of her silver dress. Ten lines of pearls work their way up her chest and neck. When her eyes meet mine, I see the abyss in them. The room goes silent.

"Leave us." She flicks her fingers at Gillies and the other BA guard, her sets of silver rings flashing.

They obey in an instant. Malloch closes the doors behind them, claiming a place silently off to one side.

"Raghnaid—" one of the onlookers starts, but another wrist twist from her quiets them.

Raghnaid Findlay strolls toward me, each click of her high heels resounding in the spacious room. "Well, now."

Her eyes sweep me in a way that makes my soul want to crawl out of my body to prove that I'm still a person even under her gaze, or to conform to the lens through which she sees me. I scramble for something, anything to say to her: An explanation. An apology. I made the wrong choice. I should never have left the lower city. I don't belong here in this exquisite, terrible place without mist or silt or soul. Its perfection devours me and spits me back out with every silted breath.

I search for the parasite's presence, but all I find is the cold and the fatigue, larger and more consuming than ever. The memory the creature fed me so often over the last day arises like heartburn: *'I get odder the more you know of me.'*

It's comforting this time. I truly don't belong here, but when did I belong anywhere? I will exist just as I always have, even if the lifeless floor strains against me and these grand statues of prosperity can't hear me from behind their pearl-studded earrings.

"Raghnaid Findlay." My smile slips up too far on one side,

turning it to a smirk. "I was told that you might have a solution to my problem."

Raghnaid's expression doesn't change. "Perhaps." She loops her pinkies together and sets her hands on the back of the chair at her side. "How did you come into possession of this creature?"

She doesn't ask for my name, and my introduction turns to a lump in my throat. My willpower slips just an inch. I force my grin not to falter. "I made the mistake of picking it up while it was free moving, and it refused to let me go."

The selkies behind Raghnaid exchange glances, shock and curiosity dominating.

Raghnaid's thin lips twist down. "Where is it from?" This time the question sounds more like a demand.

I can't lead her back to the Murk, no matter how thoroughly the place has denied me. "Not from your stock. I'm sure you would know if that were the case." It borders on a taunt, and I hope it has just enough pleasant wrappings to shut down that line of questioning without shutting me down with it. "I want it gone."

Four of the onlookers erupt at that.

"Do we have the means to force a release?"

"The lab would surely—"

"What would that do to a human mind?"

"If it's already embedded, then—"

"We will remove it." Raghnaid cuts them off, sounding so much like Tavish's diamond-edged voice that it makes me search the room for him, as though he'll materialize through the blue silk curtains or the sea-covered skylight just to echo her. "By whatever means necessary."

A buzz of panic rattles my spine, and I can't tell if it's mine or the parasite's. Both, probably. I sharpen my smile, wishing I had something to flick between my hands to distract from the fear leaching into my organs. "I'm offering you this aurora on the basis that I live through its removal, Mrs. Findlay. If you've no guarantee of that—"

She doesn't take her eyes off me as she picks up the sleek, black wall phone and speaks into it, "Join us in the boardroom, immediately. Bring your strongest bindings."

The panic grows. I search for something to say, but all my best lines flee from my grasp like butterflies into the fog. I could mention my connection to Tavish, but will it make things better or worse? With his distance from the family business and his certainty he means so little to it, what kind of action would his name spur?

A room member in a sheer wrapping dress drifts forward from her place near the back, her strawberry blonde ringlets bobbing as she walks. "Mother, don't you see? It's latching to him." She pauses beside Raghnaid, towering over her by a full head. While her frame is willowy and long, she has the voice of a Findlay, and it does what a Findlay voice seems made for: it cuts. "If we destroy him for the aurora, then we throw away the chance to study a living human host. We may never have another."

"And if we refuse to take full advantage of this rare opportunity to add to our collection?" Raghnaid snaps in return. "You should not even be here. You are clearly still in mourning."

As though speaking them made the words true, I notice the deep circles beneath the younger Findlay's eyes, the red tinge to her whites. She takes a step back. "We shouldn't spit on the chance to better our company. All our current technology and knowledge didn't stop Alasdair's murder, did it?"

Raghnaid's abyss eyes catch flame. "Ailsa! Your whimsical opinions are unneeded here. Go find somewhere you're useful."

Every onlooker flinches, starting with me.

"Aye, Mother." Ailsa's full height seems to collapse inward. She vanishes through a door in the far end of the room, not with dramatics or defiance, but as though she's simply floated herself out of existence.

My one advocate and she's as viable as the Murk mists. I make a sound that's meant to be something bigger and stronger—a bitter laugh or a dismissive snort perhaps—but it falls flat. "You've never seen this before, have you?" I wave to the parasite with a delicate swoop of my hand. The fuzzed and broken strings of my fishnet gloves look shabby in the harsh light. "You've seen auroras. You've studied them, but never one latched to a human. You're *lacking* in that." I hope she reads into the comment: in all this wealth, you're still missing something. I don't know how to feel about that something she's missing being me, though. Neither, it seems, does she.

Her lips part, but they linger there, her tongue pressed forward. Instead of speaking, her expression twists. The double doors spring open.

A slew of people in pristine workers' uniforms sweep in, creating a perfect arc around two more black-clothed bodyguards. One hands a pair of thick manacles to Malloch. Their lips tighten, but their worry doesn't seem aimed in my defense.

Raghnaid steps forward, and I cringe back, the parasite shrinking even as I hold my shoulders straight. She may be shorter, but she never seems to need to look up at me. "Your aurora comes from the South—where you're from, too—is that not correct? One of those little colonies along the Manduka River, perhaps? Do your people have more of them?"

With weak knees, I lean toward her. "Work with me instead of against me, and maybe I'll tell you." I sound like a steamship and feel like driftwood. Half my mind throws up flares while the other half searches desperately for an escape route. Too many workers block the entrance for me to dodge all of them, but the doors behind the silk curtains might be reachable if I move quickly enough. I prepare to spring.

Raghnaid motions to the bodyguards. "Take him directly to the head of research's external offices—*not* to the Trench laboratory itself. They will see he gets there."

At that, the parasite finally blazes to life. Terror suctions up my limbs. This time the emotion comes with no push to fight or run, just a crushing debilitation. I struggle against it, but the devastating panic holds fast like the roots of an ancient mangrove. The parasite's connection to me grows with every defeat, turning its fear into my own.

Malloch grabs my wrists. I stop breathing. Stop existing. Some part of me hangs in the air, weightless and useless, numbly drowning but still far too much alive. Whether I see it with my eyes or feel it in my skin or sense it with the strangled leftovers of my being, I know the parasite has dug itself deeper.

Breathe, breathe, breathe. I need to move my lungs. I need to still be me.

From across the room, the slam of the door rattles the parasite loose from my brain. I come back to the sight of Tavish, a stack of papers in his arms and an expression on his face like a man going to war.

CHAPTER EIGHT

a collision of findlays

The stars are going out, one by one by a hundred.
How do you still see me through this deconstruction?
If I am already lost to the shadows within,
where do I end and the darkness begins?

TAVISH LOOKS READY TO wage war. His silver-trimmed suit lies perfectly beneath his draped sky-blue scarf, its ends tucked into his deep-grey vest. He leads his attack with nothing but the sophisticated rap of his cane and the air of a king coming home.

"Board members. Mother. Ailsa mentioned your predicament." No one can speak over him. No one can look away. "In the wake of Alasdair's death, haste isn't a virtue. I'm glad to see you're deliberating on this with such care." He may not be able to see the haste, but Tavish Findlay knows it's there, the coattails of his words creating a layered condemnation.

His mother's lips part, but his own move faster.

"We are the power of this city, both in the literal and the metaphoric. We are their sole supplier and guardian of fuel, but more importantly we are the stability—the authority—the entire city relies upon. If we crumble, so does Maraheem." He plants his cane against the tile, his attention turned toward those I assume must be Raghnaid's board members. His unfocused gaze is stunning in this moment, determined to the core and just wistful enough to draw in the room. "Yesterday morning, we appeared to all the world as immovable and untouchable. Then my brother was murdered."

None of his shock from the gate remains, but a perfectly manicured flash of grief crosses his stoic face, not mourning tinged in melancholy but the rage of an avenger. Alasdair means little more to me than a name the lower people hate, but the way Tavish looks now, I would kill for his resurrection. The board members clearly feel the same, all lips tipped down and eyes shining. Even the workers nod along.

"Our people already interpret Alasdair's death as a sign of our waning authority. And despite all efforts to control the ignation leakage, they will soon brandish that as a failure in our abilities as well. We stand in these grand halls, and we crumble." He needs no curse to amend his claim because his entire sentence is an oath of its own. It cuts through the room, a diamond blade sharpened to the finest of points.

His mother's eyes narrow.

"Adding a single aurora to a collection the populace has already lost awe of will do nothing to fix this," Tavish continues. "We need to strengthen ourselves beyond the ordinary, not to patch up our cracks but to give the city—and the North Seas—a new reason to bask in our power. And by the grace of the Trench, we have been handed that on a silver platter."

A flicker of the parasite's warmth bubbles in the back of my mind, repeating the phrase 'Bask in our power,' and then, 'That sounds tough.' I don't know what to make of it, whether to see it as a reminder that Tavish is a Findlay, and Findlays have more power already than any single family should, or that Tavish doesn't quite believe in that power, even if his heart and soul seems crowned in it right now. My confliction shatters the spell he's set on me, and I catch the slightest tremble in his fingers as he motions in my vague direction.

"Never before have we seen an aurora implant on a human. This is the scientific breakthrough of our time! We are the only ones with access to it, the ones with the opportunity to unlock the future, and every new advantage it might grant us." Tavish pauses there, letting his claim solidify in the enraptured room.

Raghnaid's interruption comes so sharp that I can already feel it knock the first crack into his argument. "You seem to have given this much thought." It sounds like the start of an execution, her breath after the pull of the blade in preparation to swing for the throat.

Tavish doesn't give her the chance. "Indeed. And as Findlay Incorporated's public ambassador, it's my duty to arrange for surveillance and study." From his papers, he produces piles of forms, gliding a small device over their titles before setting them neatly onto the board table in easy reach of the members. "I have proposals here from the heads of our laboratory and ignation engineering departments, signed delayed-disclosure agreements from everyone who saw the subject entering the upper city, official press releases for distribution to the other company heads, and, since the subject is not a part of any specific big seven company's holdings, I've informed the assembly and received temporary waivers from them allowing for immediate instigation. Sheona is currently working with the laboratory staff to prepare a secure quarter for baseline recordings."

It's a pity that Tavish can't see the expressions his mother slips through, her cheekbones lifting and her lips pursing, then falling, a choked rise in her shoulders and finally her entire body going taut. "Well thought through indeed. It seems nothing more is needed—for the moment." Her low words carry like a threat. She waves her fingers, flipping on her heel. "Have the copies delivered to my assistant immediately. This meeting is adjourned."

Each step she takes clicks like a thunderclap as she exits the door opposite Tavish's. A bustle of voices immediately overtakes the room, board members and workers each talking on their individual sides with exclamations that overlap exactly.

"Rubem?" Tavish sets the rest of his papers down and holds out his free arm.

"I'm here," I say, as though I might be anywhere else, as though I have any choice in the matter. Everything I could add, both good and bad and all the in-between, lodges in my throat. He rescued me from his mother—rescued me through a feat he must have been planning since long before I arrived in this boardroom. And I know he's likely not here for me as a no-man's lander named Rubem, but as a responsibility and a tool he's decent enough not to let break, but it feels nice all the same.

I press my palm to his arm. Three different people call his name. He grips my elbow, and I can't tell whether he's holding me in place or just plain holding on to me.

Sheona bursts into the room with a bundle of folders. She takes one look at the chaos of the attendees, all of whom seem to want Tavish's attention, and clears him a path out with the discretion of a howler monkey. Tavish leads me through the gap she creates, half pulling, half falling back toward the door he'd first entered from. His cane clanks into its frame. It catches there, and he catches, too, jiggling it uselessly.

I nudge it off with my toe and help him into an empty, sweeping hallway.

"Wait for me while I hand these off," Sheona grumbles, still holding her folders like she might bludgeon someone with them. Her attention fixes on me, and though her only other weapon is her snarl, calm and precise and calculated to perfection—so different from Lilias's reckless fury—it alone fills me with dread. "You will treat him like your life depends on his well-being."

"I do," I say.

Her eyes narrow, but someone tries to badger their way past, and she grunts, yanking the door shut before they can.

I shudder from a mixture of relief and fear and a million other things I can't identify. Some part of me never imagined I'd get this far, not when my legs never seem to step in the right direction. Without Tavish, I wouldn't have, and the power he now holds puts me at the mercy of his whims. If I'm offering him this kind of control, I can't be apathetic about it.

Tavish may have this handled, but he can't be the only one.

I draw myself straighter, trying to put together the kind of words that will be a match for his own, but as I turn to him, I no longer find the king from the boardroom. Tavish's single sliver of fear—that one tiny tremble—has multiplied itself into an earthquake. He clutches his chest. His knees wobble.

"Fuck," he sobs, too fast, too shallow. He leans against the wall, supporting himself between it and his cane. He slips toward the floor.

My chest tightens. I catch him, grabbing his forearms in mine. He flinches at my touch, but as I utter an apology, he clutches me back. "Easy there," I say softly. "Do you need anything? Does it hurt?"

"No," he wheezes, and for what seems like an eternity, he just leans on me, breathing and shaking. Finally, his lungs seem to loosen, the gasps deepening. "It—it's passing now." He breaks into a small laugh, choked and weak. He tries to right himself, but his legs still quiver. "I can stand. I should stand."

Hesitantly, I let him. He only wavers once. My hands feel too useless now, and I tug out the little coin Ivor gave me, tossing it into the air just to give them something to do. "You're all right? You're sure?"

"Sure enough. I haven't had an attack that strong since my first year speaking to the board. It merely shocked me, is all." Tavish's lips pull so taut they must hurt. He straightens further as Sheona returns. "We should be going."

He turns on his heels, and though each step is slow, he moves steadily toward the spiraling stairway on the other end of the chamber.

I don't follow. "What are your plans for me?"

Tavish stops, Sheona already ten steps ahead of him. His brow tightens. "To help remove your parasite."

I grip the coin so hard it bites my skin. So many times, I've done this, with Lilias, with the Murk, with the river people. So many times, I have waited patiently for the axe to drop. Waited for someone else to decide. "You of all people must have a strategy for that. I want to know it."

"We really must—"

"Now, please." It's such a weak plea, one I expect to be met with pitying condescension.

Instead, my cracking seems to break him in turn. His lips part, and the lines multiply between his eyebrows. His gaze goes straight through me, but the weight of his attention is a physical thing, gripping me to my bones, as though we are two people inhabiting the same reality, both of us ghosts, or neither of us so.

"Ah, I ken." And somehow, by a miracle or a curse, it's him who stumbles over his words. "I'm sorry, it seems I've been inconsiderate. Or, let me rephrase that: not *seems*, but *have*. I have been inconsiderate." He barely draws a breath, charging onward. "I've witnessed firsthand what my mother thinks of you—or what she doesn't think, I suppose—and I don't want you to feel as though I'm the same. I don't want to *be* the same. You are here because you need help, and if at any moment you feel I can no longer help you, then you are free to find someone else who can. But you can hardly do that when you don't understand what help I'm offering."

My fear cracks into ugly, stale chunks. Past trauma has rotted them inside, but I try to look beyond it, to hope. Tavish was an ally when I didn't even realize I needed one.

He might continue as such. No betrayal or misuse or abandonment. The thought won't silence my doubts, but it lets me sidestep them into something almost peaceful.

"All right. You're forgiven, this time." It's the same words he used, the same tone, but it feels different now: feels like every soft, tight emotion I'm holding in my chest. I take one step, then the next, and the rest just follow.

Tavish joins me.

"This laboratory you mentioned? We're going there now?" I play with my coin as we descend the stairs, Sheona far enough away that it would almost feel private if she wasn't so obviously listening.

Tavish's face twists up. Despite a full hallway and heavy door between us and the boardroom, he keeps his words barely audible. "The Trench? Och, no. It's the primary Findlay Inc. laboratory in which the auroras are kept. Taking you there would mean handing my mother full control. I may have shuffled some forms toward their department supervisors, but I don't trust them not to cave to my mother the moment she enters the room."

"But all the forms, and everything you told Raghnaid, was that all a lie?"

"I implied what I needed to in order to win this particular battle." The diamond edge comes into his voice again, aimed not at me but at something larger and farther away, the full expanse of the world, I think, or perhaps just someone who clouds his. "Nothing I've levied against her has ever held, though. The temporary experimentation waivers I received from the assembly had very specific wordage that stops any dangerous operations from being forced on you until they decide who officially owns your aurora, but give my mother a day or so, and she'll pressure or bribe or outright intimidate them into signing it over to her."

We cross a landing embedded with thin swirls of shells so lovely I feel odd stepping on them. "What will we do once that happens?"

"We, I hope, won't need to do anything because you won't be here anymore. I'm contacting Dr. Druiminn to see if she'll provide us with a medical team—she's been a fantastic partner in helping reestablish hospitals in the lower since her sister died—and there's a few Trench scientists I may be able to bribe for assistance. I'm certain Greer O'Cain would be eager to take part as well." A slight flush tints Tavish's cheeks, and he fiddles with the top of his cane. "I'm not entirely unselfish in this endeavor. Greer was the company head I'd wished to meet at the beach yesterday. They're not fond of my family and have taken to ignoring me entirely, but I hope giving them access to this might entice them into working with me in the future."

"Can we trust them though? How do we know they won't prioritize the aurora over me, hoping they can keep it after?"

"Greer is stubborn and an asshole at times, but they believe that all life is valuable, even if they seem to despise anything that can walk on two legs."

A kindred spirit, then. "You know them well for someone who seems to think so little of you."

Tavish's expression morphs into a callus stare of superiority so chillingly like Raghnaid that it sends a shiver across my shoulders. "Their misgivings do seem reasonable when you consider one particular side of my family tree—and that my father gleefully abandoned the O'Cains for it. He's Greer's little brother, and they've never forgiven him."

"Ah, a typical family feud, then," I say, as though I've been close enough to any of my living family to have had such an experience. I return to bouncing my coin along my knuckles, watching Sheona's back as she prowls ahead of us.

A guard post appears. Beyond looks like a new building, the architecture somehow even more grand and dramatic, a palace instead of a place of business.

"Welcome to the Findlay Estates," Tavish announces. "You should be safe here while my mother untangles my bureaucracy and settles things with the assembly." A grin spreads across his face, a bubble of pride in his voice so soft that it seems even he isn't sure whether or not to pop it. "She won't bother you until it's done—likely won't even think to look for you here. She'll have to cut out her own stone heart before she views you as a guest instead of a science project."

He can't see the way I cringe, nor feel it mirrored in the parasite's emotions.

We walk in silence past the guard post and through a set of pearl-crusted archways so magnificent they belong in the citadel of an undersea god. One glance at Tavish, his curls a perfect sweep away from his freckle-strewn face, and I think I'm not half-wrong. But for a kind of god, he is overly anxious. His fear still haunts him in the constant motion of his jaw as he chews on his own tongue, and he recoils from every distant voice.

Sound travels through his elegant palace like rustles in a graveyard, both too loud and too soft all at once. Water trickles down elaborate structures of iridescent stone and polished sapphires, and magnificent external windows reveal the deep blue of an endless sea, while interior glass walls give glimpses of coral and fish. The first signs of home life appear—sitting chambers completed by grand pianos or art displays, and a dazzling dining area with a chandelier of hanging crystals—but each new room seems just as uncomfortable as the last, everything spread too far apart and so empty of life it could be a tomb.

"Your family certainly doesn't know the meaning of modest." Even my faint whisper feels as though I might shatter this hall's impossible amounts of glass.

"This floor is used most for events and house parties. My parents both reside seventy-four steps above, in what my late Findlay grandmother dubbed 'The Tower.' And this," Tavish explains, leading me down yet another immense stairway, "is the floor I share with my siblings."

The shift in scenery is barely noticeable, but the high ceiling does appear a tiny bit lower, the spectacle of it all reduced, slightly. Tavish seems to fit them better, as though their precise level of regality was made for him, or perhaps more accurately, *he* was raised to suit *it*.

Sheona continues on ahead to do what she calls a "perimeter scan" and what Tavish refers to as an "overprotective time waster."

A minute later we pass a set of cracked open doors to a dark parlor lit only by the faint glow of ignation in the ceiling. A cat pokes its head out. The rest of it follows, its sleek, tabby-striped body a deep blue-grey against its sea-green eyes. Its tail twitches as it walks. It cocks its head at me.

"Hold on," I tell Tavish, slipping Ivor's coin back into my pocket. Slowly, I crouch down to the cat's level and offer it my open palm.

It watches me. With another flick of its tail, it trots up and sniffs my fingertips. I brush gently against its face. When it leans in, I scratch harder, following its body language to knead in the places it wants most. The cat releases a purr like a steam car, much too rumbly for its slim frame.

I chuckle. A meow responds, but it comes from a second cat, a fluffy, far more rotund beast whose silvery coat fades to a grey around piercing blue eyes. It places each paw like a dancer. Neither its chin nor tail come down as it paces near the door, watching me with obvious suspicion. I offer it my other hand.

It tips its nose up.

"I respect that," I say.

Its sleeker friend steals both my hands and the better part of my calves, rubbing against me like there's no tomorrow. Animals are genuine in a way people never will be. They say exactly what they mean, every time, if only we would learn to listen. They stay as long as we offer them what they need, and when they hurt us, it's only because we ignored those needs. I close my eyes and smile. The rest of the world seems to melt, blurring all the fear and anxiety beneath the soft, natural thrum of the creature pressing into my hands.

Tavish's voice shatters the peace of the moment. "The cats were Alasdair's—'his girls,' Ailsa calls them. The only companions he ever found worth keeping for long." One edge of his lips tug. "They don't usually like strangers. Or anyone, really, with the exception of Alasdair." He holds out his hand, but both cats ignore him, accepting and perpetrating his insult in one fell swoop. His smile turns sad. "They probably miss him. Last night was the first time he didn't come home to them since they were both tiny things that fit in my palm."

That thought twists my heart like a physical blow. Most of my own pets haven't seen me for weeks. Poor Sheila might still be watching the sea where Lilias's ship carried me away. I won't make her wait forever.

The sleek tabby nibbles on my hand, nearly catching her teeth on my fishnet gloves.

I massage the sides of her face in retaliation. "Do they have names?"

"Likely. I've only heard Alasdair call them by outrageous epithets, though, never the same thing twice. Except 'you dashed fool.' I believe that is reserved for when the smooth-furred one knocks things off his nightstand." He pauses, his voice going hollow. "*Was* reserved, anyway."

The sorrow in his tone makes me stand, but I give both cats one last, long look. If the grey fur of the sleeker one appears almost blue, then the fluffy aristocrat's darker points hold hints of lavender. Blue and Lavender, I dub them, though I doubt I'll be around long enough to use the names.

As we try to leave, Blue lets out a positively offended yowl. She springs herself up my back and lands on my shoulder—the side opposite the parasite. Her slight form just barely fits. I scratch her head and vow to find both her and her friend treats later.

Tavish looks like he could use a treat now. His eyebrows press together, each step dragging a little as he continues down the hall. Lavender follows us at a distance, her tail in endless motion. She keeps looking back, as though she expects someone else to come with us. Someone who will never come again.

"I'm sorry about your brother."

"Aye. Me too." A bubbly laugh leaves Tavish, augmenting the grief that lines his features. "He was shite, you ken? A real proper dobber, arrogant and selfish. It'd probably have been better for the city—for the whole damn sea—if he'd retired to some wee fishing village. But dead? He shouldn't be dead." The final word cracks, trembling through the air like a snap of electricity.

It buzzes my bones. I focus on petting Blue, trying not to drown in the sensation, but the grief creeps in, a different sort from Tavish's, old and dark and deep. It flows in the same shade as my mother's dried blood. I press a thumb to the corner of my eyes, even though those tears have long since been drained. I want to tell him that I know sorrow the way a child is supposed to know their parents, but I can't bear to leave the crust of my mourning in Tavish's home. Instead, I say, "I never had siblings."

"Some days, I wished I didn't. But other times? When I was a bairn, he used to ruffle up my hair." The admission flows from Tavish like his emotions, leaping and spinning with the urgency of rapids. Whether they charge toward a waterfall or a lake, I don't know. "Mother hated it. She loved him, though. He had her ambition and her strength, and, oh, she loved him. Alasdair, her shining boy. Alasdair, who no one was good enough for, not even the other company heirs. Alasdair, the only opinion in this family that mattered. Now look at her: dry as a desert and half as sympathetic. I'd pity him if he could see how little she mourned." He doesn't sound pitying but vindicated, as though he and his brother are closer now that their mother has left them both behind.

I don't point out that mourning looks different on each of us. Raghnaid doesn't deserve my defense. "What about Ailsa?" I'm not sure what I'm asking—was he close with her, is her grief genuine, would their mother weep if she died—but I know that this moment feels like an exhale, letting me simply exist without thinking of where I'm headed or where I've been, and I want to cling to that.

"Once, I would have sworn that even if everyone else in my family turned on me, I would still have had her. But now . . ." His brow pinches, and he runs a hand through his hair, chin still tipped toward the ceiling. "The past few years she's been caught up in her library more and more—it's that one we just passed, ten paces back and three to the right."

The silent, closed room seems to lack anything that should have alerted Tavish to its location. His cane barely even taps the floor. It's how well he knows the estate, I realize. This is his home. He was raised to it in more ways than one.

As we round the next corner, Sheona waits for us in front of an elegant doorway, iridescent inlays curling up the sides. "The floor looks clear. I'll go deliver those messages to Dr. Druimmin and Greer O'Cain, but for fuck's sake, stay put until I get back."

"Only if you hurry," Tavish grumbles. He turns to the door. Ignation pours through a box around its handle, and a light comes on, targeting his brooch. As it shuts off, the lock clicks. He smiles as he leads me inside. "Welcome to your home away from home."

CHAPTER NINE

ghost grime

The hole in my chest is black; it has its own gravity now.
If I say to you, "Reach in," I also pronounce:
"Be entrapped."

I TAKE IN THE room slowly, all too aware that this space
does not, and will never, belong to me. Smaller and blander
than the magnificent chambers behind us, everything sits
exactly three steps away from everything else, all in silvers
and blacks and blues. A massive, pillow-strewn mattress
presses against one wall, competing with a pair of clutter-free
dressers and a desk so wide it could almost be a second bed,
dozens of paperwork piles scattered across it.

The plush carpet covering most of the marble floor makes
me yearn to kick my boots off and let the fibers slip through
my toes like the clay-heavy mud at a jungle river's edge. Two
half-curtained windows on the far wall look out on a
scooping rock barrier, streams of light pouring between gaps
in the coral. An eel winds through the base. Blue hops from
my shoulder, scampering over to watch it swim. It bares its
teeth at her.

An archway leads to the bathroom, and another to the
closet. A proper undersea bedroom, except for a distinct lack

of mirrors and lights. That's when it hits me.

"This is *your* room?"

Lavender slips in just before Tavish closes the door. He slides down a physical bolt so practical and dull that I wonder whether Sheona picked it out or if he somehow stumbled across it himself. "Does that bother you?"

"No. There's only one bed, though." As I say it, my heartbeat pounds a little louder. I tug at my gloves, trying to realign my emotions the same way I adjust the interwoven black strings.

"I'm aware." A hint of red appears in Tavish's cheeks. "I can have another mattress brought in if that's what you prefer. I've no wish for you to be uncomfortable."

His honesty comes with a kind of vulnerability that feels as though he's extending his hand toward my teeth and asking me not to bite. As though he trusts me. I choke on something deep inside myself, large and tight and consuming. For him to open himself up without necessity or benefit: that, I think, must be friendship. Or the start of one, if I grab hold of it. If I can acknowledge his hand and bare my throat in return. "This is the most comfortable sleeping arrangement I've had in weeks," I reassure him. The rug alone looks twice as plush as Ivor's cot, and I can't imagine Tavish would let me sleep there without a pillow and a blanket or two after all he's done for me already. "I should thank you, by the way. What you did back there was incredible."

A smile lights up Tavish's face. "Oh, no, that was—it was nothing. Just a bit of luck, really."

I can see the excuse is half a lie. The printed papers on his desk look similar to the ones he brought to the boardroom. What looks like a typewriter with raised dots on the keys perches in front of the cushioned chair, while from within an open drawer peeks out a pile of the same little devices Tavish ran over his paperwork's titles back at the boardroom. A longer inspection of the room reveals similar aids—a clock without a front, an umbrella holder of canes, a thick set of cards whose backs hide lifted lines, a phone with unique indents around the outside of the spinning dialer.

I try to imagine him here, at his desk, notes and worries and a buzzing phone, while I drank beer to the news of his brother's death. "You must have started planning all this well before I came through the gate today."

"I've been working since last night. I slept for a few hours in the early morning and a few again while awaiting responses from the directors. Sheona helped enormously. She might not act it, but she feels guilty for not checking for you. As do I."

"You'd just learned your brother was murdered. I think anyone has a right to be distracted by something like that."

"Aye, but still." Tavish removes his shoes with the care of a glassmaker handling his masterpiece. He traces his fingers up the first three rungs of his mounted shelves and places them onto the only open space.

My own boots release a smudge of grime onto the pristine floor as I step out of the way for Tavish to hang his suit jacket on the back of his chair. He loosens his scarf and flops onto his mattress. Somehow the dramatic collapse comes off as stupidly sophisticated when he does it, his ankles landing perfectly crossed and his palms propping him up from behind. Lavender tiptoes her weighty body across the bed, as far from him as she can, and curls up on one of his pillows. Her equally elegant motions mirror Tavish's perfectly.

I lean against the desk and tug at the tops of my boots, but I don't take them off. Setting them by the door with Tavish's seems too forward, like an announcement to the world: *Hi, I'm a part of his life.* They'll only leave crust behind when I have to pick them back up again.

I sink onto the marble floor instead, tucking in my feet so they don't touch the plush carpet. Blue hops into my lap, ignoring the grime. She starts purring the moment I rub my fingers down the sides of her neck.

My mind flashes back to Alasdair and his grim fate. What were his murderers hoping to achieve? Simple vengeance? Chaos among the family? A transition in power? If I'm going to be sitting in their estate for the time being, it would probably benefit me to know what's going on here, so I'm not caught in it unaware.

I run a hand down my jaw, the harsh prickles of facial hair rubbing into my palm after so long without a shave. "If I may, who will get the company now that Alasdair isn't here to inherit? Ailsa?"

The parasite pulls up the memory of Ailsa's dispute with Raghnaid, the way her mother disregarded her. I shove it back down. *Yes, I know. I was there.*

'Here because you need help,' it tosses back.

You could help by not using Tavish's old words against me and getting the fuck out of my head. I flick it for good measure. It snaps me with a jolt of heat so stifling that I almost miss Tavish's reply beneath the wave of pain.

"Aye, probably Ailsa, though she will hate it almost as much as Mother will—she'd never have killed Alasdair for it, if that's what you're getting at. At least, not the Ailsa I knew."

That didn't count her out entirely. "If not her, then who else benefits from your brother's death? Surely he had enemies?"

Tavish stiffens. He seems a step away from slipping over the edge of his emotional waterfall, but he breathes out and sits straighter, tugging at the lines of his button-up shirt. Perhaps his emotions are not rapids, after all, but rather ignits, his power flaring until it suddenly zaps out, forcing him to recharge. "I suppose Alasdair had rivals among the other corporations," he says. "Greer O'Cain in particular despises him, but no more than they hate my mother. And I can't imagine them assassinating him like this. He was found in his parlor, his throat slit and a fish symbol drawn in red paint."

I give Blue my best spine scratch. Perhaps she does know

her owner isn't coming back after all. "What about your staff?"

Tavish groans. "We investigated ours thoroughly, but there were thousands of workers in the upper districts when Alasdair was killed, and our security isn't infallible. Besides the advantage the other big seven corps might gain, everyone from the lower districts also stands to profit from Findlay Inc. having a less ruthless heir."

"An heir like you?" I realize the implication as soon as I've said it, trenching its way through Tavish's features like a dark pit. "I'm not accusing you," I clarify. "I just want to know, if you had control of this company, what would you do with it?" Ivor's allegation rings in my head too violently not to ask. Whatever Tavish's reply, I trust that he means well. But meaning well and doing good are two different things; my own failures prove that.

Tavish's pain doesn't leave, only transforms, aimed, I think, inward instead. "That's—it's beyond my ken. I'd never actually considered it."

I gently nudge Blue out of my lap before heaving off the ground. "But if you did? If you had the chance to do whatever you wanted with the ignation and the auroras. With Maraheem?"

"You're off your head." He snorts, a refined, dainty sound that rides on a needle's point. "Everything would take so much planning. I don't have a tenth of the information I'd need for that kind of undertaking, or half the ability, or—"

"What if you had everything you needed here, to do anything you wanted, what would you choose?"

"I'd force the assembly to take down the gates." He whispers it, so low it nearly blends into the brush of his lips together. "But without the proper precautions, eliminating the harsh district divisions would throw the city into chaos. We'd need the assembly to have equal representation between the upper and lower, and new tax distributions, and so much more. An impossible amount more."

He's halfway there, at least. He means well. Someday, that intention might finally transfer over. "If it were easy, someone else would have already done it."

"Aye, right." The hint of sarcasm in his tone seems to soften the edge instead of strengthening it. His chin falls, his brow drooping. "I'm not the best person to lead a project like that."

"Probably not." As I say it, Ivor's wrinkle-lined eyes come to mind, sparking with hatred for the philanthropists unwilling to become a part of the people they help.

Tavish's brow shoots toward the ceiling, his unfocused gaze popping up before drifting back out of alignment. "You're a damn dobber, you are."

"It's not a personal failing. You just don't understand the lower city and what it needs the way the people who live there do." I slip off my boots and pad across the carpet, only realizing what I've done once they're behind me, the rug's fabric sinking between my toes and drawing me farther in. Lavender gives me an offended meow as I plop onto the bed at Tavish's side. The smudge of my lower-district grime mars the clean, sky-blue blanket like a gash. "But even if you aren't the best person for the job, you're the one with the most means. Sometimes life gives us a yoke that doesn't fit our shoulders, and it's a fucking mess, but we have to do what we can to carry it all the same." That weight presses phantom palms to my back, bearing down with the musty scent of the deep swamp.

"You sound as though you speak from experience." Tavish runs his hand up and down the side of his thigh, so close to mine that I swear I feel the motion of the air he displaces.

I watch his fingers drift back and forth, back and forth. "Between hiding from the world and letting myself be bullied into maintaining a terrible status quo, I finally accomplished something good—did my best to help save my mother's homeland." I don't mean to lower my voice, but the words come out quiet. "Though, I guess I can't recommend it. I don't think they accepted me even after I helped them. I'm here, aren't I? None of them stopped that. I can't say that if you saved the lower districts, they would do the same for you."

Tavish's fingers keep drifting. They find my arm, and I can't tell if it's on purpose or by accident. The soft squeeze I swear he gives could be nothing but my own heartbeat pressing against my skin. He drops the hand so quickly after. "You deserved better from them."

I force a smile before realizing there's no need with him. Instead, I weaken. I droop. I collapse inside. And for a moment, with his hand on mine and the fear let loose, I feel like a whole person, alive and present and able to exist without alcohol to prop me up. "If you're right, then my lack of deserving didn't stop it from happening." That little doubting voice in my head adds: *Nothing will stop it from happening again, there or here or anywhere you try to build connections.*

"You don't deserve this whole aurora disaster either." Tavish's quiet statement cuts my frazzled doubts in half. With a soft hum, he lifts his hand. "May I?"

I hesitate, but my indecision caves to logic. He's helping me remove the parasite—I can let him understand it a little better. It's a single touch, not an acceptance of everlasting friendship. Not anything more than that either. "You may."

I guide his hand to my neck. He doesn't flinch away from the parasite's velvety surface, not even when it goes from cold to hot and back again. His lips sink, then part. A stray curl tickles the edge of his mouth, but he seems not to notice. He seems not to notice anything but the fissure between myself and the parasite. His fingertips trace it, dancing between me and my enemy.

Every brush shivers through me. A part of me wants more of his thoughtful caress, but the rest wants nails beneath the creature and a liquid fire in my throat to smother it all.

"I don't care whose shoulders fit this particular load,"

Tavish says. "I'd like to try to carry it with you."

His sincerity is almost overwhelming. All of him is. The way his fingertips rest so delicately against my skin and his lips purse open just the slightest, a set of three large, auburn freckles decorating them like piercings. I shouldn't be thinking about this. I should pull away. I should wall myself back up with my stale life and my endless exhaustion. I should.

His thumb accidentally brushes my jawline.

We both jerk back, and I can't tell if it happens before or after the banging at the door.

Tavish springs to his feet. He catches himself on the side of the mattress and stands properly. I scramble up as well, my heart pounding, limbs tingling, head light. Another round of aggressive knocking startles Blue off Tavish's desk, and Lavender pins her ears back and tucks her tail over her nose.

Sheona's voice comes through the door. "Tavish, dammit, you'd better be alive in there."

"I'm coming, Sheona," he grumbles, sliding back the bolt and pulling open the door with a lethargy to rival her force.

She scowls. "Greer's people won't acknowledge your request without you present. Prissy assholes. Personally, I think we should cut off their pinkie fingers and see just how quickly Greer responds to that."

"How about we start with bureaucracy and only maim our desired allies as plan B?" Tavish asks. "Have you had a chance to bathe lately, Rubem? What an arse I am—of course you haven't. Up with you, up! There's clean water and soap and fresh everything." He waves me toward nowhere, his motions too vague to be of actual use, before grabbing his jacket and backtracking toward the door. "I suspect I'll have to finagle my way through a dozen loopholes just to be sure Greer receives my message. That should give you a few hours to freshen up. If anyone comes by, pretend you aren't here."

I don't know what to make of this sudden transition from our quiet moment—what to make of him as a whole. I don't know what to make of me, either. Through the emptiness in my chest, I piece everything I know of joy into an expression that almost mimics it. "I'm from a swamp, Tavish. The cleanest I've ever been was my escape from the womb."

Tavish bobs in front of the door, one hand on the bolt. He quirks a smile, but it wobbles. "And here you are, still a little bit covered in blood?"

I glance at my ragged outfit. "It blends with my color scheme, and the dirt has pretty much concealed it at this point." The need for a drink hits me with a subtle ache in the back of my throat, paired with a melancholy that desaturates all the color from my emotions, turning them to nasty greys and blacks. "Does your family's endless wealth ever go toward liquor vaults or only pearls and gold?"

"Aye, of course. How do you think I survive in this place?" He pops over to his wardrobe and retrieves a large bottle of deep-amber liquid. The gentle light of the window reveals a label for O'Cain Fishery whiskey. "I hope this suits your tastes well enough. There're glasses in the third drawer of the second dresser. Don't drink it all before I get back."

As he sweeps out the door, I cringe, his joke hitting too close to home. "I'll try not to."

The lock clicks into place, and I hear nothing more, the thick walls blocking out the sound of Tavish's footsteps.

CHAPTER TEN

cats on character

I, in turn, can only watch you unfold,

caught

so close to your own magnitude

that you no longer see the size of your soul,

only the spot

where the meteors hit the avenue.

I STARE AT THE whiskey bottle. It stares back, unblinking. I take a swig of it. The alcohol burns like fire on its way down, scorching out the monochromic emotions, turning them to soot in the back of my throat. I sip a few more times to wash even that away and traipse over to my shoes. The rim of grime they leave sticks to the floor even after I wipe at it with my sock, then scrub with my fingernails. "Fuck."

'Oh, good fuck,' the parasite replies, drawing up Tavish's words from way back on the beach.

That's not your voice, I hiss in my head.

The parasite remains silent, but it simmers, a sort of frustrated confusion slipping off it, turning me antsy and annoyed. I move to the bathroom. Its counters sweep in an arc around a giant tub, a single stream of light shooting from a long, high window with a ridge above it.

I hop the tub's rim and pull myself onto the windowsill, perching there as though between two mangrove branches. The walls of the Findlay estate creep in at the view's edges, but beyond them lies a clear ocean, its blue so deep and full that the sun must have finally peeked out through the grey gloom. In the distance, flashes of color gleam off a black-and-white body. The orca, still stalking me. Or stalking the parasite, more likely.

I nudge the creature so hard I can feel the poke through my skin. *Can't you tell it to leave?*

It turns my own words from the day before against me: *'You can do this.'*

I snort. *And let you sink deeper into my nervous system?*

'There. Not so cold anymore, are you?' This time it's my mother's voice, so soft and distant it could be the wind.

I leap down from the window and turn on the bath, twisting the hot as far as possible. *One kind deed doesn't make up for murder.* I don't know which murder I mean: the ones the parasite committed by my hands, or the one it's committing with each of my nerves it tugs into itself.

The parasite says nothing, but its emotions continue to drip through me, sweltering beneath my skin. I tap my foot against the tub and take a swig of the whiskey. My fingers yearn to flip something between them. I turn a few circles, but Tavish's counters are regrettably free of small knickknacks.

I catch sight of myself in the mirror. I don't look tired—the reflected man who pulls back his lips and lifts one brow to smirk seems like he could conquer an entire universe. It scares me. But the thought of my exhaustion showing scares me almost as much, the idea that people could see right through my face into my all too-empty, listless being.

I strip off my outfit, leaving only the three bronze, fang-like rings in my right earlobe, and drop the clothes into a dusty pile. The creases between my bare muscles are too gangly, a stark reminder that I should be eating something that doesn't come in liquid form. But the growl of my stomach cries only for more alcohol, for how much faster and stronger that alcohol will hit when there are no remnants of a meal obstructing it.

I can already sense it buzzing along my edges, fizzing with the joy of a life I barely remember. It feels like being me again, as though the world has turned from the stench of stagnant water to the overwhelming blaze of a hundred thousand falling flowers. I barely notice the bite of the bath's heat as I slip into it.

Tavish's soap smells of honey, and I carefully lather it into my braids before cleaning the dirt off my skin. My bath turns a gruesome shade of tan. I flush it all down the drain and fill it back up with another round of nearly boiling water, lying there in the steam and wishing it were mist until the vapors die and the room goes cold.

Climbing out is so much harder than climbing in. A long sip of the whiskey helps, and the plush towels stop my regrets from piling. I slip into an equally luxurious robe of blue and white that only covers me to my knees. After a moment of hesitation, I put my fishnet gloves back on. The rest of my worn outfit can be washed, or perhaps burned, but these I can't part with.

The whiskey bottle feels lighter now, its glass expanse a quarter empty and my arms drifting on stardust. I swirl it around once. Cups. Tavish said something about cups.

I search back through my recent memories, finding them blurred and brightened beyond use. The parasite steps in, but it moves sluggishly, pulling up the same discombobulated recollections paired with a soft laughter that might have been my own as a child. It clutches a moment just hard enough for me to make out the word *dresser*.

Dresser, dresser, dresser. I open the drawers one by one. Socks, silken pajamas, an assortment of scarves and ties, all arranged by color between perfectly spaced separators, then a collection of desk supplies, a bundle of unused notebooks, and a letter opener. I pause at the last drawer. A case sits at its center, displaying a knife so ornate it looks cumbersome. Five glasses make a neat row to its right.

"Success!" I fill one, set it aside for Tavish—it seems he should have been back by now—and return to the bottle despite the parasite's disdain. *You don't want me to feel good, is that it?*

It seethes in silence and pokes at the foodless state of my stomach. I ignore it.

The line of the whiskey sinks down in chaotic intervals, as though the time has been pulled away from me with each small slip of the sun. The hazy light greys further, letting the glow of the ignation-fueled tech around the room come into better focus. Where is Tavish?

In his absence, my hands search for something to do, tossing about each paperweight in Tavish's extensive collection before growing bored of them, moving on to the next thing. The room seems to grow smaller with each turn I take. Where the *fuck* is Tavish?

Something crashes down the hall, loud enough to penetrate both the thick walls and the haze of my drink. A scream follows it. My heart thuds a little too loud. If someone could kill one Findlay, then they could kill more. And Tavish should be back by now.

Tavish should be back by now. A vision of him in the next room over with his throat slit and a red fish painted at his side knocks into the exuberate high of the alcohol. My emotions run a flimsy battle, up and down like a leaf in the wind. Stay or go. These four walls feel smothering. And I need to know that wasn't Tavish.

I creep from his room on bare feet. The bottle of whiskey comes with me. His door nearly slips closed behind me before I remember the way his brooch had to trigger it to unlock. Stealing a few little gems out of a nearby vase, I tuck them between the door and the frame and slink down the hall, whiskey raised like a club.

Out the vast sea windows, the ocean has turned from a sapphire pool to a dark mirror, hiding its secrets behind our own reflections. White lights along the ceiling glow dimly, adding to the shimmering ignation effect, silver and rainbow overlapping. Every color cast by the ignation holds an edge of darkness. I try not to glance over my shoulder in search of the fear I feel climbing inside me. It clings to my periphery, but I won't find it, no matter how many times I turn. I will never be fast enough to see inside my own soul.

The parasite warms and sputters, launching its own worries at my monstrous cobbling of fear. It points me toward the light streaming from the crack in Ailsa's library doors. I hold my bottle close and peek through the doors.

Shelves of whitewashed wood rise along all sides of the room, enveloped by backward-facing and half-toppled books. Ailsa shuffles through the corpses of flayed manuscripts beside a pile of fallen boxes and a broken vase. Her cloak of silver feathers lies over a dress so sheer and luminous it could be made of light itself. She pushes her pink-tinged waves away from her face, revealing the edge of her lip caught between her teeth. A bead of blood slips from it, but she doesn't wipe it away.

Her pencil tears through the paper of the dissected book she's writing in. She curses. As she tugs at the rip, her chin comes up. Her gaze flickers toward me, then sticks, and her expression goes from specter to poltergeist.

"Ah. That's why he wanted you." Her eyes crawl over me. Me, clearly wearing her brother's bathrobe. She nods. "He has good taste."

"What? No." But I feel his fingers on my neck, and the shudder it brings isn't fully unwanted. Not even half a bottle of whiskey can make me tell Tavish's sister any of that, though. "I heard a scream."

"My books fell."

"Oh." All my panic for nothing. That's a weird kind of

relief.

I step back, a single, silent motion. Footsteps from down the hall seem to echo it, not in the soft, courteous patter of the staff's occasional crossings, but with the loud, purposeful planting of boots. No click of a cane accompanies them.

The parasite sparks fear down my spine, repeating the very first memory it dragged up: *'Go, Ruby. Run.'*

But Tavish's room is all the way down the hallway and around a bend, and I may be too drunk to get there in time, but I'm not drunk enough to think that I can. The boots keep approaching. They round the corner.

I slip into the library, spinning like a ghost between spilled papers and decimated books. My whiskey bottle sloshes. I set it quickly on the desk, like its sound might be infectious, and duck between the library door and the shelves, out of sight from the hall. Through the crack of the door, I catch a fringe of straight, red bangs and a bodyguard's dark outfit. Malloch. What are they doing here? Oh, right, bodyguard. Hiding seems silly now.

But when Malloch stops, a sliver of their arm just within my view—black sweater, black gloves, black vest plated in black armor—I stay quiet. No matter how certain Tavish is that his mother won't make any moves to grab me yet, I can't take the chance.

Ailsa watches Malloch with a bug-like stare and brings her pencil down on the nearest scrap of a book. Her writing digs into the document. The paper breaks, the torn piece scrunching up in a tiny worm as she continues to push. Not once does she blink.

"Dammit, Ace, would it kill you to act normal for once?" Malloch scoffs, but I can hear a shudder in their voice. Their heels squeak as they continue to Tavish's room. The retreating sound makes my bones feel wilted, like I used up all their strength holding myself in place. I remind myself to inhale.

"Are you okay?" I hiss at Ailsa.

Her shoulders bounce, making her feathered coat flutter. "Should I not be?" she replies, equally hushed. "Why were you hiding from Malloch?"

"Your mother wants to dismantle me. I thought maybe they'd come for that. It sounds a bit ridiculous out loud, though."

Ailsa taps the end of her pencil against her other wrist. "Maybe not ridiculous. They're my bodyguard, but I don't leave the estate much, so Mother and Father always send them on errands. No one cares if I'm murdered." It's such a blunt statement that I almost miss her abrupt transition. "Also they're Sheona's cousin."

"Does that mean they might ignore orders if she asked?" Hope unfurls in my chest.

It closes itself right back up when Ailsa shakes her head. "Oh, no. They kind of hate each other."

Malloch seems to have paused somewhere beyond Tavish's corner. Ailsa and I go quiet while a pair of half as squeaky, half as loud, grey-clothed guard types pass the library. Malloch's disgruntled voice greets them.

"Keep moving." It turns to near a growl at the end, so reminiscent of Sheona that I wonder how I could ever have not known they were related.

Ailsa's hands creep out over her dismembered books, reaching like a pair of ethereal spiders. One of them stops. "There's kitchens through the sitting room across the way and along the little staff hall and down the left stairs. No one will look for you there, not even Malloch." Her nose crinkles. "Especially not Malloch."

"Right." I can just go back to Tavish's room, but I suppose she doesn't know that. "Thanks." I sneak back to the desk to grab my whiskey bottle. But I pause, my fingers around its neck. "Why are you trying to help me?"

"The cats like you. Cats are the best judges of character." She says it like it's a scientifically proven fact.

Blue rubs against the back of my legs, and Lavender

plops down in the doorway, delicately licking one paw. They must have followed me out.

"The cats," I reply. "So, this has nothing to do with Tavish?" I mean, *Are you trying to help Tavish by helping me?* but she seems to pick up something entirely different.

"Oh, no. Tav sees the best in everyone, even, on occasion, our mother." She stills, and I think she actually blinks for the first time. "But if you hurt him—"

"You'll have to battle Sheona for any remaining pieces of me," I grumble.

Without a hint of emotion, Ailsa nods. "She could step on me." She slides so easily into her next question that it takes a moment to register. "Your name, what is it?"

"Rubem." It's a relief to say, as though I hadn't realized I wasn't quite real without it.

"Rubem. You can go now. They left."

As I listen, I realize she's right. I give her a quick salute with my whiskey bottle. "See you around."

The hallway is deadly silent but for the light padding of the cats. When I reach Tavish's door, it doesn't budge. Locked. I swear I'd made some kind of adjustment for this, but it takes a moment to realize the little gems I'd stuffed between the door and frame have come out of place. I take another drink of whiskey and knock. My fist makes no sound against the wood. I call out instead. There's no response.

Kitchen it is, then.

I feel as though I've already forgotten most of Ailsa's directions, but the parasite slams the blurry memory into me so hard that my feet carry me into the tight, unfurnished staff passage and halfway down the equally neglected steps before I even realize what I've done. I wrench back control with an aggressive *You can fuck off now, thanks* and slow for the cats to catch up.

'*You're welcome,*' it spits back, piling a dozen different voices on top of each other. The effect shudders up my brain stem.

But as the sensation dies out, my shoulders loosen and my heart rate steadies. I take another swig from my bottle, letting it soothe the rest of my tension, and all but topple into the kitchen.

If the rest of the estate is fancy, so is the expansive galley, but its wealth comes in the form of technology, not décor: wide sinks and chopping machines, walk-in iceboxes and ovens large enough to cook an orca. The extreme quantity of ignation flowing through the appliances casts the whole room in cascades of rainbow. Five cooks lounge on a wide island counter. They bounce to attention at my arrival, wobbling in their grey chef's uniforms.

A woman with hair buzzed down to a fuzz slips into half a bow, but her hand creeps toward the phone mounted on the side of the counter. "Excuse us?"

"Sorry, I didn't mean to startle you." I think all of those words came out in the proper order, but the chefs still stare at me as though I have their boss's prize possession stuck to my neck and her dead son's cats sitting beside my heels. "I'm staying with the Findlays—with Tavish." Tavish, who should have been back by now, right? But my wandering through the estate didn't seem to help with that, and Tavish is supposed to have Sheona with him anyway. Besides, I'm supposed to be here, not there, to stay away from Malloch. And here is where they have food. Genius. I'm a genius. "Do you think I could whip up something delectic-leta-delishable—something to eat for Tavish and me?" I smile and toss the woman a wink. "Unless I'm intruding?"

She shuffles, glancing from the phone to her fellow cooks and back at me. Slowly, her tight expression loosens. "Well, um—no. No, sir, of course not. The kitchen is always open. What would you like us to make? There is a lamb stew brewing on the stove, and there'll be steak pies for dinner in a few hours. We could whip up some potato scones or mince and tatties?"

"A friend of mine was making something called a bride or

a birdie or some such?"

"A bridie?" The corners of her lips turn up. "We can do that, sir."

"No *sirs* here. Just a tipsy disaster." *A wasted disaster.* The words sound like my own, but the parasite's warm presence feels much too mixed with my nerves for it not to be an accomplice. I set my whiskey down and fish an apron off a hook. Apron, bathrobe, fishnet gloves: I am every sort of disaster tonight. "Right, where do we start? Onions?"

The kitchen staff bounce around the room, pulling forth supplies. They start out stiff, cautious to let me lend a hand, but by the time we're folding the mix of onion, meat, and spice into half circles of pastry, they've broken into kindly chatter, nudging me around and correcting my technique with the nonchalance of old friends while the quietest of the lot lays out little meat scraps that Blue gobbles down before Lavender can overcome her arrogance-cloaked anxiety and creep up to them. I plop Blue onto my shoulder to give the rotund princess a fighting chance.

I lose track of the cooks' names in the alcohol still slurring my world, but most are level-nine workers, while the last takes back-to-back shifts to keep his family within the upper's outrageous income cutoff. When they have the time, they all pile into his apartment, which they jokingly call a mansion, and listen to a radio program about a cursed boy from a small beach town searching for a magical shark eye shell. Only three of them actually prefer onions in their bridies.

"And then, when the third scan still gives him my level-nine authorization, he clears his throat and asks which spa my face mask is from, like I'm not absolutely covered in street grime from head to toe!"

Our laughter cuts short when a series of soft clunks travel up the hallway across from the stairs. Click, slide, step. Click, slide, step. Blue hops from my shoulder, and Lavender's ears perk. I pick up my whiskey. Tavish appears in the entrance.

The chef with the buzzed hair pulls the bridies out of the oven and snaps into a line with the rest of the staff standing along the counter as precise and lifeless as the technology around them. In unison, they say, "Good evening, sir."

Tavish ignores their display. "Has anyone come across a man with a deep, honey voice—"

"I've spotted him in a mirror once!" I interrupt, giving Tavish just enough time to startle near out of his skin before I continue. "Brown skin, long black braids, kissable lips, stunning facial structure. And yes, he's here now."

"Thank the Trench! Why aren't you in my room?" There's a bite to his voice, but the crunch of his brow screams of fear not anger.

"I was worried about you, too, thanks." I grin as I detach myself from the counter and make my way toward Tavish. "Ailsa dropped some books, and I thought maybe you'd died." The reasoning doesn't seem quite sensible, not when it lacks all the worry it contained for some fantastical, imagined version of Tavish. "But then I figured you'd have Sheona anyways, and I'm a glass past punching straight, I think. It's a bit harder to tell when you aren't drinking with glasses. You do have Sheona, right?"

As I ask it, she arrives down the hallway behind Tavish like an incoming storm, grumbling under her breath.

Tavish smiles. "Perhaps I should have locked you in."

"I might be a little drunk, but I don't think that's how deadbolts work? And if you had, I'd never have made the bird-brid-iedies. Brides. Those ones." I waggle my whiskey at him, the remaining quarter of alcohol sloshing pathetically in the bottom. The world keeps swirling around the edges. Either it shines or I do.

"They should be cooled shortly, sir, if you'd like one," the cook with the buzzed hair puts in.

"Aye, thank you." Tavish's awkward smile turns his handsome face into something almost laughable.

I clamp onto his arm, preparing to make him sit at the counter to eat, but one look at the nervous staff changes my mind. "I bet we can take these delicious bundles to a more private location?"

Tavish sighs. "I've had enough dinners in my room of late. The closet park would be a nice change. It even has a bolt now, for privacy."

"The closet park?" I ask.

But Sheona is already stuffing five of our golden meat-filled pastries into a fancy basket, along with a pair of glasses and a few embroidered cloths. "Only if we're quick about it."

As she returns to us, Tavish holds out his palm. "Don't you have a few of those pesky perimeter scouts to run?"

For some reason, she looks between us. Her throat bobs, and she hands over the basket. "Don't take too long." She casts me a scowl. "And don't get too cozy either."

I have the wildest feeling that I should know what she means by that, but then I think of how cozy the rug in Tavish's room is, and how he looked at me when I pointed out that there was only one bed, and there's something different about that memory beneath the swirl of the liquor, something I still can't quite place.

"Aye, Nana." Tavish's voice holds a teasing edge. He brushes his fingers over mine, just once, as he leads me out of the kitchen without another word, the cats following at their usual, free-spirited pace.

CHAPTER ELEVEN

the man behind the aid

But fading or falling, we want all the same.
Magnitudes and black holes coming to align.
Do we have, together, enough to sustain?
Can we each be a sea or must one fill the sky,
dragging the other to their own incline?

INSTEAD OF TAKING US back up to his own floor, Tavish bypasses the staff's stairs entirely, ducking into a tight, low-lit passage of small, simple doors. Closets, I assume, though my brain still struggles to fit the idea of a park into one.

"This place is meant to be a secret—the architect wrote 'storage closet' on the designs, but someone put in a sheet of glass beneath the pool like it was meant to have an ocean viewport. When the staff found it, they decided it was too beautiful to leave bare." He stops at the last door and slips a key off the top of the frame, finding the opening of the lock with his fingers before deftly sliding it in. It clicks, and he puts the key back after. "I stumbled across it while trying to memorize the estate—I was twelve, I think?"

When he pushes open the door, I'm hit with a rush of warm, humid air, dense and floral, like the Murk made miniature. The rippling glow of light through water tumbles along the silhouettes of five lush trees and bundles of flowering plants, all wrapping around a small cobblestone walkway which leads to a patch of grass with a folded blanket.

My eyes linger on the glass-bottomed pool in the ceiling. A line of perfectly groomed lily pads floats on top of it, giving us a direct view of their undersides. The water around them shifts the light into swells of wrinkles and puddles, a sign that even in this foliage-filled paradise, we're truly a hundred feet underwater.

As Tavish bolts the door behind us, I close my eyes and breathe in, letting the garden fill me so thoroughly that I feel it might take root in my lungs and grow flowers up through my rib cage. The rough stone presses between the wrinkles of my bare feet, reminding me that I'm alive. I can take up space in this place. All I need is a wine bottle and a jaguar nuzzling against my leg.

This is what I've been missing, here in this city of metal and diamond. How do the selkies not suffocate from its lack?

Tavish drops onto the patch of grass, leaning back on his palms. His unfocused eyes ease to one side. I settle on the ground with him. Lavender hops onto the folded blanket and curls herself into a circle, her paws on her nose, while Blue clambers up the nearest tree.

We eat in a relaxed silence. The bridie tastes like the most delectable thing I've ever consumed, but with the whiskey still working its way through my system, anything more or less edible would fit that bill. By the end of the meal, we've torn the final one in half and finished it off. Little crumbs coat my lap. I give up brushing them off and splay my half-bent legs out, leaning my elbows onto my knees. My ankle bumps against Tavish's. He doesn't move away.

"We've had no luck with our contacts so far." He speaks softly, as though anything louder might break the peace we've acquired in this tucked-away place. "Everyone is too afraid of my mother's wrath if she finds out. And I understand, I suppose. The Trench scientists are concerned that she'll fire them, and they'll have to leave Mara to find anything close to the aurora research they're doing now. And Dr. Druiminn worries my mother will raise the interest price on the ignation meant to power her medical equipment in the new lower-city hospitals we're constructing, which will mean cutting back on their quantity, leaving more people without care. We still have Greer as a potential option, but only because their people haven't replied to my message yet."

"Ah." I try not to think of what that means for my future existence in this parasite-ridden body. With the alcohol still burning bright in my chest and painting my emotions in shimmering hues, it seems a waste to mar the moment. I shove the whiskey bottle into Tavish's hands. "Perhaps you need this, too."

A little laugh follows, too stale for the lush freshness of this place. He tips up the bottle to his lips, then farther, slowly lifting it until he can sip the alcohol. The swells of light from above shift across his bunched nose. "Good fuck, Rubem, how much did you drink?"

"That's none of your business, it's not yours any longer." Grinning, I grab for the bottle, bumping shoulders with him in the process.

He holds it away from me with a chuckle. "No more of that unless it's in one of those glasses Sheona packed."

I don't give up, slipping beneath his arm and leaning across his lap.

His laughter grows. He prods me in the stomach with his knee, and I shove down his leg with my own, practically climbing over him. My fingers brush the whiskey. Before I can steal it, his cane finds me right between the ribs.

I cave with a groan, plopping back onto the ground at his side. "I've been dismantled, I'm afeared."

"Bested by a bureaucrat!" Tavish manages to poke me with his cane a second time.

I steal it from him with a quick twist. "I propose a trade!

Your weapon for my whiskey."

"It's an aid," he corrects me, his smile lopsided and gorgeous.

"So's mine." I accent the claim with a middle finger to the gods. And as I do, I realize they have already damned me, because I feel as though I've fallen through every barrier that should be keeping Tavish and me apart, and with the easy joy that fills his face, I can't even find it in me to be worried. Right now, his friendship is worth its future loss. It's worth being lonely again someday, in order to not feel alone with him right now.

"How so?" His bright voice bears a weight that would make gravity jealous. "I mean that with all sincerity. I'd like to understand."

Each syllable pinches in my chest. I could sidestep the question or laugh it off. I could pretend that the person everyone else sees is a full being beneath the skin, that there isn't a dying fragment of me that the brighter parts of life drown in. It would be safer.

I tip my head back, the ends of my braids coiling in the grass, and close my eyes. The weight of Tavish's attention settles over me like a heavy blanket. But he doesn't speak, only sits beside me, warm and real and listening.

"I have melancholia. Or I suppose the new term is depression?" The words bundle in my throat, barely forcing themselves forward, but once they're out, the rest follows easily. "It isn't your usual grief or trauma—it doesn't go away when the stresses of life ease up, just keeps coming back and back again in what seems like entirely random cycles. It turns my useful emotions to ash and sucks away my energy until some days I have to pick and choose what's worth using myself up for. The alcohol doesn't remove it, but it coats it in—I don't know—a film, I suppose. Rainbows and elation."

My nerves flicker. It's a light feeling, somewhere between happy and empty, like I'm suddenly made of helium. I turn my gaze to the cats, unable to make myself watch Tavish's reaction.

"I'm sorry," he whispers, his tone marring a sigh with the peeking of the sun through rain clouds. "That sounds challenging, and highly uncomfortable. If there is anything I can do to help you with it, you'll tell me, won't you?"

The tension that binds my heart to my body settles, smoothing me back into place. This must be what friendship feels like. "I will. Thank you."

He hums and his lips part, a curl of his hair tickling one corner. "If you let me pour you a glass of the whiskey, you can have *that*."

"You're murdering my aesthetic, Tavish," I grumble, as though the bottle somehow turns my apron, bathrobe, and fishnet gloves into a functioning ensemble.

"My dear fellow, I intend only to plague it for the night." Tavish takes a swig from the bottle before digging out one of the whiskey glasses Sheona had tucked into the basket. He fills it so slowly I can't decide if he's in more danger of underpouring or not hearing it overflow.

"You know, I did put some aside for you, back in your room. I was considerate."

"A true saint." He hands over a crystalline cup filled perfectly to the highest whiskey line.

I watch him. The light from the ceiling casts silver ripples across half his face while leaving the other half in shadow. It's like the picture of him in my head come to life: part gorgeous and part haunting, an enigma of compassion and wit and anxiety. I draw my fingers up and down his cane. "How do you do all of this?"

He pauses from his drink, the bottle pressed gently to his lips. "All of what?"

"Pour whiskey and move around the city and be a public ambassador?"

"The same way anyone else might, only a little different." He sips his whiskey. "At this point, I have a map of the city carved into my bones—the upper districts, anyway—and no one in Maraheem would deny me directions if I needed them. The drink pouring is just sheer practice, but I read with braille, and my aids make the world a bit more accessible. I perceive a contrast between light and dark, too, which can help."

I try to imagine growing up with my hands and ears as my only practical means of taking in the world. My heart lurches. I would miss the way the first plumes of fog roll across the water. No touch or rhythm could ever replicate its dance. "Is that why the bed's so low? Some kind of aid?"

Tavish laughs. "It's low because my shite sleeping habits used to roll me off it. Smacked my damn nose into the ground enough times to give up. That could happen to a sighted person just as easy."

I turn toward him. "Am I being rude?"

He lifts his whiskey toward me. "I think you're being drunk."

I clank my cup against his bottle, harder than I intend, my arms moving in fluid lunges when I mean them to be small sways. "Fuck."

He jolts, laughing, and takes a swig so long he could almost rival me. "I'll be drunk, too, in a few minutes."

"Lightweight," I tease.

A leaf tumbles from the trees, and Blue pounces on it, rolling into Lavender as she does. The princess releases an indignant mew.

Tavish lifts his chin with equally dignified annoyance. "Have you ever tried being drunk *and* blind?"

"Have you tried being drunk and *not* blind?"

"Fair enough." A strand of his curls falls over his left eye.

My fingers ache to draw it behind his ear, such an electric, carnal sensation that I force my thoughts elsewhere, settling finally on his irises shining the perfect grey of water vapor. The color of fog and freedom. "Back home, we have mists that spill out of the deep swamps so thick that it's almost like going blind. There, sound and silence are the difference between life and death. Your selkies would need all the aids in the world to survive. But you might do all right."

"That's the way of things, isn't it? We adjust for what's most common. Anything that isn't gets left behind."

That dangerous curl still hangs across his face. I flex my fingers, stretching and coiling them, stretching and coiling, as though he's a planet and I am a lonely rock caught in his orbit. "Anyone would be a fool to leave you behind."

He gives an awkward, mangled laugh. "Aye, right." His sarcasm runs nails down my heart. "You saw me at my best. There's a long way down from there. Everyone else has witnessed it."

"Are you sure?" My memories still swim with light and life, but from what I recall, that boardroom looked enraptured, enthralled, certain that Tavish could give them exactly what they needed. And then he'd convinced them that he had, even while taking what he really wanted instead.

But he scoffs, a sound so bitter and rough it barely seems to come from him. "They might not show it, but they watched me grow up. They've seen my mother demolish my petitions time and time again. They ken that no matter how often I equal her for a moment, I will never rise above."

That only convinces me all the more that Tavish is wrong—wrong about them and about himself and about his future. But I can't make him see what's right in front of him, not if he's so determined to close his eyes. Metaphorically speaking. "If it's any consolation, I, too, am a raging disaster."

The corner of his lips quirk. "Och, you disgrace me, Ruby. I still have a bit of my life together!"

"Ruby?" The word forms in a whisper, the sound of blossoms opening and mist slithering through the trees.

"Sorry, it just—it came out." He picks at the skin along his nail, nearly spilling what little whiskey remains in his bottle in the process. "I won't—"

"My mother used to call me that." It's her voice that

makes the flowers flourish and draws forth the fog, I realize. Her voice, resonating through my memories, still a part of me even so long after the rest of her has left.

No one else has been with me long enough to imprint upon my life like that, to transform pieces of me from the inside out. No one else. But the sparkling buzz in my head and the pounding of my heart yearn for it afresh. My gaze goes to Tavish, but even if he is good, and kind, and he gives more than he takes of me, even then, he will never actually come home with me. He'll be a passing moment, a few days of friendship that I can look back on and smile about. Nothing more.

But perhaps a few days might be better than none.

"You can call me what you wish, you ridiculous princeling." I don't know why I whisper.

"Unacceptable. I'm not a prince." His freckled lips pucker slyly. He lifts his head, and his breath curls against my chin.

I tremble. "You are, compared to me."

He slips his palm along my shoulder, and even through the thickness of the robe, I feel every curve of his hand, every wrinkle and freckle and perfect imperfection. I embrace the touch, closing my eyes and bathing in his presence. He finds my collar, and his fingers rise over it. Then, he stops, caught between skin and aurora. Between me and an intruder.

He traces it. His caress lightens, then vanishes, leaving me hollow. Empty.

He seems equally so, his fingers drooping into his lap. And I can't blame him. His dead brother's cats have curled around each other, Blue finally calmed enough to settle onto the blanket and groom the back of Lavender's neck. Whiskey can only brighten a dark world so much.

I take a long gulp from my glass, trying to chase the tail of my high, even for a minute, a moment, a heartbeat. To be happy while I can. While I have nothing else to be.

I break the silence with a hum. "Would you turn into a seal, if I asked?"

Tavish goes so still I think he may be a rabbit frozen before a pair of headlights. His shoulders shake. Laughter bubbles out of him, chaotic and contagious.

"Was that rude, too?" I chuckle, slamming down the rest of my whiskey. "Gods, I don't usually interact with people while drunk."

"No, no, it's fine. It's cute." Tavish wipes the corner of his eye. "But I would have to be naked to shift."

"I've seen you naked before."

In the low, drifting light of the pool, the embarrassment in Tavish's cheeks is unmistakable.

I cringe. "We can forget this ever happened."

He laughs again, the sound just as warm and vibrant as before. He lifts his whiskey bottle. "Unfortunately, I'm not quite that drunk. Yet."

I clink my empty glass against it.

Tavish finishes off the whiskey and flops backward into the grass. The shift in his weight rubs his calf against the side of my bare foot, his skin so close beneath the fabric of his pants that I can almost feel it, soft, smooth, scented in his honey soap and littered with tiny freckles.

I dig my fingers into the grass. I want not to want Tavish. It makes no sense. This is not the time, not the place. He is at most a passing fancy who will choose to stay in Maraheem while I flee home.

But that doesn't stop him from being gorgeous or sweet or funny, and it doesn't stop my heart from thudding just a little faster when his lips part in a sigh. Or, maybe I only want Tavish because it's been years since I had the courage and charm to pull a stranger into a back alley of the nearest village, him always too drunk to notice or mind my Murk heritage, and me too drunk to care that he would shun me the moment we were sober.

Tavish can't see that heritage either. But neither would it bother him.

I tip my head back, staring at the ceiling. I can almost feel the way the water-strewn light ripples across my face, can almost imagine that for this single moment we are the only things in existence. Can almost dare myself to kiss him, even knowing that it'll be a terrible idea whatever the outcome.

My heart stutters as a tall, black-clothed selkie plunges into the pool above us. Instead of swimming or thrashing or transforming, he sinks slowly, bubbles streaming from his mouth. His hair splays around him, but it can't mask the glow of the purple stone wrapped to his neck. Purple—the color of ignits that release paralyzing energy. Most likely the bodyguard still lives, but by the looks of it, not for long. Not unless the ignit's energy runs out, or someone removes or deactivates it.

My fingers twitch. But I shouldn't go charging through a place that isn't mine to rescue someone I've never met, not when the more I involve myself in this mess, the longer it might keep me here, away from my pets, my life, my home. Tavish shifts at my side, his leg sliding against mine once more, and the parasite echoes the motion by drawing up a stream of recent memories, each one boasting Tavish's smile, his laugh, his kindness to me. My chest tightens. But he's safe at my side here. Staying put is the best thing for us both . . . right?

Another paralyzed, black-clad body falls into the pool. I recognize her immediately, her figure slight and fluid compared to the man's, and her gracefully curved eyes stretched wide.

I scramble to my feet. The world sways, then steadies.

Tavish groggily rubs one eye. "What is it?"

"Sheona—she's in the pool—she's not moving." I yank him up as I speak.

His pinkie finger trembles, but he seems instantly awake. He tightens his hands around mine. "The stairs we passed coming here lead to the room across from the pool. It's two flights up."

"Bolt the door once I'm gone."

"I'm coming with you." He jogs after me, his cane clicking at twice its normal speed and his footfalls light, like he's prepared to take back any wrong step in an instant.

I glance at Sheona's sinking body. The last of her air slips from her unmoving lips. In the time it would take me to force Tavish to stay, she could be dead. Besides, Tavish is no child. He has a right to place himself in danger, no matter how much I wish he wouldn't. "Keep behind me."

We rush out of the garden, down the hall, and up the stairs. The first landing opens to a staff corridor near Tavish's room. He urges me onward, to the floor above it, where everything is a little too huge, too impeccable, too lifeless. We leave the staff chamber through a foyer and cross the hall to a set of double doors. They're locked by the same scanning system that guards Tavish's room.

Light bursts chaotically through the machine before peppering out. The crystal tubes and tiny grooves where the ignation normally flows hold little of the iridescent fuel. What remains slips slowly toward the floor. It leaks under the crack beneath the door, its rainbow flare gone pure silver.

I shove my shoulder into the door. Sparks leap from the lock, and it jerks open, the rest of the ignation pouring out its front. The liquid drenches the rolled-up sleeve of my robe and trickles down my forearm, soaking into my fishnets. A chill runs through me.

I burst into the room.

Its marble-tiled floor stretches beneath a ceiling so high it seems to lose itself in the darkness, and little, silver lights shine down from grooves in the walls. The pool extends along one end, its lily pads floating peacefully beneath large, white flowers. The drowning bodyguards still sink beneath the gently rippling water.

In the room's center, a different kind of execution takes place. A gagged woman in an elaborate nightdress lies on a pure-white sofa, her hands bound to the wooden curls of the sofa's back. Her head bobs lethargically as her eyelids flutter, her cheeks slack and her brow tight like she's trying to think away the lump on her temple. The expression differs so vastly from what I saw in the boardroom that it takes me a moment to recognize her as Raghnaid.

Below her silken slipper-clad feet, a person in a hooded cloak paints the bright red symbol of a fish. The symbol they found beside Alasdair's corpse. My gut turns, solidifying the dread I'd been gathering there since hearing that first radio announcement. Alasdair's murder was never about him. It was about the Findlays. And there are other Findlays.

Findlays I would prefer to keep living.

CHAPTER TWELVE

lament of the sober

Perhaps I offer: I will be your moon.

For you I will rise and for you I will fall,

for you I'll ignite and for you I'll withdraw.

Forever circling,

rigidly in tune.

But never quite touching, lest one be consumed.

TAVISH COULD BE NEXT.

In the instant it takes me to come to terms with that, the assassin glances up. A full mask richly painted with silver swirls hides their face. They stall. The paintbrush slips from their fingers.

I sprint at them. The assassin jolts into motion as well, snatching up an ornamental knife in place of the brush. But they don't raise it against me. Instead, they turn and dive for Raghnaid, blade aimed at her throat. I crash into them just as they connect—just before or just after. A muted scream leaves Raghnaid, and her eyes lurch open, but the assassin grabs the back of my neck, taking my attention with it.

They flip their knife around to drive it toward my stomach, but their grip on its handle wobbles. I slide to one side and slam my fist into their ribs with such force their whole body jerks. When I hit their wrist next, the knife tumbles from their hand. It scrapes across the tile as it rolls toward the double doors.

The assassin grabs my collar and shoves their knee into my gut. A harsh ache shoots through my insides. The parasite writhes against the sensation, and I can feel its unhappiness in the same inescapable way it must feel my pain. Like a fist clenching, it pushes against me—into me—straining for something. I strain, too, barely ducking the assassin's next punch as I grit my teeth against the parasite's unnamable desire.

Splashing rises from the pool, undercut with Tavish's worried muttering. As I block the assassin's next attack, a wave of panic rushes over me. "Pull off the netting but don't touch the ignit!" I shout. Whether he hears me—whether he understands what I'm talking about to begin with—I don't have time to check.

The assassin bursts forward, catching me between the ribs with their fist. The parasite shoves at me with the same force, as though trying to meet the blow, tearing me up from the inside out in the process. I slam my heel into the assassin's stomach. They stumble backward.

I glance toward the pool. Tavish holds Sheona by the shoulders as she sits bent over at its edge. Water streams from her hair. A series of rough, wet curses leave her.

"A gun," Sheona growls, lifting her head. "Get me a damn gun."

The assassin stalls. Their hand goes to their waist as though they're checking for that very thing, but their palm only bumps against their cloak. They take a step back. Turning on their heels, they flee the way we'd come, only pausing long enough to swipe their knife off the floor.

I lunge after them. My fingers graze their cloak. If only I could shove myself a little farther, a little faster. If only I had less alcohol intoxicating my system and more of that furious strength from my one-sided fight with the poachers. If only I could end this here and now, then Tavish might be safe.

As though the mere thought opens the floodgate, the parasite rips into me.

It winds through my shoulder, pressing down my arm, and writhing along the ignation-soaked fabric of my bathrobe sleeve. It crashes through my nerves, its heat blistering as it grabs for the ignation there with an excitement so vibrant that a laugh spews out of me. I fight the feeling. Every inch I gain, I lose a mile. The parasite digs into the skin between my fishnets, tearing needle-thin gashes of color from the tips of my fingers up my right arm. Its warmth surges through my brain, polluted with color and light so bright and bold I can taste its presence on the back of my tongue, metallic and salty.

I cough, and blood comes out. A sob follows. *Stop, stop, stop, stop.*

My legs buckle, spilling me onto the floor.

I receive a reply in my own voice, *'I get odder the more you know of me.'* With it, the parasite finally stops its invasion. It doesn't retreat, but it watches through my eyes, like a guard dog on high alert. A guard dog who guards the body it means to take over and not the person still trying to live inside it. The crisscrossing gashes of color it sliced into my right arm remain.

The assassin is gone. Sheona holds her gun, but she's slumped to one elbow beside Tavish, still coughing in rough, gurgling hacks.

Raghnaid groans from the sofa. A red line snakes across her cheek—that first swipe the assassin got at her. I must have shoved it away just in time. It's so light the bleeding has already stopped, but the gag is mere threads now. She tears it in two with her teeth. "Tavish!" Her voice is crystal even when hoarse. "Untie these."

Tavish goes still.

Raghnaid calls him again, stern, sharp, just enough scolding to sit squarely between mother and queen. "Now,

Tavish."

"Aye, of course," he mutters. His cane rattles against the floor as he tiptoes toward her voice.

My veins course with an energy not my own. I lurch to my feet as though standing fast enough might leave the parasite's presence behind. As I do, I realize the other bodyguard still lies, forgotten, at the bottom of the pool. Raghnaid's bodyguard. It's been so long since he was dumped in. Too long. I try to cling to my earlier ambivalence, but now that I stand at the edge of the pool, I can't just leave him there.

I drag his body out, but he doesn't breathe, not even after I carefully peel off the net-bound ignit and toss it away. By the time I've confirmed his pulse is gone, Raghnaid stands before the red fish symbol, rubbing her wrists. She's even shorter without her heels. She picks up her feet with Lavender's dainty delicacy, stepping between the wet paint, nose wrinkled. With half of it shielded by her dress, its familiarity hits me.

It's the same marking the workers were covering near the lower-district gate when I fled Lilias. Same color, same rugged, minimalist style, even roughly the same size. The assassin might have worn a fancy mask and carried an ornamental blade, but this symbol is a thing of the lower districts.

I lift my hand to rub my face, but the tiny lines of color cutting through my skin stop me.

Raghnaid picks up the end of the netting I'd tossed aside, careful not to touch the paralyzing ignit still glowing at its center. Her nostrils flare. She looks at me. "You are meant to be in a lab."

I'm not sure who she speaks to—me or the parasite. I'm not sure she's ever seen the difference. She tosses the paralyzing weapon at me.

My body moves, not on instinct this time, but on the will of the parasite. I grab the stone in my color-scarred hand. It vibrates, pulsing its purple energy. But instead of paralyzing me, its power slides up my arm like the first sip of booze. My fingers circle the ignit.

I crush it.

The solid crystalline energy stone shatters to powder in my grip. Its glow sinks beneath my skin and swirls up my veins, electrifying. Raghnaid chokes on her own voice. I take a step, my motions half my own now. But only half. Raghnaid moves back, not a retreat but the preparation for a pounce.

I follow her. "I just saved your fucking life," I hiss, letting the ashen remnants of the once-luminous ignit slip in a trail through my fingers. The net flutters after it. "How dare you throw away mine."

Raghnaid's lower lip wavers between the start of speech and the gasp I see forming in her every time her eyes go from the parasite to the miniature gashes on my arms to the pieces of disintegrated ignit. The back of her knees bumps the love seat, and she falls into it. My fists tighten. With this much power, I could do something here. I could do what the lower districts have wanted for ages.

"Rubem?"

Tavish's voice yanks me from the delusion with such force that I can't tell whether it was even my own, or something parasite-born, morphed by its tingling power and wanton determination. The more I dwell on it, the more foreign the desire feels. And the more it eats me up inside. I step back from the sofa.

"Rubem?" Tavish repeats.

Ending Raghnaid might let her scientist help me without fear of her wrath. Or it might throw the whole system into such a mad transition of power that the assembly decides to lock me in a cage until it's sorted through. I can't risk that. "I'm here."

A pair of bodyguards appear in the room's entrance: Malloch with their face pale and their lips drawn back, and the final guard who appeared at the boardroom meeting. Their gazes both come down on me. I should leave. If I need to contend with both of them and the guns at their belts, I doubt my new ignit-destroying abilities will save me.

Sheona must realize it as well. We meet on either side of Tavish. She coughs still, dripping, but she holds her gun like she's been trained to shoot her way through death itself and come out the other end.

"Malloch and your mother's other guard are here," I mutter to Tavish. "We're leaving."

He offers me his arm, and I take it, keeping my ignation-mutated skin as far from him as possible. I guide him between Raghnaid and her bodyguards—both the alive and the dead—careful not to step on the assassin's still-wet symbol. Malloch has already gotten a smudge of it on their otherwise perfectly polished boots. I wait for Raghnaid to protest, but her lips remain clamped. She watches me leave with the serenity and determination of an empress.

The parasite's touch doesn't retract as we descend back toward Tavish's floor, but it blends into the rest of my perception now, one stage closer to becoming me. In the dying fizzle of the alcohol, I want to rip it off my neck with my bare hands.

Blue and Lavender meet us at the bottom of the stairs. Sheona's and Tavish's footsteps ring along the quiet corridors, clipping and scuffing against the marble, and the cats' gentle paws form a soft rhythm just beneath. Mine remain silent.

'You're a wee bit odd.' This time the parasite pulls up Tavish's regurgitation of its favorite phrase. A spark of affection follows, but whether it's from me or the creature, I don't know. It's worse not knowing.

We file inside Tavish's room. Sheona latches the bolt into place and retrieves a pair of lower-city algae bulbs that come to life in swirls of emerald when she shakes them. They slowly settle after she sets them down. Lavender patters over to a pair of pearl-studded food dishes someone—perhaps Sheona—delivered here in our absence, and I catch the faintest whiff of litter box from what looks like a private cat-sized clam in one corner.

As soon as Tavish sets his shoes on the rack, Sheona wheels on him. She grabs him by the shoulders, her fingers digging into his thick arms. She doesn't let go. "You fucking dobber, an assassin murdered your own damned brother—murdering him *to death*—just yesterday, and the first sign of chaos, you go racing into it!"

"'To death' is the usual meaning of murder," Tavish grumbles, but his unfocused eyes form a sheen. "You were the one dying. I couldn't—"

Sheona latches her arm around his neck, gripping him in something between a choke hold and an embrace. Her words come from between tight teeth, whistling like the spin of a projectile. "You do not risk yourself for me. My job is to save you—to die for your fucking fool of an arse if that's what's needed. If you go rushing into danger in my place again, so help me, no one will need to murder you because I will splay your guts all over the fucking ceiling my damned self."

With a scrunch of his shoulders and a dramatic wiggle, Tavish frees himself. "Trenches, Nana, that child you were hired to protect is long grown. It's my choice to risk myself, for you or for anyone else." His hair sweeps disastrously upward, and a ruddy rise grows in his cheeks, but he holds his chin high, dignified beyond adulthood and into divinity.

"I'm not demanding, Tavish." Sheona's voice slides, thick and heavy, saturating the hallway. "I'm begging. You are good, and strong, and brave, and the world needs that, more than they will ever need me."

All the indignation leaves him in a single breath. "Nana."

Something creeps at the edges of my memories, a shadow I could identify if only I could touch it, but it turns to smoke in my fingers. The parasite tugs at the silhouette of my mother: slim and strong and far too young to die. Far younger than I am now. The vision of her stirs a deep cavity in my gut.

"If something happened to you because of me—because I couldn't—" Sheona's voice catches.

I'm an intruder here, barging into a conversation too intimate for someone like me who doesn't quite belong. My insides continue to tighten. I'm no longer drunk enough for this.

Neither of them seems to notice me grabbing a light and slipping into the bathroom, the ache of sobriety landing on me with every stride. Their conversation continues, a string of frustrated hisses and tiny sobs and soft consultations repeating itself. I close the door over it.

I look tired and disheveled in the mirror, my earrings twisted at an odd angle and my braids piled awkwardly in a half bun I can't recall having tied. A strip of dried blood coats my upper lip and trails out of my nose, from the parasite or the ignation or perhaps the fight with Raghnaid's assailant. I dab at it with my saliva, wiping the crust away. One long look at my outfit, and I strip off the kitchen apron.

Delicately, I pull up my right sleeve to examine the damage the parasite wrought there. Though my fishnets hide them somewhat, the thin, straight, black lines of the parasite's infection course with a vibrancy that seems almost toxic, their gleam noticeable any time I flex or release the muscles beneath.

With a shudder, I drop the sleeve back into place. I let my braids down after. They cascade over my shoulders, black as coal, their coppery beads too rough and resilient to be paired with such a plush garment. I wish I could discard the robe, pile back into my rugged browns and reds, and vanish through the steam of the lower districts.

"Rubem?" The sound of Tavish's diamond voice slices through my contemplation, burying itself in my chest. Rubem, not Ruby, as though the intimacy he shares with Sheona has drawn the line between casual friend and more than. However close I am to Tavish, there are others who come first. And I understand why. But it still hurts.

"I'm here." I tighten my robe around me, trying not to feel like a trespasser as I move back into the bedroom.

Tavish stands at the dresser. The smudge of dirt I left on the floor earlier rubs into his socks, forming the faintest line along one silvery-blue edge. He searches through a drawer— the one I took the whiskey glasses from earlier. The drink I poured still sits, homeless, off to one side. The coiling melancholy in my gut tells me to down it, to chase my vanishing happiness a little longer. But it won't help now. Not after all that's just happened.

Tavish pauses. "Did you touch something in here?"

"Only the glasses." As I bumble back through my earlier actions, finding nothing but stained-glass images in a blur of black, I groan. "I think. Your whiskey is blinding."

"Is it now?" It's not quite flat, but not quite a joke, either, as though Tavish is still lost in his thoughts. Then, he shrugs, collects a fresh tie for his hair and a neatly folded pile of clothes, and heads for the bathroom.

The light seems dimmer without him. I tap Sheona's light, making the little luminescent flecks move again. "These are from the lower city, aren't they?"

"Aye." She bounces her shoulders. "I find them more natural than ignation."

"Were you born there, in the lower?"

The pound of the shower starts up behind the closed bathroom door. As it whines on and on, it seems she won't answer. Finally, she shakes her head. "My family is, but the most inclined of us train from a young age, make ourselves indispensable to these rich diddies. I was the best. I got my top choice." She tips her head toward the bathroom. The drop of her chin after that offers no room for further questions.

"I left your breather on the counter earlier," I say instead.

Sheona shrugs again. "Keep it. It's no good to me

anymore." The strength of her voice seems at odds with the draw of her features, so taut they might be a bowstring ready to snap.

I don't ask about the spouse who once used it. I don't ask if it was her fault that they left or theirs, or if there's just certain people fated to be abandoned. I don't ask, but her gaze snaps to mine, and we know, the way addicts know one another.

She makes me bolt the door behind her after she leaves. Her knock makes me jump a few minutes later, but between her gruff voice and the outer lock's response to her brooch, I relax. She tosses me a pair of grey pajamas that actually fit my tall frame. They're indulgent, but not quite the whisper of silk or the cloud of the robe, just a regular soft that feels good against my skin. I don't take off my fishnet gloves when I put the new outfit on. Without the netting, the parasite's crisscrossing lines on my arm would be undeniable, and I have so little of myself left that I can't bear the thought of losing my fishnets too. If I do, there might cease to be a me altogether.

Sheona plants Tavish's desk chair directly across from the door and roots herself to it, a pistol propped in her lap, as though she's prepared for someone to break through the bolt just to get to us. Perhaps it should make me tenser to know how worried she is, but having someone to guard my sleep for the first time since Lilias took me from my pets feels comforting. I grab a pillow and blanket off the bed and flop onto the rug, just out of her way but near enough to wake if something happens. The moment my eyes close, the first waves of sleep creep in, turning my thoughts to a heavy smoke and blurring the edges between myself and the parasite. Its voice wiggles through my head, whispering urgently in words I can't decipher. I turn, tossing the incoherent demand away, and knock straight into someone's legs.

Tavish yelps. "Och! Ruby, are you sleeping on the floor?"

I groan, bundling my pillow into the side of my face. "The floor, yes. Sleeping? Not anymore."

He prods me in the side with his slippered foot. "Have you felt the size of my bed? Get in it! In!"

"You could be a little less demanding," I grumble, climbing up.

"And you could move a little faster." There's a warmth in his voice that means more than the words themselves.

I'm still trying to figure out what it all means—whether he's implying anything, as a friend, as more, as neither—when he pulls the covers over us. Blue settles between our heads, and Lavender between our feet. Still, he's so close. An arm's reach, and I could grab him, touch him, pull him to me. Yet that gap feels like a longer expanse than the floor to the mattress. It feels like forever and a day, like the sight of him retreating into the distance when we part. It feels like a loss.

I turn away from him and tuck my arms over my head, a shield against the world. Even a shield can't block out the soft sounds of Tavish's breathing. If we had met in the Murk, him a colonist and me a nothing, would our paths have tangled? Maybe, with no ties forcing him to me, with no aurora in my neck and no destruction looming before me, he would have walked away the moment we met. I trace a finger over the parasite. *Is this your fault, then?*

It replies with the memory of a soft laugh, an eerie compilation of every piece of humor it can reach its ruthless tendrils into.

I drift off again, this time to worry and wanting. Darkness scoops me up, but it pitches me to and fro, as if warning me that each minute I lose rolls me closer to the edge of a cliff, the waves far below crashing against rocks like teeth, hungry to tear me apart. That's when the dreams start.

CHAPTER THIRTEEN

me, you, and us

What does it mean to balance an ocean,

to give oneself up to become a foundation?

Then will every collision be an extinction?

And every new motion a strict calculation?

MY SLEEP DROPS ME from one tangled mess of black to another. Jumbles of color and incoherent whispers filter in. They settle around my feet, becoming a plain of grass in blues and teals, an orange sky giving way to pink at the edges. As I turn, its colors flutter and drift.

Warm air brushes through my braids. My ignation gashes prickle. I hold up my arm. The colors yank themselves out of my flesh, peeling up like centipedes and leaving the red of an open wound behind. They drop to the grass. Forming together, they build on each other, rising to my height. Arms sprout from a torso, and a slew of braids spill from a head, until I'm staring back at a fractured version of myself made of wiggling stained glass.

"I get odder the more you know of me," it whispers. Raising one color-cracked hand, it points to its own chest. "I," it repeats. "I get odder."

Odder. Emotions coil up inside me: a flickering confusion

that masks a realization I refuse to look at. Instead, I want to flee, into the Murk or through the gap in my empty chest. I refuse to be as shattered by this as the other me is.

Its fingers come apart into colored threads of glass and light. I feel myself turn over in my sleep, and our hands, the physical and the dream, neither or both, clasp an arm. My confusion blooms into fear.

The weight of whatever we've clasped turns into a full presence. It sucks us into itself, like the parasite had shoved itself into me, only in reverse, and as it does, we're hit with a suffocating feeling, something dark and weighted. We float within this new being's existence, taking up parts of its body, seeing through eyes that aren't eyes at all. A tank surrounds us. Beyond lies a giant room, silver-ornamented windows and graceful chandeliers hanging high above tables of research equipment. A pair of white-coated scientists hover around a woman with her arms and legs bound to a table. She bares crooked teeth and familiar wild eyes. The conspiracy theorist—Jane, or Jean, definitely Jean. One scientist pins her head down while the other plunges a syringe of rainbow-glowing ignation into her neck. Jean screams.

Somewhere beyond the rims of the tank, Ailsa shouts in protest, "What are you doing—that's a person. Where are the dogs?"

"Don't worry, dear," a man's voice replies. "No one will miss her."

I jerk upright.

Lavender releases a protesting mew from where she's snuggled against my knees. Light streams in through the cracks in the stony façade outside the window. The covers tangle in a mess around my ankles, and my sweat sticks my pajamas to my skin. Tavish's side of the bed is empty and cold. The shower runs, but he must have convinced Sheona to use it, because he sits at his desk, fully dressed in a casual, blue-and-grey overcoat and scarf, scribbling away at

133

a set of papers with a system of indented rulers as a guide and his ignation-fueled reader pressing along behind the words. He seems to be doing less writing, though, and more combatting Blue's desire to sprawl across his notebook.

I flop back down. Those few drunken hours last night were a much-needed break from reality, but they weren't enough. I feel worn still, from my sore limbs to my exhausted soul. If I could only postpone life a little longer, use another bottle of whiskey to turn it all off again. But time would still continue its usual trudge. The parasite would dig itself deeper. My pets would curl themselves up on my porch for another week.

I feel the parasite unfurl itself. It slides through my mind, and I want all the more to cast myself straight out of this existence, out of any existence where a foreign sentience is slowly taking control of my body and leaving me to sit, helpless and hurting, in the backseat. The thought propels me out of bed.

The blankets come with me, pulling a very unhappy Lavender along. With a hiss, she scrambles across the floor and dives beneath the lowest shelf of shoes, somehow squishing her extra weight in there like she's made of liquid. She glares at me.

Tavish's pen stops. "Ruby? Are you all right? You sounded restless, but I wished not to disrupt your sleep."

"I'm alive." I force myself to exhale as I strip my moist top off and lift my braids away from my back. The parasite perched in my neck warms uncomfortably, casting off emotions that make my skull itch and raise the hairs on my arms. It crashes back through my dreams, bundling them into a memory it can shove at me. They make me shiver despite my sweat. "I had nightmares, though."

Tavish swivels his chair toward me.

I perch myself on the edge of the desk and bounce a paperweight between my hands. The first part of my dream twists around my chest, forming a knot I can't untie. It feels too personal to explain and too nonsensical to make use of. I skip directly to the lab part, sharing my view from the tank, the way the scientists injected the conspiracy theorist with ignation, and Ailsa's objections. When Tavish doesn't respond, I toss the paperweight into the air, catching it with one hand. "Maybe it's nothing. Just a compilation of all my fears from the day."

"Probably," he replies. "But we also ken so little about the way an aurora latches onto an intelligent host. What if it's sending you a message? Or worse." Neither of us speak this other option out loud, but its static touch transfers between us: my dream might have been some kind of vision.

"If that lab is real, we have to stop it." They aren't quite my own words, shoved desperately out of my mouth through the sheer fire of the parasite's combined fury and anguish. I try to force away the foreign emotions—this is sad, yes, but it isn't my home. It isn't my fight. I'm only here to get this damn parasite out of me. How can I save a corrupt city if I can't even stop my own body from being corrupted by a nonsensical aurora?

And another, more wrinkled thought follows: why the hell is the parasite so determined?

Then, it clicks, the pieces of the dream coming together. Whatever is happening in that lab, perhaps it's not just hurting people. Perhaps, somehow, it's hurting auroras too.

The fury takes hold again, stronger than ever. I choke on it. Somewhere beyond the haze, Tavish speaks.

"You can't have seen my mother's primary laboratory, where they keep the auroras. It's in the business end of our building, and Ailsa never goes there anymore. Besides, every research project is screened through multiple scientists. If they were injecting humans with ignation, I would have heard something." His voice lowers to a mumble. "A secret laboratory would violate a slew of old assembly regulations, though."

Blue rubs against my tense fingers, nuzzling her face into

my palm. Her gentle purring settles over me like a calming blanket, and again, I don't know whether the feeling comes from the parasite or me. Does Blue soothe me because I like the cat, or because the parasite also holds some strange affection for her? Or do one of us appreciate her only because the other does, because there are parts of us too entangled for the otherness to feel foreign any longer? I have to bury the thought before it can take hold of me and tear me apart.

Tavish appears lost in his own head, his fingernails pressing mindlessly into his cuticles and his jaw set into his tongue-chewing sign of worried concentration.

I toss the rest of my borrowed pajamas to the side and head for my clothes stacked on the dresser beside the door. A few rips and stains still mar it, but a light floral scent replaces the grime and stench. I don them in a rush.

With my long vest's flowing material flaring around my knees, and its ruby accents shining against the black lacing of my billowing shirt, I should feel more at ease with myself. But the parasite's presence still hovers between each thought. It tickles my consciousness when I quiet my mind, as though its own intellect runs at a whisper beneath mine, sharing pieces of my brain to use for its own, indecipherable deliberations.

As though snapping back to himself, Tavish bursts to his feet. "Ah, I forgot to tell you— apparently unethical experimentation is the lesser of our worries. We received this while you slept." He offers me an envelope, the shimmering silver wax seal already broken.

The note within is written in delicate, sweeping letters on stationary trimmed in iridescent loops and swirls. I read under my breath, just to let Tavish know I'm processing. "The assembly is in the process of working out a contract that will grant Findlay Inc. the sole rights to the foreigner's aurora. You may deliver him to me by noon. I have already canceled your eleven-thirty meeting with Dr. Druiminn's lower-district hospital reformation committee so that you might not be preoccupied."

There's a threat in there somewhere, and it takes me a moment to pick out its layers: first, that Raghnaid can cancel her son's meetings on a whim; second, that it's this meeting, the one where Tavish feels confident and knows he's doing good for the city; and third, that she knows Dr. Druiminn won't stand up to her over it.

Tavish picks at the skin around his nails, his scowl so deep it seems it might fold into his face. "I knew it was only a matter of time."

This is it. Our position dawns, sharp and dark and red, like a sailor's warning. If we can't convince Greer to take me in—against the assembly's judgment—then my only options are to flee from Maraheem or hope that when Raghnaid rips the parasite from my neck, it lends me a swift death.

I set down the letter. My hands shake.

"What will you do?" I ask. Tavish has sacrificed so much of his time and his energy for me already. If his mother forces him to pick between the good he's doing for his city and the good he might do for a single, potentially doomed foreigner, his only sane option will be to choose his home. Something substantial, something permanent. Not the ghost that is me. And I could forgive him for it, nearly.

"If Greer would only reply to me." He almost snarls the words, his diamond voice turned into something husky, entrapped in emotion, and his brow tightens as though its tension is the only thing that keeps him together. "It might not save us, but it would give me options."

I can taste my own relief, almost sickly in its sweetness—he's going to keep trying to aid me, at least for now. I run my palm down my face. Dreams, secret laboratories, plans falling apart. It's all so much. So much I want either to charge headlong or collapse.

Sheona's shower turns off.

The coin Ivor gave me appears between my fingers, unbeckoned, and I flip it, as though if I move my hands fast enough, the rest of the world will fall in line around me. It flows and twists, leaping and falling like a thing alive. I slap it onto the back of my hand and look to Tavish. "Isn't there someone else in this city—this country, even—who knows about auroras and isn't afraid of your damned mother?"

Tavish yanks so hard at his cuticle that blood blooms in the crack, filling across the underside of his nail. A grunt leaves him. "Technically, yes." He wraps a handkerchief around his bleeding finger. "But you aren't going to like him."

CHAPTER FOURTEEN

rainbow blood and cherry-red rebellions

If we are the moons and the tides, then is a heart like a spark,
no end to the blaze so long as it's stoked?
Or is it the wood, with each piece used, used up for good,
leaving less and less flame till we're alone in the gloom?

AS OUR WINDING PATH through the Findlay Estates takes us closer to the city's apex, the décor bleeds ostentation, with sofas so plush that I think they might digest the people who dare to dirty their velvet exteriors, and gilding thick enough that it fights with the ignation glow for the prize of most dazzling. Raghnaid's visage stares back at us from sculptures and paintings. Sometimes a man with a triangular beard and a gaunt face lurks behind her, but more often she reigns alone, swathed in wealth with an expression like a jaguar standing over its kill. When I turn away, I swear I see the blood of her prey dripping from her chin.

We ascend a sweeping staircase that leers above the rest of the city through ceiling-to-floor windows. Below us sparkles the brilliant glass and polished metal of tunnels and domes and bridges. None of the lower districts' grimy, rusting exterior is visible from here. The haunting stillness of the climb seems to wash me out. I can feel myself fading away, piece by piece. The parasite shudders. A wave of exhilaration leaves it, fire and terror mixed together, bringing me back to life.

At the top of the stairs, Tavish holds his brooch to an ignation-fueled reader. The lock opens for him. We pass half a dozen doorways and parlors and finally stop in front of the library entrance. I take a breath. Sheona glares as stiffly as she did during his entire explanation of our situation, but Tavish gives her arm a little pat and pushes the door open.

This library must be triple the size of Ailsa's literary crypt. Its ceiling rears toward the ocean surface, a dozen mobile ladders coating the monstrous shelves, while its far windows view out over the glimmering city. Books pile between the central desks, stacked in neatly controlled pillars. Malloch leans against the far wall, arms crossed and expression so empty they might not even be awake.

Ailsa bobs beside them. Her strawberry curls swirl back and forth, and she digs little indents in the stray papers she holds. The nibbled cut in her lip has grown into a ruby gash. She clamps her mouth into a harsh line as her gaze meets mine, pooling a drop of blood that slips onto her chin. She rubs it away with the back of a scarlet-smeared hand.

A man who could only be Lachlan Findlay swoops to a stop in the middle of placing a worn paperback on an already towering pile. He blinks at us from behind a pair of overlarge glasses. His angular beard and gaunt face resemble the portraits perfectly, but his scraggly head of thinning hair boasts more silver than red, and his near lack of freckles makes his skin glow pink against his dark-blue and green sleepwear. Or perhaps that's the beginning of a blush.

A grin takes over his face. "Well, what a surprise! Tavish, and the guest! I was hoping Ailsa would drag you both up here." He shoots his daughter a scowl that evaporates again the moment his attention turns back on us. "Science, you know, it waits for no one."

I mean to introduce myself—the words are already piled

up behind my tongue, ready to turn this into a different meeting than the one I had with Lachlan's wife. But they stick there, trapped beneath a feeling of familiarity and a creeping dread that winds itself through my ribs. As though to confirm my feelings, Ailsa takes a step back.

"Come now, come." Lachlan waves us into his literary labyrinth, tripping over his own slippers in the process.

I hesitate, but the look of desperation on Tavish's face gives me something adjacent to courage. Resolve, perhaps. The knowledge that this might be our final option. If I can embrace it, maybe I can get something out of it in turn.

As we weed through the books, Lachlan dislodges a series of open tomes from a couch. "Not much space right now, but you can sit here—no, just Tavish." He pulls me back. "You, let me get a look at that."

Before I can resist, Lachlan yanks the collar of my shirt over one shoulder. I swallow down the bile that rises in my throat, trying not to think about the sweat on his fingertips or the way his voice prickles in my head. He prods the parasite, examining the lines excavated into my flesh by its dark expanse. They appear black at first glance, but a harder look reveals streams of a different color hiding in each. Heat pulses through them in time with the parasite's feverish interest.

"Brilliant, absolutely brilliant," Lachlan mutters, his tone skittering across my eardrums in an eerily familiar way. But whatever I can do to get closer to removing the parasite is more important than the goosebumps Lachlan raises between its rainbow-flecked strands. He sweeps by me and lurches open drawer after drawer in his web of desks and cabinets. He drags out some kind of extended eyewear and flips the lens, testing different combinations. "And you're still you? Still maintaining full physical and cognizant abilities?"

"I'm still mostly me, for now at least. It's straining to entrench itself deeper into us—into *me*—when I—we—gods—" My brain seems to spasm, the parasite digging its grimy fingers into it. I grit my teeth and think of it gone, dead, shriveled and pathetic at my feet. A spark of pain zaps through my skull. "Fuck off!"

Lachlan stares at me.

I try to offer a smile, but it comes out as a grimace. "Sorry, that wasn't for you. The damn aurora is playing with my brain."

"How fantastic." Lachlan straps on his lens concoction. He grabs my arm and shoves the eyepiece up to the parasite. I try not to ghost away from him as he flips in and out of various lens. "This is monumental. Just incredible. First of its kind."

"Indeed." It *would* take a specially fucked up creature to want to latch to me. But why choose me—why chose a human at all, when every single other of its kind all host in sedentary invertebrates and plants? Mobility, opposable thumbs, the ability to kill? None of those were things the other auroras sought after. I shudder. Perhaps my aurora is different. Twisted. A proper parasite.

This time, the parasite's flare is weak enough to tickle. '*I get odder the more you know of me.*'

So you keep saying.

"If I could take a sample?" Lachlan licks his lips, making their chapped surfaces glisten. "I have a place, just around the corner—it has everything we'd need."

Papers clutched tight to her chest, Ailsa finally speaks. "Mother will find out."

"Don't worry, dear, I will deal with her." Lachlan dropped to a musical mutter, stretching a hand toward her.

Don't worry, dear. It echoes through my head, matching with the same words in the same voice, turned a little hazy in the light of day. *Don't worry, dear, no one will miss her.* The parasite springs to life, pulling back up my dream and slamming it into full focus once more. Panic flares through us, bitter and sharp. We have to be free of here. We have to find that lab, that tank. We have to—

None of that. I have to do none of that. I shudder, drawing in air like the fresh oxygen might poison the parasite and clear the fear from inside my lungs. With a precise wiggle, I slip out of Lachlan's grip.

He seems only to notice after the fact, staring at his empty hands before dropping them with a smile. "Off to it, then, shall we?"

Ailsa gives me the tiniest shake of her head. As though I needed another reason to stay out of a laboratory conducting unethical experiments under the supervision of a man who never bothered to ask my name.

I lean against the arm of Tavish's couch, as far from Lachlan as I can reasonably get. "We'll do what we can here, for now."

Tavish's fingers bump against my leg. They stay there.

"I see." Lachlan's expression droops, making his skin seem to slide a little on his gaunt face.

He looks irrationally moist. I swear his eyes bulge. He turns to a completely different desk from the one where he first retrieved his lens device and deposits it in the top drawer.

While he's distracted, Ailsa slips by me. She presses a torn piece of paper into my hand, never once glancing back as she winds her way through the room and ducks past Sheona, out the door. Malloch trails behind her like the world's least enthusiastic guard dog. I unfold the note to find a short scribble: *My library, fifteen minutes. You and Tavish. Please.*

It's the *please* that gets me. A little splatter of red covers the *e*, blood born from the same kind of anxious picking that mars Tavish's cuticles. Whatever Lachlan is doing in that lab, it scares her.

I can't let it scare me, too. I can't let my own emotions drift too close to the parasite's. I fight down the wave of anxiety and tug my shirt back up, flipping the collar to cover as much of the parasite as possible.

Lachlan turns toward me once more. His previous disappointment transforms into sweaty ecstasy, his smile a little toothier than before. "So, you said it's trying to latch? How does that feel? Let's start there."

If this is the start, I want to ask where he intends to end. Whether I'm alive in it. Whether I'm me. "Terrible, but not physically. Whatever it's doing, it seems to be taking me over without destroying too much."

"Terrible," Lachlan says, and I can't tell if it's a reply or just him repeating my own answer. He drums his fingers along the top of the desk, his movements like crabs compared to Ailsa's spidery motions. "But are you stronger from it?"

I don't know which of us slams into the memory of the ignit we crushed in front of Raghnaid, but it turns my stomach like a monsoon. Between that and the extra speed and intensity during the fights when it has dug into me, stronger seems accurate. I nod. "How does that happen?"

"We don't know!" Lachlan's gaze still sticks on me, interjected only by the occasional set of rapid, wet blinks. "But we've never seen any noticeable energy loss from those in the Trench, even when creating ignits. In fact, quite the contrary—the aurora seems to provide the host with additional energy. The hosts grow larger and stronger than their aurora-free counterparts and become increasingly more difficult to kill without cutting out the aurora entirely, which is, itself, not an easy task even with the proper tools."

"Brilliant," I grumble.

The parasite ruffles through Lachlan's speech, poking at a few earlier phrases with an intensity that makes my head itch. *'Even when creating ignits, additional energy, even when creating ignits, additional energy.'*

I almost refuse to ask out of spite, but the weight of its emotions rise, bumping against mine until our curiosity gets the better of me. *My* curiosity. Or its curiosity, bled over me until I've drowned. I don't know which anymore. "If the auroras and hosts don't require any extra energy to form ignits, and ignits also produce energy themselves, where does all that come from? Do they just create it?"

"That's the dominant theory. But not the only one!" Lachlan snaps into motion, displacing half a pile of books onto the one across from it and rustling through the folders underneath. "There was a manuscript here somewhere—ahh! It's from a finfolk, and you know you have to take everything they say with an ocean of salt, of course—even less advanced than the humans, they are. But this person writes like they know what they're talking about. By the Trench, they could almost be a selkie." Lachlan pauses to take a breath.

I manage to get in a question before he starts off again. "Who are the finfolk, exactly?"

"Oh, them? They're generally weak-minded—"

"A group of mer who share the sea with us," Tavish cuts in, his sharp Findlay voice tearing through his father's words like a knife through melting butter. "Selkies haven't been the kindest to them over the centuries. We reached a truce a few decades ago, and now they pay the Mara Diplomatic Assembly a heavy tax to continue living within the North Seas."

The thought makes my chest tight. "I'm feeling better and better about my life choices," I grunt, wishing the assassin's blade in my memories was a little closer to Raghnaid's neck. The parasite tears the thought away, replaying the moment Lachlan mentioned the finfolk manuscript. *I was getting there,* I snap. But I take the hint. "What do those papers say?"

"Yes, right," Lachlan mutters. "A few decades ago, we analyzed records of aurora-host energy consumption and emission and concluded that the energy produced by ignits appears out of nowhere—it's created. Such a startling revelation that it rewrote our very laws! Energy cannot be created or destroyed—except through the knitting of the auroras." He flips through the pages without reading, turning each in a ritualistic rush. "But this finfolk claims that we shouldn't be so quick to excuse the energy in ignites as created just because there's no other easy explanation. They propose that our initial theory that energy cannot be created or destroyed is still true, and the energy auroras use for their ignits is being pulled from a secondary place."

My heart sinks. This is useless to me. But the creature still builds like pressure in the back of my mind, as though it's trying to force some kind of knowledge into me.

'Pulled from a secondary place,' it repeats, following it up with that same stupid sentence: *'I get odder the more you know of me.'* It slips deeper into my mind, nudging at the inside of my skull.

I cringe away from its warmth, physically flinching right, then left. *And you're trying to drag me there, too? Trying to pull me into whatever the fuck is happening in Lachlan's lab and your feelings toward those mutants the poachers were after? I won't let you. You can't have any more of me. I have my own problems and my own home, and I'm going back to them.*

'That sounds tough.' It shoves the words at me with such force that my jaw clenches in a combination of my own disgust and its unbridled determination.

Yes, you are, I reply.

At that, it fumes, its frustration sinking into my bones and making me itch to pace. *'I'm trying to save,'* it hisses.

I know where that sentence was meant to lead—a soft *I'm trying to save you* whispered to my precious crocodilian Sheila when she was only a hatchling tangled in a fisher's leftover netting. The word *you* cut off at the end means more than the rest of the phrase combined. This parasite isn't trying to save me. It's condemning me to save something else.

"I received another paper by the same scientist earlier this week, but I haven't gotten to it yet. So much science, so little time, you know. Could be useful though." Lachlan tuts. "Oi, Sheona, fetch it for me! It's in my suite, in the stack beside the rightmost desk. Should be titled something about dimensional theory and the motion of energy through space."

Sheona hesitates. The wrinkles around her eyes tighten.

"We haven't all day!" Lachlan snaps. "No one is paying you to ignore orders."

Tavish's grip tightens on his cane, but he nods to Sheona.

"Untwist your pants, I'm going." She shoots Tavish a worried scowl as she steps out of the library.

"The possibilities though—as I was saying—the possibilities of a secondary place from which ignits and auroras draw energy are endless. What we could do with that knowledge if we could uncover it!" As he speaks, he shuffles through another of his drawers, blinking rapidly and giving little shakes of his head like he's trying to dislodge it from his body. "And you—you could be the first step! With proper lab equipment, we can compare your energy readings to those in the Trench. What happens when your energy is drained through exertion? Through lack of sleep or food? You produce no ignits; does this alter the amount of energy your aurora creates?"

I fight the urge to look away from him. In the Murk, no one takes their eyes off a predator. I think the same is true with the exceedingly wealthy.

But the longer I watch, the stronger my panic returns, opening a floodgate through which the parasite's feelings rush, blending us back into one person. One person aghast and terrified and even more furious. One person who would tell Lachlan, '*Yes, take me to the lab,*' if the words would only come through the lump in my throat. I need to go there, I need to help—

Fuck off, I hiss, but it feels more like a plea. My fingers ache as if they need something to do in order to be mine. I tap them restlessly against my thighs and focus on my breathing, counting the pattern of blue and gold in the floor titles.

It takes so much of my concentration that I almost miss

Lachlan when he leans back toward me—toward the side of me not occupied by the parasite. Something pinches my neck. The parasite's anger fixes to mine, but as we both lift a hand to swat him away, I can't quite see the motion out of my periphery, my vision shrinking around the edges. My fingers bump numbly into something—my own neck? The parasite's furious shrieking dims. My world turns on its side and snaps out.

"Father, what was that?" Tavish's voice sounds distant, echoing from outside my hazy burrow.

"Oh, dear, seems he's passed out!" Lachlan shuffles about, nearer but still a thousand miles away. "Better take him to the lab, yes, best—"

"Passed out?"

Something squeezes my upper arm and pokes the tender skin inside my elbow. I try to yell, or whisper, or even moan, but my lungs clamp up. The parasite struggles with me, fluttering around in my head. It burns at the fuzzy edges of the world, slowly bringing them back into focus—destroying whatever chemical Lachlan used to knock me out, I realize.

"By the Trench, Father, what is happening?" Tavish shouts, clearer or closer, possibly both.

"Ah, nothing, nothing. He seems stable. There's a gurney in the lab, we can send for that."

I force my eyes open. Light floods in, and as the blinding whiteness clears, I find Tavish hovering a little way off. He cautiously nudges his cane toward me, his face ghostly pale. Lachlan kneels at my side, almost out of sight as he bends over my arm. When his gaze catches on mine, his own cheeks sallow to match his son's, his throat bobbing. He moves faster.

A rush of energy floods from the parasite, coursing through me.

I yank away from Lachlan, struggling to pull myself to a sitting position. A needle pokes out of my inner arm, quickly filling a vial with my blood. The sight jolts me to a stop, a wave of wooziness crashing through me, not simply because of the blood taken without my consent, but because it doesn't *look* like my blood anymore. Iridescent shimmers and soft, sparkling, white flecks glow through the dark-red liquid.

I tear out the entire contraption, needle and vial together, and pinch my arm upward to cut the bleeding short as I scramble farther away from Lachlan. My back hits Tavish's legs.

He startles, then steadies as his fingers brush my shoulder. "Rubem?"

"We're leaving." I grip Tavish to help pull myself up. I'd rather have my consent stolen by an insufferable body-stealing parasite than by this creep.

"Well, now, don't be hasty," Lachlan has the audacity to say.

Sharp, disgusted anger flows through me, resonating between the parasite and me. The half-filled vial of my blood still rolls listlessly toward me, and I slam my heel into it. The glass cracks, slipping rainbow-laden blood across the floor. No good to me. No good to Lachlan, either, and that's enough to satisfy both the parasite and me at the moment.

Tavish holds my arm. "Are you hurt?

"Other than the drugs your father injected into me and half a vial of blood lost? Not one bit."

"That's not exactly—" Lachlan tries to argue.

But Tavish's expression turns to stone. Or perhaps to diamond. "You're right. We *are* leaving. And we are certainly not coming back."

He charges with me toward the door, swinging his cane aggressively in front of him as he goes. The tip of it catches on a stack of books. The pile sways.

Lachlan's eyes widen, his whites swelling. He lifts his hands, but he's too far away. The books topple, slamming into the stack beside them. The labyrinth goes down one pile at a time in a mismatched mess that leaves single towers standing amidst a sea of splayed pages. The catastrophe quiets into the fluttering of papers, and the final victim falls from the edge of Lachlan's desk with an excruciating plunk.

Lachlan rounds on us, a vein popping in his left eye. His lips peel back. Before he can release the sky-shattering shriek that seems to be building in his throat, I yank Tavish out the door and slam it closed behind us. We don't stop, hurrying down the hall so fast that I nearly black out again. It could be the remaining drugs in my system or the fury and terror and indignation that hits me in waves, or it could be that I underestimated my blood loss and Lachlan has a series of vials he hid away before I woke up. But the thought of going back to check only makes me feel fainter.

Tavish catches my arm. Maybe he never let go. "Are you really all right?"

"Yes, I think so," I answer honestly. "Shaken and a little woozy, but it should pass. Even if he's my only option, I don't feel comfortable letting him touch me again until we know more about this lab of his." I lower my voice. "Ailsa left us a note to meet her. There's time, right, before your mother shows up?"

"You're the one who can see the hands on the clock."

I cringe at not having checked the large one ticking away above Lachlan's door. In the moment, the one counting down against my neck had seemed more important. I'd forgotten it wasn't the only thing due to explode soon.

But Tavish sighs, picking at the skin around his pinkie. "It should be around forty till. And it's on the way to my rooms, which is where Sheona will head once she realizes we've gone. I assume the paper she was sent after was a ruse to get her out of the room. I didn't think my father had it in him."

"It wasn't your fault."

His brow pinches. "Still."

We hurry through the halls, slowing at the stairs just long enough for Tavish to grab my arm, holding firmly despite his perfectly timed strides never once missing a step. The cats mew at us when we enter the Findlay siblings' floor. Ailsa's library doors sit a crack open, and we push the rest of the way inside with a quick knock from Tavish.

The vast ceiling windows let scattered grey-ocean light filter in through an army of dust motes. Books still clutter the room in every state of dismemberment, pages torn and piled and sentences cut apart, their meanings turned as enigmatic as the executioner herself. The same ragged handwriting on my note covers all the free paper, tearing itself in lines and swirls, blocks and circles, digging so deep in some places that they split holes and gashes. Little splotches of blood mark a few of them, left to blur through the pages.

Ailsa lies beyond the desk, her strawberry blonde hair gleaming with pinks and golds, the tips made two tones of red by the cherry-red of a fish symbol and the deep scarlet of the fresh blood.

CHAPTER FIFTEEN

all in the execution

Is each day together a gift, or is it a roulette?
The glass is half full: we are blessed to have met.
The glass is half empty: we brace, knowing
the shot saved for tomorrow still comes to collect.

TAVISH SEES NONE OF the horrific red. It's a blessing and a
curse, and it suffocates. First Alasdair, now Ailsa, mere
minutes or even moments before our arrival, perched on the
line between fate and luck. Her blood still oozes, sinking
deeper and deeper into the white carpet beneath her.

"Tavish . . ." It must be the weakness of my usually rough
voice, or the tightness with which I grip his finger, but I see
the knowledge hit him squarely.

"Has something happened? It smells off." One of his knees
gives out, and he leans his weight against mine, a hand over
his mouth. "Oh. Oh, fuck. Is she . . .?"

With an arm around Tavish's back, I press through the
dust motes, working us around the desk. Ailsa's blood drips
in slow trails from the great red gashes on either side of her
throat, a bead of it dried on the ragged, self-inflicted wound
in her lower lip. It slides through the upturned feathers of
her cloak and feeds into the stain on the rug. The circled, red

symbol of a slim fish bumps up against her splayed hair.

Her eyes are already closed, long eyelashes brushing pale cheeks. The body seems too perfect to warrant a death proclamation, as though it's all not quite real enough yet, but with my free hand, I sign out the two most basic words: *become one.*

Where the fuck was Malloch? I don't need any help to remember our first meeting in this room, Ailsa's voice so flat: *No one cares if I'm murdered.* Staring at her corpse now, her bodyguard nowhere in sight, the statement makes me bristle.

"The assassin must have found her waiting for us here." I draw my palm up and down Tavish's arm as I speak, an awkward, uncertain motion that I hope comes off as supportive. "I'm sorry."

Tavish wipes a glimmer from the edge of his eye. "Is there somewhere I can sit?"

I unclutter a chair of dissected book spines and help him into it. I feel his sister's corpse at my back all the while, guilt and grief hitting me in turbulent waves: guilt from me, and grief, well, I assume the grief comes from the parasite, its rush too distant and unreal, too disconnected from Ailsa, but the creature's warmth in my mind feels dormant.

In the swirl of the library's dust, I see the petals that fell around a different body. This *is* my grief. It's just not meant for Ailsa.

"I'm sorry."

"Aye, me too," Tavish whispers. "We were nearer in age than either of us to Alasdair, and we'd played as bairns. She was the only one who would, with me. She'd yell at the others with that voice of hers, so like Mother's and Alasdair's, the one that cuts through sound like it's a blade." His words dip, more ice than crystal. "I always wished I could speak like that."

"Now you do," I remind him. "You figured it out."

"No. No, I imitate, but it's not the same." Tavish straightens his shoulders, setting both hands firmly on the chair's armrests, his cane crossed over his lap. Another tear streaks down his cheek, but he doesn't move to wipe it away. "Right. What else do you see? Clues, notes, anything?"

"There's that red fish the assassin painted last night."

"It's probably the same as the one they found with Alasdair's body: the weaver fish symbol the last rebellion used, back before we were born. The venomous spines behind its head are shite to step on."

The phrasing pulls to mind Ivor Reid's bar, one of the cardplayers shouting above the rest of the talk, *See, they can't step on us forever!*

"Anything else?" Tavish asks. "Anything new?"

"I don't know. There's a lot of decimated books." I step through them on feet that barely touch the floor, as though I'm walking over Ailsa's grave instead of around her life's work. "It looks like they're primarily some kind of science— odd diagrams and equations and charts. She wrote notes over everything, but I can't read most of it." At a distance, Ailsa's scrawl through margins and between lines looks like a pattern of lace or vinery instead of genuine script.

"My reading aids could never pick up her handwriting, it was always so atrocious." Tavish draws a long, ragged breath. "She practiced her penmanship just for me."

I slip around the edge of the blood stain. This side of the room resembles the other, but from here I can just make out a bundle of papers forced between the hardcover of a plain green novel, the whole thing caught beneath Ailsa's dead grip, half buried in the feathers of her cloak.

"She kept a notebook." I slip it out, picking through the pages as though they might turn to dust under too much pressure. Their torn edges look half-decomposed already. "I can't read most of the text, but this seems aurora related."

I scan the words for anything legible. One line sticks out, circled twice: *explosions transport to second dimension?* The idea of another realm reminds me eerily of the twisted version of reality in my dream.

'Pulled from a secondary place,' The parasite murmurs.

Another place. Another dimension. None of it tells me how to rid myself of this thing in my neck.

I set the notebook aside. As I stand, the shine of light on metal beneath the desk catches my attention. I lean over Ailsa's corpse, careful not to touch her cooling body, and nudge out a long, elegant knife with a blood-stained edge. It takes me a moment to recognize it.

"Gods is this fucked." I handle the weapon gently, hoping I'm wrong. "Tavish, I think I might have found your knife."

Tavish jolts out of the chair, barely catching his cane before it topples to the ground. "That's not possible—it's been in my room—my lock was never tampered with."

A curse rises in my throat, coming out in my voice as a twisted snarl. "I left the door propped open when I came here last night. I was drunk, I didn't think—I'm sorry."

"Perhaps it's only a similar style." Tavish holds out his hand for it, and I tuck the hilt into his grip. He slides his fingers along the elegant patterns of sapphires and pearls to a small, swirling pattern on one side. His face goes slack with horror. "It's mine," he whispers.

The squeak of polished boots resounds form the hallway, already too near to run from.

"Really, Ace, I don't think it's necessary for me to—" Malloch freezes in the doorway. Their face pinches, and they draw their gun, not taking their eyes off Tavish and me as they shout down the hall for help. Through their teeth, they hiss, "Put the weapon down."

I wait for Tavish to speak in his diamond-edged voice, to cut through Malloch's condemning glare until it, too, lies dead on the plush rug. Instead, he reaches for me with a floundering hand. I grab him on instinct, both pulling him in and pushing him toward my back. As I do, I slip my hand into his, giving it a squeeze before easing the ornamental blade away from him. He presses his freed fingers against the center of my back. They shake.

"You drop yours first." My upper lip curls.

Tavish finally finds his voice then, if only in scatter scraps. "She was like this when we found her."

Both library doors clatter, flung wide by a flurry of four grey-uniformed guards. They stop short.

Malloch releases an angry scoff, more polished and perfected than Sheona's parental grunts but laden with something dark and emotional. "Found her like this, did you? With her blood on Tavish's blade?"

"We saved Raghnaid from the real assassin last night!" I object.

"So you say, but when I arrived you looked ready to slit her throat." Their lips roll, and a sheen grows along their lower lid. It's the most emotion I've ever seen from them, and it pulses in a way that's too genuine to be an act, as though they're trying to inflict a mask over it and failing. "Tavish has the motive. With someone skilled enough to help him carry it out, then why not? He is a Findlay, after all. And who else would she have felt comfortable enough with not to call for me?"

"You can't truly think—she's my sister." Tavish's words hold only half an edge, the trembling of his fingers worsening the longer he speaks.

"And the new heir to the company," Malloch says. "Is it a coincidence that all the assassin's targets are those in line above you? Or that you push yourself into boardroom meetings you weren't invited to, stealing specimens out from under your mother? Or that you spend as much money as you can wring out of Findlay Inc. on your personal projects?"

"I don't want . . ." But in this moment, Tavish looks entirely unsure of what he wants. His voice slips, panic taking over. "You—you guards, you believe me, don't you?"

One of the guards looks at the ground. Another swallows. Finally, the third speaks.

"We saw only you two coming this way—wouldn't have let anyone else through. That'd get us fired, or worse, you ken."

As she says it, her hand skates the hilt of her electricity stick, and by then end, she makes her choice. She pulls the weapon out and powers it up. Her companions barely hesitate before following her lead.

I struggle for one last argument. "Why would someone as smart as Tavish use their own heirloom as a murder weapon?"

Malloch's determination wavers a moment, their grief and fear peeking through. But they clearly don't care. Whether they truly think we've done this, or they just don't want the blame levied against them for letting it happen right under their nose, they will keep finding reasons to see things their way. "An heirloom no one would have checked up on if you'd been faster. Who *would* kill someone with an heirloom, anyway?" Malloch moves toward us, crushing dissected papers underfoot. "If you would both come quietly, it would make things better for you."

I grip the knife all the harder. One blade against four sticks of electricity and a pistol. If I were alone, if I could vault off the desk, over their heads, and flee, then maybe. But I'm not, at least for now. I can't leave Tavish to their mercy.

He squeezes my hand so tight it almost stops his shaking, and the beautiful, brilliant fool steps out from behind me. And lets go. "I'll come, but not him. He stays."

"No, Tavish." After all he's done for me, he's not allowed to sacrifice himself like this now.

Malloch's lips curl, and they rattle a pair of cuffs. "That wasn't an option. Whatever the BA decides, someone is waiting for the foreigner's aurora. His life was already forfeit by the assembly half an hour ago."

Tavish sways.

"Excuse me if I don't plan on being here long enough for that." Because I'm not alone, on more than one front. As much as I despise it, the parasite's presence still coils through my brain like a python lurking amidst my memories.

In a rush of thought so loud I hope it rattles my brain, I shout at it, *If you're going to be here, you might as well work.*

The parasite bursts to life. It stirs through my memories of the last few moments and flutters back to grab a sight I'd nearly forgotten about: the ignation-mutated orca calming beneath my influence. With it, the parasite flings some of my first words to it back at me, *'You can do this,'* but this time it blends together the kitchen staff's approval of my bridie suggestion into an amalgamation of voice and emotion, pounding hope through my parasite-fused veins. *We can do this. We can do this.*

Something smaller and weaker beats against the conviction, something that sounds like all of me and none of it. *This is how it takes you over.* But I can't think of that now, not with the guards flanking us on both sides and Malloch holding a pair of handcuffs like they're a torture device.

I ignore the *me* in myself and dig into the parasite's touch. My senses stretch beyond the library, spilling out into the sea above us. I feel the beat of a hundred hearts. Anger at Malloch swells through me, echoing between the parasite and myself and ricocheting outward. Like a sound wave made entirely of emotion, it crashes into them. With each stanza of my violent appeal, the parasite latches deeper, tearing its black tendrils into my flesh. It twists itself up my arteries, reaching for my lungs. But I can't stop, I can't—

Fingernails dig into my side. Tavish's perfect Findlay voice cuts through me, jerking me back to life. "Rubem."

My senses plunge back into place, leaving me tired and empty. Malloch reaches me. They press their pistol to my chest, but they don't pull the trigger. One advantage to being a commodity instead of a person, I suppose.

"Whatever you're doing, you'd better stop," they hiss, fear shining in their eyes. I don't have to look down to know what they see: the parasite, woven farther into my flesh, forming ebony lines beneath my skin, each gleaming with rainbows.

In a burst of color, the ignation-mutated orca rams itself

straight at us, slamming into the glass ceiling. The skylight shudders, and a tremble runs through the room, stirring papers and churning the dust. Two of the guards scream and Malloch jumps. I take advantage of their distraction, wrenching their pistol from the bodyguard's grip. A pained hiss leaves them.

As the orca rears back for another dive, I point the gun at Malloch. "I wouldn't follow us if I were you."

Rage bundles in their gritted teeth and clenched fists, and a tear finally slips from the edge of their eye. "You damn—" Their fingers curl. But they swallow and give a little nod to the guards. "Let them go."

I back Tavish toward the library entrance.

The orca crashes against the glass once more, pounding it with a strength no natural sea creature of its size should possess. The sharp clink of shattering follows. A single crack splits across the ceiling. I continue to move, keeping my gun trained on Malloch. Fear tingles in my lungs. Maraheem must have protections against major flooding, but that will do nothing for me if an entire ocean surges into this library while I'm still in it.

When the orca hits a third time, it produces a sickening crunch, then a soft, terrible drip, drip, drip. A bead of seawater hits my cheek, slipping down to my chin. I turn and shove Tavish out of the library. Behind us, three of the guards watch the ceiling in horror, leaving only one to lunge at us, but they're fast, their stick slamming into my arm. The parasite engulfs the electric energy, but the force of it still throws me off balance. My feet slide on Ailsa's flayed books. I miss the doorway and slam into a bookshelf.

An alarm blares through the building, and a massive metal slab rises up from the floor of the entrance, tearing the library's wooden doors off its hinges as it climbs toward the ceiling. My heart launches into my throat an instant before I throw myself through the remaining space. The tip of my boot catches on the slab. It continues to rise, the sea pouring into the library behind me with a crushing roar.

I wrench my foot free and roll to my feet just in time to make out the guards scrambling to activate their brooches, Malloch already twisting into seal form. The water lifts them alongside Ailsa's body in a swirl of paper and blood, her personal notebook rising to the top. A tiny wave slips over the lip of the metal slab. Then the seal locks, cutting us off from the room entirely.

The skylight above the hall reveals a sliver of water between here and the next layer of the Findlay estate. Through the gap I watch the mutated orca crush one of the seal-form selkies between its teeth, releasing a cloud of red. I'm almost hopeful it's Malloch, but a creature with their star-shaped brooch slips by the preoccupied orca, diving into a tighter water channel with the other three guards close behind. At least this high in the city, it will take them time to swim for the nearest gate.

"Rubem!" Tavish shouts over the blaring of the alarm.

"We can't talk here."

Distant commotion bombards us all the way down the hall, and even though we see no one, Tavish's door still feels like a flimsy barrier between us and eventual doom. I pull the deadbolt immediately.

"That was a breach alarm!" Tavish doesn't lower his voice, its diamond edge snapped nearly back into place.

"The library ceiling caved in." I scramble into the bathroom as I explain. Sheona's breathing device sits right where I left it. "I had to stop Malloch somehow."

"By dousing all the evidence that might have exonerated me?" Cracks form in his words. "Now it'll be the word of Ailsa's bodyguard of seven years against the black sheep of the family who inherits the company now that she's dead."

I force myself to breathe. Each inhale seems to press against a warm rubber band tied in knots around my lungs. Knots made of darkness with rainbows in their centers. "Fuck."

"What am I going to do?" His stable exterior breaks, revealing panic etched in something darker and fuller than fear, something that resembles the moment before an empire collapses.

"You tell the BA you're innocent the same way you told that boardroom you needed me!"

Tavish's pale face turns so ghostly that the red flush that blotches between his freckles looks like a rash. "I cannot— this is not what I've practiced for. With how much I panic— they'll see right through me. I'm sorry."

"You don't have to apologize." A part of me thinks he's wrong. He can do this, whatever he says. But I can't convince him of it if he doesn't want to believe it. Just as with our innocence, the only piece of evidence I can offer comes from personal anecdotes: the way my knees grow weak when he steadies his shoulders and my heart skips a beat when he walks through the world as though he could turn it inside out with a flick of his cane.

Now he does the opposite, half collapsed and half strung up, and from the way his voice trembled back in that library, it's too much to ask any more of him. He just lost his second sibling in two days, while his mother runs his plans for me into the dirt, and the universe seems bent on dragging the foundations of his life out from under him. This would be too much for any single person to bear, even him.

"Is there anywhere you can hide for a bit?" I ask. "Someone here that would shelter you?"

"This *is* the one place that should shelter me!"

"What will happen to you if you stay?" I almost don't want to know.

"They probably won't hurt me. I'm a Findlay, after all." This little laugh is broken and bitter. "But if the assembly puts me on trial, it will cause a power war between the big seven. With Ailsa gone, I am, technically the last Findlay heir to the company, and most of the other heads will be thrilled to push Findlay Inc. out of our family's hands, even if they have to play a long game to do it. If they have no one else—no one with obvious guilt—they might lock me up or deport me to one of the other smaller cities just because they can."

"So we find them someone who looks even more guilty." I don't have time for this—I know I don't have time for this. But with Tavish's future on the line, I can't just leave him here to suffer. "The weaver symbol is the sign of the lower districts' revolution, you said?"

Tavish's brow tightens. "Aye, but the assassin used ignits as weapons. Even the wealthier upper citizens barely have access to those, and every loan is recorded and signed for."

"Lilias has some." The full picture hits me, not like a wave or an avalanche, but like the rising tide, something I've felt creeping in around my ankles for hours and simply needed to open my eyes to notice. "She brought back a whole bag of them from the South. She's from the lower, wants to gain control of the auroras, and has a stock of ignits and few enough morals to consider murder a good option. She might also have access to the upper city—she's determined enough that I doubt she'd let the gates stop her." The only thing that theory fails to cover is her fighting style, but my encounter in the pool room is too blurred by alcohol to tell whether the cloaked assassin's attacks match with what I know of Lilias's or not.

"She just got back to Maraheem," Tavish protests. "Alasdair's death was the very day you escaped her."

"And she came to the city right beforehand, left me alone in Falcre just to visit Maraheem. Is that a coincidence? She has a partner working in the city. They might have set things up for her." The thought of tracking her down makes my skin tingle, tracing sparks along each of the veins the parasite has woven into. "If nothing else, we know she's up to something—something the big seven won't be happy with." My gut twists. Am I doing their dirty work for them? But Lilias deserves this, and Tavish and I deserve to see her behind bars instead of him.

He still doesn't look convinced. "If we run, I'll appear all the more guilty. And unless we find the culprit, that will only make things harder on me later."

"You could always leave Maraheem." I can feel myself tense under the words just as surely as he does. "I'm not saying you should, but it's only an option as long as you're still free."

That seems to drive a stabilizing wedge into Tavish's fissures. "No. This is my home and I won't abandon it." He closes his eyes. "But you have to save yourself; find someone who can coax that aurora out of you. I'll be fine here, one way or another. It's you I'm worried about."

Then come with me, I want to say, but his decision already takes up too much space in my chest. I knew our friendship would always be short-lived. My goal is still to sit on my porch again, just me, my pets, and a bottle of wine. Tavish was never going to be a part of that.

The alarms finally cut out, the distant clamoring of a small crowd taking its place. Tavish shifts from one foot to the other, gnawing on his tongue so hard it looks like it hurts. He says nothing. Waiting for me.

I force a breath. "Just don't let them step on *you*. You can't help anyone from a prison cell, least of all yourself."

It feels like a harsh, badgering good-bye after what we've gone through over the last two days. But it's all I have to give. He doesn't respond.

The moment I open the door, the commotion down the hall seems to eat me up. I slip away from it, making my way to the kitchen before my feet or heart can rebel. Only three chefs remain in the kitchen, whispering fiercely while kneading dough, their expressions tense. They startle when they notice me, but I recognize two of them from last night. When I explain my situation, they give me a roomy, grey staff outfit to don over my clothing. I wipe Ailsa's blood from the knife and fit both it and Malloch's pistol into the rim of my pants, hiding it under my disguise. One of the chefs whisks me down a workers' hall to a back exit with a cracked brooch reader and a security guard who barely glances at my uniform.

Blue mews from behind me. She hesitates, giving Lavender time to pad daintily up to her side before stepping toward me. I shake my head, hoping some part of her understands. They're safer here. Lavender rescues me by wrapping her tail around Blue's shoulder and guiding her back toward the kitchen. The tabby offers me one last blink before vanishing.

I can do nothing but close the door on them, sinking into the realization that I'll probably never see them again. Or Tavish. It shouldn't matter. The cats are not my pets. Tavish is not my family. This is not my home.

I turn my back on it.

The exit whines as it flings back open behind me.

"Ruby?" His voice is nearly diamond again beneath his gasping and wheezing, and I feel it cut into my heart like a physical blade. He rushes out the door with his cane extended, his grey staff uniform only half donned over his outfit. His curls bounce around his face, one of them falling into his open mouth.

He nearly crashes into me before I manage the words "I'm here."

A tainted sort of relief floods his features. "You're right. Not about leaving Maraheem, but the rest of it."

It's the best I could possibly expect of him, and it fills me with a thrill as bright and fluttering as a rush of butterflies. "I'm glad you're coming."

"If we want to do this, we'll need Sheona."

"I get the feeling she'll find us." I laugh, and the sound is already half out of me by the time I realize it's genuine. A little jittery, a lot tired, but still genuine.

I am out of options in the upper, fleeing with an aristocrat who will require energy I so desperately need for myself, yet I can't find it in me to despair. Perhaps that's the thing about hope, though. It's sustainable for however long you choose to hold on to it. If the bottom of the well runs dry, you can always keep digging.

Keep digging until it kills you.

Tavish runs a hand through his hair, and the curls tangle up on one side of his face. "This whole thing is absolute shite, you ken that, aye?"

"Oh, I know."

The pristine alleyway beyond the staff entrance winds around to a main street, just as lavish and vacant as all those I traveled on my way into the Findlay Estates the day before. I tuck Tavish's cane beneath my arm, lest anyone recognize him by it, and walk with the tips of our fingers touching. He takes us down and down and down again. After a final slew of wide stairs, he leads us to a gate. A small line of level-eight and -nine workers wait on the other side, peeking around each other as one of the guards shouts into a phone beside the two open archways.

She waves an arm at no one in particular. "I'm not closing the whole gate for some fucking air lock alarm ten stories up. For fucks—you, you there twiddling your damn thumbs, check the radio! They giving another citywide call or not?"

A young man leaning against a brooch scanner snaps into action.

I pull Tavish through the gate behind him. The security gives us half a glance, too preoccupied with some crackly, clearly upper-city voice announcing on a portable communication device. As we pass under the lower districts' archways, a muffled groan arises from the woman on the phone, and one of the younger guards slaps a coin into his grinning fellow's palm.

"Gates are closed!" the woman shouts. "Better luck tomorrow, folks."

The metal barriers slam shut behind us, stranding Tavish and I in the lower districts. I grab hold of his wrist, drawing him down the steps and into the hot, steam-strewn world of bustle and chaos. He lifts his hand, sliding his fingers around mine instead. Holding to me. And maybe it's nothing more than a thoughtless repositioning to help him maneuver better. But right now, that one purposeful touch feels like the physical incarnation of all my hope.

I don't let go.

CHAPTER SIXTEEN

the effect of the foot

I want to call you mine, to be the only one you hold.
I want our path to intertwine into one smooth, golden road,
not the landslide, the grave, the all-too-cleansing rain,
a universe apart and always just out of range.

WE STEP INTO THE anarchy of the lower city, and the flow of traffic takes us over. A hundred thousand sounds fill the silence of my own footsteps. The humid air swelters in my lungs and draws sweat along the back of my neck. I pause us to pull off most of the chef's outfit and tuck it under one arm. Tavish can't do the same, not without displaying his upper-city garb.

As soon as we start moving again, he bumps against a passing selkie's shoulder. I return his cane, but his first swing of it hits the feet of three separate pedestrians. His expression pinches. He tucks the aid against his chest and scoots closer to me, looping his arm through mine. I wish I could make his path clear, so he could walk on his own, exactly as I know he's capable of.

As we cross the square, a spot of fresh paint catches my attention, slapped onto the metal floor with no regard for symmetry. A hint of red pokes out one side. The assassin's symbol, or a copycat.

Tavish's crystal voice cuts through the lower-city bustle just as easily as it did the lavish boardroom. "So, where do we find your Lilias?"

"I don't now—yet. We'll ask around. Lilias isn't exactly a subtle person."

"I suppose this means we should strike up a conversation with one of these jolly vendors?"

"Careful with that aristocratic speech, you might scare them off."

His lips quirk. "You ken that, do you, you wee, canny dobber?"

"Fine, fine, you've slain me, silt-breather." I laugh in a way that's too light and soft for my sobriety, the sound itself a thing of rejuvenation.

As soon as the sound fades, though, all its confidence and joy slip away. I have to fight to draw it back, piece by piece, but every breath drains me again, leaving a larger, darker melancholy than before. The parasite's warmth twists along the emotion's edge, watching in silence. I swat at its presence, but I'm met with only a gentle humor, darker and softer than my own, as velvety black as the creature it comes from.

I shudder it off and pull Tavish out of the way of a sprinting woman with a bundle of newspapers on her back. "I know a place we can start. It's a bar in a pretty low district. I saw Lilias between it and the central gate, and the locals seem like the sort who might recognize her name, if nothing else."

"Then lead the—" A yelp leaves him as his boot catches on a crack in the sidewalk, nearly plummeting him off the curb.

I pull him closer with an arm around his shoulders, guiding us toward the steam trolley stop. We pay with the coin Ivor gave me, receiving a piece of change that has value only in the fact that its size flows perfectly between my knuckles, and crowd on board. The machine rumbles and rocks as it twists its way through the streets.

Tavish tucks his face toward my shoulder. "It's busier here than I imagined. We always drive through most of it with a cart."

"You don't have Sheona and your fancy clothes scaring people off, either." I tilt my head toward him as I say it, and the jostle of the trolley bumps my nose into his hair. The urge to feel that mess of curls between my fingers hits me like a monsoon, fraught by other urges that don't have any place, not here, and not with him. I swallow them down and look away.

"I never really understood—" He is cut off by someone shoving into him while working their way toward the door. "I knew the populace estimates were high, with all the factory work available, but I certainly didn't imagine this."

We chug around a corner. Through the shifting steam and the busy foot traffic, I make out a board of worn fliers fluttering against a dirty wall. "Some of these people were lured out of that town we met in—Falcre, was it? Taken from the fresh air and a world full of choices and trapped in this mess of vapor."

Tavish doesn't reply, but his jaw twists and turns beneath a heavy brow.

We depart the trolley a street away from Ivor's place, close enough to see the brush-marked red letters on the metal sign: *Reid's Bar*. The tune of the radio spills into the street, mixed with laughter from a throng of workers crowding the counter. We enter just in time for all chatter to quiet as its jolly music fades to the announcer's booming voice.

"We got the news in, you wee scunners! And you aren't gonna believe it."

The other host replies with a scoff. "They believed it last time. Maybe you just aren't giving them due credit?"

"MacNair, MacNair, my love, my one and only, why ruin this for me?"

"It's my lot in life, I'm afraid." A long silence lapses, in which the bar's populace exchanges the sort of exasperatedly bemused glances I imagine the radio hosts must be giving each other, before MacNair pipes back up. "Well, you gonna tell the poor folks?"

"Aye, scunners. We've heard right from the source, the gates are reclosed because of a second murder. A second Findlay murder."

Scattered mutterings nearly block out the radio's sound until the host continues, "And do you want to guess who died this time?"

"Was it our future job opportunities with dear Bubble?"

"It was, in fact, Ailsa Findlay, found murdered in her own library!"

The bar erupts with cheers and shouts, and a few roars of "Slit Raghnaid's throat already." The radio continues on, running through a series of jokes that bounce uselessly off my eardrums as Tavish wilts. He reaches out, finding the bar's wall just in time to stop himself from crumpling. His delicate fingers look out of place against its rough, red-green tinge.

I touch his shoulder. With the strength of a lapping wave, I nudge him toward me. He collapses into my arms, letting me wrap him up in the kind of devouring hug that could turn two people into one if they're not careful. But I don't know how to help him further. I don't know, and I mourn my lack of experience. I mourn for him.

"I'm sorry," I whisper.

Tavish sniffles, grabbing a fistful of my shirt as if to anchor himself. "They're right, Ruby." His voice might be a rustle of glass wind chimes or a clink of porcelain. "Damn assassin should've killed my mother instead. Not Ailsa. Not Ailsa . . ."

I hold Tavish, wishing I could do more. But if I knew how to make grief dissipate, then maybe the wounds in my own heart would have healed over by now. So, I merely let him stay within my warmth, giving him a place of safety as best I can, trying to tell him with my body, *You can have this for as long as you'd like*, even though I know it's a lie.

"These people didn't know her. They don't ken how much of her was genuinely good, how similar she was to all of them, how our family hurt her, too, with my mother's disdain and my father's disregard." His broken tone can't compete with the celebrating crowd. He hiccups back a sob. "And now they never will."

Someone from across the bar gives us an odd look, but they don't bother coming over. Tears must be common in the lower districts, coming in quantities far larger than the numbers of handkerchiefs. We're all a little worn here.

"I just have to ask the owner about Lilias. Are you all right—"

"I can manage." It isn't quite an answer to my question, but perhaps it's what he needs to hear from himself. He pulls away.

I leave him sitting at an empty table.

The bartender pauses from pouring beers long enough to give me a suspicious glance and state that Ivor Reid won't be in until late. When I ask about Lilias, he freezes.

"Lilias Erskine?"

My heart bursts into a frenzy, the parasite leaning against my consciousness with such a mix of eagerness and fear that I almost slap the side of my neck to knock some sense into it. "I think so. She had a brother who died recently during an expedition, if that helps?"

"Aye. Lots of people around here got caught up in her reckless nonsense before she left, even more now that she's back—people who should know better than to put their lot in with a fiend like her." His words have the sort of edge that implies his gripe is nearly as personal as mine.

"Do you know where I can find her?"

"Why you asking? You aren't BA," he concludes after a momentary double glance. His lip wrinkles. "She sway you, too?"

"She fucked me over, is what she did." The parasite weaves through my mind and curls down my arm in tingles. I itch to scratch at it, like ridding myself of it is a kind of revenge. Maybe Lilias isn't responsible for the assassinations at all. Maybe this is just an excuse to make her pay for *something*. I give too few damns to care. "I won't bother anyone she's working with. It's just her I'm after."

That last statement takes the pinch out from the bartender's brow. He leans in. "Try the Breac building, three blocks up. Last I heard, she's got the rooms above the brewery. Stinks of malt—you can't miss it."

I add my own amalgamation of dread and hope to the emotions I share with the parasite. "Thank you."

He grunts in return. "If Ivor asks, I told you nothing."

The foam on the next beer he refills makes my mouth water, and I leave before I can impulsively start checking my pockets for spare change.

I nudge Tavish. "We have a heading."

As he turns to come with me, he laughs, his crystal voice slicing through the melancholy that seems to linger in the air around him.

I don't know whether to be happy or worried. "Is something wrong?"

"Aye, most things. But somehow, it still feels a little right, you ken?" He almost smiles. Almost. "Though I could never manage it without your help. I should thank you."

"You helped me first." My next words stack up, but I have to force them out. To know what he thinks of them. "You could have saved yourself back in the library by putting all the blame on me. I was the one who caved in the ceiling, after all. I had access to your knife. I have experience with killing. I have a grudge against your family. You could have thrown me under the boat." I expect something, anything—shock, confusion, dramatic balking—anything but the knowing look he gives me, his eyes focused somewhere past my face and his expression filled with the sort of harsh openness that could crack the earth.

"It would've been easy," he says.

That answer cleanses and haunts all in one. Because he chose not to betray me. But he saw the opportunity, saw a conclusion no truly innocent person would have come to. He saw it, and had to make a decision, and maybe it was an easy choice for him, or maybe it was a coin flip. I tug the change from the trolley out from my pocket, flicking it between my knuckles. For everything I know of him, Tavish is too fair a person to truly consider selling me out, but he did waver on coming with me. He could waver just the same in the future and end up landing the other way. I have to be ready for that.

The atmosphere of the streets has changed during just the little time we spent in the bar. Guards pass in bundles, driving ignation-powered carts. Lower-district civilians lurch out of their paths, avoiding eye contact. The paths clear as most people move into the buildings, and I try to keep Tavish and myself tangled in the few remaining crowds, swerving us through tunnel alleyways whenever the guard carts come too close for comfort. We cross the corner where two days ago Jean the conspiracy theorist waved her fliers in my face. Only her pamphlets remain, most of those already scattered across the streets. My gut churns.

By the time Lilias's building finally comes into view, my thoughts spin a mile a minute. The stench of beer suffocates the whole block. I pull Tavish up to the door beside the brewery and yank at the knob. It refuses to budge. "Locked. Looks like a basic key system, though, none of your fancy ignation and lasers."

"Can you use those little sticks to open it? You ken how to do that, don't you?"

"Pick it?" I laugh despite the guard cart on the street behind us. "I've done my share of terrible, but I'm not that kind of criminal."

'I get odder the more you know of me.' The parasite's

warmth tingles with a strange fondness. It tears through my heart, cutting me in half. I try to find its destination, but I keep arriving back at that moment I first said those words, as though the parasite is pointing at me.

Stop that. You don't own this body yet; you're not allowed to be protective over—

It cuts me short by curling around my consciousness, almost smothering, its sudden rush of panic tingling through my veins. The echo of the guards leaping from their cart curdles in my ears, sharp in an otherwise dulled world. I glance up the street. My vision twists with the parasite's touch, but it centers on the three guards heading our way. They grab the few remaining bystanders, confronting them with a picture that could only be Tavish's face.

We have to get out of here. I shove my palm against the door handle. The parasite's warm pressure twists along my arm, and its black gashes in the back of my hand dance with color. It lurches from my skin, pressing into the lock. The guard's demanding voices almost block out the tiny click as the door opens. I pull Tavish inside.

We stand at the bottom of an empty stairway. My skin burns where the parasite lingers amidst my flesh, so dark my worn fishnets appear grey against it, like a stenciled glove compared to the real thing. A shudder runs through me. I had barely suggested we work together, implied it without a conscious thought, and the parasite used that as an excuse to bury itself further into me. But as it coils in the back of my head, leaking fear and tugging distractedly at the memories of Raghnaid's stare in the boardroom, I don't know if I can blame it.

Tavish and I ascend the tight stairs. Another door sits at the top, this one wooden. It opens with ease. I press my palm to Tavish's chest, signaling for him to stay put.

Not a sound comes from the small apartment. It resembles the rest of the lower: aged metal and grime, too small to be properly habitable, its contents messy and cheap.

The central room holds a set of crooked furnishings cluttered with signs of life, from empty cups to a cluster of wooden animals arranged across the end table. Sheer curtains drape the front windows, and a pair of bioluminescent bulbs in yellow glow faintly from a holder in the low ceiling.

They light the half circle of worn sofas and rickety chairs—enough for a decent-sized clandestine meeting. Lilias is planning something, and I'm well enough acquainted to the violence and pain that's come with her past ventures that I doubt I'll like this one any better.

Across a stool lies the schematic for some kind of ignit-incorporating earpiece titled *energy reflector*. The paper looks old, creased from many foldings and torn twice, and it bears the signature of an expert ignit mechanic who'd been unlucky enough to arrive at the rivers around the Murk a little after Lilias. I hope the older woman recovered from the ordeal.

Small, rusty tools and bits of metal clutter the schematic's edges along with a single, nearly completed version of the earpiece. I pick it up quietly, flipping it between my fingers as I examine it. The empty slot in its side would hold an ignit no larger than my thumbnail. Lilias toted a mixed bag of similarly sized ones from the Murk—there's no telling which color she intends to use in it.

As I set the earpiece back down, I notice lines beneath one of the paper's tears. I lift it, revealing a map of the coast underneath. A circle marks a little inlet of water north of the dot for Falcre, but there's no town labeled. I let the paper drop back into place and slip between the mismatched seating.

The assembly overflows into the archway of the tiny kitchen, all staring toward the open entrance to an even smaller bedroom across the way, where metal gleams from within a deadbolted wire cage: electricity sticks and pistols. The room feels far smaller suddenly, breathing down my neck. I shudder.

This is what she's planning: a rebellion. A rebellion of stolen weapons against a society made of ignation. A rebellion at the cost of whomever she convinces to hold those weapons. But a rebellion those same people sorely need.

I stop just before the kitchen entrance, begging myself not to think too hard, not to look back over our history from her perspective. Lilias arriving at the Murk in search of anything that might free those she loves and finding a wealth of auroras and ignits to rival the one used to suppress her people. Lilias turning to violence and threats to get it. Lilias watching her brother die in the process, immediately losing the aurora, one of the only things she had managed to bring back from her trip, and striving forward anyway.

A paper flutters silently beneath my foot. I move to reveal the red symbol of the assassin's fish. *They can't step on us forever.* But who will be poisoned when the fight finally breaks out?

In the kitchen, someone shouts through a phone speaker—a masculine voice, I think—but the distance and static mar it. A stool clamps against the metal kitchen floor, followed by a curse.

"I was plenty awake—" Lilias barks. "Well, it's your fucking fault for making me hold forever." She raps her nails against wood. "So, it's done? Did they take the bait? They're targeting the youngest Findlay?"

We don't need a victim to blame, it seems. We have the real thing after all. I watch Tavish for signs of breaking, as his whitened fingers grip too hard to his cane, but he holds himself steady.

"Don't you worry," Lilias says. "We'll put Raghnaid's head on a pike soon enough." A brief sputter from the other side of the line leaves her shouting, "When have I ever been reckless? This is the best time, probably the only time—" She releases air through her teeth. "Aye, fine! But you'd better get back here soon."

I waver on the soles of my feet, the rebellion flier still lying too close for comfort. Whether or not Lilias's motives are good, there's only one real option here. I shuffle my memories back around: Lilias finding a place that's been repeatedly hurt by foreigners for the last three hundred years and being willing to destroy it for her own gain. Lilias, who could have worked with us, who could have sought our help as a friend instead of demanding it as an enemy, stealing what little the Murk has retained to fuel her war. Lilias, who murdered my favorite caiman just to hurt me. This is the Lilias framing Tavish. This is the Lilias about to find us standing in her living room.

I move on feet of mist. For once I feel myself in total agreement with the parasite, neither of us overwhelming the other, every strained muscle and thought aimed solely at Lilias. We hate her in equal proportions for what she has done to us, to our home. The time for fear has passed.

I had tucked both my stolen pistol and Tavish's ornamental knife under my pant line, against my back, lest the guards catch notice, but as I pause to retrieve them, the phone clicks back into the box. Lilias immediately rounds the corner of the tiny kitchen.

I abandon the still-holstered weapons on instinct and slam my elbow against Lilias's jaw. She sputters and sways, but she rams her shoulder into my stomach. I twist away from her, into the kitchen.

Lilias growls, the light in her eyes more feral than any of my jaguars back home. She launches herself at me, fists flying. I try to back out of her reach, but the edge of the kitchen's metal counter hits my side like a blunt spear. Pain shoots through my ribs. The parasite's warmth meets it, interweaving into my agony and turning the sensation into a dull ache, then into nothing.

I knee Lilias square in the stomach. She grunts and slips back a step, just enough for me to follow it up with a proper kick. This time she stumbles away, her back to the kitchen entrance and her boots skidding along the rough floor. A knife appears between her fingers.

The parasite bundles inside me, preparing to take over. I resist, reaching for my weapons instead. Lilias lunges.

From behind her swings a line of silver and blue. It slams against Lilias's head. Her lashes flutter. She crumples, revealing Tavish's stocky figure behind her, cane still raised.

CHAPTER SEVENTEEN

even the villains

Things to remember when you're no longer here:
The wind-whipped splendor of our salt in the shallows,
intermingling on the altar with the sweat and the tears.
A perfect surrender of our joy and our sorrow.

I SNATCH LILIAS'S KNIFE off the floor. "How did you know that wasn't me?"

Tavish's chest heaves once. He brings his cane down, resting it pointedly in front of him. "Her, I can hear."

She groans, struggling to pull her elbows under her, but I shove her onto her stomach, yanking both her arms behind her back. "There's a bundle of cord on the couch to your right—no—no farther. Not that far."

Tavish grumbles under his breath, launching the spool of mechanical wiring at me. It nearly sails over my head, but I catch it and wrap it around Lilias's wrists and ankles. She's still off-kilter and blinking when I set her in a chair, but she finds the energy to glare daggers at us both.

Her gaze rips into the parasite on my neck, her lips twisted and orange hair splayed across uneven shoulders. "So, you've managed to hold on to it. I thought for certain the Findlays would lock you in some dark hole and rip it from your bones piece by piece."

I twist another chair around and sit in front of her. Tilting forward, I stare at her, expressionless and lingering, before releasing both weapons from where they're tucked against my back. I covertly set the pistol behind me and withdraw Tavish's knife, holding it between us to examine the hilt. Its blade nearly nicks Lilias's chin as I twist it around, but she doesn't flinch. I relax, crossing one leg over the other. "You say that as though you had planned to do any different."

"I need the aurora." Lilias scoffs. "It's consuming you anyway. How much longer do you think you have? A week? Days?"

I flip the knife. My left hand slips, my fingers not quite grasping through the feathering rope of my fishnet gloves, but my right makes up for it, faster and stronger beneath the parasite's black ripples. A crest of color shines within each dark groove. How long *do* I have? How many more times can I fail to resist the parasite's lure before all that's left of me are the parts that entwine neatly with its presence and conform perfectly to its will?

Lilias tracks the flow of my blade. One side of her lips catches in a smile so bitter it draws metal in the back of my mouth. "Or maybe you've only got hours, by the look of those fingers."

"What would you know?" I snap my hand closed around the knife hilt. My fishnet glove snags on it, ripping.

She grins, all bite and no glimmer. "Nothing more than you do. Doesn't it gall you that in a city of the most advanced minds in the world, the only person helping you is a blind philanthropist who isn't even liked by the people he claims to aid? Maybe they ken something you don't."

Her words sting. *'Princeling'* repeats in my head, the parasite nudging me into it, egging me on. I bare our teeth. "I would shut your mouth if I were—"

"No, Ruby." Tavish's words cut through my ire. His hand appears on my shoulder, his little finger brushing the side of my neck, tickling against the parasite.

It curls its warmth toward him, drawing up the happy thrums of my precious felines. *'Princeling.'*

"She's right," Tavish continues. "The people don't like me, and they're justified. I threw money at charity projects, and maybe that's done some genuine good in the moment, but at the end of the day, I left this place so I could huddle within a family who continued to quash the less fortunate just to build themselves up."

"What more could you have done?" I realize those are the wrong words the moment I utter them.

Tavish's features fall. "Nothing, I suppose. If I had existed outside my corrupt family, perhaps, or if I had possessed the courage or the ability to demand our company change its nature from the ground up instead of simply patching their wounds after the fact."

Lilias's head plunks against the back of her chair. She stares at the greening ceiling, and a scratchy cackle leaves her. "Are you fucking kidding me?" she grumbles. "Rubem Veneno, befriender of great crocs and jaguars and mer-snakes and now a damned Findlay. You have no standards. Or very strange ones."

The parasite laughs at her wordage, and it comes out my mouth. I cut the sound short, letting it flow into my voice instead. "You know, that was never really my surname." I return to flipping the knife, watching the silver and blue swim as it switches places. "But yours—Lilias Erskine? Is that what you want them to shout in the streets when you take down the big seven? Or is that the name they'll curse when the upper city crushes them?" I tip the blade toward her. "Or maybe it's the name that'll be spoken before an execution sentence for playing a part in the murder of two Findlays and the framing of their innocent brother."

"This revolution will come," she snaps. "Even if you turn me in to the BA, the lower will just burn them down. Whether I'm the central blaze or the spark that ignites it, it won't make a difference once the big seven are all ash."

Her conviction flings me back to those images of Lilias as savior instead of destroyer. But this rebellion, as righteous as it might be, doesn't deserve to come at the cost of the Murk. If Lilias's rebels want so badly to make a better city, they should have joined someone who wants the rest of the world to be better, too. "That was your partner on the phone, wasn't it? The one who slit Ailsa's throat? Who is he?"

Lilias tips her head to one side, her eyes moving down my face. "Unlike you, I don't betray my own." She clicks her tongue against her teeth. "Now, this has been a fun chat, but I have an appointment with a man about a cow."

Her boots screech as she lurches out of her chair, ramming aside my knife with her bound wrists.

I let her rise just enough that her forehead comes to rest perfectly against my pistol. She freezes in the presence of the cold barrel. All color but red drains from her freckled cheeks. Slowly, she sits back down.

I keep my aim steady. "Tavish, would you be so kind as to fetch more of that wiring from the chair beside you? I don't think the gate guards will appreciate being delivered a half-escaped predator."

Through his slight confusion, amusement quirks at his lips. "Aye, Ruby." He traces down the chair and grabs the spool.

Lilias leans toward me with such cautious movements that the determination in her eyes seems to be a part of a whole separate person, as though she, too, is trapped between herself and a parasite. "We chose not to kill your precious Tavish," she hisses. "He'd never be condemned for the murders the way they would someone from the lower districts. Maybe they'd put him in a posh, little prison, but he'd never suffer the way we have. He'd even be safer there once the fighting started." Her voice comes faster by the end, almost desperate. Soft. "We killed the villains, Rubem. We killed the villains."

Her words twist up my heart, trying to find a place to take root. But they're met with only the hard velvet of a dislocated aurora. I grant her a single shrug. "You hurt the Murk."

Lilias opens her mouth, but all I hear is the squelch of her boot into my dying caiman. When I yank her to her feet, all I feel is the fading heartbeat of every swamp-born creature she didn't find worth sparing, and when I bind her wrists tighter, all I smell is the innocent blood she's spilled to reach this point. But it doesn't quite cover the shuffling coming from the bedroom, or the way Lilias stiffens, the color leaving her face.

"Please," she whispers.

I want to reply that whatever she's asking of me, she won't receive it. Then, the bedroom door swings open a little farther. A small boy steps out, clutching a wooden cow in one arm, a tattered blanket wrapped around his shoulders. His muss of orange curls nearly covers his bright green eyes as his gaze flows over us, brow ever tightening.

He lifts his free hand, almost losing his blanket in the process, and signs a familiar word, "Mama?"

The motion tingles in my fingers, so close to the sign I'd used as a child. This time it's not warmth that travels up my arm, but a prickle of pain that digs itself into my chest.

Lilias jerks against the cords on her wrists, and she mouths a word: *no* or maybe *go*.

But the child steps closer, watching my pistol with such confusion that I can't imagine what Lilias must have told him about the weapons. He slips his little cow figurine into a pocket in his oversized bed shirt to make use of both hands. His signs stray from the dialect the colonists of the South picked up from the Murk, but I catch his meaning well enough: "Mama, okay?"

The pistol weighs more and more the longer I hold it.

"Ruby, what is it?" Tavish asks.

"A child." The word rubs wrong against my throat. "I think he's deaf."

"If you touch him . . ." Lilias's threat sweeps like a miasma from her quivering lips. Within her weakness, her desperation, her obvious, terrifying love, I have never been more afraid of her.

I take a step back, not daring to lower my pistol even if I don't dare fire it either. A knock at the metal door reverberates through the space, tearing my gaze toward the stairwell.

Lilias crashes into me. Her forehead hits the underside of my chin with a crack that sends stars across my vision, and the pistol flies from my grip. It skitters along the floor, flickering in and out of view as it passes under a row of chairs and finally comes to a stop beneath the sofa nearest the bedroom door.

As I latch my arms around Lilias's shoulder, fighting to keep her in place without accidentally driving Tavish's knife into her arm, the pounding at the entrance grows stronger.

"If those are the guards—" Tavish starts.

A gruff voice through the door cuts him short, muffled by the metal. "Lilias! You going to let us in or not? The streets are crawling."

"Get the spare, dammit," Lilias shouts. "The aurora's here!"

I punch her across the jaw. She totters on her bound feet, and another hit sends her sprawling. Her plaid shirt lies crooked over her heaving chest when she sits up, the shine of her crab-shaped brooch peeking beneath her collar. She knows better than to ignore an attacker while she's down, yet her attention flies to the gap between the chairs, fixing on her son. My heart jolts with the remembered ache of a boy watching his mother in pain.

But the child looks oblivious. He sits on his knees, the fluff of his hair shielding him from the sight of us as he reaches beneath a sofa. And draws out the fallen pistol.

The world turns glacial, freezing us in a quiet so complete I can hear every soft brush of the little boy's fingers on the pistol's metal. He cups the base of the barrel, twisting it toward himself as though inspecting a new toy—a toy his mother's been keeping locked away. His nails tap the trigger, slipping over the sides without pulling it. Each beat of my heart breaks me anew, repeating my mother's death in reverse.

The sight holds me in place as though a vine connects me to the gun, its thorns growing through the edges of my eyes. I have to help, but my bones lock, the parasite's warmth not making it past the cold horror in my muscles. With the prickling agony of rending flesh, I move my hands.

"That will hurt you," I sign, my usually fluid motions shaking. "Set it down. You have to set it down."

The child notices my movements and lifts his head from the gun. He fumbles it in his grip. Each centimeter his little hands slip around the barrel takes a thousand years and half a heartbeat.

A sound not humanoid, not even animal, leaves Lilias, breaching her like a void coming open. She kicks the back of my calves. As I fall, she dives onto my knife, haphazardly cutting her wrist bindings across it in mid-roll. Blood rises in a line up her forearm, but she plunges onward, crashing over a stool and lunging for her son. Her hands clamp to the barrel of his gun, yanking its aim away from his stubby legs in the same instant his fingers catch on its trigger. It fires.

The explosion hits me late, a distant blast I can't quite hear, then an endless tinging over silence. Lilias's eyes widen. Blood pours from her left hand, streaming from the spot two of her fingers should have been, and angry burns sear up her palms. Pain peels itself in ribbons across her face, the sort of shock-silted agony that coils deep and reemerges eternally.

Her son shakes, but besides the red sprinkles on his bed shirt, he looks untouched.

Somehow Lilias pushes through her anguish and takes the pistol from her son's trembling hands. She scoops him up, burying her face in his messy hair, staining his back with streams of scarlet as she clutches him. A sob leaves her, wet and relieved. For one blessed moment, the scene is almost peaceful. Tavish even leans out from his cover between a cabinet and the living room windows.

Then, a key rattles against the downstairs lock.

Lilias scrambles into the bedroom with her son. He vanishes behind the metal wall, and she reappears with the pistol, her hold on it precarious. I jerk back into the kitchen as she fires. Her bullet ricochets near my feet. Across the living room, Tavish folds himself into what little cover he can, the window at his back.

I cup my hands around my mouth. "I'll break the glass!"

Tavish's nose wrinkles. "Rubem—"

But I'm already lugging the stool away from the wall phone. Two sets of feet pound up the stairs, bringing two men with them just in time to see me launch the stool across the room. Lilias's next bullet whizzes by it as it flies through the spread curtains, past the now open windowpane, and into the air.

"They unlatch," Tavish says, so flat I nearly choke.

I burst out of the kitchen to a rain of bullets, Lilias's at my feet and her friends' zipping around my head, too close for comfort.

"Don't kill him, he has the aurora!" Lilias's shriek follows me across the room.

You better not let us die here.

My thought sparks a rush of warmth.

I scoop up Tavish, plunging us both out the window. Tavish screams, but I hold him close, angling my back toward the ground. The parasite digs through the flesh along my shoulders, biting lines of black into my skin. All my better instincts fight against it, but I restrain them, waiting for the ground.

We hit the street so hard the impact sears into my bones, where the parasite consumes it, turning the energy from the fall into a feast for itself. As it devours, it digs. I roll us under the shelter of the brewery's lower overhang, focusing on blocking the parasite in its tracks. The thought retaliates, as though I'm placing my own fingers in my mouth and biting down. The parasite cringes and goes quiet, not pulling back from the gashes it just made, but not tearing further into me either.

That was the last time. The words are for me, not it. I have to believe them. I have to make them true.

"A little warning in the future, please," Tavish groans.

"How about we just don't jump out any more windows."

I pull him up. He sways and clutches his cane in a death grip. The few locals left on the street watch us with a mixture of dread and curiosity, their gazes darting to the open apartment window. An empty guard's cart stands a few strides away, and the thrum of another approaches, but the soldiers themselves are nowhere to be seen. Lilias's friends charge out her front door, both their pistols already aimed at us.

I step in front of Tavish. The black marks now cutting up my arm, over my shoulder, and down one side of my back all ignite in preparation. But before the pair can decide whether to shoot me down, the cart's troop jogs out of an alley across the way—four of them. Electricity already pulses through their sticks. One drops a bundle of fliers at the sight of us: two assumed felons held up by a pair of ragged lower-city men with polished silver guns that look as though they were stolen straight off the Findlays' personal security.

"Lower your weapons!" the guard in the lead shouts. One of Lilias's friends swaps their aim to her. She freezes, but the rest of her team fans out on either side.

I motion vaguely toward the rebels. "They helped kill the Findlays!"

My words only draw two of the guards to us instead.

Tavish digs his fist into my shirt, clutching it like a child, but when he lifts his voice, it cuts in the way only a Findlay's can. "These people are in defiance of the thirty-ninth statute by bearing projectile weapons within Maraheem without the permitted documentation of a personal bodyguard. For the safety of the city, it's your duty to arrest them and their supplier, who lives in the apartment above us." He steps out from behind me, his grip slowly settling. "We are unarmed and persecuted under false pretenses—"

"I have your knife still, princeling," I whisper, holding it as nonthreateningly as I can manage.

Tavish swallows and starts again. "We are *less* armed and persecuted under false pretenses. Your first commitment is to the well-being of this great city, which is threatened by the very existence of those pistols."

His words ripple like a physical force through the street. The rebels waver, as though Tavish is a bright light they can't look directly at, much less aim for. When they turn both their guns on the guards, they're met with straightened shoulders and buzzing electric sticks. The onlookers creep farther back.

A motorcycle turns the corner behind the guards, compact and agile but with an engine so loud, it seems to beg to be let loose, its silver sides glowing from swirling lines of ignation. A figure in black dismounts. As they pull off their helmet, their bangs resettle around their forehead.

"It's Malloch again," I hiss to Tavish.

"We have proof!" he exclaims. He waves for them, delicate as a diamond. "Those rebels are blocking the apartment of the woman who arranged for the murder of—"

Malloch cuts him off with a sound even more powerful than a Findlay voice: the ring of four consecutive bullets. In a row, blood blooms from the guards' chests. One by one, they drop, sticks clashing across the ground.

Malloch turns to us, bearing an unnerving grin. "Would you look at that? They just dropped dead."

CHAPTER EIGHTEEN

the easy way out

Stalled at the crossroad,

where yours and mine interact.

When you continue for home,

will you even look back?

THE TRUTH COMES TOGETHER, piece by piece: Malloch's twisted smile, their determination to peg the murder on Tavish and me, the upper-city gleam to Lilias's weapon stockpile. The red smear of paint on their boot in the pool room and the way they flinched when I grabbed their pistol in the library, as though that wrist had been hit recently. It was never Lilias under the assassin's cloak. It was Lilias's partner. It was Malloch.

They train their pistol toward us.

The parasite jolts me with warmth, urging me to act, to fight, to run. Malloch shot the guards, not us. They still want us alive, then. I hope.

The guard's cart stands a few strides to our right, its absent door gaps inviting. I grab Tavish and pull him toward it. Shots follow us, but they scatter somewhere over our shoulders. We slide into the cart. A pipe of ignation flows through its console. The keyhole is empty.

"You can't run from this," Malloch calls, polished tone reaching a melody. "Felons won't go free in this city for much longer."

Tavish latches to my arm. "Can you make it go?"

"I'm trying." In the split second it takes me to wonder how we'll start the cart, the parasite flares. It slams my palm against the keyhole, moving me through its black gashes. As it does, other tendrils of it dig deeper into me as well. I jerk, hissing through my teeth.

"We were going to let you live, Tavish." Malloch's dark silhouette appears in the cart's vapor-blurred side mirror. "If you come out now and bring our aurora back to us, we might offer you something better. You wanted to help the lower city? Why don't you finally do it? We could use a mind and voice like yours."

Tavish goes taut. His unfocused eyes look even more distant than usual, as though he sees into the future, calculating each possible choice and running it to its end. The contemplation in the look spears a little more panic into me than I'd like, but he only whispers, "Whatever you're doing, hurry."

His worry fuels my resolve to leave, and the parasite slips beneath the emotion, taking advantage of it to dive into the keyhole. The ignation engine whirs to life with an electric hum, blackened rainbows pulsing and shining off the silver in its console. The parasite's pressure weighs on me, the empty exhaustion left behind in my chest so overwhelming that all I feel is it and the creature and our mixed fear.

Once we're safe—once we're safe, I'll stop relying on the parasite. What good is it to die now, after I've already given it so much, if one more inch can save us? I'm still me. We're still—I'm still—still me.

I slam down one of the pedals. Nothing. I push the other instead. The cart blasts forward at nearly twice the speed of a sprinting human. Tavish's hand finds my thigh, and I swear he grows claws.

Malloch curses. A spattering of bullets follows us down the street.

"You do know how to drive this, right?" Tavish shouts.

"How different can it be from a boat?" I tuck the knife into my belt and yank on the wheel, finally spinning it when nothing else will make it move. We turn with a screech, clattering down an alleyway. Three pedestrians plaster themselves to the wall as we roll by. I cackle, the laugh something between cynicism and insanity. "All I need now is a stiff drink!"

As we launch from the tunnel, the ruthless purr of Malloch's motorcycle follows us. We turn into the street, narrowly missing the chugging trolley. A billow of vapor slides around us. As it clears, a third body appears in the cart, hovering at Tavish's far side, black clad and snarling. I nearly swerve into the closest building to knock them off before I recognize the intruder.

Somehow Tavish knows who she is just by the way she plunks into the seat next to him, still half hanging out of the cart. "Sheona!"

"Told you she'd find us," I grumble, but my heart lifts all the same. A group of shoppers cusses us out because I refuse to slow for them. They dodge at the last moment.

Sheona scowls. "Seemed a bad sign when Malloch arrived at the gate and immediately took off into the lower city. Tracked them here, the bastard."

"They're the assassin," I explain, "working with a rather shifty rebel group."

Sheona hisses through her teeth. "Fucking—turn left here."

I swing the wheel, and we launch into a descending tunnel. The cart rattles over every step, jolting my teeth against each other. Tavish holds tight to me. I grip the wheel for both our lives, hoping with each step that our back end won't rise to flip us. Sheona rides the plunge as if she's done it a thousand times, screeching at the pedestrians to get out of our way.

As we peel off the final step, I glance in our mirrors. The lights of Malloch's motorcycle cascade along the tunnel wall.

"Go right," Sheona shouts. "Then left again down the next set."

I spin the wheel, turning us in an arc around a cluster of startled schoolchildren in shabby, brown uniforms, and dive our cart into another descent. "Where are we going?" My speech rattles with every bounce.

"To the dredges?" Tavish asks.

Sheona nods, or maybe her chin just dips from the jolting. "Aye."

Tavish must realize my confusion because he explains, "They're the ruins of the original Maraheem, the one built by the finfolk. Now they're only used for waste transport. The homeless congregate there, and the criminals."

A stairway later, the road opens onto a balcony above the ancient city's remains. The metal walls rise into thick domes that feel almost like the spacious glass ceilings of the upper districts, but for the stench and the decay. Crumbling stone structures make elaborate patterns on the ground four stories down, forming decrepit walls and archways, a wobbling current of smog and steam shifting in their cracks. The heat feels oppressive here, targeted and angry, so sweltering that the stink of sewage and chemicals becomes a part of the temperature. Vapor shoots in constant sprays from the massive forms of machinery that rise up nearly to our balcony.

We turn onto a new stairway that winds and drops through the old city's clutter, a rickety railing on one side. Few people traverse these stairs, but through the gloom on the ground are hunched selkies, sleeping or huddling around cooking fires. In the distance, a series of red and blue canopies cover what sounds like a party but looks like half a war and half a funeral.

As we drop off the edge of the stairway onto hard-packed

dirt, Malloch appears above us. They lean over their motorcycle and shoot. Dust stirs at our side.

Sheona returns fire, forcing Malloch to pull back. She reloads once, then again, but at the end of her second magazine, she curses. "I'm out."

Malloch responds with a fresh bombardment of bullets. The cart rattles when they hit us, piercing along the dash. The tubing in the console cracks. Ignation spills into the center of our seat. My heart stutters as it douses Tavish.

"Dammit." Sheona whips off her cloak and hands it to him.

He wipes himself down with a wrinkled nose and crunched lips, his unfocused eyes adding to the look of disdain. I wait in horror for the ignation to gash colorful lines into his hands, barely watching the road as I veer our cart into the maze of decrepit buildings. But Tavish's freckled skin stays as smooth as ever, the silver shimmering harmlessly across the front of his blue-and-grey overcoat.

I grab his fingers just to be sure. "Why isn't it mutating you?"

"Mutating? Ah." Tavish pats my hand. "It's harmless on the skin. The mutations only seem to occur now that animals have had long periods of internal exposure—ingestion, I assume, though Lachlan's lab might be using injection. We wouldn't have this stuff running through our walls if it changed us with one touch. And we wouldn't be having this mutation problem now if we ken that it even did this at all."

His explanation makes so much sense that I should have figured it out myself, but hearing it out loud clicks a switch in my mind, one the parasite is all too happy to nudge at excitedly. "You've had ignation for decades."

"Nearly a century," Tavish corrects.

"And you've never seen the mutations before? In all that time?"

Tavish's brow shoots up, half of it burying beneath an overturned lock of his ridiculous curls. Sweat pastes the hair to his forehead. "You think something has changed?"

"Something must have, right?"

The parasite shoves against me, hot and frustrated, its indignation pooling in my bones. It growls, a mixture of all my pets' anger combined into one atrocious sound that rattles my mind. Something *has* changed. I just have no way to uncover it right now.

The whirring of the cart turns to a sad sputter, and the vehicle chugs to a stop, the last of the ignation dripping from its console and pooling on the floor. The chemical-filled fog creeps in through the cart's open sides. Sheona pulls Tavish out of the vehicle, leading him through the ruins at such a speed that I have to jog to catch up. Malloch's motorcycle hums nearby. We duck under a low archway and run through a field of deteriorating pillars, almost falling over a cluster of vagabonds asleep in the low-lying haze. A beer bottle tumbles away from my foot, liquid still sloshing inside it. My anxiety and fatigue both bombard me with desire, but I'm far too sober to try whatever lies within the grimy glass.

"Why are we down here again?" Tavish wheezes, stumbling into Sheona when she stops us at the edge of an empty street that cuts along the side of the thick metal wall.

Lights flicker beyond a break in the stones to our right, and a pair of grey-uniformed workers pull themselves toward a landing three stories above using a hand-cranked elevator, but the world remains silent. Holding its breath. Or perhaps, in this place of toxins and sickness, the world doesn't breathe, because it's a corpse long gone cold.

Sheona leads us across the road and down a spacious metal tunnel. "We're here because this is the only place besides the gates from which anything leaves the city."

On one side, thick cables lower massive wastebins from a chute in the ceiling. The sorting station below it is empty, as are the containers marked the same as the massive, smog-spewing machine that rumbles a little way down. The tunnel ends in a pair of glass chambers with air locks that form a seal between the humid, chemical heat of the dredges and a patch of deep-blue seafloor, both open on our side. Food waste half fills one, while the other remains empty but for damp scraps coating the bottom.

Tavish balks. "No. I refuse. I will stay here and face my fate before I—"

Despite Tavish's stocky form and Sheona's slight one, she sweeps her arms under his legs and heaves him onto her shoulder. She lugs him to the mostly empty garbage chute and drops him, unceremoniously, inside.

Tavish grumbles under his breath. His entire face scrunches up as he removes the grey chef's uniform in dramatic yet precise yanks, tossing it to the side and folding his scarf, coat, and shirt carefully for Sheona to tuck into a waterproof bag. He presses his brooch firmly against his bare collarbone, and it sticks there.

My gaze catches on his skin, finding the layers in his freckles, the transition between the heavy patterns across his face and the gentle spotting on his shoulders that turns near white across his chest, where his dual scars cut clean, silky lines below his nipples. I stop myself from accidentally following the rim of his pants as he draws them down, half out of respect and half because, despite our present situation, I'm still aching just a little with the desire to slide my hands along the curve where the bulk of his stomach and his gracious upper thigh meet. Imagining the sounds it might raise in him is the very last thing I need right now.

Swallowing the disastrous thoughts, I pull off my boots and add them to Tavish's bag along with my vest and shirt. As Sheona seals the clothes up and lops the cord over my shoulders, I flip her breathing device between my fingers. It occurs to me, finally, that she's removed none of her own outfit.

"You're not coming?" I ask.

She smiles, a thing more sad than happy. "Someone needs to release the chute."

My mouth opens, but I don't know whether to object or thank her. If it were only Tavish and me, would I have stayed back? I glance at him, and I want to say yes, but the reply comes forced through a memory of home. The home I'm still just as many steps away from as I was when I caught him on the beach. I feel weak around the edges.

She grabs my chin between her fingers and thumb, the slight wrinkles around her eyes growing as she stares at me, fiercer than fire and older than stone. "If you return him with a single hair missing, I will make such fine slices of you that you'll be mistaken for a pile of fleshy locks."

My soft grin feels crooked beneath her scrutiny. "His safety will be my top priority."

Sheona lets me go, her expression as loose and open as I've ever seen it. As she steps toward the garbage chute's controls, though, a familiar hum reverberates through the tunnel. Malloch's motorcycle whirls toward us.

They use the vehicle as a shield as they skid it to a stop. Crouching on their knees, they fire over the top. I dive in the corner between an empty wastebin and the metal wall. Sheona ducks as bullets whiz above her head. They crack against the front of the garbage chute, making tiny splinters in the thick glass. A trickle of blood joins them. Clutching the breathing device tighter, I follow it up Tavish's arm to a light graze in his bicep. His hand lifts toward the tiny wound, the color leaving his face with the same intensity it fills Sheona's. Before he can touch it, she slams a lever on the chute console. A hiss of steam fills the tunnel, and the glass slides down in front of Tavish.

Malloch fires again, but this time they aim toward the console. At Sheona's exposed back. Red explodes from her chest. She wilts to the floor, where she gasps, drawing in a sob and letting out a growl. I feel the sound like a knife in my gut.

Tavish's voice echoes through the sealed glass, calling out her name questioningly. Water fills his chamber. His brooch shimmers, a wave of color-imbued black dancing out of it, and he shifts from human to seal. Sheona watches him, clinging to the console with one arm. Her blood looks black where it saturated her dark clothing, but it plunks to the floor in scarlet drops, quickly forming a small puddle in the dirt.

I flick the breathing device between my fingers and try in vain to drive down my chaotic heartbeat. Malloch seems not to notice me hiding, but one wrong move could catch their attention. I can't leave Sheona like this, though. I can't stand here and watch Malloch kill her. Despite the pain pinching her features, she looks as if she might leap at them were they not aiming for her chest.

"Are you going to finish me off?" she hisses.

Malloch steps over their motorcycle, each stride so polished they hardly seem real. Even the dust doesn't stick to their perfect black boots, the red paint from the pool room long since removed. "No, I ken you're already finished." They smile, something between a taunt and a reproach. "But I could save you."

"What do you want?" Sheona snaps.

"Your allegiance." Malloch stops, planting both feet firmly into place, looking so eerily like an image copied from the upper districts and pasted here without regard for the grime and stress and death of the dredges. "You're the best in our family—I'm not so daft as to forget it. If you joined those who want to make this city right instead of siding with the bastards who have kept us as little better than slaves in their cycle of poverty, we would welcome you with open arms." Their upper lip curls. "I know you used to hate the Findlays as much as I."

As Malloch speaks, I slip the breathing device into my pant pocket and shift, ever so slowly, willing myself to be one with the curling vapor that swirls along the room's edges in the wake of the chute's release. The mist creeps in. I move with such silence that my bare feet leave nothing of themselves, not sound or print. Not even Sheona seems to notice me drifting toward Malloch's back.

"I never knew you felt like this." Sheona's eyes dig into her cousin, raking them as though searching for a conscience beneath the refined exterior. "I guess you weren't brave enough to voice it."

Malloch's façade slips in a twitch of anger. "I didn't have the privilege of your skills." Their aim shakes as they jab the barrel of their gun toward Sheona. "If I'd spoken my mind, no one would have hired me. But you were worth it to them." The words bubble with venom. "Did all of Tavish's pampering change you?"

Sheona goes silent. A thousand emotions pile through her features, running into each other too fast to make out. They land on desolation. She exhales, her sigh leaving nothing but exhaustion in its wake. Exhaustion, and a ghostly blanching that contrasts the red of her gushing chest.

Malloch laughs, but there's something else in there, a hoarse kind of wetness. The beginning of a sob. "I didn't let them get to me. I killed Ace—" Their voice hitches, but they breathe out. "I killed Ailsa. Because it didn't matter what else she was—she was still a Findlay. So, have they corrupted you, or not? Are you too soft for them, or will you join us?"

"It's just one Findlay I'm soft for. And you shot at him." She closes her eyes, slumping a little lower against the console. A red stain follows her journey toward collapse.

Malloch snorts a sound that mimics the Findlays' diamond tone so precisely that it shatters through their argument. "I should have aimed for his heart."

The way that aristocratic snivel aligns with their perfected composure, their self-righteous commands, it hits me: they don't want to simply remove the Findlays. Some part of Malloch, large or small, subconscious or not, wants to *replace* them.

A tear slips down Sheona's cheek.

I grip Tavish's ornamental knife as best I can manage

amidst its inlays and ridges and tackle Malloch from behind. The blade slides easily between their ribs. With my free hand, I clutch at the pistol in their hands.

They react sluggishly, caught between a gasp and a shudder. Then their training kicks in. They bring their arm down on mine, twisting and shoving with a speed I can barely track. I block their swivel as they try to turn their pistol toward me, and ram down on their already injured wrist. Their gun flies toward the console. They lunge after it. I catch them by the shoulder and stab deep into their side once more.

Sirens blare through the tunnel, a deafening alarm bell that makes my bones shake.

"You have to-to leave." Sheona sounds like a pale imitation of the fierce bodyguard I know. She holds herself up against the console, her blood coating the ground in a trail between us.

"Not without you." I latch onto Malloch and slam my knee into the gash I just created, drawing a mangled scream from them as they struggle.

"There's only one place I'm going, and I don't want Tavish joining me there till he's old and grey." She coughs, a fresh stream of scarlet flowing from the corner of her mouth. Through the blood, she wheezes, "He'll need you, you ken."

I want to rebut her—he doesn't need me, he needs her, too, I could never replace her—but the deep-red pool forming beneath her makes all of that meaningless. Tavish will have me or he will have no one. So he *will* have me, for as long as I can offer that.

"Thank you, Sheona," I manage, because to say *I'm sorry*—to apologize for her limited number of future heartbeats—is to declare that there is something worse to come after that final breath vanishes, and I wish not to believe that for anyone, least of all for her.

Shoving Malloch away, I leap for the half-filled garbage chute. The instant I squash into the mulch, Sheona, shaking and teeth grit, creaks down a second lever. The door descends.

As it closes, I shove the knife back into my belt and reach into my pocket for the breathing device. My fingers find nothing but lint. I grope at the emptiness, my chest filling with a hot, heavy panic that water will soon replace. No, no, it was just—

But through the locked glass I find Malloch half-hunched but holding the glimmering silver of my borrowed breather. Their polished features twist into a smirk, breaking free of their perfect formal mold and bending into something grotesque and bitter. As their smile reaches its peak, their pistol fires, Sheona's finger on its trigger.

The blood that surges from Malloch's chest blends with the black of their clothes. Flecks of it splatter their chin, red freckles on their brown ones. They stand there as the water floods in around my bare feet. The breather slips from their fingers. They collapse.

The water keeps coming, blasting up my legs. I manage a single breath before it encircles my head. The trash around me lifts, filling my vision with mold and peelings. Then, the door at my back opens, and everything drifts toward the sea.

I search for purchase within the chute, pounding on its door. Sheona still holds Malloch's pistol, slumped in a sea of her own blood. Her lashes flutter my way, and her fingers twitch toward the console. Joint by joint, they fail. She slides to the ground, her chest still.

My grief swells, and I yearn to sign her a death proclamation, but my rising panic overcomes all else. It clenches my worn lungs and screams for me to breathe. I slam my palms against the glass separating me from air, but I only succeed in shoving myself backward, setting me adrift in the sea. The lights of Maraheem rise in a chaotic wall above, the nearest gate too far away to reach and teeming with people who will kill me in worse ways than the water. Even farther off, the hazy, blue surface of the ocean peeks at me from beyond the garbage chute.

It silhouettes Tavish as he fiddles with his cane, catching it in his mouth and spitting it out again. If only he could swim to me.

But he doesn't know I'm about to drown. He doesn't know Sheona is dead. He knows only enough to fidget, soaked in his anxiety but unable to act. Through my panic, I wonder if this is the real restriction of his blindness—that by being silent, we withhold from him his agency.

The screaming of my lungs shatters the thought, seeming to sever every nerve but its own. The parasite reacts by screaming in turn. Its fear magnifies mine, but it also knocks me to my senses. This will be the last time. It has to be.

I take hold of the aurora, as though I'm grabbing each side of its beastly face and shaking it. Then, I pull it closer.

'Can't breathe,' it shrieks in a voice that sounds like my own, the original tone lighter and laughing. It's not laughing now. But I ignore it and call for a different kind of help. Despite its terror, this parasite tendrils leach into me, its subconscious taking advantage of every moment I use its power.

Help me. If you want my body, then save it.

For the heartbeat it takes for the parasite to answer, I feel a piece of me siphon away in the trickle of bubbles that slip through my lips. 'Aye.'

Together, we call for aid. As we do, it lodges in my lungs. Its tendrils lock into the lobes, going from velvet to stone as it holds them in place. Dark spots form in my vision. I try to inhale as my brain gives one last cry, but this damned parasite—my parasite, talons digging into my consciousness with all its might—won't let me. I choke, not on water but on stale, empty air. The world closes in, losing shape. As I float, I feel two things: Tavish's soft fur brushing my side, and parasitic tendrils stretching toward my heart. And I see, darting through the blue, a glimmer of color.

CHAPTER NINETEEN

every righteous thing

Does it even matter in the least

if your backward glances don't sway your feet?

If you'd only stay from my knuckles turning white?

Voice rigid, heart rapid,

I cling too tight.

I FLOAT IN NOTHING, black and empty. It feels like a languid cavity, where each second of sadness stretches into a millennium, eating back through the joy of the past. Beneath it all, lurks me. My parasite and I. *Mine.*

I don't know where the possessive term comes from: me or this creature—my creature—wrapping through me. Part of me.

'*Mine.*'

Life bursts back into existence as the nothingness turns to sky and ground. Our lungs tear open, drawing in fresh, blessed air at my parasite's command. With each breath, the sensation of our body returns piece by piece. My body. My body, mostly, but within it I feel the coil of something more still working its way toward my heart. In a sob of panic, I strangle its crawl, battering it in an onslaught of rage. My parasite recoils like a guilty animal, winding back into my lungs where it oozes stark petulance.

Above me extends a listless grey sky. I force myself to sit up. Sand sticks to my back, and water brushes up and down my legs. I glare out to sea, barely spotting the ignation orca as it retreats, a pair of mutated dolphins at its side.

"What in the fucking Trench—" Tavish sputters as he settles into his human form, his diamond voice clipped and choked. "Ruby? Ruby!"

"I'm here," I reply, reaching for him even though he's a few strides away. "We're safe now."

"What took so long? Were those dolphins guiding us?"

"Yes—it's complicated." I drop my hand to the bag. Our clothes nearly slip through my fingers as I bundle his up and press them into his arms. "Change. I'll explain after." Withholding knowledge from him leaves a sickly taste in my mouth, but I don't think the words will come just yet.

Tavish doesn't argue. He ruffles his hands through his curls and slips back into his clothes, his abnormally fast pace the only sign he's bothered by the wait.

I lift my shirt, but my arms tremble. My gaze tracks my bare skin where my parasite weaves itself into my muscles. The black lines knit together in patterns smaller than my littlest nail, working themselves up my right arm and over my shoulder in a design almost like a fishnet. A fishnet engraved into my skin, gleaming with flashes of color in its deepest depths. A fishnet that will become me.

The ferocity of my indignation makes my jaw hurt. Fishnets are my aesthetic. This damn body thief can't take them away from me. But it seems to think otherwise, flinging my resentment back at me. I scoff and yank on my shirt, turning up the collar and tugging the sleeves down to my knuckles. My parasite reacts by stealing the use of my right arm and rolling the left sleeve back up.

I roll it down again.

It protests loudly.

Before we can start a shirt war, I trudge us up the beach

to where the grass stretches over moors of green and grey, wipe the sand from my feet, and shove on my—thankfully dry—boots. The seawater in my pants immediately seeps onto them. My parasite sighs with my lungs, and I can't even object.

"At least we tried?" I grumble.

'*Wet ball of lint,*' it replies.

No beer for you.

And to my surprise, its borrowed laughter feels genuine. I shake my head, releasing another deep exhale for the both of us. Tavish joins us—me—on the hill. He slips on his shoes, arranges his scarf to precision, and plants his cane into the dirt.

"My clothes are donned. Now tell me, what utter shite was that back there? Why did those dolphins carry us here? What in the Trench is taking Sheona so long?" His expression remains dignified, but cracks ring through his voice, just as they appear at the corners of his too-tight lips and the unsteady squeeze of his fingers.

If this news breaks the fragile hold he's gained on his grief, I don't know if I can forgive myself. But that's no excuse for keeping it from him. I rub my hands down the front of my face, one striped in black and the other clean brown beneath the damp, fraying fishnets.

And I tell him, expanding on every detail, my parasite pulling at the memories whenever I miss something. I end with *She's dead* and *I saw it.*

Tavish's jawline quivers once. He lowers himself to the ground and collapses backward, his breathing so slow that he must be putting in great effort to control it.

"I knew . . ." His words come out strained, as though shoved through a grater. "I knew from the moment she was assigned to me, despite how young I was then, I knew that this could be how it ended. It was a hazard of the job. But she is—was so much more than a bodyguard."

"She loved you like family." I plop onto the grass beside

him. Last night there was a moment like this, I recall, but I was on his other side, and we were safe, and Ailsa and Sheona were alive, and the world was, perhaps no more right, but at least a lot less wrong. "In my culture, we proclaim over the dead a series of blessings toward both them and the living. Do you mind if I . . .?"

"Please."

I sign the words, but I speak them, too, low and heavy, nearly a chant, reciting the full proclamation as well as I can remember it, having given it only once and far too young. "We mourn for a life, both taken and given, for the dousing of a spark, unique, never to be replicated. We mourn for the loss, the tear it forms within the world, the rip in the heart of each who feels the absence. We mourn for the love that was to come, for the dances cut short, the relationships severed by an unbreachable divide. May you, Sheona—" I pause, realizing I'd never learned her last name.

Tavish rescues me. "Aris."

"May you, Sheona Aris, provider of stability and strength, worthy protector, may you find peace as full as the quiet of the womb. May the tears of those who weep for you become one with the sea. May the fruition of your life, your love, and your loss carry those you left behind, guiding them into the future. We proclaim you ours, in life and in death. Be at rest."

Tavish stares at the sky. Small, gleaming tears slip unhindered out of the corners of his eyes so quietly I don't think he even realizes. He doesn't move, even after my final sentence has rolled across the waves.

"We can't stay here, you know." I don't add that Sheona died to bring him this far. That her loss literally carried us into our future. But he knows.

"Aye." Tavish shoves both hands into his curls and scowls with more dramatics than true emotion, as though he's covering up something too raw to let the air touch. "This is fucking shite. How do we prove my innocence now?" He releases a grunt that vanishes as quickly as it forms, eaten by the sea breeze and the rushing waves. "I suppose the Gayles of Sails and Co. bring their fleet in and out regularly. If we can flag one down before they can port, and they've not heard of my involvement yet—if they still believe I'm accepted as a Findlay—then perhaps we could—"

"I can't." The words hurt, bringing with them an echo of my last promise to Sheona: *his safety will be my top priority.* But as I rub at my parasite's velvety blotch on my neck, failing to find where it ends and I begin, they're too true to deny. "I have to focus on removing the aurora from my neck."

Tavish jerks upright. "But Lilias—Maraheem—the rebellion!"

"Tavish." I catch his hand, pressing his palm to the place where my parasite molds into my skin, its hide and my flesh so indistinguishable than it could be a natural part of me. "I'm so far gone, Tavish. I need to at least try to remove it while I still have a chance. Last hope, and everything."

In reply, my parasite twists within my corrupted arm. It pokes me in the fleshy side of my neck, so reminiscent of what I did to it for our first day that I don't need its wave of bitterness to piece together a meaning: Just as it was a thing in me for a time, I'm now becoming a thing in it. As it's grown larger, I've grown smaller. Soon I'll be nearly as small as it was the hour I first let it in.

"I want to help you return to your home," I say, however much it kills me. And I find, against all odds, that it's true. Thinking of those bullets aimed for him, of the streak of scarlet that dripped down his arm, of all the rest of the red in his life right now, I would have pulled his chute no matter what it meant for me, if the alternative was his death. But he's not the one dying now. "If I assist you now, though, there might not be a me left by the time we get there."

"Trenches, I'm sorry. I didn't know." Tavish's fingers slide across skin and parasite, leaving a warmth like whiskey in its wake. They settle beneath my jaw, his thumb fitting there perfectly.

I never want him to pull away. "It's not your fault. You can't see the way it's crisscrossed through my muscles."

"Fuck." He lets go.

The lack of his touch sobers me. I draw out his ornamental knife and flip it, letting it twist in the air in front of my face before catching it again. My parasite's arm always snatches it faster, stronger, more precisely than my own. If it would even let me attempt to cut it out of myself, I'd bleed to death before it was done. I try not to think about how little of me there will be left in the best of circumstances. Maybe too little to carry me home. Too little to help Tavish either. I'm no doctor, but I have the strangest feeling that a human can't survive without their lungs.

I can't give up yet, though. There must be one last hope for me. I will dig until I die, or I might as well have never started.

"The finfolk," Tavish exclaims, so abrupt that a pair of seabirds take flight.

I put back the weapon. "What?"

"The finfolk," he explains. "Lachlan referenced one of their scientists as having those revolutionary ideas about the auroras taking energy from other places. If anyone outside of Maraheem can help you remove it, I bet it will be them."

My instincts say no. Every search for a scientist's help so far has ended with someone looking at me and seeing only an aurora to play with. But maybe that wasn't because they were scientists, but because they were Findlays. And maybe this close to being consumed, I'd rather die knowing those that the big seven have oppressed the most will learn from my loss than bleeding out in a human hospital where they won't know enough to stop my parasite from latching to a new victim.

"Right." I pull myself to my feet. Each motion feels like it might be my last. "Where are the finfolk, then?"

With what must be every ounce of theatrics he can

muster, Tavish stands, too, cane in hand. "Glenrigg is their only village in Mara that they haven't been run out of yet. It's tucked into a tiny, mountainous firth about a half day's walk north of here, which they cohabit with a group of outcast pixies from the mainland. If this scientist lives anywhere permanently, I suspect that's where they'll be. But the village has an ignit that makes anyone who approaches it lose their mind. Few who go there come back alive, and those who have report waking from some kind of hypnosis after being bound and hooded."

"Perfect. I lose my mind on a regular basis." The idea sounds almost desirable in my current sorrow-saturated and alcohol-free state. "I doubt it will be a problem for me, though—ignits don't seem to affect me the way they should." The purple paralyzer disintegrating in my grip proved that without a doubt. "But you'll still be caught in its pull."

"I trust you'll guide me through it." The words are out of him with such speed and confidence that it makes my heart warm and ache all at once.

"Then we go to Glenrigg."

As I turn toward the northern hills, I can't quite put Tavish out of my sight: his tussled, damp hair twisting in the breeze and his rumpled wealth, such a contrast to the landscape's rugged desolation. He deserves someplace safe where he can plot his return to Maraheem in peace. But if I tell him outright that he need not come to Glenrigg, I'm too afraid he'll realize it's true. He has better things to do than to follow me.

I loop my arm through his and set off, not giving myself the time to wonder at the ethics of my selfishness.

Though we walk as straight a line up the coast as we can, our conversation meanders like a wild vine. We strangle meaningless topics while avoiding anything resembling our current predicament, as though the recent past infects it. Tavish informs me that the skies are grey here more than they aren't, and I taunt him with descriptions of the southern sun, the way its warmth seeps into you no matter how cold the air is. I explain the way the Murk hosts festivals of light that cut rainbows into the nighttime gloom, and Tavish scrutinizes all the despicable revelries the inland loch kelpies are said to partake in, too many of which involve stealing humans—either to marry or consume live, depending on who tells it. Tavish listens to my recanting of the myths of the South, and in return I learn that selkies are generally home-loving folks, of whom only the Gayle family have instigated much travel, but those few adventurers bring back wild stories that are passed like delicacies from person to person.

As the sun drops toward the horizon, the hills turn mountainous, forcing us onto a ragged beach that eventually veers inland. It leads to a narrow inlet of sea—the firth Tavish had mentioned—cupped by monstrous hills that cast the whole region in long shadows. As we move into their majesty, I spot a vine-enveloped tower in their crowning rocks before trees shoot up around us, blocking it out.

With each step, Tavish's hold loosens, until he's draped from my arm. A sloppy grin engulfs his face, ghastly in the low light and the lingering grief of losing Sheona. "Isn't this a good, good night? The sky smells of air, like it's meant to be breathed." He loops away from me, swirling his arms out.

I step back to avoid being jabbed by his cane. "It's certainly better than the stuff Maraheem pumps out."

A hint of ignit energy buzzes in the back of my mind, not near as strong as the power I drained in the pool room, but far more constant. It slips into my pores and fills me up, making the world clearer and each step swifter, easier. My parasite curls contentedly around me, reverberating with a soft happiness that's nearly intoxicating all on its own. I almost snap for it to stop, but the feeling eases our joints, letting our fears relax.

Tavish slows, knocking his cane into a rock with a sluggish curiosity.

I take his arm and pull him along. "So, this is what losing

your mind looks like?"

"Lost what now? I must have put it somewhere." He ruffles awkwardly though his pockets before reaching for the ones in my vest.

I wrap my fingers around his and guide him along. "It's all right, you can share mine for a bit."

"How thoughtful." He plops his head against my shoulder.

I brush back a lock of his curls. He hums, such a soft sound that it loses every hint of his voice's usual diamond edge. Without the characteristic Findlay tone, he seems smaller, younger, less prince and more poet. Less serpent and more dove. I find I like both versions of him equally; one does not seem complete without the other.

I wrap my arm around his back. Beneath the smothering purple sky, this almost feels peaceful. And it's that feeling which prickles fear in little bumps along my arms.

Tavish twirls his cane in lopsided circles, knocking it unceremoniously into so much of the thickening forest that I have to slip it from his fingers for fear he'll snap it. He barely protests. Each of his steps comes a little faster, as though he's being yanked onward by a puppet master. Or a form of hypnosis.

The trees give way to a clearing littered by a few large boulders and shrubs, the firth's waters lapping at a rocky ledge on the far side. In the center of the outcropping, a vibrant-yellow ignit nearly the size of my head glows from the top of a boxy machine. Great cords connect the machine to metal dishes pointed at us—targeting the ignit's effects away from Glenrigg. The tower I noticed earlier must have informed the town to activate it, making potential intruders distracted and hypnotized by the time they reach Glenrigg's entrance, easy pickings for the pair of sentries seated on a little wall, their rifles still in their laps.

One look beyond them proves just how thoroughly the town depends on their ignit defenses. It spreads out from the rocky ledge on stilts over the water. Its inhabitance must be impervious to the cold, because the wooden buildings are little more than floors, columns, and roofs; the privacy of their interiors protected, not by walls, but by trellises of climbing roses, wispy-fabric draperies, and small, potted trees with dainty leaves. The light from colorful glass pots within the wall-less houses cascade into the darkening evening, illuminating the bridges hanging between buildings and the walkways floating on the firth's surface, ladders made of wood and cord connecting the two.

Tavish tries to step from the edge of the trees, his attention fixed on the Glenrigg ignit. I pull him gently back. As I do, a swirl of grey blooms in the center of the ignit. My parasite snaps our attention to it. The grey patch bursts through the stone like a storm, sucking in the light. The thrum of the ignit's power fizzles and zaps out.

Tavish blinks suddenly, jerking upright. "Good fuck, that was a nuisance."

The statement has barely left him when the ignit rights itself, color spilling back through it, overtaking the grey until it's no more than a tinge at the stone's center. Tavish's momentary sobriety vanishes.

Alarm vibrates through my parasite. It tightens around my lungs. I choke, planting my feet to keep from falling, and reach with my mind for the panicking creature. *Easy there, easy.* The gentle coo is hard to push out, saturated by my parasite's emotions and dragged down by the undercurrent of my own shock and horror, but together we cling to each other, slowly winding back into something resembling stability.

'*Something wrong!*' it cries, repeating my words over and over, each time more frantically than the last.

No, unfortunately, I think you're right. There's something very, very amiss with that ignit, something that I've never seen before. Something even the creator of ignits has no knowledge of, despite being the only one who truly knows how they work. *But we can't fall apart now. Tavish needs us.*

At Tavish's outburst, the sentries have stood, their guns at the ready. Behind them, Glenrigg's inhabitants glance our way, some like we're a curiosity, others a warning. They usher their children down streets, toward the center of town, but the wilted way it's done seems not out of fear—at least not fear of us.

My parasite unfurls at the thought of protecting Tavish, and I feel it bury its panic until what's left brushes against my own emotions without taking control. We both focus on the sentries.

One shines faintly, teeth pointed and eyes reflective orbs in the low light, his body delicate in a way that off-puts his clear marks of a predator. A pixie, I assume. He comes barely to the waist of his taller finfolk companion, her hulking body forming a menacing shadow. Dusky teal tinges her skin, and her dark hair flares like each strand is made from a silky version of the fins along her limbs and the webbed flippers that curl over her otherwise humanlike feet.

She checks her rifle. "We're shipping these ones back, aye? There's only two of them."

"Better safe than sorry." The pixie balances his weapon against his shoulder. "One's definitely a selkie. And the other . . ." His eyes narrow as he says it, flicking back toward me. His brow tightens. "What the—"

Holding Tavish by his arm, I lift my free hand as nonthreateningly as I can. As nonthreateningly as any ignit-immune scientific marvel in frayed fishnets can possibly be. "Please, don't shoot."

The pixie's flash of confusion turns to shocked terror. His rifle lifts in a motion too definite, too automatic. He shoots.

All the energy I've absorbed from the ignit roars through me as I grab Tavish, covering him with my lamentably thinner body. The impact of the bullet feels like fire and fury. But just as soon as it comes, the pain dissipates, the metal pushed from flesh, replaced by new black stripes in our back—my parasite's black stripes in mine.

A growl leaves us—or me—or us. Definitely us, emotions compiled, anger and affection so unanimous I can't separate mine from its. We snarl, "That was exactly what I said not to do!"

The finfolk responds by shooting as well. We take this bullet as we did the last one, but I feel our energy diminish. And with this second shot, I feel, too, the way my parasite leaches through the muscles where the metal hits, spreading and sinking deeper, crisscrossing itself along what little untouched skin remains on my back. I can't take another hit. And I can't give up another inch.

But my parasite keeps impelling, tearing, penetrating. I gag as it lurches up my neck, digging into the soft tissue beneath my jawline and splintering along the inside of my skull. My vision wavers, pops, and slides. The colors flicker, turning to a silvered veil. Through one eye, I see pieces of a person, or perhaps a person in pieces, the same broken shards my parasite used to mimic me in my dream.

That will not be me. I scream—me, and me alone.

My parasite flinches so hard it makes our body twitch. I feel its flesh resting in every place it dug, now filling down my back and netting parts of my cheek, just above the bone, but its presence curls into a whimpering heap beside mine, bringing all of its emotions with it.

The change feels like having the life zapped out of me. It takes all that I am to focus through the sudden exhaustion and pull Tavish behind a boulder. He flops to the ground with an intoxicated giggle. I join him, trying to collect the last slivers of my energy. Even with my parasite pulled in on itself, the ignit's waves still turn into power beneath my skin. It helps.

Across the clearing, the pixie and the finfolk argue.

Tavish grabs my face in both hands. His eyes stare straight through me, but some deeper, fuller part of him stares into me instead, like he's examining the pieces of me that aren't visible from the outside. "I think I'd like to love you," he whispers. "I think that very, very much."

Through my confusion and fatigue come little, heart-aching bursts of hope. It's all I can do just to look at him, this beautiful, precious man. I'm not entirely sure what he's confessed, or whether he even knows himself, but whatever it is, I want it.

And it galvanizes me in a way no ignit energy could match, as though my heart is falling over itself to agree: *Me, too, I feel the same.* Impossibly and irrationally, I feel the same.

"I think I'd like that, too." I squeeze Tavish's fingers in mine. "Just not right this minute."

Letting him go, I launch over the rock, sprinting and leaping the line of cylinders that project the ignit energy in the same motion. The sentries both take an instant too long to aim for me. I tackle the pixie, knocking his much smaller body down with a swipe of my foot against his calves and an elbow to his face. Blood trickles from his nose. I twist his rifle from his grip. With a twirl, I aim it toward his finfolk companion.

She slowly lowers her weapon.

There's the tiniest splash, then a grunt, and the click of a pistol being cocked. My whole body goes numb. In those six seconds of distraction—those six seconds where I turned this pixie and finfolk's world upside down—the same has happened around me.

An older finfolk stands with us on the rocky ledge, water still draining from the bundle of ropes that fall over her flat chest. Her stringy, sea-green shorts stick to her legs, an ornamental rope holding them up. The finlike locks on her head flare and twist like a thousand coiling snakes, completely devoid of color. She points her readied pistol into the clearing, where a swaying Tavish hovers over the machine. The ignit's yellow glow reflects oddly off his disconnected eyes, blending the whites with his grey irises, and he smiles in a detached way, completely unaware of the bullet prepped for his head.

My parasite coils back through me. It presses against my edges, doubling my panic with the weight of its own.

"Don't." I drop my stolen rifle. It clatters on the stone; the chaotic, ruthless rattle mimicking the feeling in my chest. Anguish spills from me, coming from places so dark I'd forgotten they existed, soft as a rain of little, pink petals and fetid as my mother's stale corpse. "Please, don't shoot him. We're here only for sanctuary and to speak to one of your scientists. We don't want to hurt anyone." I swallow, glancing at the pixie, who has his nose pinched in both hands, eyes watering. My heart pounds. "Please."

The finfolk gives me one sidelong peer out the corner of her eye, not enough to waver her aim. "He's a selkie." Her voice is guttural and dusky. It reminds me of the things that lurk at the bottoms of deep lakes.

"He can't change that." My protest comes like a plea, gracious but for the wail right down its middle.

Her finger holds firmly to the trigger. "A wealthy selkie." Her eyes narrow, slipping across my face and down my neck. "But you are not. Are you human?"

Part of me yearns to agree—I am human, human enough; I have to be. But peace floods from my parasite, saturating me until no more protests remain. Together, we form the commitment behind the worlds, even if it's my mouth alone they slip from. "No. Not anymore." The statement comes out too strong, too accepting, but I can't help it. I can't stop it. "I'd like to talk to your scientist about that."

The elder finfolk stills, a single wrinkle appearing between her eyebrows. In the silence, my gaze latches to her pistol, to the way it still tracks Tavish's slow bobbing as he basks within the ignit's glow. He walked here at my side, not a single protest, all while understanding this was the fate most of his people met upon entering. How many selkies must have died while staring at that ignit—died by the bullets of a desperate town, a town Maraheem would have long since wiped off the map if the retribution for trying were not so harsh.

It isn't right. None of it is.

"Please, we need sanctuary." I hear the crack in my own voice, but I don't care. "Both of us. We'll do whatever we can to earn it."

She tips her head toward Tavish. "His coat still holds ignation?"

"Yes. But that's not mine to offer. You'd have to let him past the ignit's energy, ask him instead." My gaze hops back to the stone, catching on the speck of grey polluting its brilliant yellow. "Please, just let him speak for himself. If you intend to kill him, you should know who you're murdering."

She watches me like a statue surveying the ways of the living. Beneath the fins and the leathery skin, I wonder how old she is, if she might be like the elders of the Murk, ancient and seemingly immortal. "Go get him, then."

The buzz of the ignit's energy reappears as I step over the line of cylinders. I wrap an arm around Tavish's back. He releases a happy sigh and leans against me. My heart wants to snap in two. I could grab him and flee, hope for the best. But with the way my parasite still trembles from its own repressed panic, and how I have to dig deep into my bones to find the strength to put one step in front of the other, paired with the multiple rounds in the elder finfolk's pistol, I know that hope would be miniscule.

As I lead Tavish away from the ignit, he plants his heels. "No—no, where are we going—I have to—I'm missing—I'm missing—"

"I know," I whisper, and I scoop him up, cursing at the ridiculous amount of weight he manages to pack into his short form. As we walk, I wrap my arms tighter around him, so instinctual that I don't realize I've done it until I'm burying my fingers into his soft overcoat.

The instant I step past the line of cylinders, Tavish's whimpers turn into a grunt. Pink crests his cheeks, and he lets himself out of my arms, flowing right back into his poise as though he'd never lost it. He fixes his outfit, scowling at everything and nothing.

The elder finfolk clears her throat. "Selkie—"

"Tavish." He brushes his curls out of his face. "Tavish K. Findlay."

She accepts the name without comment. "Our ignit is failing, but with the ignation in your coat, we could maintain it a little longer. Would you give it to us?" Behind her words, I feel a promise, not in her tone but in her entire town's history. Tavish can hand over the ignation now, in life, or his death can leave it to be pillaged.

But Tavish, dear, pampered, princeling Tavish, for all his wit and cunning, can't sense it. This is still bureaucracy to him. He has not grown up arguing his worth with a gun to his head, has not had to prove at every turn that he is enough of a person to be judged equally. He can't comprehend the kind of rage that comes to a boil over an entire lifetime of being demanded proof of a right to exist.

"It's my *coat*." His cutting words catch at the end, as though his knife-edged voice has gone dull. "This is all I have of my home, of who I am."

It hurts not to immediately tell him that he must keep it, must fight to remain himself even as I slowly lose pieces of me in the process. But I can't, despite the pain. I'll make it up to him before I go home.

And if you can't because you're dead? It's my thought, but it twists the way my parasite does, weaving into me, bubbling against my hollowed core.

"Then will you not let us have it?" The finfolk's face droops, her expression turning sad. No, not sad. Tired. Exhausted. Like all her pain and rage have eaten her from the inside out, leaving room for nothing else. She looks like me.

Tavish doesn't see it, nor the way her pistol begins to lift once more or the panic that sears through me. I step in front of him.

"There must be another option," I say, as though options are things that can be hunted down without the cruelty of the universe towering over them, pulling them constantly from the reach of some and placing them like gems beneath the feet of others.

"You need this ignation to protect your town, aye?" Tavish asks, his voice thoughtful. "To prevent those from Maraheem taking their tax?"

The barrel levels with his head, his head through the center of my neck, from where I stand between them, my palms outstretched. But she doesn't shoot. "Aye. To keep what little we have."

From somewhere beyond the nearest buildings, behind the tense scattering of adults, comes a child's laughter.

Tavish tips an ear toward it. His pain is palpable. "Take the ignation, then, please."

He tucks his cane under one arm and reaches for his brooch with both hands. His trembling fingers slip, catching on the clips. Carefully, I remove the device for him. He lets me take it, his fingers trailing across mine as he gives it up. The moment it leaves his custody, he pulls away, pressing both palms to his cane and directing his attention everywhere but toward me.

I offer it to the finfolk woman, my voice low. "May we have the brooch back when you're done?"

"It will be returned in the morning." She closes her fingers around it until the silver glow vanishes. With her other hand, she tucks away her pistol. "I assume you're seeking the ignit cycle physicist Dr. Elspeth Coineagan? They're only a part-time resident, but they should be here to inspect our ignit sometime tomorrow." Her lips peel back, just a little. "We will put you in the lodge for the night. You'll have what hospitality we afford all who seek aid from us, but if you prove my allowance misplaced, I will float your bodies toward Maraheem myself."

Tavish nearly drops his cane as he transfers it back into his hand. "Thank you." But he sounds a little distant, a little desolate. "May I ask, what is your name?"

Her weight shifts, turning back toward the ignit, but she pauses halfway through the motion. "I am Beileag, head of Glenrigg's governing committee." After another moment of hesitation, she inclines her head. "Come. I will take you to the lodge."

As we follow her, I snake my arm through Tavish's. A bit of the tension slips out of his shoulders. After all he's lost today, I want to make this one night the happiest possible. Tavish may not have his home or his bodyguard or his siblings or his coat—he may even think he has too little ability to pull himself out of this—but for now, he has me. And for now, I still have him.

CHAPTER TWENTY

a taste for seal

Teach me what it means to let go.
I feel you
in my cells,
in every ridge and plateau,
and I cannot,
I cannot
surrender.

BEILEAG LEADS US THROUGH the town, over bridges and along second-story boardwalks, passing houses with walls of brush and hanging planks of bark and a thousand dried leaves stitched together. As we walk, my eyes adjust to the subtle light that streams from beneath the firth's surface. It comes from sheets of multicolored curtains hanging throughout underwater buildings that mimic those constructed above them, all simple support frameworks with nets and fabrics and seaweed forming the basis for walls and floors. Finfolk swim along them, their fully extended feet-fins propelling them gracefully through the water.

I watch it all in awe. "You've put together a lovely place here."

When Beileag remains quiet, I worry I overstepped, but

she finally sighs. "We are a town of refugees, but I have never wanted that to stop us from creating something beautiful. We have peace here, at least. But our wounds still heal slowly."

It leaves a little ache in my chest. If Manduka had such a society, I might not have spent so much of my life alone.

A few shops spring up as we near the center of the town—a general store, a bakery, and an apothecary—but in terms of size and life, the lodge dominates them all. Half a dozen little rooms—perhaps temporary housing for new refugees while more permanent housing is built—fill the highest story, while some kind of council chamber sits on the lowest, but a communal dining hall takes up its central floor, visible through the trailing loops of the vines that take the place of walls. The smell of fresh bread seeps through the place. Brown rolls appear from the kitchens alongside cooked vegetables and whole fish, set into the center of family-sized tables. My stomach gurgles.

Tavish stops, though, his cane trembling against the threshold of the lodge. "Sheona should be with us."

"She should." I could say more: That she sacrificed herself so he could be here instead. That she would want him to make the most of this time. That she loved him more than life. But she practically raised him. He knows their relationship deeper and more intimately than my words could ever describe.

Instead, I pull him into my arms. He cries without tears, but the motion seems to force a few of his fragmented pieces to seal back together. Not many, I think. But maybe enough for him to survive the night.

It seems as though everyone in a mile radius cranes their heads to look at us as the staff leads us through the crowded dining space. We're given a table in the back, a tiny ball of bioluminescent algae at its center. The whole place is a little disjointed—a chalkboard along the far wall lists its staffing and resources on a rotating system so complex that much of the town must participate in it—but it holds a kind of cheer that neither side of Maraheem possesses.

We're brought two portions of the evening's simple meal of bread, butter, and vegetables, along with a cooked fish with scales and fins intact. Its hollow eyepits stare into me. Its gaze is almost as hard to avoid as those around us, theirs ranging from bitter to cautious to curious.

The beer only comes after I shout for wine twice, each request receiving an odd look and no reply. I down the first glass they bring in one guzzle. It's too light and starchy for my taste, nothing like the dark, heavy stuff Ivor Reid supplies at his bar in the lower. I immediately wave back the finfolk serving us.

Tavish shovels food into his mouth as though there's somewhere else he needs to be, only to chew too slowly, swallowing like he can't quite get it down. Every attempt he makes at a conversation sputters out, and he ends up gnawing on his tongue as much as his food.

I finally order him a beer too.

"I've never had much of a taste for it," he protests as I slide his into position at the right upper corner of his plate and set to work on my second.

"You don't have to drink it. But it's okay if you want to just live for tonight. It doesn't mean you aren't mourning her, that you don't miss her, or wish with every piece of your being that she were here. It doesn't mean you won't shatter a little, next time you need her advice, or her love, or just her arm wrapped around you. And by drinking it, you aren't denying that. You're just existing in the moment. The moment is a precious thing right now."

"I can't—" he starts, only for his lower lip to tremble. "I can't stop imagining it—what it must have been like. The sound of her dying. I didn't even know it was happening."

My chest aches, the effects of alcohol not yet strong enough to mute my own anxiety and sorrow. *The rebels still would have framed Tavish, whether you were here or not. One way or another, Sheona still would have died helping him*

222

escape. This is not your fault.

But a part of me, a part that might be me, or might just be curling through me in black strands, retaliates: *Maybe I don't care whose fault it was.* Maybe, I can wish I had changed it even if I didn't cause it.

The thought leaves an acidic taste in my mouth. I wash it away with the beer. "She was just the same as ever. Strong, brave, loving you like you were her own flesh and blood. Because you were safe, she was happy. The sound of death isn't always ugly. Some elegies are beautiful even while they tear you up inside." Sometimes mothers died beneath flowering trees, bleeding out in a rain of petals. "So, if you want, then drink to Sheona." I lift my glass before downing the rest of it.

"To Sheona." He takes a sip, then a longer one. A little half sob, half giggle leaves him. "This isn't bad, actually. I wish they made it like this in Maraheem."

I almost laugh. "You're a fool of a princeling."

"I could have you beheaded for that, if Sheona—" He doesn't trail off as much as crash into a wall. But he picks himself up, taking another drink, and concludes, "She would be happy that I have you with me. Especially after that entrance into the town. Were they shooting at us?"

He doesn't remember, perhaps none of it, not even the things I was hoping he'd expand upon. My stomach flops. I lift my glass, only to recall it's empty. "Just at first."

Tavish accepts that with a slight scowl that vanishes almost as quickly as it comes. "That ignit of theirs must be incredibly large." He pauses, trailing his fingers around the outside of his drink. "I admit, I never memorized the kinds of energy they give off. Those variations are eliminated when it's turned into ignation, so there didn't seem much point."

"Glenrigg's ignit is a standard yellow—a color seen commonly in the South, though not as plentiful as say a red, which provides heat. All the other yellow ignits I've seen have been far smaller, and could, at most, attract fish or rodents from a short distance away, soothe cranky newborns, or distract an injured caiman. They've been very helpful when I've had to calm a young jaguar enough to set a leg or stitch a gash." I motion for the server. He pretends not to see me. "Even I don't know all the colors though. There's a whole rainbow of them, some so rare that their effects are undocumented."

"I will believe that when I see it." He almost, *almost* smirks. "All this rainbow nonsense, in fact. Colors sound quite fake to me."

I laugh, but my gaze catches on our centerpiece's bulging head, and it turns to a huff. "Don't they have real meat here somewhere?"

Tavish pauses with his fork halfway to his mouth. "Did you just refer to a fish as *fake* meat?"

"Well, not fake, but disingenuous. I bet seals taste much nicer."

Tavish sputters. "We do not." He pokes my shoulder with his fork. His grief seems to slide off, like he's tucking it away, piece by piece, and when he turns back to his food, his lips quirk. "But there is more than one way to eat someone. I'm not opposed to all of them."

Now it's my turn to choke, heat blazing across my cheeks and running like an arrow between my hips at the very vivid scene his words create in my mind and the way he'd be moaning in it. I wave at the server again, lifting my glass and pointing aggressively. I'm still far too sober for this, here, now, with my life-consuming parasite and the curious looks of the Glenrigg inhabitants and a too-gorgeous selkie making inappropriate jokes.

I could let the comment go. Or I could carry it forward. Maybe I won't be here forever, but for one night, if it turned out he craved the thought of this the way I do . . . *if*.

"I wouldn't want to eat you any other way." I barely manage to force the sounds out, and the din of the dining room covers it over immediately.

The only sign he heard is the tiniest tint of red in his cheeks. He ducks his head and returns to his food. I feel like the butt of a joke, like the monkey who crawled too far down a weak branch only to be surprised when it snaps beneath him. What if it was all intoxicated nonsense? Not flirtation, not a heartfelt proposition, just the rambling of a man out of his mind.

Fuck.

A thin silence settles over us, Tavish sipping from his beer. The dining crowd seems to have finally accepted our presence—or possibly just grown bored of us—because only a few of the younger ones peek our way now. I toss a bread roll to keep my fingers preoccupied while I search for the server.

As Tavish's glass empties, the remainder of the tension loosens from his shoulders. "You use ignits readily in the South, aye? Does everyone ken as much of them as you do or that a trait reserved for animal-obsessed recluses?"

"They're as common as your ignation." I tap my nails against my still-empty glass. "But I did run an ignit cartel for a month."

Tavish drops his fork. "You did what?"

"No dirty work, I promise. Or, not *much* dirty work." I spot the server and wave, half standing. He immediately dodges behind a pillar. With a grunt, I sit back down. "Lilias wrangled me into it, back before I had the aurora in my neck and I was just trying to get her away from the Murk as quickly as possible. But I didn't object all that much; kind of suggested it, actually." A host of emotions hits me, and in the midst of it, I feel my parasite's encircling warmth, curling around me like a melancholic pet. I shake it off, trying to dislodge the memories in the same motion. Trying to ignore the pain they sprout in my chest.

But Tavish nudges me, his expression too soft to say no to. "Did you want to join them—the cartel, I mean?"

Outside the bright, jovial room, rain sweeps over the town like a veil of silver. I think it must be raining in me, too, that hollow pattering accompanied by a chilling ache. "No. But I was lonely and out of wine." As the server slips around a table two away from ours, I grab a bread roll and hurl it at him, nearly taking out a tall pixie who happens to stand at just the wrong moment. "No one had ever wanted me, not in the Murk nor the river towns. But here was a group that few others wanted. I hoped, maybe, it could be my chance to belong somewhere. In the end though, they turned on me too." Everyone always did: betray or abandon. I look at the man beside me and am glad that isn't true of him yet.

"I'm sorry." Tavish picks at the already raw skin at the corners of his nails. "And I understand, in a sense. I've been trying to fit myself into my family's company, yet I keep feeling like a circle forced into a square hole, just waiting for someone to notice that I ruin the puzzle for all of them."

"What if you don't?" I take his fingers to stop him from peeling himself bloody. "What if you're making this puzzle into something better, something new? You're not a circle in a square hole but a fresh color on an old painting."

His mouth twitches, making a sound so soft it could be a sob or a laugh. "You do realize that is the worst metaphor you can use on a blind man? But thank you."

"I'm always happy to offer you my terrible analogies, princeling." The moment seems to settle over us, the rest of the world fading beneath the pressure of my hand around his.

His fingers stiffen. He opens his mouth.

"Is this enough?" The server cuts him off, fins bristling as he plunks two pitchers of beer on the table hard enough to slosh some out the sides.

I wink at him. "You, my friend, are brilliant."

He huffs and turns on his heels, marching back to the kitchen.

Tavish lets me go and finds his beer. He doesn't drink it, just holds the near-empty glass, chewing on his tongue. "Ruby."

I don't like the tone of his voice, too serious, too ominous, too eternally warped around words like *once this is over* and *good-bye*. I can't hear it now. So I distract us both. "The problem with Glenrigg's ignit must be related to whatever's causing your ignation mutants to form. And maybe the reason my aurora decided to bind to me instead of a proper host, too. It feels like there's something wrong with the whole system."

Tavish sips his beer. "It does all seem a bit extraordinary, doesn't it?"

"I bet your secret Findlay lab is exploiting it, somehow." I refill both our glasses. Mine is half empty again just as quickly. I feel the buzz of its combined effects softening my world around the edges.

"Aye," Tavish mutters. "If only we had gone to Ailsa sooner."

"You didn't know, Tavish."

He only chews on his tongue in response.

By the time we conclude dinner, I've drank through most of one pitcher, Tavish finishing off the last bit. He already wobbles more than I, slack and a little overzealous in his movements, enough that I have to guide him through the now half-filled dining hall as he swings his cane a little too precariously for it to be of use. Beileag sits at a table with two other translucent-haired finfolk and an ancient-looking pixie, but she points us toward the disgruntled server as we near.

"One room or two?" he asks, his voice flat as a board.

"One," Tavish replies.

I don't question him. If he needs me there, then that's where I'll be. Even if it ends with me staring at his back, wanting more of him than he's willing to offer, his shoulders rising and falling just beyond my reach. Maybe there's a bathroom I can slip off to while he sleeps—fuck knows I'll need some kind of release after the mess my body keeps trying to make of me.

The server directs us to room three, up the stairs and to

the left. It takes a bit of searching with a bioluminescent orb to find the number, painted in lilac on a piece of bark to one side of the curtain doorway. The room holds nothing but a washbowl of cold water and a central mattress placed, like Tavish's, directly on the floor and covered in furs. Thick cords of bark grant us privacy from the rest of the lodge. The external barrier of dangling dried flowers looks out over a shimmering town and distant mountains obscured by a stream of silver rain. Except for the occasional laugh, only its heavy pounding can be heard.

"Well?" Tavish asks.

I set our light on a little wire holder in the ceiling. "There's a bed."

"Fantastic." He detangles himself from my grip. With an overzealous helping of dramatics, he unloops his scarf from his neck, folds it into a neat square, and holds it out. I take it from him. He removes his coat and boots next, doing the same with each. I pile it beneath his scarf as he slips out of his pants and hands those over too.

I shake my head, but a smile encroaches on my lips. "I'm putting them beside the water bowl."

"Dear Ruby, exactly how terrible of an idea do you ken that is?"

Pausing, I glance between Tavish's cane and the wide-rimmed basin and amend my decision. "I'm putting them as far from the water bowl as possible," I say, settling the bundle in the corner beside the door.

"Which is *where*?" he demands, playfully. The pretentious twist of his nose looks ridiculous when he wears only a half-buttoned, silver shirt that brushes his thighs like a toddler's nightdress.

I can't imagine a reality where he said *two rooms, please,* a reality where I don't watch him, brash in his vulnerability, and feel so warm and vibrant that the affection seems to fill in all my melancholic valleys until I overflow with it, while the lust fills something else entirely. I want him the way a river wants to run downhill, ever seeking the sea. And I'm just tipsy enough that it's a damn struggle to try to swim upstream.

As I watch him, I'm glad he isn't clinging to his grief the way I did mine. I can still make out the edges of it, the way it mellows and softens him slightly. But it seems a part of him, unlike the darkness I held to my chest after my mother's death. He is proving that while a hole taken from a heart cannot be refilled, new joy and warmth can still be added elsewhere.

My own heart wants so badly to do the same.

"Where isn't important," I growl, soft and teasing. And I tackle Tavish onto the bed as a friend. A friend who wants him desperately.

He yelps. His cane clatters across the floor, knocking into the pile of clothes. "Ruby!" By the time he finishes shouting my name, he's laughing, high and light and perfect, a set of wind chimes in a downpour.

We sprawl where we land, bundles of fur beneath us and the simple wooden ceiling above. Tavish's back pins down one of my arms, but instead of rolling off, he scoots closer, laying his head over my shoulder. In our silence, the wind picks up. It churns the rain, pounding it sideways against the roof, and ruffles Tavish's hair. But the water never reaches our open room, its frosty presence just a thrill against the combined warmth of my parasite and Tavish's body.

"The rain's not coming inside," I mutter.

Wonder shines on Tavish's face clear. "Times like these, I do believe there's a bit of magic in this world."

"Says the man who's turns into a seal."

"Och! That's science! We're practically just humans with a good helping of deactivated genetic coding." He pokes me in the ribs. I arch away from him, laughing, but somehow he ends up nearer than before, almost pressed against my side as he plays with one of my little braids. "Your ghostly feet, on the other hand? Nothing in the natural realm can be that soundless."

I don't flinch at the comment, and between the soft smell of him and the ease of lying here, I realize it's because his gentle observation didn't hurt in the way of other accusations. Despite my soundless steps and my liminal existence and even despite the aurora weaving through my body, he still holds to me like I'm substantial. Like I'm a kind of universe all of my own. I smile. "Maybe there *is* something unexplainable afoot."

I close my eyes and live in the weight of his fingers through my hair, their tips brushing against my chest as he reaches the end of the braid. My parasite curls through the sensation, basking in it as much as I do. I can't tell it no, not with the warmth it's adding to my heart. We love this.

"What does it feel like," I ask, "to have a different body? Is it weird?"

"Never." He says it with such ferocity that his malty breath curls against my chin. He lets my hair go to tug at his collar where his brooch should sit. "I think we're made for it. Not having that—that other part of me at my fingertips, that's what's weird." A snicker leaves him, crooked and unkempt. "Though the communication of seals doesn't have near the specificity of this form's vocals. As wonderful as a good dip in the sea is, there's a reason we conduct business inside a glass casing of air."

I watch the rain fall, but in my mind, I hear the squeal of the cart as Sheona directs us to the only possible ocean escape route from the lower. I try to estimate the number of bodies inside the lower's walls compared to the few seals I've seen swimming through its ornamented and manicured waterways. "When there aren't contamination warnings in place, are the selkies from the lower allowed outside Maraheem?"

"Aye, absolutely! There's still regulations, of course—we can't have everyone going for a swim at once—and heavy restrictions on what they can take with them to lower potential water pollutant levels, and appropriate fees to cover the maintenance costs, and—" His enthusiasm fades. "Oh. Oh, I see what you mean." He whispers it, as though he can change the realization if no one else hears it. "I suppose, then, not exactly. Or, perhaps, yes, actually: allowed. Allowed by the good graces of the upper, given permission to, occasionally, do what should be their continuous right." He presses a hand to his mouth, breathing out against it, a shudder beneath the exhale. "I lived my whole life there, and I never looked at it like that before. What does that say about me?"

"I don't know, Tav."

In the quiet and the rain, my thoughts press in, dark and taunting, all the harm I've let slide by me now creeping up at my back. All the pain I could have stopped had I cared enough. My parasite—my stupid, controlling, cruel parasite—draws up memory after memory in response: rescued pets, small children grinning at my parlor tricks, my efforts to protect the Murk even when they refused to protect me. It nudges them toward the darker, calloused parts of my past, twisting itself beneath the layers of my apathy.

'I get odder the more you know of me.' This time it turns the words as velvety as its black hide, tender as the wind still brushing over my skin.

Oh, fuck off. But I feel better, whether from the recollections or the warmth of the damn creature clutching my soul. I turn toward Tavish, letting our breaths mingle. "I don't know what it means, but I know that you're a good person, here and now. That's what matters most, isn't it?"

Tavish's mouth tugs out of his grimace, but it falls again just as quickly, his brows descending. "A good person who has shite to show for it."

I draw myself onto one elbow. "You still helped the people of Maraheem where you could. And . . ." I should stop there, but the words slip through the crack the alcohol wedged open, "You came here with me."

"Of course I did." He lifts himself, ending up with his lips hovering so close to mine that I swear I can taste the freckles that coat them.

My whole body warms, the sensation shooting between my hips. I should pull away. Or I should lean in. But I can't find the courage for either.

He shifts his legs, and his foot hits the top of my boot. His nose wrinkles as he jerks away. "You're still dressed! You heathenish fiend! Trenches, man, off with those shoes."

The exclamation releases me from his thrall, and I cackle softly, rolling away from him. "Do selkies even follow a religion?" I tease, tossing my boots toward the pile of Tavish's clothes. I heave my vest after it, then my shirt, returning to the bed in only my tattered fishnet gloves and my Murk pants, their thin fabric doing a terrible job at hiding the full extent of my want from anyone who isn't blind. "How can I be a heathen to a godless people?"

"We did worship a pantheon once," Tavish points out, drawing back the top layer of furs. "Now, we are our own gods, in a way."

I climb in beside him. "Should I be calling you my almighty instead of my princeling?"

"I'm not a prince, remember," he grumbles, but a coy smile creeps into the protest. He rolls into me, pinning my arm once more. "Would your gods be offended if you did?"

"Probably." I try to sound a little less breathless than I feel. "But I'm not sure they can see me this far north."

"Do you miss the South? The rivers and the swamps and jungles?" As he lifts his hand, his fingers brush my bare chest. He stutters, but instead of retracting, he delicately weaves his leg between mine, hooking his foot beneath my ankle like he's afraid someone might try to pull him away.

I inhale, and suddenly I can't think straight enough to decide whether he's doing this on purpose. "I miss them constantly," I whisper, as not to further taunt whatever northern deities might currently be looking down on us. Tavish's wild curls tickle my cheek. Slowly, driven by courage and fear and nothing else, I sweep back his hair from his unfocused eyes. My netted fingertips graze across his forehead, the dark strands worn and fuzzed now from wear.

He hums, lips turning upward. "Why the fishnets?"

"Why not fishnets? There was a pair in a market I snuck into as a teenager, and I've made a point to wear them ever since. Leggings, too, back at my house." I tuck the stray curls behind his ear. "Are they obnoxious?"

"Aye." Tavish grins. "And perfect. So is this." He turns his head, nuzzling against my palm.

My heart launches into my throat, leaving my mouth only one option.

I nudge his face back toward mine and kiss him. His lips part in a moan, and I've barely moved before his tongue steals into my mouth, his head twisting to deepen the kiss. It makes every ache worth it. I press my fingers through his hair, feeling nothing but him, the soft sea scent of his skin and the pressure of his chest on mine.

When he pulls back, a diamond laugh spills out of him. His shirt hangs lopsided, revealing the scar beneath one of his nipples, and his tousled curls drift in the wind. "Good fuck, I've been waiting for you to do that since last night."

"Waiting for me?" I bark, half humor and half shock.

Tavish only laughs again. "You think I'm willing to risk accidentally missing your lips on the first kiss? I could never have lived with myself." As though to prove his point, he leans forward, his mouth brushing first my nose, then my cheek, before he finally catches my upper lip, tugging it gently between his own.

I moan, both at the act itself and at the carnal pressure that builds beneath my hips. "I don't think anyone who can draw forth a sound like that should be ashamed." My voice goes low near the end, honeyed words turned raspy and needy.

I kiss Tavish again, my fingers working their way down the last few buttons of his shirt, until I can run my palms along his stomach. He nibbles his way to my earlobe, laughing as he finds the set of three fang-like rings there, and I trace my pinkies tenderly at the rim of his soft underwear.

He pauses, nose buried in my hair. "If you lived alone with your pets, then have you ever done this before?"

I snort. "I was an outcast, Tavish, not a fucking monk."

"So, a non-*fucking* monk?"

"Not—" I break into laughter so murderous I feel as though I'm sobbing. When I wipe a hand under my eye, it comes away wet. "I'm sorry, you dear, dear god-prince, but damn you." The exclamation comes in a wheeze, and I pull myself together before continuing, "I *meant* that I have slept with other people before. Other men, technically—only men. I only like men. Gods, all these words are not working. What the hell did you do while you were in my mouth?"

"Nothing you didn't feel. But thank the Trench, I was about to be vastly over-experienced. Though not just with men. I can be a terrible fool for anyone with a voice as gorgeous as yours and skin this delectable." Smirking, he preoccupies his mouth with the skin in question, his teeth brushing the stubble along my jaw.

I fiddle with the rim of his underpants. "I will admit, most of my previous experience happened in alleys behind taverns." All of it, technically, but for that one beautiful Murk boy at sixteen, who had loved the secrecy of us until it seemed his carpentry apprenticeship would be revoked if anyone found out. The memory nearly makes me cringe. I force it away. I have no delusions as to where Tavish and I will end up, but I'll deal with the hole it will leave in me when the time comes and not a moment sooner. "Even that was a while ago."

I feel Tavish's smirk in his voice. "Your body certainly still recalls what to do with itself."

He presses up with the leg he's slipped between mine, rubbing his thigh someplace highly inappropriate and absolutely perfect. Before I've finished moaning, he finds my mouth again. I draw down his underpants.

We explore, gentle caresses turning rough and needy as our moans grow ragged. It feels like everything I imagined, and so much more.

By the time we finish, the bioluminescence in our light has faded to a few tiny flutters. We hold each other, the rest of our discarded clothes tangled somewhere near our feet and the furs pulled up to our shoulders. Sometime in the night, I know he'll turn away from me. I'll watch as his back gently rises and falls. But for this moment, this one night, I'll also be able to slip my hand around his waist, and draw my thumb over his scars, and press a chaste kiss to his shoulders while he sleeps. That has to be good enough for now.

As I lie there, my parasite flickers in the back of my mind. This whole time, it was there, warm and awake and happy. And I barely even noticed. Neither did I bother to think of what I might become once I finally attempt to remove it, and how alone that could suddenly leave the wonderful man in my arms.

CHAPTER TWENTY-ONE

more than one reality

My wants devour.
The stars, I said,
the stars are going out.
Cinders in the hearth,
darkness like a shroud.

I WAKE TO THE sounds of the village coming to life: splashes and thuds and soft voices paired with the occasional shouted hello. Despite the subtle ache in my muscles and the dryness of my throat, I feel alive, as though last night was the first night I ever truly slept. I reach across the bed, but I find only cold furs.

"Tav?" I mutter, opening my eyes to the silvery light of the cloud-marred morning.

Tavish answers with a grunt. He sits at the edge of the bed, dressed in his pants and shoes with his shirt tucked in and his coat splayed across his knee. He scribbles lopsidedly onto a scrap of paper, even though his ignation-powered aid that would let him reread the lines must still be back in Maraheem. Maybe it's just the motion that helps him think.

I scoot toward him, pressing my hand to the hollow of his back. A soft *good morning* forms on my lips. Before I can speak it, he bursts into a scrambling explanation, his words bouncing into each other.

"I've been thinking, once we break back into Maraheem, we'll need to turn Lilias's rebellion over to the BA ourselves—if all I have to offer the assembly is my word that Lilias is the culprit, it might not be enough to appease them. I doubt Lilias is a diddy, so she'll likely have already moved to another location. But there are already so few routes into the city without permission from a big seven family, and every way I can think of will reveal our identities too quickly." His paper crumples as he tightens his fingers on its edge, his pen slipping carelessly across the writing. "The longer we wait, though, the harder this all becomes. We should hurry if we can."

The light in my chest fades. I ache to take away his frustration, to give him back the relaxed, happy world of last night. But I feel my parasite lurking in the corners of my mind, and I can't ignore it forever.

"All of this comes after we see Dr. Coineagan, right?" They're soft words, but somewhere under them I feel a flicker of the pain I share with the finfolk.

Tavish must hear it, because he sets his papers aside to fumble for my hand. "Of course, of course. You're our focus right now. Your life is more important." He squeezes my fingers. "There's nothing I can do while we're in Glenrigg anyway."

I try not to wonder whether that dedication would waver if he could leave for Maraheem this instant. How close is this choice to a coin flip? I chide myself: I knew he would leave. I knew this was temporary, a source of pleasure in a painful situation. Now that I've kissed him, though, I also know how badly I want to kiss him again. And again. And again.

I don't want to lose him.

The knowledge aches in my chest, tight and a little furious, and perhaps I've only known Tavish a few days, but it feels like a few days longer than I've known anyone in all my adult life. A few days that have felt so very right, as far as Tavish is considered. But I'm not losing him to Maraheem yet. The least I can do is take advantage of the time we have left. "How about, before me or Maraheem, we start with breakfast? Beileag might even have your brooch ready for you. I know you'll feel a little better with it on again, even if it can't transform you."

"Aye." Tavish's shoulders drop, but he gives me the smallest of smiles. His fingers creep from my hand up my bare arm, and his lips bunch, teasing. "Or perhaps a little something *before* breakfast? If you're still in the mood for seal."

I laugh, and I kiss him with all the hunger of the hundred thousand days we're not likely to get.

By the time we've had our fill of each other, the sun is a bit higher, though the sky no less grey. I watch Tavish dress, committing every elegant crest of him to memory before shoving on my own clothes. I button my shirt as far as I can, letting the sleeves dangle over my knuckles. In protest, my parasite uses the arm it's woven through to roll up the opposite sleeve. I shake it, trying to dislodge its control. It hisses in my mind, stealing from my pet's sounds of frustration until I give in, one sleeve rolled up around my worn fishnet gloves and one tugged down, hiding all but the final gleaming hints of my parasite's hold.

It remains quiet while I slide on my boots and vest. I turn up one side of my shirt collar. It turns down the other.

As I pass a little mirror hung from cords against our makeshift wall, I freeze. Wrapped through the iris of my parasite-infested eye shines a glimmer of a rainbow, the usual dark brown turned to a midnight black. I swear I can see the faintest streaks of color beneath the skin of my cheek, too. From three steps back, it's all indistinguishable, but up close, I am clearly an aurora's host. If Coineagan can't help me, that's all my body may ever be. I have to turn away before the panic can set in.

I fiddle with my empty fingers as I wait for Tavish to tuck his supplies into his coat and take my arm in his. Even with his cane gently tapping, he trips a little on the stairs.

"They're steeper here," he mutters.

I feel the weight of his words in my chest.

We eat quietly, our comments limited to the appeal of sweet or savory breakfasts—of which I'm neutral and Tavish veers heavily into savory territory—and by the time we finish, one of Beileag's underlings brings us the now drained brooch. Tavish clips it back onto his shirt collar, looking a little more whole than before. But only a little, and whatever peace it returned to him collapses again as the messenger warns us of a BA squad traversing the coastline.

"Dr. Coineagan saw them while coming in earlier this morning—they may even have moved on already. Beileag mentioned you wanted to speak with the doctor? If you hurry, you'll find them down at the ignit, tweaking the stabilizer."

"We'll hurry."

We do, so much so that I nearly lose Tavish at every turn.

I catch glimpses of the ignit through the buildings' stand-in walls. It now shines with its activated glow; the Maraheem selkies must be near. My gut clenches as a sliver of panic runs through my parasite. *They won't get to us,* I remind it. *That ignit will stop them, even with its degradation.*

My parasite curls itself close and, tucking into my corners, tries to bask in what little calmness I possess. But something about its reaction confuses me, though it takes a moment for me to piece it together. *You could be trying to stop me from seeing Coineagan; I'm planning to remove you, and you're only putting up a fuss about my clothing choices and whether or not the scientists are friendly.*

It flings Tavish's words at me. *'You ken that, do you.'*

I've told you to stop that. It's not your voice to use.

239

'*I get odder,*' it snaps in reply. Its emotional residue barely changes but for a hint of something I can't identify, a void that seems as though it's trying its hardest not to bleed into me. '*Refused to let . . . go,*' it says, twisting my words to Raghnaid.

I grit my teeth. *I could very well make you.*

A slew of memories confronts me, starting with Sheona's final breath, then Malloch's falling body and Ailsa's corpse, scrolling back through every death I've witnessed until it finally lands on a spot of blood beneath falling flower petals and the sound of a much smaller me crying for his mother. That final image sets me aflame, annihilating any indecision I might have held. *Maybe I'd prefer that to living with you inside me. Maybe I'd rather die and know you're gone than live and have to deal with your reign on my life.*

I expect rage or aggression, laughter or bitterness, but all I feel from my parasite is an overwhelming wave of sadness as it backs away, twisting itself into my past and vanishing to a distant warmth. I leave it be as the ignit comes into proper view and warn Tavish before breaking into a sprint.

A pair of sentries—two pixies this time—stand at attention while a finfolk tweaks the ignit's holder. After Lachlan and Ailsa, my expectations of ignit-loving scientists have twisted more toward twitchy and impulsive, and it seems the universe has obliged me in the most unexpected way possible. Coineagan mutters to themself, moving with the same restless energy as the science-minded Findlays, but unlike the Findlays, they are immaculate under the eccentricity.

Their dusky brown, purple-tinted skin sparkles beneath a pinstripe top that pulls in a V from both shoulders and knots just about their waist, a tight necklace of black metal with purple stones gleaming at their throat. Their baggy, black pants tuck into tight wraps near their fin-covered feet, a pair of leather gloves flopping out of a side pocket. They bend over a black walker with shimmering purple grips, using it to stand back up to their incredible height of what must be a half a head taller than even me, broad shouldered with bulging arm muscles. Their thick rows of deep-purple head fins flare out behind them, the tips brushing the backs of their knees.

I lift my hand, calling as I approach, "Dr. Coineagan? I have a problem I'm hoping you can help with."

"You might have noticed, I'm a little busy right now," they grumble, but they turn to me, and their eyes latch on my neck. Their mouth falls open. "You have a—you're a—ah, fuck me sideways. Come here, let me see it!"

Their lilac pupils shine in a way so reminiscent of the hungry gaze that Lachlan and Raghnaid and even Lilias gave that it terrifies me. I shudder, but my parasite pulls me back to my senses, focusing on the rounder edges of the finfolk: on the dimple that bunches up their left cheek and the wrinkling at the edges of their round eyes and the excited little bounce to their shoulders. I came here because I wanted my aurora to go to the finfolk.

I step toward them, but a bell clangs from within the mountainside watchtower. Its metallic din echoes eerily through the firth: a warning, despite the brilliant glow of the hypnotizing ignit. My parasite coils anxiously, leaning into my own worry. If we trap ourselves here, if they take us back to Maraheem, if Lachlan's lab rips us apart—

Part of me knows I'm here to ask Coineagan to do just that, but it's a small part tucked beneath a mound of hope, and my parasite overwhelms it all with our fear of the Findlays. The selkies who round the bend, though, are as far from the Findlays as possible, their clothes duller and thinner than anything in the upper. Behind them comes a third intruder. Even from this distance, I recognize her, not just the red curls or the determined stride, but the wrinkle of her nose and the bandages around her hand.

Lilias found us.

CHAPTER TWENTY-TWO

the cross hairs of another's war

Each tightening of my grip forms a silent plea:
ignite yourself; shine into me.

I HAVE JUST ENOUGH time to connect the dots—the firth Lilias had circled on the map in her apartment, along with the schematics she'd labeled *energy reflector*—without quite understanding the picture they make before one of Lilias's lackeys aims a weapon at Dr. Coineagan. My legs move at the same speed as my lungs, slamming me into Coineagan the instant that my warning bursts from my lips. The bullet grazes my shoulder, my parasite consuming the tiny cut immediately. I shift myself underneath Coineagan as we fall, catching them before they can crash face first into the stone. They grunt and roll once.

Another bullet rattles Coineagan's walker.

They shake a fist, even though the ignit's mount blocks them from Lilias's group. "Stop shooting Berti! What has she ever done to you!" Lying in the dirt, their legs splayed a little and their top drooping off one shoulder, they look so young, perhaps barely into their twenties.

I grab their walker, tugging it toward them. "Dr. Coineagan, we need to get you to safety."

"I have never once been safe in my life," they reply, so

profoundly calm despite the gunshots Lilias's lackeys and the sentries now exchange above our head that I almost believe them. "And it's Elspeth, El if you must. Dr. Coineagan is my father."

"Rubem!" Tavish calls to me from the nearest building, his bulk tucked behind a column a bit too thin and skinny to properly protect him.

"I'm safe—find cover!" It's not a lie, technically. For now.

"What cover?" Tavish shouts back.

Around him, the town seems to agree. Finfolk drag their children into the water, while pixies dart as far from the shore as possible, some taking the plunge with the help of their mer-friends. I peek over the ignit.

Lilias rushes toward me, another three lackeys guarding her from behind while the first two continue firing at the sentries who duck behind the little stone wall. A red hole blooms in the center of one the pixies' heads, and the woman drops. Her companion screams for aid.

It seems, for the moment, I'm the only aid available. I grit my teeth. If I keep telling myself that this is the last time, one of these times really will be the last, whether I want it to or not. It better not be this one.

I launch over the ignit's mount, making it into arm's range of Lilias before any of her lackeys get a shot off. Her lips peel back, her eyes catching fire.

"Thought you'd be in pieces by now." She punches.

I slip to the side, slamming my elbow across her jaw. "Only emotionally."

I've fought her enough times to feel the difference in my movements. We should be equals, but now I move with a speed that she can't quite match, each blow pushing her back, slamming her down. With a sudden rush of exhilaration, I realize: I can win this.

Until her lackeys close in around us. Around me, around the ignit, and around the one person who might, maybe, possibly be able to give me back my life.

Dr. Coineagan—Elspeth—clambers up their walker and shouts, "Touch my ignit and I'll drown you in glitter," at the five selkies with guns. I'm beginning to heavily doubt the intelligence of scientists at this point.

One of the selkies takes hold of Glenrigg's ignit and yanks it out of the machine. Its brilliant yellow light vanishes in the depths of a leather satchel. Two of the other four shift their aim to Elspeth.

If the world would turn a little slower, I might see a way to stop them both: the selkie carrying away this safe haven's only defense and the bullets about to rain down on my last hope. But the triggers are already being pulled.

I vault to Elspeth, shielding their body with my own.

As Lilias's lackey carries away the Glenrigg ignit, my parasite urges me to follow. I almost give in to it, fear for these people I don't even know, slamming headfirst into the knowledge that I came here for one thing: to find Elspeth. And this—this is not my problem. I do not have to be this town's savior, no matter what the absurd creature sharing my body seems to think. Not when that salvation may cost me my only remaining hope and myself along with it.

I rage against my parasite's urging, rage against everything that tells me to protect this little makeshift town of outcasts, even though it sears through my chest to do it. Slinging Elspeth's walker under one arm, I push them in front of me and half run, half trip to the town. I expect bullets in my back and the invasion of my parasite as it attempts to cover them up, turning me more into itself with every deliverance. Instead, I hear Lilias shriek.

"Don't kill him—we need his blood!"

My blood.

Malloch must have realized that Lachlan had taken it and delivered that information to the rebels before Sheona killed them. My stomach churns with an echo of wooziness formed of fear and memory. Whatever use Lilias might find for my shimmering, inhuman blood could not be good. Or, if it were good, at least not moral.

A pair of Lilias's lackeys sprint at me, but they're caught in the fire of fresh Glenrigg sentries. It drives the selkies back. With a final unhappy screech, Lilias orders their retreat.

My heart still pounds all the way to the road, my parasite's fear pulsing in time with mine. Lilias is leaving. But Glenrigg's ignit will carry her straight past the BA, letting them to take her place. I have to force my lungs open and closed again, resting one hand on the frame of a shop.

"Rubem?"

"I'm here."

Tavish's cane hits my boot first; then he finds my arm. "Was that Lilias?" He doesn't wait for an answer—doesn't seem to really need one. "We have to capture her again; this could be my chance."

"If we follow her, we'll run into the BA soldiers."

"Then we'll tell them what she's done! We'll take her back to my mother—"

"Tavish!" I grab him, a little more desperate than I mean. A little more angry. "What about the physicist? What about my aurora?"

"We'll bring the physicist."

"They can barely stand!"

The finfolk sits beside their walker, their legs shaking as though they've just run here all the way from Falcre.

"Then we don't!" Tavish replies. "We wouldn't need them. My family still has the better technology." His words are made of graphite instead of diamond, brittle and grey.

"They will kill me. You know that." Fear and anger cloud my thoughts, pulsing through me in time with every new flush of pain. The emotion seems to wrap around my parasite, tugging it inward. Toward my heart. Toward what little remains of me.

It shrieks. I echo the sound, high and nearly musical, a scream and an elegy wrapped into one. We sway, knees giving out.

Tavish scrambles to catch me. His cane clatters to the floor. I slip quickly through his arms, landing with a thud beside it. My lungs tighten, suffocating. My parasite takes them over, forcing them to fill and contract, fill and contract. Tavish crouches beside me, and I lean against his chest, clinging to that small part of myself that's purely me and kicking back at the impending darkness.

"Ruby?" Tavish brushes back my braids, desperately patting my head and neck as though he might find a reset switch. "Ruby, please—"

"I'm here," I manage.

A little sob leaves him. "We'll go with Dr. Coineagan, aye? Can you move?"

"I'll manage," I say, because I'll have to. I force myself to stand, turning my attention on the scientist I let Glenrigg's ignit go for. "Dr. Coineagan—Elspeth—you *can* help me, right?"

"If your problem has anything to do with that aurora, I can certainly try." Their legs tremble as they lean so heavily against their walker that they seem to hold themself up on arm strength alone.

A second alarm rings beside the original bells, creating a spine-chilling harmony. This one means something different. Where the Glenrigg inhabitants had reacted to the first by hiding or congregating away from the town's entrance; at this bell, the real panic sets in. Our server from last night rushes from a house three intersections down, a stuffed bag slung over one shoulder. He leaps through the open walls to avoid the walkway, where people scramble in all directions, some hauling belongings and others carrying makeshift weapons.

Tavish might not see the commotion, but the terror of it seeps through the air itself, requiring no interpretation. "Can we do something to help them?"

"Not anymore." My chest pinches. I slap away the memory my parasite flings at me, the selkie shoving Glenrigg's ignit into a satchel. But it keeps pulling it back up, molding it into a fresh blow with each repetition.

'*Done something,*' it snaps at me in Sheona's voice.

It wasn't my fight! I want to shout that I helped when it was about my homeland and not some random town that nearly shot me instead of granting me shelter, but what I did for the Murk—stole from them—now winds through my brain, criticizing me. I try a different tactic: *Saving Glenrigg would have sentenced Elspeth to death. What right do I have to sacrifice one person for the sake of a village?* But that hadn't factored into my decision in the moment, and we both know it.

My parasite's disapproval lingers in the back of my mind; a rough, thick feeling like a blanket made of sandpaper.

Elspeth interrupts our internal feud. "If you'll be wanting my help, there's a few things I need from my lab across the firth. I assume an epic escape awaits us after? Or probable death, but I do have a preference." Before I can respond, they roll off the edge of the walkway, plunging into the firth. Their head fins fanning around them as those tucked over their feet unfurl to the length of small paddles. "Carry Berti, would you," they shout. "And keep up!"

I grab the walker in one hand and Tavish's shoulder in the other as I jog after Elspeth.

The edge of the village comes up suddenly, the chaotic patterns of Glenrigg's three-story buildings giving way to a dock. A few families toss their belongings onto steam-powered vessels, leaving a series of rowboats to bob sadly off to one side. Across the water a cliff made of natural black pillars surrounds a huge wooden door. Elspeth swims toward it.

I help Tavish into a rowboat. He sits at its center as I paddle, his arms tucked around his stomach. Scarlet fills in the space along the side of his pinkie nail, but he keeps picking at it anyway.

"We couldn't have caught Lilias," I say.

"Maybe the BA still will." He presses his palm to my knee. A drop of his blood seeps into the dark fabric. "And maybe Elspeth *can* help you, the way my family couldn't. I hope so, at least." There's something behind his voice, deep and heavy and hidden so well I can only see the outline. "And if they can't, there will be someone else. There has to be."

"There will be." But I don't mean it, not anymore. I think this is what it feels like to die. It's the point where hope finally runs out. Where the future stops being a tunnel before you and starts looking like the top of a well you've dug so deep that there's no redirection, no chance of something new. Elspeth's help is all I have.

As we pull into the dock, something between a drizzle and thick fog begins to fall, cutting us off from the town with a barrier of chilled quiet. I retrieve Elspeth's walker, and they open the door in the side of the cliff, ushering us inside. They flip a switch.

A steam machine chugs to life somewhere to our left, and one by one the lanterns on the hall's high ceiling flicker awake. Their orange glow reflects golden off the black rock. Cautiously, we follow the path of the light through a wide kitchen of low counters and past a bedroom with dark-purple drapes tied around the bed's three and a half posts, a couple crooked paintings of sunsets layered beneath pinned diagrams boasting things like half-dissected sirens and ignit classifications and elaborate chemical formulas. One looks eerily like the cross section of a Murk's aurora-latched mangrove.

At the final bend the hall opens to a massive chamber. Glittering strings of silver and black beads drape between each peak in the ceiling, surrounding dozens of purple-glass lanterns. A few of the finfolk's glowing rainbow curtains drape between them. The smooth floor looks like a small explosion tore out chunks of it. Shelves with glass fronts embed the polished, black walls, some filled with oddities, from organs in jars to wavy vials of fluorescent liquids, others with thick tomes and skinny notebooks.

Between the shelves hang blackboards packed with chalk scribbles. A row of dark aprons and a few cloaks fill the only empty wall space. Low, black tables that sparkle like they were painted in glitter take up the center of the room, many with a railing curling off one side. A variety of machinery clutters them, and a chemistry set winds through it all, tubes running over microscopes and flasks balanced on elaborate radios with twisting antennae. Two silver metal balls clang against each other, the first shooting the second forward only to be hit back the way it had come a moment later. A small tunnel twists upward off the end of the lab, but it looks like a back entrance, rugged and unrefined.

We all flinch when someone pounds at the front door and shouts, "By order of the Mara Diplomatic Assembly, come out with your hands up!"

"Sorry, better luck next time!" Elspeth calls back at them, shoving a lever beside the lab's entrance. The floor rumbles with the clicking of gears, and wall of metal and glass lowers, blocking us off from the hallway. "My blast door should hold them back for somewhere between indefinitely and ten minutes," Elspeth explains, waggling a hand my direction. "So best to get moving."

"What do you need?" I ask

"First, a look at you." Elspeth reaches for my neck, and I force myself not to pull back. Their eyes narrow, then widen. "It hasn't latched?"

"No, but it's trying its damnedest," I reply. "That's why I've come. And since you wrote what I'm told is a rather inspired paper on ignit energy, you seemed like as good an option as any to help me remove it."

"You're outrageous. I respect that." They grin, and I can't tell whether I'm outrageous for trying to remove my parasite or for asking someone like them to assist me in it. Their smile wanes at the clatter of soldiers against the blast door. "Wheel out the cart under the table for me, won't you,"

Elspeth says, leaning against their walker with one arm to don a cloak in a dramatic swoop.

"Can I be of help?" Tavish drags his cane across the floor, fidgeting from one foot to the other.

I kiss him on the cheek as I pass. "Sorry, princeling. You do the talking, I do the lifting."

His laugh hurts to hear.

Elspeth and I wind through the room, them pointing and me loading, filling the cart with a series of small machines, books and papers, blueprints and tools. They add in a case of glitter and a bottle of whiskey at the end. "Glitter for the aesthetic, whiskey for the victory."

"You're a genius." I wink at them, trying not to flinch every time the selkies in the hall slam against the blast door. "Where to now?"

"Up, up, and away." They flick their fingers in the air. I swear a tiny shower of glitter halos their head for a moment. With a sigh, they point toward the ascending tunnel. "That's the back exit. It leads out to the other side of the mountains."

I grab Tavish, and together the three of us work our way up Elspeth's exit tunnel. The lights grow farther and fewer between, and by the time we reach the end, my parasite forces my lungs not to turn to ragged wheezes. Elspeth unbolts the door, this one the same solid metal from the lab, and leads us onto a bluff with a large garage.

Inside sits a monstrous, steam-powered vehicle that must be a truck, but everything about it gives a slight middle finger to the concept of labels. Its smokestack curls like horns over its canvas roof, and one of the high sides of its bed flips down into a ramp when Elspeth hits a button. They crawl through the open gap to the main compartment and settle into the hugest driver's seat I've ever seen, complete with gears and steam pipes and a row of water bottles.

I wheel our cart into the truck, latching it to the bed, and sit beside Tavish in a giant bag stuffed with something squishy.

"This can't possibly be safe," Tavish mutters. He crosses his legs daintily over my lap, his grip on his cane squeezing all the blood from his knuckles.

"I don't usually have guests. But I think you'll probably live!" Elspeth jabs a button on the console, and the engine whirls to life, shooting steam so thick that it fills the garage before we pull out.

CHAPTER TWENTY-THREE

communication crisis

But if you burn yourself to be my light,
if you fight my dark by flaring bright.
You may be ashes in the aftermath.
Soot scattered across an empty path.

I HOOK MY FEET under loops in the truck floor and wrap an arm around Tavish's back to keep either of us from bouncing into the bed as we peel out onto a worn dirt road and head down through the hills. Elspeth controls the car like the boats back home, their arms moving between their wheel and an assortment of levers with ease. After a series of dramatic drops and tight turns, the path meets up with what looks like a main road, though the nearest vehicle is only a steam smudge beyond the hills.

By the time the BA round the coast to collect their own land transportation, we'll be far ahead of them. Somehow, that knowledge doesn't shake free my anxiety. Or my guilt.

My fingers ache to be used, and I run them absentmindedly up and down Tavish's thigh.

He pauses from chewing on his tongue to curse. "By the Trench!"

"What is it?"

"My hormones. I didn't think to pack them when we left for the lower yesterday."

"Can we find you more?"

He shakes his head, his brow tight. "Druiminn Health is the only place I know that produces them."

I don't understand all that this means to him, but I see the pain it pinches across his features.

"There are a few organizations producing them in Alkelu," Elspeth says. "I know that's not helpful, you being here and not there." They roll their fingers along the wheel, their gaze straight ahead. Their fins flutter, dislodging a few shimmers of silver caught in their hair rays. "I've thought about taking them myself, but I don't know if I'm ready yet, or if I actually want them. This is—it's new. Well, four years new. But that feels like no time at all when you have to rediscover yourself."

Tavish moves to pick at the edges of his fingers, but I catch his hand, squeezing it. He breathes out and leans into my side. "I ken that."

Elspeth nods. They finally glance at Tavish, a soft gleam in their eyes. "When did you know?"

A flush spreads up Tavish's neck, saturating into his cheeks. "I was six. My mother ordered us all suits for the yearly family portrait, and my tie matched hers and Ailsa's. I told her I wanted Alasdair's tie, because I was going to be a boy when I grew up. I couldn't even see the patterns; I just heard the men's were different, and I knew I was meant to have one of those instead."

"Ailsa and Alasdair?" Elspeth slams on the breaks.

The truck screeches and slides. My stomach flies into my throat as I brace against the console, holding tightly to a shrieking Tavish. My heart still thumps out of control by the time we finally slide to a stop, dust and steam stirring around us.

"You're the third Findlay child." Elspeth slaps the wheel, cackling. "I'll be fucked sideways *and* backward. Tavish Findlay!"

"You couldn't tell from the mixture of blind and devilishly handsome?" I try to make my voice light, to stop the worry from creeping into it. What if Elspeth won't help me now? What if—

"The statistical probability of blindness in selkies isn't documented among any credible resources outside of Maraheem, handsomeness as an aesthetic quality is highly culturally based, and the existence of devils has never been scientifically proven. So, no." Elspeth stares at Tavish, the quirk in their lips an unnerving contrast to their narrowed eyes. "They're saying you killed your siblings."

Tavish scowls. Slowly, precisely, he straightens himself out of my grip, adjusting his outfit and running a hand through his hair. "I have not killed anyone, least of all them." His voice turns to ice. "But if I knew a knife was flying toward my mother, I would not stray its course."

As though that's all they needed to hear, Elspeth lurches the truck forward again. "You, Rubem was it?"

"Yes, that's me." More than ever, it feels nice to be asked for my name, one of the few pieces of me left that's truly mine.

"You came to me because of my paper on how the energy of the ignits isn't created, but taken from some other place?" They shake their head. "Long distance, or perhaps cross-dimensional transportation, that's the key. I've been monitoring the energy differentials caused by ignit explosions for years, but no proof yet."

It sounds a bit like nonsense to me, but so does the thing taking over my body. "Beileag called you an ignit cycle physicist? That does include auroras, right?"

"Auroras, ignits, the stones ignits react with. I also built Glenrigg's hypo-wave transmission system. Had to gather a nonsensical amount of data first. I even went to the siren seas for a few weeks, almost got eaten twice before I stumbled into one of the cohabitation groups. Turns out sirens are excessively decent when you both have a common language! Or a translator, at least. But that's not related to your problem, I don't think." Their eyes narrow. "Or mayhaps it is."

My brow hurts from trying to piece through their story. "Maybe my problem is sirens?"

"Communication." They smack the steering wheel. "See, I figure the auroras are sentient in some capacity. Now, I know what you're thinking: they appear to be parasitic entities of a single-cell type. How can something be smart if it doesn't have a brain? Do *you* even have a brain, Elspeth? But the really peculiar thing is the way the auroras release specific rhythms of electromagnetic waves, not just in response to environmental factors or in a repeatable array of songs, but in true code-like fashion. They *speak*." Elspeth draws their hands in an arc, wiggling their fingers like a street magician. At the same moment, the truck hits a pothole, and the wheel twists left. They yank it back. "And if something speaks, it must be sentient!" As though in direct protest, the engine grumbles.

Tavish gives a little snort.

My parasite's laughter fills the dark corners of my mind, sounding as blundering and honeyed as my own drunken guffaws. The humor it seeps through me feels genuine, though, tinged in affection. It presses against me, echoing physical memories of the warmth I feel toward my pets.

I rub my face. "You're more or less right. It thinks you're adorable, by the way. Like a kitten."

Elspeth screeches the truck to another chaotic stop, but this time I'm prepared for it, latched in place like a leech. Tavish still yelps, and he continues to hold me even after the vehicle settles, his expression such sheer shock that it seems he thinks I've grown a second head instead of a second consciousness.

Elspeth twists in their seat. Their glittering gaze fastens on mine. "You can hear it?" They don't wait for a response, or maybe my fatigue is answer enough. "Then my subsequent hypothesis must be correct, too. Since an aurora binds itself to its host's organ systems, in the case of a human that must include the brain, the endocrine system, and the neurons. It would therefore be able to manipulate those systems, mayhaps not fully, but at least to a degree." They tug a little notepad out of the truck's dashboard, and a stubby pen seems to materialize from behind one of their pointed ears. "What's it saying to you? Besides my physical relatability to small, furry creatures, of course."

"It can't speak directly, so it replays pieces of things I've already heard. Mostly it's a silt-breathing pain in the ass who doesn't always make sense." I drag my fingers over its initial latching place on my neck, even though I can't quite feel the difference between it and me anymore.

Tavish presses his hand to mine. "I'm sorry."

"So, you want me to remove it?" Elspeth asks. "An asshole in your head *would* be annoying."

"I might be able to handle an asshole, but it's taking over my body." My voice sounds distant, as though I've already lost myself. "Having my memories tugged up is one thing. No longer being the person who makes them is another."

"And if it can't be done?" Elspeth speaks with Lachlan's straightforward candor, but where he held only an unfeeling curiosity, Elspeth watches me with a gentler gaze, impulsive maybe, but not calloused. "I'm no surgeon, but something that's integrated itself so thoroughly into your body should be impossible to extract without killing the patient. What will you do if disengaging it proves too much?"

I fold my free hand into my lap, trying to ignore the way the black gashes that crisscross the skin mimic my fishnets so well. "I won't exist as background noise for its life. I've already felt left out of my own far too often."

The blare of a horn makes me flinch. A car scoots around us, filling the truck with steam as it passes.

Elspeth taps their nails against the steering wheel. "I assume it has control of parts of you already?"

I bundle up my swelling emotions, tying a bow around them for later. "I know for sure that it's buried into my right arm and down my back, as well as through my lungs."

Elspeth nods. They pull free one of their many water bottles and take a sip. A few drops of water trickle from delicate gill slits in their neck. "But you're still commanding those areas at the moment? When you wrap your arm around Tavish, it's your action, not the aurora's?"

"That was, yes. It only bothers taking control when it doesn't like something, or to amplify what I'm already doing—make my own actions faster or smoother—or when my body might die otherwise."

"So, it *can* control you, but it chooses not to most of the time."

The phrase presses against my chest. *Chooses* not to take control. As though it's doing me a favor, letting me use the arm it wove itself through against my will. I grunt. "I figure the effort isn't worth its trouble yet, since it doesn't have all of me."

Elspeth's brow lifts. "Have you asked it?"

"It might just lie." It's an excuse and I know it, cringing before Elspeth even continues their prodding.

"Or mayhaps it won't. I always think it's better to ask the question even if you can't trust the answer than to hold it inside and not trust yourself instead."

I nearly object—I'm a bit more trustworthy than Elspeth's giving me credit for—but Tavish rubs his palm along my arm. "What if this is how you remove it?" he asks. "If there's something more that it needs from you, something that isn't your actions or your memories, perhaps we can convince it to leave by finding it another way to obtain that goal?"

However dastardly I know my parasite is, and however much I don't believe we can persuade it to let me go, I have too much at stake here to object. "All right. I'll ask it."

I press my lips gently to Tavish's, and when I straighten, I turn my attention to my parasite. It takes no effort, the motion far too much like sliding into a secondary part of myself, as though the creature inside me is merely the back of my mind. The back of my mind waiting patiently to make me the back of its own.

Well, silt-breather? What have you to say for yourself?

Its presence yawns and stares, but I have the feeling it's been paying very keen attention to this entire conversation. *'Who doesn't always make sense,'* it says, toneless.

I don't know why I even try with you. "The damn thing's laughing at me."

Elspeth notes it down. "In what way? Do you feel the humor, or is it drawing on memories?"

I look for both, only to realize it's offering me neither. Whatever unknowable sentiment tumbles beneath its emotions contains no humor after all. "I suppose it's just being a sass."

My parasite repeats itself with more vigor, hints of its frustration leaking into me: *'Who doesn't always make sense.'*

You don't *make sense, you're right about that.*

'Communication.' It growls as though that will make its obvious insult more clairvoyant.

I can see that, you fucking—and then it hits me. I groan. *Well, you could have been less of a butt.*

'You wee scunner,' it replies.

I sigh and pick a piece of slim metal off the floor so I can dance it between my fingers. "It couldn't tell me the answer even if it wanted to. It just doesn't have enough vocabulary using my memories. It can only draw from so many at once, and the unusually small number of conversations I've had over the years probably doesn't help."

I feel the influence of my parasite on my right hand every time I flick the piece of metal toward it, the way it slips beneath my actions, propping them up, making me faster and more accurate. I hate it. I hate it because it's not actually cruel. However despicable and intrusive my parasite is, a lot of what I blame it for might be . . . inaccurate?

The realization comes not in a single stream of thought but a bunch of lumpy, disconnected threads, yet I know my parasite can sense them. Now it does laugh.

Silt-breather. But the longer I focus, the more my bitterness leaves the word, drowned by the soft brush of my parasite's presence, its humor warm and friendly even while I'm still contemplating chopping it into pieces.

As its laughter fades, it turns stoic. It rifles through my memories, drawing up the ones of our shared dream: the mirror of me built of my parasite's pieces and the way we fell into Lachlan's lab tank together. *'Communication,'* it repeats.

"It does want to tell me something," I admit to Elspeth.

They nod. "Something about why it's latching to you?"

I know it's right the moment they say it, because my parasite leaps excitedly, its energy flowing into mine, making me giddy in turn. I have to force my breathing slower to calm our anticipation. "But I still don't understand *what* it's trying to tell me."

Tavish squeezes my hand, and Elspeth jots a note. My parasite doesn't back down, only curls around me, nearly smothering. I can't seem to throw it off, so I leave it there, let it bleed through my thoughts and meld its emotions with mine. Maybe if it influences me enough, it can figure out how to get the information it wants to me.

"Mayhaps I can fix that?" Elspeth smirks.

Another car honks at us as it swerves around. The driver pauses to glare. They blink a few times and speed away a little faster.

Elspeth lurches the truck forward again. They veer into the grass at the next halfway decent opportunity, pressing through the hills until a set of them block the road. We come to a halt beside a stream cluttered in grey rocks. Elspeth shuts off the engine.

"What are we—" Tavish begins, just as I say, "So, how do you plan—"

But Elspeth cuts us both off by cranking a lever on their seat. Metal peels back from its sides, revealing giant wheels, and a sliver of the floor spins and expands to let the chair roll free of the truck. Elspeth halts it beside the vehicle's bed and holds to the bed's railing as they retrieve one of their smaller radio-like machines. Tavish and I join them.

"With this we can pick up the unique waves of energy your aurora produces and convert it to speech through the coding system I developed," they explain. "It's about as perfect as I am, which means, obviously, flawless." Their smirk scrunches. "That was a joke, by the way. Though I am spectacular, the translation will be imprecise."

Hope swells within me, amplified by my parasite's yearning. "Do I need to do anything?"

"No offense, but you are the least necessary aspect of this equation." They waggle the ridges along their brow line and flick the machine's switch.

Static comes from the speaker. It bounces in and out, as though focusing on something. *Any time now?* I try to push away the worry, to give my parasite a more soothing nudge instead of my usual aggressive snapping, but its fear rattles in my chest.

'It's trying its damnedest.' It turns my earlier words on their head, following them with a statement I once grumbled over a limping monkey. *'It's not broken. It's not broken!'*

Whoa, easy there, let's not give us a panic attack. I cling to what little calm I have left, trying to release it into my parasite the way it leaks its emotions into me. It writhes, but each breath we take steadies it. It curls against me. I let it. *So, you're trying to talk with your electric-whatever, but it's not working?*

'Broken.' The statement comes in a soft rush this time, a shattered sound. Then it whimpers, *'It's trying its damnedest.'*

"Is it—" Elspeth begins, but my parasite lifts my hand for quiet.

"It's trying, give us a moment." *You could do this before, right?*

'*Live in this Murk,*' it replies.

I put the pieces together. *You haven't tried since the Murk.* I feel its agreement like a wail. *Take your time. Don't give up.*

I regret my encouragement immediately. My parasite shifts around my consciousness, drawing on both our energies as it strains. Pain shoots along our spine, and our vision wavers. We collapse on a nearby rock just as the world shifts, colors altering, removing, going dull.

"Ruby?" Tavish grabs my shoulders.

I hold to him, breathing against his shoulder.

'*Broken,*' my parasite repeats.

"It gave its all, but it can't make those waves you want. It might only be possible when it's fully latched." The mere thought still sends a shudder through me. *I heard of the way your old host turned to ash when you left it. If you keep this up, will my body do the same?*

A pause follows. It shuffles through my memories, finding one where I replied with a simple *probably* and no other explanations. My heart drops.

"I don't think I can come back from that," I continue. "Any option where I alone am not in control of my body isn't an option at all, not to me." I feel like I need to justify this desire, to myself just as much as to Elspeth and Tavish. This is my choice. It's my right to make. I shouldn't feel guilty for it.

"What if it writes?" Tavish asks. "Maybe it doesn't need to speak. You said it can control your arm; can it write to us instead?"

Elspeth whistles. "Ah, you're a genius."

I kiss Tavish's hand before letting it go. "Can we borrow the notepad?"

Elspeth pushes it into our grip. They scoot their chair as close as possible, leaning so far into my field of view that I have to nudge them back a little. A single piece of glitter flutters along the notepad page.

I wait. My parasite doesn't ask for permission, but it takes control of my muscles gently, as though expecting me to protest. It drags the pen, forming loops and lines. As the text unfolds, it's obvious it's not writing at all, but an elaborate series of connected swirls in an intricate arrangement.

I slap down the pen. "That's nonsense."

It retracts like a wounded animal. *'It's trying its damnedest.'*

The desperation and pain leaking from it turn my stomach into a knot. *I'm sorry.* I feel like it should be harder to apologize after everything it's put me through, but the more I look back over our last few days, the less I'm convinced that it's done anything to hurt me after all. In the subconscious cracks of my memories, I feel its fondness, feel the love of a dangerous creature who wants desperately to be held, wants to believe its sharp claws don't cut just as easily on accident as they do on purpose. Maybe some of those times it saved my body, it was trying to save *me*, too, even if it can't quite seem to also protect me from the tendrils of itself that dig a little deeper with each salvation.

I don't think it's your fault, I add, trying to be gentle. *You are trying your damnedest, and I appreciate that.*

My parasite responds by curling around me, burying itself deeper into my consciousness as it trembles. I tremble with it, us, together. We grieve.

Elspeth scrutinizes the pattern. "Mayhaps this isn't nonsense, just something we can't yet make sense of. An aurora's form of writing?"

As they try to take back the notepad, my arm jerks under my parasite's will, hope rushing through us. My parasite snatches so hard that the paper comes free. It flips it over and draws on the back, its motions ragged and frenzied now. When it finishes, there's a picture of a stalk topped in dozens of feathery tentacles.

I stare at the alien thing, my own confusion warring with

my parasite's optimism. I know what it is, yet I can't picture it. I can feel it, though: the creature I connected to—inhabited, perhaps—at Lachlan's secret lab.

"It sketched a feather duster worm." Elspeth's gaze shoots expectantly to Tavish.

"They're the Findlay Inc. auroras' hosts, aren't they?" I ask.

My parasite warms in response, a deep purr rattling it. *'Communication.'*

So they can help us speak. I slide my fingers over the drawing of the strange underwater creature. *You connected us with one in that dream. Can you do that again?*

Its uncertainty bleeds into me so strongly that I almost tell it to stop whatever it's doing. Too late. We move, our arm reaching out, but this arm—the one attached to this me—it stays cradled around pen and paper, even as I can feel deeply, firmly, from my fingertips to my bones, that we are grabbing someone's hand. The world snaps into three.

The grassy hills, Tavish and Elspeth staring at me. Lachlan's secret lab, a white-coated figure blocking most of the view. And another place, one dark and quiet, hauntingly familiar, just not to me.

The other hand grips ours tighter, and I feel, again, the sensation I couldn't quite identify last time. It feels like weakness. Like struggle. Like pain. An idea spills into us, not in words or sounds or even emotions, but in something more primal, like one magnet being drawn to another: *'Come.'*

My parasite agrees with everything in them. This is it, my solution, its purpose, our answer. But finding our way back into Maraheem, through the upper and the Findlay Estates and all the way to Lachlan's secret laboratory—

'To the Trench laboratory itself,' my parasite corrects. Its use of Raghnaid's voice sends a shiver down my spine. Reaching the Trench might be a little easier, but not much.

If I find a way to get you there and see whatever you want through, then you'll leave me be?

Its sincere agreement floods in, mixed with tinges of sadness.

Then why not leave now? I'll complete my end of the bargain, and you can latch properly to something else while I do.

'The aurora seems to provide the host with additional energy. The hosts grow . . . stronger.' Its presence throughout my body tingles, and a mixture of emotions bleed from it, desire mixed with distrust. Distrust I probably deserve.

Silt-breather. I think I'm talking to us both. As the thought fades, I realize what this means, for me, for Tavish, for the terminally ill *us* we've been nursing fruitlessly. It means one more journey, one more shared destination. A little stability before the eventual coin toss.

One more last hope.

"If we can reach these auroras, they can help. I think they can tell me what mine is saying or at least what it wants."

Tavish taps his nails against his cane. "If we could get into Maraheem and the upper, maybe there's a chance I could slip us into the Trench, but that all means nothing, since the moment we come within sight of a gate, they'll arrest us."

Elspeth slips the drawing of the feather duster worm from my hand and squints at it. "Finfolk built the original city of Maraheem. There're ways into the lower that your selkies don't know about."

Hope lights up Tavish's face. "How do we get to them?"

All the fight deserts me suddenly, the last of my mental energy rushing away. I have nothing to add to this conversation. As Tavish was useless earlier, now I have no purpose. No purpose, but for a pair of legs that twitch to move and two hands in desperate need of something to bounce between them. I stand, giving Tavish a soft peck on the cheek, and leave them to their discussion, letting my anxious body wander so my mind doesn't have to.

But no matter how far I go, I can't wander away from the

presence in the back of my mind, anxious and determined and almost as terrified as I am.

CHAPTER TWENTY-FOUR

louder than words

In this war of multitudes, we climb the embankment.

Instead of a question, here is a statement:

"I am not the reason we're falling apart."

The consequences of most lies don't emerge at the start.

ELSPETH TAKES US JUST past the abandoned selkie town, to a locked shack with an assortment of odd supplies and dusty scientific tools. They retrieve an atrocious watertight helmet of rusty brown, which comes to my shoulders and sputters air in awkward surges. After a quick explanation, they find a second one for Tavish.

The nasty thing blocks most of my vision and stinks of metal. It rattles ominously as I slip into the water off Elspeth's equally ancient-looking boat. The flippers over the finfolk's feet unfurl, and ripples in their neck flare into proper gills. Their clothing seems made for this, not soaking in the sea like my pants do, but gliding through it with the ease of an oiled seabird.

As we sink below the surface, the water rushes in around me, turning my helmet into its own little world, the only sound the gentle thrumming of the currents. Tavish grabs my arm, digging in his nails. His chest rises and falls so fast he almost appears to tremble, and little bubbles slip out the sides of his helmet. For all his life, the sea has been his home. This is the first time he's had to fear it.

I pull him close until our helmets bump. "I'm here," I whisper, even if he can't hear me. "I won't let anything hurt you."

It's not a promise I can rightfully make, in part because I'm no god, and in full because I won't be beside him forever. Just like he won't be beside me.

But the pressure of my touch must calm him, because slowly his panic lessens. Each step he takes across the sandy floor grows a little stronger, his grip on me no longer cutting off my circulation. Still, I hold to him the entire trek through the water, my parasite clinging to me in turn.

Elspeth leads us through kelp beds and into a castle of rocks where the only light streams from our helmets' headlamps. Every time the constricted space seems to creep inward, flaying my nerves and dragging the air from my lungs, my parasite forces me to breathe deeper and curls its warmth into my stomach.

Finally our underwater cleft opens upward. We break the surface into a cavern, half lake and half flattened rock, with a metal door in one wall and an array of chests beside it. Tavish sits with his head in his hands, little hitches in his breathing, while Elspeth digs out a pair of gloves, a wig of shaggy, auburn hair, and a case of makeup to go with their black cloak. When they plop into the compact, low-backed wheelchair tucked behind the chests, they could pass for a dark-skinned half selkie obsessed with purple makeup and glitter.

Tavish pulls himself together enough to put on a fake beard. He strokes it so often I have to remind him not to accidentally pull it off, but it's better than him picking apart his cuticles. I settle for a wrap of brown and black that flips up into a massive hood and tuck my hair inside it.

Tavish wants to immediately search for Lilias, to place all

our bets on restoring himself as a functional, guilt-free member of the Findlay household and using bureaucracy to grant us access to the Trench, but I remind him that even when we knew where Lilias was, we still failed to bring her in. Whereas I know Ivor Reid's bar fairly well and suspect that whatever path to the upper he refused to tell me last time, we could convince him to give it up now. Elspeth sides with me, and Tavish reluctantly gives in.

"I've been using this entrance for ages," Elspeth explains as we leave their secret cave through a weathered metal door that leads into the dredge's ruins. The mist coating its floor churns behind us, the fumes burning in my nostrils. "Mostly to aid my research. I've traded a bit with the dredgeheads for chemicals and, you know, other things."

"The dredgeheads are the crime leaders down here," Tavish adds before I can ask. His cane catches on an empty bottle, but he barely seems to notice.

"They aren't so bad if you don't infuriate them—wait, no, Tavish, the pillar!" Elspeth leans in their wheelchair, as though they can redirect him by sheer thought alone.

Tavish startles and follows their guidance too well, almost hitting a broken wall as he overcorrects. I consider stepping in, but the added chaos seems to distract him from his anxious twitches and incessant tongue chewing.

By the time we've worked our way up a rickety elevator out of the dredges, we're all hungry. The lower's bioluminescent algae lights shine at their full potential, and steam hisses from the ceiling. People crowd in and out of the tight alley passages and pile into dingy dining establishments. My parasite nudges me harder and more aggressively until we stop to pick up street food with a few spare coins that Elspeth supplies. As my sausage roll sinks into my stomach, it seems to stir the anxiety lingering there in nauseous bundles.

It only grows as we reach Ivor's bar.

The sign above hangs unlit, the cage-like garage fronts

pulled down over an empty room of ghostly barstools and tables topped by their own chairs. The soup kitchen sign is propped against a corner. A light still shines from the floor above, and a single, fiery voice echoes through the metal walls, just loud enough to make out the ire but not the words. It skitters along my brain without quite landing.

I can think of nothing better to say than "Fuck."

I direct Elspeth and Tavish to wait at the resale shop across the street while I call softly into the bar. No one answers, despite the obvious commotion above. Attracting more attention by shouting seems reckless. I give the garage gates a little rattle instead. The lock near the floor clatters tauntingly.

My parasite could open that with ease, but I don't trust it not to take me over the moment I do, if only by accident. It gives a soft, hurt vibration. I cringe.

'Well, it's your fucking fault?' It uses Lilias's words from at her apartment, but in a far more teasing tone.

Shut up, I grumble, but there's no bitterness now. Before I can scare myself out of it, I let the thought form: *What would you do with me if you did latch?*

It responds with a series of flashes: its disdain for my extra guzzles of whiskey, its fighting with me over my rolled-up sleeves, its nagging for me to eat, to breathe, to care more fully. It would not take me over or destroy me the way I had assumed, but every little emotion it would meld into me, every choice it would take, every piece of me it would slowly turn into something new—that would result in a decimated me all the same.

I can't.

It doesn't fight me, gently settling at my metaphorical feet instead.

With a sigh, I let it crack the bar's lock, releasing a little more of myself in the process. We cross the dining area and slip around the bar. I lean hesitantly into the storeroom. Light spills down the stairway to the apartment. I cup my hands around my mouth to call out, already feeling like an intruder, but the conversation from the apartment stops me dead as the familiar, fiery voice solidifies in my mind.

Lilias. This close, I can just make out her words. "If they find him, they'll have one more weapon against us."

"With Malloch dead how can we know that any of this is accurate?"

"I trust my informants," Lilias snaps.

Someone else backs her up. "Even the chance of it is bad enough!"

"We should act now. We have the Glenrigg ignit. The longer we hold on to that, the more danger we're in."

A much closer voice makes me jump.

"Breaking and entering's still a crime in the lower districts, laddie." Ivor Reid stands behind me, a parcel under one arm. His smile sharpens.

"It's a shame to see your famous bar so dim and lonely." I try to make my voice light, but the edge still comes through. We can both hear the conversation upstairs. We both know that we both know.

"It's my brother's birthday." Ivor's expression doesn't change, but he seems to turn from flesh to stone all the same. "Seemed right to do something a little different today. Avenge him, maybe. He's dead, you ken, a martyr for the last revolution—sixteen years old and the upper executed him in the square with our mother watching."

I taste metal in the back of my mouth. "You're helping Lilias Erskine." In my revulsion, the words slip free, my mind still wheeling to make sense of them. "For what? What could you possibly be getting out of her schemes?"

"Me?" His shakes head, his upper lip lifting at the edges. "I'm doing this for Mara, not for myself. We're gonna split the monopolies, shut down the gates, install a proper governing system where people from the entire city—the entire coast— have a say, and help the new government redistribute enough wealth throughout all levels of Maraheem that no one goes hungry or homeless or lacks medicine or a proper education."

They're good goals, honest ones, the kind I'd expect from a man like Ivor. But he's brought Lilias into them, and she's a taint even on the best of objectives. "You think aligning with her will do that—any of that?" The laugh that leaves me is maniacal, but I can't help it. "She'll destroy this city first."

Ivor moves forward like a rolling boulder, closing the little distance between us in an instant. He presses his palm to my collar, not grabbing, simply imposing his presence onto me. "Hear me this, laddie," he whispers. "Something in Maraheem needs to change. If Lilias Erskine is the only one who's brave enough to do it with me, then so be it." Within his unyielding stare is the compassion of his soup kitchen and the man who let a stranger sleep in his back room. "I know what she's done to you—I ken it hasn't been fair. But life hasn't been real fair to her long before you came around, and she might make things fairer for a lot of wee bairns who've only ever experienced the shite end of existence."

I want to blame him for the pain she's caused me, but the rush of anger my parasite lurches through me makes my focus rise above my own suffering, grabbing onto all the things I shouldn't be caring about. "She's bad news." My stomach ties itself into a knot, binding the statement in an acidic certainty. I press my own hand to Ivor's, letting my nails dig. "That ignit she has was the finfolk's. She let the BA overrun them for it. How fair is that to *their* children."

"I heard." Ivor's wrinkles multiply. His grip on me slips. "But what's done is done. It'll save lives here. If we want control of the city long enough to establish anything new, we've gotta capture the heads of the big seven and take what they've kept from us. We're gonna hypnotize the upper city with the ignit and bind them before they recover. Less fighting, less death. But I'm not gonna claim I've done all good here. No matter how hard we try, more people'll still die from this."

Lilias's voice rises again as she shouts a word that sounds an awful lot like *killing*.

Alasdair, Ailsa, Sheona, Malloch—every side has suffered, even the ones who never realized the lines were being drawn. My eyes lift to the smaller version of Ivor's sign, nailed above the bar: a slightly darker red, deepened by age, but still the same aggressive color as the symbol painted beside the Findlay's bodies.

"It was you." I can feel his presence in my past, haunting me each step I took, just as thoroughly as I know that the knowledge itself changes nothing. I still stand here, now, bearing the weight of every consequence. "You were Lilias's partner on the phone. You had Malloch murder Tavish's siblings and came up with the plot to frame him. You let Lilias hold me hostage, and when you realized who was walking out of your bar, you sent her after me again." No bitterness mars my words, just a sad emptiness. It turns out that the inside of my rage is hollow.

"Aye." Ivor's brow casts dark shadows over his eyes. His hand flattens against my collar. When he speaks, it's with all the emotion I lack, tight and desolate, stubborn and hopeful, fierce and solid. "I have to keep believing that this'll all be worth it."

"And if it isn't?" I whisper.

Ivor looks across the street, his gaze shifting from one exhausted, anxious face to the next. "It will be. It'll be worth everything it's cost."

I don't know what to say to that. Instead, I drag my hand down the front of my face and grit my teeth, trying to sort through my hatred for Lilias and Ivor's hazy morality and my own empathy for the lower city's plight. The pieces of each can't quite fit together in my mind. Maybe they aren't meant to. Maybe some situations aren't right or wrong, but a mess of everything in between.

A mess that doesn't involve me. But I'm already here, already so close to the Trench. My parasite shifts through my consciousness, and I know what it wants to say as though our communication barrier has cracked right down the middle: *We're* already here. We could do so much, together.

But the Trench awaits us, the Trench that will bring me closer to my freedom and my parasite's original goals. Their mess is not my mess. It's not our mess. I have to repeat the reminder until my parasite relents.

"So, are you going to drag me to Lilias now?" I ask, knowing he can't. Not with the rainbows now pulsing beneath my skin. But Ivor could still make my quest to the upper very, very hard.

"No. The time an aurora might've helped us has passed." He still looks at me with the wary presence of a viper who isn't sure whether to bite or flee. "But if I let you go, what'd stop you from sending the BA raging through this district, a petty vengeance though it'd be?"

I glance to the stairwell and shake my head. "Going to the BA would cause more damage than good, for both of us." Not for Tavish, though, who might waltz back into his estate to open arms if he can bring the rebels down first. But I can't consider that now. I came here for me. I can focus on him after.

Ivor releases a heavy breath. He steps back, stiff with tension, or perhaps fatigue. "Why *are* you here, Rubem?"

Across the street, Tavish and Elspeth argue over the feel of a cloak so adamantly that Tavish even smiles, Elspeth badgering him like they've been friends for years instead of hours.

I ignore them both. There's no need to mention their involvement in this. "The auroras are in trouble, something so rare and bleak it's scaring mine. I need to get into the upper city—all the way to the Trench—without being seen. Whatever fate befalls Maraheem, this is a problem larger than just the city, or the selkies, or even the whole North." I feel guilty leaving out what all this might do for me—the fact that I might not be trying to sneak into the upper at all if removing my parasite weren't one of the things I'm likely to get out of it.

That doesn't quite feel true anymore, though. With my parasite clogging my veins, I can't pick apart where my love for the Murk meets its devotion to its kin or at what point that has turned into an affection for the full span of this world. But no matter how this whole mess has skewed my feelings, the auroras' presence is a major part of the Murk and its ecosystem. They have a place there, just like the jaguars and the mer-snakes. Just as I should have had. Just as the creature inside me should, too.

Ivor's brow lowers, his lips taut. As he hesitates, a cheer rises from the rooms above the bar, followed by the clatter of people rising. He presses his palm to my shoulder again. His fingers tighten on my vest as he leans in close.

"There's a back entrance to O'Cain Fishery from the office ceiling of the abandoned warehouse on Seagrass and Rock Ridge. I hope you consider this a kind of repayment." He slips a small key into my hand and pulls away. "But you should leave it be, laddie. If whatever nonsense is plaguing the auroras can wait, I'd suggest you all get the fuck out of Maraheem." The seriousness of his tone is only amplified by his exhaustion. "We're trying to save as many as we can, but we gave up enough already. We'll give up more on both sides if we have to."

I can't tell if the ache in my chest is for the losses to come or those I've already witnessed. Maybe Ivor is right and reaching the auroras should wait. But the rush of corpses my parasite brought to mind earlier sits too fresh, too real for me to ignore. Something bad is coming. Perhaps something worse than a rebellion.

"Stay safe," I reply, and slip the key into my pocket.

As I leave, the lights of the bar blink back on, but Ivor locks the front again, behind me. No soup kitchen tonight. For better or worse, there's a far more violent compassion about to go down. And for better or worse, I'm walking away without trying to stop it or aid it. Guilt and doubt hang on every step.

But I don't pause. I take Tavish's arm with a soft "I found a way into the upper."

I don't mention that the rebellion is rising or that Lilias is here alongside her and Malloch's partner in their crimes against the Findlay family. Later, there might be time for that. Later, when I don't have to worry that this knowledge will be enough to make Tavish flip that fateful coin: his innocence or my future.

My parasite balks at me, crashing through my chest with a flush of irritation. *'Don't let them cover up the truth.'*

It'll only be for a little while. There will be time for him to get on with his life soon enough.

It tosses back a pair of my own statements from one of my last days in the Murk, pairing them together to form something new: *'Since they abandoned you'* and *'I think I'm justified.'*

I take a moment to piece the phrases into a single declaration. *You think I'm clinging to him because I lost everyone else.* There's something more, though, something in my parasite's bitter edge that I don't want to admit. Just because they abandoned me doesn't make it right to hold Tavish here.

I shove the thought away. That's not what's happening. I just know I can't help him take down Lilias right now, so why put him in danger of her? My remorse only grows, though, with every tortured wrinkle on Tavish's face and every taut step he takes.

We find the rusty signpost for Seagrass and follow it all the way to Rock Ridge. Ivor's key unlocks the door to the warehouse on its corner with ease. My nerves tingle through our silent slink across its empty main floor and up to the overlooking offices, where a trapdoor in the ceiling opens to a tight mechanic's tunnel that runs between the lower and upper cities. Then, those same nerves go so flat I could be a walking dead man. I heave Elspeth's wheelchair into the mechanic's tunnel and pull them up after, holding their hand as they reposition themself back into the seat. Their legs continue trembling. They seem not to notice, stretching out their arms before wheeling themself along in front of Tavish. His cane makes a faint click, click, clank as he accidentally taps it into Elspeth's chair.

A tiny line of steam shoots from a crack in the pipes along the dingy, brown floor of the lower-district ceiling, but every so often a channel of ignation twists through a mechanism in the wall between ourselves and the upper. When we find another ladder, we take it up, despite the inconvenience of carrying Elspeth's chair.

"The easier access points to Findlay Inc. are all in the highest levels of the upper districts. We should get as near to them as we can before we exit. It will take us through Greer O'Cain's place, though." Tavish chews on this tongue for a moment. "The BA thinks we're long gone, and I can deal with any staff, so we should only have trouble if we run into someone important. Greer's is one of few estates with no internal surveillance—they don't trust Callum & Callum's tech, and they don't have the kind of leverage over them that my mother does by controlling the ignation all those systems run on."

After climbing four more levels, the tunnel tightens too far for Elspeth's wheelchair, forcing us out of the walls. We backtrack to a door and creep into the silver ghost world of the upper. It's obvious from the first room that we're in Greer's living quarters, though they appear no more occupied than the Findlays'.

The only active lights come from the rare lines of ignation in the walls, their glow casting shadows against the teal and grey furnishings, making the metallic garnish stick out like veins beneath elderly skin. Even without his sight, Tavish seems drawn to the mere existence of the ignation, his empty brooch listless and dull in comparison. Every swish of motion from a distant room sounds as though it comes from the nearest dark corner. I swear I spot the bulk of a well-dressed selkie leering from a far hallway and a maid at the top of a stairwell, but each time they vanish, and no alarms sound after.

At first Tavish leads us based on guesswork and whispered descriptions, but soon he grows more confident. "We must be in the west wing. There's a side door into the city through Greer's secondary office. We should be able to slip out that way, so long as they're not using it."

We take a few more turns before reaching its massive, arching hallway.

"All the rooms look dark," I whisper, the empty silence nearly consuming my words. Still, the eerie ease through which we traversed this place seems wrong, as though the estate has rolled away from us as it prepares to crash down like a tsunami. My parasite coils closer in agreement, the vulnerable, pleading nature of its worry creeping into my bones.

We slip through the fourth door on the left and find the silhouette of an exit across from us. It stands in the faint lamination of a huge glass wall, so many small grey sharks and dancing silver fish swarming beyond that it must be a proper fish tank. A desk takes up most of the room's center. The collection of small, sea life-inspired sculptures guarding it form haunting silhouettes.

My breath catches.

Behind the desk, a flame sparks to life at the end of a small box. The holder lifts it to a cigar caught between their teeth, illuminating the scar that twists through their thin lips and along their cheek. They draw in a breath, and on their exhale a gust of smoke leaves, lingering in the air for a moment before a little machine behind them sucks it up.

"I thought my lack of response should have been clear enough." Their voice sounds rough, their words twisted with something between bitterness and humor. "So, why the fuck are you in my office, nephew?"

CHAPTER TWENTY-FIVE

for every ecosystem, a genocide

Fear festers
until all I have in me is a curse.
All I am is a thirst,
sweltering.
Gods be damned.
For the consequences of our own actions.

THE TENSION BUILDING INSIDE me contracts like a snapping viper. It sends my parasite into a defensive growl. I press my palm to Tavish's back for my own support as much as his.

Greer O'Cain leans over their deck, cigar between their first and second finger, and flicks on a small lamp. It illuminates their shadowy corner, revealing the bespectacled selkie to have more freckles than clear skin and just as many wrinkles, their frizzy, grey hair drawn back in a series of elaborate braids. A whiskey cup with an inch of amber liquid sits beneath their other hand. They twist it, running the bottom edge against the black wood.

They are everything Lachlan isn't—stout and solid and resolute—but there's a mechanical aspect to them that the siblings share, something about the manner in which they move and the way their lips quirk. My heart doesn't hammer in their presence, but I think, perhaps, it should. The same way it should have with Lachlan, even from his very first awkward fumble.

"I wasn't sure whether to believe it when my head of house said they'd spotted you wandering through the estate. But here you are." Greer props up one foot, then the other, their dirt-caked boots conflicting with the pristine state of the office. "Give me a reason not to call the BA. Or, better yet, your mother."

I want to launch over their desk and give them the very best reason of all, but as I shift, Tavish's hand slips over mine.

Though he holds his voice steady, I feel the tension in his shoulders, the way his breath trembles ever so slightly as he draws it in, and how he takes too long to release it. "There's something wrong with the ignit cycle. It's present in the mutants Raghnaid is trying so hard to hide, and the latching of an aurora to a human. I've even experienced an ignit failing at random—a situation too atrocious to contemplate if it starts happening to our ignation. My mother has been doing nothing to stop it, so I have no choice but to deal with it myself."

Greer's eyes narrow, their cigar dangling from perfectly manicured nails. "You? With these two shadows you pulled out of the lower? You're a murder suspect to the assembly, an opportunity to the other company leaderships, and the head of your own family is furious with you. How do you plan to make any real change, boy?"

Tavish straightens his shoulders, his jaw so stiff it almost trembles. His voice comes out soft despite the diamond edge, as if he's testing each word with care. "My mother has a lab in her tower, a private one never approved by the assembly. There's an old regulation on clandestine research I uncovered last year while digging through clinical study permits in my mother's office. If I confront her about it—"

"Confront her?" In the wall tank, a small shark skitters away from a larger one, fleeing out of its path. Greer watches it, their expression darkening. "Blackmail her, you mean? And how long do you think that would grant you any control? As long as it takes to call your bluff? Render your regulation invalid? Put a blade through your chest?"

Tavish's lips part, but he takes too long to form his thoughts, and Greer presses on.

"You could have brought the aurora's host to me when you fled your estates, but you knew there was nowhere in the upper that you would truly be safe from your mother. You knew that in the end, she always wins. It's the same reason I've never agreed to your meetings, because when your mother finds out, the backlash will be unprecedented. You may wrestle a win here and there, but you don't have enough power to stand against her, not for a proper war." They draw their boots off the desk, pressing both palms to it instead, fingers lifted to hold their cigar away from the wood. "You have a bright mind and a good heart, but you don't have the kind of strength it takes to eliminate someone you know to be a poison. Or, maybe you're like me. Maybe the stability you have now is worth more than the risk of standing up to her once and for all."

Tavish's nostrils flare in disgust. His fingers find his empty brooch, bloodied calluses around far too many of his nails. "You're selfish."

"I like to think of it as entitled." It's the emotionless statement of a person who looked in the mirror ages ago and decided everything they hated in it wasn't worth the effort of changing. "I am the result of my upbringing—we all are— beneath the shadow of Findlay Inc. We have just barely enough, always."

Tavish scoffs, but his voice shakes again as he repeats, "Just barely enough?"

"No one studies the ecosystem or runs a charity hospital from a jail cell. Or a lower district." Greer continues to watch him, unblinking. "I would be a hypocrite to blame you for doing the same, cowing under your mother the way we all do, dancing around her instead of stepping up to her. It's pathetic, really. We're pathetic, you included."

Tavish throttles the top of his cane. I can see the determination slipping away from him, all of his worries closing in. I want so desperately to give him my strength, to convince him that he is already enough just as he is. But as I try to brush my fingers against his arm, he moves away, sinking deeper into himself. His retreat hurts, forming a lump in my throat that only my parasite's rumbling can clear.

Greer taps their cigar against their ashtray and sighs. "But I'd also be a fool not to tell her you were in my house." As they speak, they lean back, shifting toward the shadow of a phone box on the wall behind them.

I don't know who flares first: me or my parasite. But neither of us accept this. The one thing that slows our outrage is the understanding that, while Greer can do nothing to us here, alone, that once we're gone, they could tell anyone. They could stop us from reaching the Trench without ever leaving this house.

'Plan to make any real change,' my parasite tosses the phrase with determination.

Even if we have to tie Greer up or drag them with us or bury a knife in their chest?

'This'll all be worth it.'

For Tavish. For the auroras. Maybe it won't come to that though. If Greer likes dramatics, I have plenty of those, so many teeth that I might not need to bite at all.

I cross the room, three strides carrying me to the desk. I don't have to think about the motions: my own hand reaches instinctively for Tavish's ornamental knife stashed in my belt while my parasite uses our other hand to toss back my hood. It returns the arm faster than I could imagine and somehow just as fast as I expect, catching the knife perfectly as I toss the weapon from one hand to the other.

Greer puffs on their cigar, but their neutral expression flickers, their eyes widening ever so slightly as they fix on the gleaming black lines engraved into my skin. "You're the one they brought before Raghnaid, aren't you? The first sentient host on record." Their fingers twitch as though they might reach across the massive desk to grab for me. Their gaze sweeps across my cheek and down my neck, and I can feel my parasite sparkling beneath it, warm and a little savage. "If things were different . . ."

I should want them to be different, but I find the desire to fling myself at scientists has vanished entirely. Maybe it's my parasite's fault. It told me I couldn't—wouldn't—cut it out, and now I feel certain—it feels certain—we feel certain together, that once I've done my part, it will leave on its own accord. "What Tavish said about the auroras was the truth." I waver between sounding like him and sounding like me. Between a diamond knife and a drunken sledgehammer. "Ignoring it because you're scared and selfish isn't an excuse."

"It's not just the murderers who make genocide possible," Elspeth adds, as though they can't help themself.

I twist Tavish's ornamental knife along my knuckles and flip it into the air, catching the hilt between two fingers. "We're not here to play politics. If it's your blood I need to draw to stop the ignation mutants from multiplying and the ignits from failing, then you had better hope that red fits with your color scheme."

Greer stares, the creases of their lined face too hard to read in the dim light. They lean slowly, but not for the phone. Instead, they flick a cane free from the shadows of the shelves, pulling the end off to reveal a blade beneath. They swipe it at me over the desk.

I block it with the ornamental knife, my parasite coursing through my arm as I swing. The sword cane fumbles in Greer's grip. I grin without mirth. "Careful. I have an aurora, and it makes me stronger."

"I see that." Greer slips the sword back into the cane, the motion decisive, almost mechanical. One edge of their lips quirks. Their eyes gleam when they meet mine again. "You're going to do what it takes to fix this problem with the ignit cycle?"

Of course. The reply leaps to my lips, but I hold it back, trying to pick my own feelings out of the tangled mess they make with my parasite's. It's impossible; we are too linked, too melded together, as though it's woven its love for the auroras into me just the same as it's woven its own body. Whatever is wrong with their ecosystem, I must help. "If not us, then who?"

My parasite curls closer, affection spilling off it.

I'm still getting rid of you though, I remind it, soft but stern.

'Silt-breather.'

The term feels like a pet name instead of an insult.

Greer stares at us—my parasite and me—and we stare back, like smirking into a mirror, one predator to another. I can't locate that shocked, disgusted man who was so ashamed of killing the very same poachers he would never have lifted a hand to save, who let Lilias wield him like a weapon because he was too tired to fight back. All I find now is determination and fury and the shimmering beast entangled with me. It feels an awful lot like justice.

Greer takes another long inhale, then blows out a gust of smoke so thick it could be a rising mist. Slowly, they stand. "However strongly I think you will fail, if you have the courage to go the distance, I suppose it would be just as foolish not to let you try."

I give the knife a final flip and slide it back into my belt. "Frankly, I don't give a damn what you think."

But Tavish does, even after all Greer has revealed themself to be. It's clear in the pinch of his brow and the tension in his lips. He clears his throat. "If I find something that will get my mother out of the way, not just work around her, but do what you want—replace her even." His diamond voice stutters, but he tightens his jaw and asks, "Would you stand by me, then?"

"If you plan to do that, you call me." They walk around their desk, cane still in hand. Their gaze passes from Elspeth to me, then to Tavish, landing there with certainty. "We *are* all entitled, every one of us company heads. If she does come down, I want to be there for it." They extend a little card to Tavish, pressing it against his hand until he takes it. "This is my radio frequency. Don't use it unless you have a proposition that will work." Their eyes narrow. "Do you know how to wield a sword cane?"

They tug Tavish's cane from him and press their own model into his hands instead. The black wood and silver accents fit him perfectly. Tavish slides his fingers over it, his expression softening.

So does Greer's, somehow, turning almost timid. Almost brave. "The uh, insulated hilt should keep any of the BA's shock sticks from affecting you. It was your grandmother's and her great-grandfather's before her—no Findlay's ever touched it. Use it in a way that'd make her proud or don't use it at all."

"I will," Tavish says, and his diamond voice has never been more his than this, not a thing of Findlays but of power itself.

Greer huffs as they return to their desk and snatch up their glass. "I still don't want any of you in my house. So, fuck off before I change my mind." But as they lift their whiskey, I swear their lips twitch up.

I almost want to warn them about the rebellion that'll surely be arriving for their head soon. Almost. But when I told Ivor I wouldn't bring the BA down on them, I had meant it. So I usher us from the room without another word, stepping from the deep shadows into the bright desolation of the upper city. It feels like skipping time, the world moving forward while my emotions still recover from the last ordeal. I force myself to breathe and walk, and to think only about what lies in front of us.

With Tavish's expert guidance, we traverse the upper districts through backstreets and deserted alleys. We see little more than the occasional high-level worker, Tavish pulling us back and redirecting us whenever we come near a potential threat. Every ominous click of heels from a larger path and gentle whir of the passing trolley still wears on me, but the silence somehow scares me worse, too empty and echoing, as though the upper city holds its breath for the coming rebellion. My parasite watches everything I do with the kind of interest that demands attention without actually taking control, reminding me of how Alasdair's blue tabby would perch on my shoulder.

Even with our roundabout travel, we reach the lowest level of the Findlay Estates within the half hour. The guard at the workers' entrance has vanished, leaving the door locked, but we slip inside as a pair of whispering maids exit. Bowls of rising dough clutter the otherwise empty kitchen. I duck into the pantry to swipe a bottle of whiskey, taking a few long drags of it. It burns down my throat and lights a hearth in my chest. Even without the blurring buzz the rest of the bottle would offer, those few gulps steady me. I pause, the bottle dangling between my fingers. My hand moves on its own, leaving it on the counter. It's not my parasite's doing, and it's not mine. It's just ours.

We move deeper into the estate, navigating through the staff hallways once we reach the siblings' floor. On feet like a ghost, I sneak out into the main corridor to check for the cats. They're nowhere in sight and neither are their little, pearl-studded bowls or their clam litter box. I hope that's a good sign. They don't belong in this extravagant mausoleum alone.

Tavish leads us up a final set of stairs and through a door separating the estates from the corporation. From there, we have only to wind our way down a stairwell and enter the sentinel station surrounding the Trench's only entrance.

It takes me one perfectly aimed punch to knock down the man guarding it. I bind him with his own handcuffs and leave him in the supply closet. His security monitors display choppy, grey images of halls and rooms throughout the corporation, but none of them seem to show the Trench's lab itself.

Tavish runs his fingers over the series of bolts and ignation-fueled boxes that bar the door to it. His brow tightens. "I don't understand. The unlocking mechanism on this has been disabled. No one can pass through this door now, not even my mother."

Elspeth grins. They toss their wig to the side and stand with a dramatic flourish, one hand still grabbing the wall for support. "You want to bet on that?"

They draw the tiniest activated red ignit I've ever seen from a thick leather pouch at their waist, holding it delicately between their gloved fingers. Its glow looks as warm as it must feel against Elspeth's skin, for they quickly place it on top of the locking mechanism, shaking out their hand once free of it. "It fuels a heat pack for my back muscles. It's easier to keep them continuously activated instead of worrying about a transitioner," they explain.

Next, they unwrap something small and cloth covered to reveal an eruptstone, black but for a vein of rainbow that twinkles down its center like an aurora. Leaning away from the door, they drop the eruptstone onto the ignit. The moment the two rocks collide, the ignit burns white. Light expands from it in a small orb, silent and so bright it's impossible to see through. It covers most of the locking system, eating through the door around it. Just as soon as it had come, it vanishes. Everything its light touched is gone, leaving a clean-cut circle where nothing but air now exists. Elspeth plops into their wheelchair.

The door to the lab opens so quickly that I have to drag

the chair back to stop Elspeth from being run over. Three scientists scramble out. Shadows droop beneath their eyes, and their red hair hangs in a mess of frizz and oil.

"May we go? Trenches, is the lockdown over?"

Tavish steps toward them, every bit the compassionate princeling. "How long have you been in there? Who initiated it?"

The lead scientist releases a sound somewhere between a sob and a laugh. "The Trench has been locked for a week. Raghnaid's orders. No access in or out, not since—well—"

My parasite rumbles, tearing through my memories as if searching for words my life has never contained. It finds only my recollection of the dying ignit and the thousand curses I've uttered since I first set eyes on the thing sharing my body.

"Since what?" Tavish asks.

"Go see for yourself. That's why you're here, isn't it?" With that, the scientists leave, their footsteps rapidly vanishing down the hall. In one of the sentry monitors, half a dozen BA soldiers pace outside the front of the Findlay Inc. building.

My stomach flutters and drops, churning with a mixture of my own dread and my parasite's fear. "It's now or never."

We move through an entry chamber, past hanging lab coats and marked lockers and a little table piled with empty food containers, and into the main space of the lab. Dim, blue lights illuminate the room with an eerie underwater atmosphere that matches the massive tank at its center. A glass tunnel runs through it, but rocks block its nearest side, obscuring what lies within. The lab's ceiling stretches high above us, and the metal floor rattles faintly beneath our feet, nothing but empty air and descending darkness visible through its gaps.

I think I mean to stop, but my legs carry me up to the tank, hand extended. It thrums softly against my palm. "Elspeth, the translator?"

"Coming right up." They remove it from their watertight

bag and flip it on. Only static buzzes out. They wheel toward the tank.

"Wait—I have to do this alone." I don't know it until I say it, but it seems right. The aurora chose me. As much as I'm glad for Elspeth's help, and for Tavish's very presence, they don't have the same connection or dependence on this exchange that I do.

Elspeth's eyes shine with desire, but they give a terse nod and hold out the translator. "I respect that."

I take it, tucking it against my chest, and step up to the glass tunnel that leads through the tank. The rocks rise on either side of it, but as I enter, they wane outward, giving me a clear view of the tank's contents.

A hazy door slides down behind me, sealing me in a silent world of rainbow shimmers and water ripples. My parasite sings, not with words or tune, but with emotions, its excitement and terror and joy all rising in a crescendo as we stand amidst the Findlay auroras.

Beyond the tunnel's glass, their feather duster worms rise as tall as me, long stalks opening to flurries of wispy tentacles swirling slowly like feathers in a breeze. Unlike the mangroves in the Murk, these auroras don't hide within their hosts, but display themselves vibrantly in gashes of black that tear up the worms' sides, luminous colors radiating from within. Between the darkness and the rainbows, though, stretch a different kind of wound: blurs of sickly, ashen grey striping out the auroras' centers.

My parasite's song turns into a sob.

CHAPTER TWENTY-SIX

treachery in the third degree

In a single push, you're on the run.
One moment of fear. One solid shove.
I pulled the trigger, even if you held the gun.

THEY'RE DYING. LIKE THE ignits, they're degrading.

With the translator still tucked against my chest, I sink to the floor. It all fits: the ignit's failure, the sense of wrongness I felt when connecting with the auroras in the secret lab, my parasite's assertion that something terrible is happening, even Raghnaid's insistence that they collect my parasite—a functioning, healthy aurora—immediately.

And it all hurts, from the love my parasite has inspired in me to the knowledge that whatever is happening here will come to the South sooner or later. To my home.

The translator buzzes, and a convoluted mess of overlapping voices rises from it.

"This one is new."

"I do not think—"

"Are they not latched?"

I cover the speaker with one hand and raise my voice, hoping it transfers through the walls. "Please, one at a time."

"It can understand." The translator degrades into

unintelligible syllables, then dies to static before a single voice returns: "You, host, speak: why do you do this?"

I don't know if the odd phrasing is natural or a failing of Elspeth's translator. I choose to ignore it. "I'm from the South, where your kind live in trees and are left to do as they wish. I've come because I want to help you—because the aurora inside me wants to help you."

A buzz rises from the translator again, too many auroras speaking at once for the machine to catch them all accurately. When the chatter finally gives way to a single being, it sounds sharper somehow, despite the monotone of the translator's preprogrammed voice. "The origin of our failing is of the place from which our energy comes. We feel it like a dream, but we are here, not there, and we are too weak to pass between. We cannot see the cause, nor the solution."

I leap to my feet, leaving the translator on the floor so I can pace. "Then what the fuck can I do?"

The translator spits out static so empty and useless that I feel it in my chest like a knife. When the aurora finally speaks again, I nearly miss its voice. "The sickest of us were taken to another place. They are in pain, so much pain. We feel their screaming. They may give to you their remaining strength, that it will help your aurora see into the place from which we fell—see what the cause of this dying." That term for the ancient beings sounds odd coming from the translator, knowing that Elspeth programmed it with the only word they had to describe the creatures and not the one the auroras use for themselves.

"Another place? You mean Lachlan's laboratory in the Findlay tower?" As I come to the other end of the hallway, I turn, but my gaze catches on the space where the final two feather duster worms must once have stood. Only chucks of rock remain, splintered at their centers as though someone hacked into them.

I rub my face. *Do you agree with them? With enough energy, can you find out what's causing this death in the first place?*

My parasite releases a rush of agreement combined with flashes of larger and larger ignits that I take as its indication of the ridiculous amount of energy it requires, but it still twists and churns anxiously. It draws out my blade and flicks it between our fingers. The Trench auroras' plight is only a small piece in a larger puzzle. But if I can help the auroras in pain, then they can help me. Can help us. I don't have any other options. And our time to choose is running out.

I turn back toward the Trench auroras. "Is there anything I can do for you before I go?" The moment the question comes out of my mouth, I feel both the echo and the initiation of it from my parasite, its longing to help so strong it's more a part of me than my own limbs. "Feeding on ignation made my aurora stronger. Can it do the same to you?"

"Perhaps. But perhaps we, like our kin, are too far gone." It pauses; the static seems like some kind of thoughtful hum. "Return, when you are able, and we may see."

I give the knife a final flip and slip it back into my belt. "I'll try."

I feel as though my entire being is still just a reverberating question mark, but I can think of nothing else to ask. I shut off the machine. The sound of the auroras' overlapping voices remains, replayed in my head as I stare at their withering owners. It hurts, a physical pain that squeezes my heart.

My parasite curls closer. Gently, it tugs at my memories of death.

I know. Their dying hurts us both.

But as much as I feel its agreement, frustration mixes in. It pulls up the dream it gave me, back when I slept in Tavish's room, focusing in on the image of its recreated self, so like me yet twisted, oversaturated, a stained-glass version of the person I see in the mirror. I recall the way it pointed to itself: *'I get odder the more you know of me.'*

My stomach twists. *You're dying, too, or will be, at least.*

This time its affirmation is endless and sad. It finds a new memory, this one of Lilias threatening me from my own porch. The pounding terror and guilt of that day rages through us, the emotions that forced me to make a deal with Lilias even though I knew there was a high chance of things ending badly, because the other option was to let her ravage my home—the only other option I could see at the time, anyway. Just as no one would be here to save the auroras without my parasite.

A thought creeps in from some backwashed crack, like it's lived in my head all my life, just waiting to be noticed. I try to swallow it down, but it won't go. Now that it's reared its head, I have to let it run its course. *If we can't figure out how to fix this, will I die too?*

It draws up a memory of monsoon clouds so thick I can smell the coming storm. *'Only hold off a little longer.'*

I breathe out. *Then we'll do this quickly. We'll figure out what's causing the death and stop it. Soon you'll be back in a mangrove, happy and healthy, with your kin the same.*

Its warmth floods through me as we leave the Trench. A quiet lab greets us. Tavish holds a little portable radio in one hand and fiddles with Greer's card. His gaze seems to stare straight through the rocks around the tank and to the auroras within. He slips the radio away. I glance at Elspeth, but they shake their head. He didn't call.

I hand Elspeth back their translator. "The Trench auroras are failing like their ignits. Two of them were taken up to Lachlan's lab. If I can get to them, there's a chance my aurora can figure out what's causing all of this."

Tavish scrapes at one of his cuticles. "My father's lab must have been converted from one of the old tower rooms— it would be too obvious to build an entirely new chamber."

"I saw some of it in my nightmare." The haziness of dreams still clouds its edges, but with my parasite wrapped so firmly through my mind, we pull it up in an instant. "Fancy, high ceilings, lots of glass."

"Until last year, my mother hosted small, elite parties in a ballroom attached to the Findlay tower's underside by a spiral staircase—apparently you can see the entire city through the glass tiles of the floor. She closed it when a maintenance report came in that the support holding it to the tower had rusted through, but no one has ever finished the repairs. Hosting a secret lab inside could certainly be a reason for that. We'd have to walk though most of the estate to get there though."

"What about the private elevators?" Elspeth asks, pointing across the room to a set of gleaming metal doors with a high-tech brooch reader. "It has to lead to somewhere in the estate. Since the front entrance was disabled, they'd still be bringing out the samples and carrying in food from somewhere, specifically a somewhere nobody else in the company would notice."

I grunt, not feeling the level of relief I'm sure I should be with all my parasite's lingering agitation still in my system. "Do you have another eruptstone for it?"

"That was my only one."

Tavish fiddles with his brooch. Its crown pattern shines once more with silver streams of ignation. "Elspeth refilled it from the lab's supply." He swallows. "There's a chance the elevator might open for me."

"It's worth a try." My grimace of a smile feels wrong pressing against my cheeks.

Elspeth rolls their chair back a little. "You two go on. There must be documentation of the auroras' states here somewhere. It would improve our understanding of their situation, show us what they have and haven't tried yet, what they might have learned in the process. I want to find it."

I nod. "If we haven't returned by the time you do, leave without us. Don't wait. Take what you can and help these auroras."

"I'll save the day for you, don't fret yourself." Elspeth smirks. "Just be careful, you two."

Our walk across the lab seems to take a thousand strides. Tavish chews on his tongue as he holds his brooch up to the lock. The light glides over it, once, then again.

My parasite and I exchange hopes. Our heart catches.

The lock beeps. Slowly, the elevator opens.

Tavish's grip on his brooch tightens to the point of fragility, as though he might break himself on its edges. "If Mother programmed it with my coat, then she must have planned for me to be included at some point." His voice hitches with something. Longing. Sentiment. Melancholy. The sound of a coin flipping. "This all might have been different had I been working alongside her here."

'Just barely enough.' My parasite repeats Greer's words with a sardonic twist. Even after all he's done, all the pain and poverty he's witnessed, he's still entitled.

He takes one step forward, one step into the elevator. Then he stops. "Helping the auroras is imperative, but I'm no more use to you storming a lab than Elspeth is. I came with you, but what have I managed to actually do for us, except give up the last of my inheritance in Glenrigg? I'm no fighter, no scientist. I'm not a rebel or a leader or a savior. All I ken is to swing a bit of bureaucracy in my favor, to win a couple battles so we all get by." Tavish's voice quavers—breaking glass in place of a diamond. But it stays in one piece. "That is something I *can* do though. I'm my mother's only living child. We're made it past the BA already; I think I can convince her to take me back and defend me, innocent or not. If I spin your quest to save the auroras just the right way—"

"You are not telling her about that!" My fear is cold as ice, but beneath it burns something like outrage. Raghnaid spent her life abusing the auroras. She has no right to be a part of saving them now. It doesn't matter that I, too, have caused them pain—caused pain to one in particular. I still won't work with her. We won't work with her. "You're not telling her about me." I almost say *us*, but I don't know which us I'm referring to—to my parasite and me, or to Tavish and my presence here.

"Then I can distract her! I'll go through the company, throwing such a fuss about the auroras dying and her incompetence that she'll be focused on nothing else for hours. She won't even think to look for you until you're long gone. I can do that. I can be of help that way."

"No!" I object, stepping into the elevator to face him even if he can't see me. "You shouldn't have to put yourself under her control again." I try to breathe, but each inhale is like a billow stoking the fire. "I know that back in the pool room, you wouldn't finish what Malloch had started with her, but that might be the only way to set things right here. Could any of the other heads touch you if you were the one in control of Findlay Inc.? Could anyone stop us from helping the auroras however is needed? You're strong enough to do it. I believe that."

"Maybe I don't want to *be* that strong! I don't want to risk losing my home if I fail. And I don't want to kill her." Those last words come out so small, so soft, they seem to exist for too little time to have been real, but the desperation on Tavish's face is undeniable.

"I know," I whisper. Because I felt the same, once. I didn't want to risk my own home, and I didn't want to kill a villain. Now there's no *I* in that emotion, only a *we* burning so brightly I swear I could light Lilias on fire with a single look. But whatever Tavish's feelings, there's still a *me* that knows his path doesn't have to veer from mine just yet. He can crawl back to his old life later.

Tavish tightens his fingers, his chin lifting. "But I do have the skills and the strength to buy you more time. This is my way to help us both get through this."

Us both. But not together. "And possibly be thrown in prison afterward? That's absurd!"

A line of blood drips from one of the scabs along the side of his cuticles. It reminds me of Ailsa. "At least I'd still be in Maraheem."

Perhaps the longing in his statement should hit me like an anvil or a hammer or a knife, but my heart had broken itself already in preparation for this moment. I knew it would come. I knew anything we had would be temporary. "And me?" The question seems too delicate for something that splits me apart so. "Where will I be?"

Tavish's chest heaves, just once, and he tips his chin away from me. "You wanted to go home."

Somehow, this is what hurts. Not that he wants to stay, but that he knows I want to go. That he's known that all along. Both of us playing this game with each other while knowing whatever we felt, whatever we wanted, it was liminal.

We were liminal.

But what can I say to that? That I've changed my mind? That I'll stay here with him, if only he doesn't put himself in danger on some bleak, reckless mission? It wouldn't be the truth. I tug fiercely at my fishnet gloves, trying to tuck in their frays and only making them worse. Worse in the same way I've made this worse, the way I've drawn it out and frayed it into ruined smithereens.

As though sensing my silent motion, Tavish finds my hands with his. He lifts one of them to his chest—the one striped with the black of my parasite, though I'm not sure if he knows. His fingers shake. "Ruby . . ."

I want—I need—just one more hour of him before I go back to being no one from a no-man's land. It won't ruin his chances at returning to his old life, if that's still what he's bent on. If he wants to worm his way back into his mother's good graces, he'll still be able to do it afterward.

I slip my palm into his hair, clutching him as though I can keep him there with just my touch. "You're coming." I grip his head in both my hands. "We're doing this together."

Pain twists Tavish's lips, but he swallows it in one solid gulp, leaving only cracks behind. "Ruby." This time he forms my name with determination.

It's no longer a coin toss. He's made his decision. I make mine.

I step back, tugging him forward, just a step. A single step, putting him fully into the elevator. The polished silver walls reflect back our haggard outlines, our anger blurred and our fear intensified. The doors automatically close behind Tavish.

The sound of their locking hits him like a physical blow. His face hardens, his edges growing sharp. His fingers shake.

Guilt hits me like a handover. He may be entitled, but I am worse: I'm justified.

I wait for him to cut me to pieces with his diamond voice, but instead, a set of sirens roars to life, piercing through the quiet of the elevator in the same rhythm as the signal for the closing of the gates. My stomach twists. "Lilias must have convinced the bar to do it tonight." I realize what I've said a moment too late, and realize, too, that I had forgotten—forgotten I couldn't tell him everything.

Tavish's brow goes from furrowed to pinched, from confusion to pain. "Lilias? She was there?" He strangles his words just as he does the top of his cane.

I cringe. "She and Ivor are running the rebellion together."

"You didn't tell me!"

"You would have wanted to go after her, like at Glenrigg," I object. "Then, where would we be? She would have killed you, and I would never have made it here!"

"I might have been willing to let her go if you'd asked." He shudders. "But that—that's not—you hid it from me. You didn't even respect me enough to—"

"I'm sorry!" And I mean it, but I also know I wouldn't change what I did. He would have left. He would have left if he'd known, and then Lilias would have put a bullet through his head, and Ivor would have likely let her do it, and I—

'I think I'm justified,' my parasite whispers, but it sounds like my voice, feels like my thought. A cringe runs through us, formed of my guilt and our shared disappointment.

"Maybe I didn't tell you, but I had good reason." I add softly, "At least, I thought I did. I'm sorry, Tavish."

"You say that as though it can change something."

"And you said I was more important!" I realize it only after the words come out: *Your life*, he'd said. *Your life is more important.* Not me. Maybe never me—the me that was always temporary. That understanding twists into me like a row of thorns, piercing me painfully in place when I should be falling. I feel as though I bleed bitterness and breathe humiliation. As though either the man standing before me isn't the person I've thought him to be, or else I'm not that person. "I *am* sorry I dragged you into this. You're right. You should not be coming with me."

"Well, I'm here now." He says it like a threat instead of a promise.

As we rise, he fiddles with his brooch, rubbing his fingers along the ornamental waves, his lowered brow casting heavy shadows over his detached gaze, and his expression unreadable. He seems like the same man I pulled into bed this morning, the one I moaned with. The one I laughed with. The one who wanted me back.

And I still, despite it all, want him too.

Hesitantly, I reach out. The moment my fingers brush his shoulder, he withdraws. The recoil feels no less painful than a punch, a brawl without the release of physical contact. I wish he would truly hit me instead.

As the elevator comes to a halt, I feel no relief, not even hope, my raw heart beating a little too fast. I burst out of the opening doors, carrying myself into the empty Findlay tower on ghostly feet. I trip over a cat.

Lavender hisses and pins back her ears as she scampers out of range of my flailing limbs, her silver fur fluffed up. The sound of her anger carries down the hall.

"Can no one catch that damned cat already?" Raghnaid shouts, the click of her heels following.

A click that comes steadily toward us.

Lavender curls herself beneath the nearest ornamental end table. I am not so fast.

Raghnaid's blue dress mimics a stormy sea, swathes of sheer grey fabric curling off it and swirling behind her in ringlets as she enters the hall. She wears all ten strands of her pearls spooling downward around her neck until they are buried in the lace of her high bodice. Her silver hair streams in majestic waves, and her heels click like a pair of champagne glasses. She sees me, and her brow shoots up.

I yank Tavish's ornamental knife free of my belt, but she draws her own weapon with the same speed. The pearl-studded pistol must be a recent addition to her outfit, but she holds it expertly. Her manicured nails fit perfectly over the trigger.

"I didn't suppose you'd be the one to return," she says, her Findlay voice piercing even now.

From the corner of my eye, I can just make out Tavish standing in the elevator. As he steps forward, his cane bumps my boot. He tips his head toward his mother, and with three assured strides, he plants himself between us.

I want to shout at him to go back, to let my parasite and I take our chances. We ate bullets in the pulse of Glenrigg's ignit, maybe we'll be strong enough still. Even so, Tavish's dedication stirs something in me, fierce and full and warm, edged in guilt and torn by shame. Maybe I'm not the most important thing in his life, but mine is still worth something to him. And that's better than I can say of most anyone else.

The sight of him removes all trace of Raghnaid's shock. "Ah, my son."

Tavish spreads his arms, making himself larger. "I don't know if you care enough to listen to me, not after the murders that I've been wrongfully levied with, and perhaps not even before, but whatever you do to him, let it be done to me first. If he dies, let it also be the end of the Findlay line." He speaks with her same crystal edge, every inch a Findlay as she is, every inch as determined and beautiful and dangerous.

As diamond cuts diamond, it seems to pierce her. "Tavish." Her lips dip, her brow quickly following. "I did you a disservice. If you had my tutelage, you could have been Alasdair's equal, even his better. I never allowed you to grow to your full potential." She steadies herself, as if that one moment of sadness is all she needs to move on. "I would like to change that."

"Maraheem has already lost itself," Tavish snaps. "The auroras are dying, and you hid it, even from me."

She casts him a stern look. "Something may be amiss with the auroras, but Maraheem has not fallen yet. We still have enough ignation flowing through our walls to run this city for a millennium. We will put down this petty, little uprising like we've done each before it. And then, we can start afresh, with a new aurora. We can even work to turn the lower into a place where uprisings are unnecessary. Haven't you spoken of a healthier city? Is that not the world you strive for with your charities, one where there's no talk of revolt, no unhappy lowers?"

Tavish takes a breath, and then another, and with each, he seems to find himself. "It *was* what I wanted."

My heart skips as though its beat dances between our separating paths. Despite my parasite's warmth, our chest seems to freeze over. We stutter, not in shock, but in fear. In agony.

"This is where that future starts, with knocking down the current upheaval." Raghnaid's face doesn't change, but her voice turns sparkling and bright. "Help me, as my heir. I will personally deny all charges against you with whatever force necessary. I will prepare you as I did your brother. Your great-great-grandmother may have been the Findlay who turned this city into a gem, but you could become the

Findlay who finally polishes it."

Her offer fades into silence as Tavish stands there, shoulders back and his grip on his cane loosening.

"Tavish, please." I don't know what I'm asking for, only know that my heart hurts. And that this is wrong, for him and for us and for me. "Tavish . . ."

He inhales, drawing himself into something peppered in fire. "I want a part in managing the aurora research. I will not be kept out of what's rightfully mine, nor will I see our company ruin itself through recklessness or ignorance."

"You have your brother's ambition and your sister's caution. It puts me to shame." Raghnaid's fingers brush the lace of her dress, absentmindedly flitting just above her heart. "You will be the first person I consult on any decisions related to the auroras."

"Including the one behind me?"

"Including that one."

I feel numb.

Slowly, Tavish lowers his arms. "I accept then, and I will hold you to it."

"You would not be a child of mine if you didn't," Raghnaid replies. She calls behind her, and her bodyguard appears with two other black-clothed fighters I don't recognize, each holding a pair of sparkling electric sticks. "Disarm and bind the aurora's host. We'll deal with it once the rebellion is quashed."

Tavish holds up a hand. "Allow me."

In two steps he's at my side. I have to lower my knife to stop from nicking him. He props his cane against an end table and draws his fingers down my parasite-wrapped arm. My devastation is so stark that we can't move, can't resist, can't even think as he pulls the weapon from our grip.

He smiles. "Trust me, I *can* do good here."

My lungs force themselves open and closed in reply, my parasite doing the work of keeping us standing as I sob inside. Questions, demands, accusations, confessions all whip through my mind, blown on a wind too violent and shocking to pin down. The words that do finally come are bitter and black. "You could never let the stability of this life go, could you, *princeling*? It's just barely enough for you, isn't it?"

And how much can I truly blame him? This palace is his home, and he wants the normalcy of it. He wants to walk down his streets and file his paperwork and be the voice of reason in his twisted family. And as long as his voice is good and reasonable and working for the betterment of the city, then maybe he can tell himself that's enough.

But it never will be.

I am justified. I am so very justified, my resentment scorching through me to spill from my lips. "Nowhere without gilded walls and marble floors would have suited you anyway."

To his credit, he flinches. His hand on my wrist tightens, and his voice lowers, dark as mine. "You're right, I imagine. I'm certainly not one to lie drunk in the grass. Or to find keys above doorframes."

He pulls away from me in one fluid, perfect, terrible motion and strides past, moving through the room with so much purpose that he doesn't even trip when his foot catches on the edge of a rug. And he's gone. I'm here, and he's gone.

CHAPTER TWENTY-SEVEN

the bright and the bitter

Barrel smoking, fist empty, the bullet no anomaly.
Your forgiveness or not, I offer an apology.
Never were you the moon, even if I were the sea.
Caught in my gale, tossed to and fro,
you were merely a ship
that I should have let go.
Fist empty, barrel smoking.
One shot too late.
Once my waters are calm, might I still change this fate?

TAVISH ABSCONDS FROM MY life without flourish or tarnish, there one moment and absent the next. Raghnaid follows him down. The bodyguards advance, electricity crackling along their sticks. They say something and wave me threateningly toward a set of double doors at the far end of the hall—the opposite direction from where Tavish has vanished—but their words seem to bounce off my ears in a sea of static.

Tavish left me.

I take a step back, my legs weak and my head light. My silent feet seem to not quite touch the ground. One of my heels hits the cane Tavish set down when he took his knife back. He must have forgotten it.

But when have I ever seen Tavish forget something, much

less his aid?

The guards' incoherent demands grow louder, reverberating with the roar inside my head. I grab the cane. Its blade slips out with a quick twist. The rapier feels unfamiliar in my hands, but it makes no difference—the guards are too shocked to block my first few frantic lunges.

I cut through the outside of the nearest one's leg and twirl to slash the back of another's arm. The blade slices so clean I can almost believe I didn't make contact until the blood spurts forth, pulsing like a heartbeat. The last guard swipes her electric stick against the sword cane, but her expression pinches as the current never reaches me. My parasite cradles around me, our desperation melding into something nearly feral. We grab the stick, eating up its power, and shove our blade straight through her shoulder. It sticks there as she stumbles to her knees. We let it go.

I'm certainly not one to lie drunk in the grass.

Tavish hadn't simply contradicted my statement but referenced the garden beneath the glass-bottomed pool, even the key above the doorframe. A key which could hide me in a room known to none of the other Findlays, where I could wait in peace. Wait to see if Tavish returns for me before the rebellion flips this estate upside down with their yellow ignit. If I had let him go when he asked, if I had told him all that Lilias and Ivor were planning so he knew the scope of their threat, if I had considered his desires as real options so I could have helped him better help himself—if I had put my trust in him then—maybe I could also put my trust in him now. But even his best intentions will be ruined by the things I didn't tell him.

There will be no lying drunk in the grass for me tonight, at least not here.

I could run back to the coast, find a bottle of something amber and a lush, green lawn. I could let the auroras in Lachlan's lab suffer until their final breath and hope my parasite and I live long enough for us to find the energy it needs somewhere else—back in the Murk, perhaps. Maybe the person Lilias dragged across the sea wouldn't have. Maybe, after so much failure, he would have finally given in, been happy just to spend his final days drinking on his porch, knowing the creature consuming him would die sooner or later, too. But that same creature roars through me, all adrenaline and rage and love. Behind those ballroom doors is something it wants. Something we want.

Fuck it all?

My parasite reflects the feeling in undiluted agreement.

Two of the guards struggle to right themselves, calling for aid. I dash past them, down the hall, and through the dramatic double doors that must lead to Lachlan's lab. I take the stairs beyond in tremendous, perfectly silent bounds. Lavender speeds past me. Each of her leaps lands in a clunk.

The steps twist, leading beneath the tower proper. They end in an air lock. My parasite and I slip through it, slamming the locking mechanism the moment the door seals.

An elegant hallway extends ten strides before me. Gilded arches line its peaked ceiling, its frosted-glass floor carved with patterns that twist and turn like a sea breeze. A set of hanging tarps block the far end behind a cluttered supply of building materials and brassy helmets, its *closed for renovations* sign hanging crooked. The sounds that echo from beyond the screens are too pointed to be construction: the clink of glass and calm, almost hushed voices.

I crouch behind the makeshift walls. Lavender curls so tightly around my calves I think she means to become my second parasite. Carefully, I peek through the gap in the screens to survey the main room.

The original ballroom still lurks beneath the laboratory's transformed surface. Chandeliers of pointed diamonds dangle from the ceiling, though most of the lighting comes from clinical overbright bulbs on stands. Behind shelves of vials and chemicals, the wallpaper boasts silver-and-gold inlay swirling in majestic waves, and where a band might play atop a polished marble dais now sits a series of monitors that resemble those from the security booth in the main lab. Glass sheets form huge tiles of the floor, revealing the upper city sprawled below, its towers and tunnels and domes all gleaming in the night. We are so near to the giant channel where submersibles descend to the central gate that I feel I should be able to spot the war currently happening there.

The Findlays' careless waste of all this wealth prickles along my skin, but it's nothing compared to the fury that burns through me at the sight of the ignation mutants imprisoned in glass cells near the ballroom's giant viewing windows to my left. They pace within: Cats striped in vibrant colors, and dogs with splotches lined by sapphire and emerald and ruby. A family of wolves howls across a barrier, even the pups covered in the rainbow gashes. Their vocalizations agitate two walruses with lacerations of red and orange cutting up their tusks and into their eyes. A white bear lies in a heap in the cell beside them, its side barely rising beneath wide tears of color that seem to extend into its bones.

My parasite rattles within my rib cage, our anger shaking its way through us as we fix our gaze on the final cell. The conspiracy theorist from my dream sits at its center, her already ragged lower-city garb torn and sullied. Jean, her name was. But she's not Jean anymore.

The colorful gashes line her skin, cutting up her exposed limbs and across her face. They sear up her cheeks and through her irises, slicing open a hole that seems to extend eternally. Those terrible eyes track through the lab, furious and fascinated, and when she moves, she does so in mangled twitches, as though she hasn't quite the measure of her own body.

I have to smother the pure fury my parasite and I share before it can overwhelm us. Despite how bound our emotions are, this wrath feels a hair different from mine, almost religious in nature. Where I see a horror that defies ethics, my parasite finds a trespass on all that it stands for, all that it is, all that it holds dear. It feels like the heel of Lilias's boot hitting Blossom's side over and over and over again.

It takes every leftover part of me to shush us, gently containing the rage until it's directable. *We'll fix this, whatever it is. We'll make it right.*

Not-Jean focuses on the other side of the ballroom-lab, cocking her head in sharp motions, and I shift the tarp screen slightly to follow her gaze.

Twenty feet to my right, a couple white-coated researchers stand by an enormous tank set against the wall, a small stairway allowing them to reach inside the top. Two dying auroras lie within, their stalks attached to broken pieces of the trench rock. Their greying forms are more ash than velvet, lashed and maimed, their glowing veins of blues and greens and reds pulsing between strains of grey.

A shudder runs down my spine, peeling off in waves through my parasite. We almost can't watch as a researcher heats a blade edged in the dark, rainbow-strewn eruptstone that Elspeth used to detonate their ignit. Her gloved hands reach into the tank. We tremble with shared misery when she cuts into the aurora's velvety exterior, searing a chunk free from the already mutilated creature. The aurora's feathery tendrils jerk and writhe. Beneath my parasite's anger comes a sob, and I barely hold back the whimper that rises in our throat.

The researcher crushes the severed piece and dissolves it into a vial, bringing it to a white lab bench where another scientist works at a microscope. "This might be the last sample we can take today without overstressing the auroras."

"Lachlan won't like that."

The first researcher snorts. "If Lachlan is so convinced we'll find this mystery compound, then he can be the one to kill the auroras himself."

She leaves the microscope bench for another pair of researchers standing at a row of tables a little farther away.

Even from this distance, I can clearly make out the substance they load into their tiny syringe, the liquid twice as shimmery and iridescent as ignation but with a base that isn't just silver, or even white, but a color deeper and stronger than that, something so bright it clings to the back of my eyes and turns black as I blink. I'm ready to dismiss it as some new ignit product, but my parasite yanks up a memory of my blood in Lachlan's lab, encircling it feverishly. My skin tingles at the resemblance, as though they took that blood and removed the red.

They gather around one of the tables, where they've strapped down a half-shaved dog on its side. It jerks against its bindings and growls as they wheel ignation-filled metal equipment around it, using pulleys and cranks to aim lenses like giant guns, and flat plates like shields.

"Ready?" the one with the syringe asks, waiting for the others to flip a series of switches before injecting his terrible mixture into the animal. "Start the clock."

The test subject's eyes go black, lit from within by a plethora of colors. As one, the ignation mutants all turn toward the injected dog. The animal's fear seems to spread through them the same way the mutated orca had manifested my calm on the beach in Falcre and my desperation in Ailsa's library. The canines bark and howl, the cats hiss and cower, the bear growls, curling tighter, and the walruses roll over each other in their fright. A maniacal laugh leaves Not-Jean, as terrifying as it is terror filled, sharp and so high it could almost be a scream. She clutches her arms over her face, shuddering.

My parasite freezes, and my blood chills with it. This is more than unethical—this is perverted. If my gods could see this, even they would shudder.

Lavender seems to understand the situation in a way the scientists clearly do not, and she tries her best to shoot into the folds of my flowing vest, digging her claws into me as she climbs. It kills me to pull her off and set her back onto the floor. I scoot her into a gap between two crates, promising to bring her with me when I leave.

Slipping out from behind the tarp screen, I creep along the benches at the edge of the room and grab a metal tube rack as though it's a club. The scientists freeze when they spot me halfway between the entrance and their tables. Confusion, then panic crosses their features. One points the eruptstone-tipped knife at me, but his weak grip and lopsided stance take all intimidation out of the motion. I dash forward and catch the knife between the rungs of the tube rack, twisting it from his grip. It clatters into the gap just below the aurora tank.

"Stay back." I mean it as a straightforward demand, but it comes out a hiss, dark, almost deranged.

They obey, joining the others around the injected dog with their hands raised. The animal releases a piercing howl that seems to crack the inside of my head, and the darkness in its eyes sloughs off. A thick, black liquid drains from the edges of its closed lids. It still breathes, but barely.

The laboratory door bangs so loud we all jump. A bodyguard charges through the tarps, the three I took down earlier following behind, bandaged and scowling.

Panic rebounds between my parasite and me, increasing into a crescendo. We lunge for the stairs to the aurora tank, but the first bodyguard comes in too fast. My parasite keeps reaching, though, even as I try to turn back to fight. We trip against the first step, dropping to our knees. The guard slams his stick square across our shoulders.

I stiffen as a jolt of electricity burns through me. My parasite flinches, its focus turning to the guard an instant too late to protect us. We take another blow, and a third. The world flickers and twists around us.

The guards grab our arms, dragging us across the floor, and before we can find the strength to struggle, they slam us down on one of the tables. The air leaves our lungs with such force that not even my parasite can breathe through it.

Someone shouts, and leather shackles clamp around our wrists and ankles, binding us to a table by short chains. I tug against them, and my parasite tries to slip into their locking mechanism, but the guard slams their stick into our gut at each attempt.

Tavish's voice echoes through my mind: *Trust me, I can do good here.*

And for some gods-forsaken, silt-breathing reason, all I can think of is how I shouldn't have held on to him so tight. Shouldn't have been so selfish with him. I could have accepted that it was time and let him go with one last kiss, could have had something of him to savor during this pain.

Damn me.

High heels click their way down the stairs. I lift my head to watch Raghnaid enter the lab, her dress fluttering, Lachlan behind her. Her attention momentarily catches on the creatures beyond the glass and the scientists moving the unconscious dog into a kennel in the corner.

"Well, well, dear husband, you've been up to something useful after all." Her gaze lands on me, and her mouth fixes between a grimace and a smirk. "Thank the Trench I was prudent enough not to leave you imbeciles for long."

Lachlan pushes his glasses farther up his bony nose. A curl of stringy, greying hair falls into his eyes, but he seems not to notice. "We've found a substance in his blood that, when injected into a subject, makes the mutants responsive to the subject's desires and emotions for a time. With a steady supply, we could craft an army, a workforce, whatever you desire."

"A twitchy workforce or an impulsive army that responds to a single person? I am not trusting anyone else with that much power," Raghnaid snaps, her voice consuming his. "Besides, the longer the aurora stays in the foreigner, the harder it will be to remove."

"We may be able to rein in the substance's effect or transform it into something that could be controlled at a distance by you, or even myself." Lachlan seems to add that last part in with an eager sort of hesitation, like he hopes she wouldn't quite notice. "If I had more time and resources to explore it—"

Raghnaid barely glances at him. "Draw what blood you can, but start the necessary scans while you do it. I won't sacrifice a perfectly good aurora for your whims."

"As you wish it." His cheek twitches though, and he watches, bug-eyed as Raghnaid approaches me.

"Was that promise you made Tavish a lie?" I demand of her, trying not to be consumed by the way she dismissively scans me in return, as though I were a smudge of dirt she's about to wipe off her trophy.

She doesn't answer. Instead, she flicks her fingers at the nearest scientist. "Record this: the foreigner acted out against our gracious security and in the process endangered his own life. In order to save the aurora, we were then forced to initiate removal procedures. Date, time, sign."

"Yes, of course." The scientist ducks his head, scribbling down in an official-looking notepad.

"Prep the full body mapping," Raghnaid announces. "I want to be able to cut this aurora out by the end of the hour."

My parasite tucks itself into my subconscious, coiling so small that the exhaustion I hadn't even realized it's been pressing to the side for me slinks back in waves. I don't push through the fatigue—I can't, its bulk too endless and annihilating for one person to conquer—but I fit it into my fury. Tired and disheartened, I can still choose not to give up on us. I can choose one last hope.

"If you pull it out, it won't latch for you!" I shout. "The auroras are intelligent creatures, like humans and selkies, and you've trapped them and cut them apart for your own gain. Even if you remove it, it won't bow to you. *We* won't bow."

In the silence, I can almost hear Raghnaid's stare. "Then

I'll tear you both apart and find a use for your scraps."

My parasite whimpers, and I can do nothing but hold to it.

The scientists scurry around the table with their machines. Lachlan dances through the fray, setting up tubes and bags. When he tightens a band around my arm and pokes an eruptstone-tipped needle into the crook of it, my parasite tries to close around the insertion, but the eruptstone seems to fight it right back. The liquid that runs into the nearest bag shines so brightly with those rainbow-radiating, too-white shimmers that I can barely see the red beneath. Raghnaid watches from a distance, but I feel her presence more strongly than the frantic beat of my own heart or the cold metal against my stiff back.

Our panic grows as our blood keeps draining. The machines run through a series of beeps and shifts, one scientist moving and calibrating them at consistent intervals. Time seems too slow and yet too fast, moments or minutes or hours between each bag of blood. A scientist stops to distill one into three shining vials while the rest of their team shut down the machines. The world turns a little hazy at the edges, and a slight rush resounds in the distance, like death is coming for me in the form of a waterfall.

My parasite's emotions slowly detach from mine as it writhes with a mixture of guilt and growing determination.

'Was prudent enough not to leave you,' it says, repeating Raghnaid's earlier words with a mournful twist, before adding a line from Malloch, *'Going to let you live.'*

You're what? I fight to find meaning it the mismatched phrases.

Instead of replying, it stirs. Inch by inch, it pulls itself up, a strand of it slipping free of my arm. Leaving me. Letting me go so my blood will turn red again and they won't have reason to dissect me. It's a ridiculous proposal: I could give Raghnaid and Lachlan my parasite on a silver platter, and I doubt they'd send me anywhere besides a watery grave at

313

this point. But the fact that my parasite offers it at all makes me almost laugh and almost cry.

As it pulls itself farther away from me, though, the freed tendril of its body changes. The rainbow of colors deep within its black form flickers out as the velvety surface turns brittle and ashen. It cries, its pain so violent it tears into me.

With every ounce of strength I have, every small piece of control I share over it, I pull it back into me. It shivers, curling through me like a hug. Slowly, the greyed-out slice of its body returns to normal.

You'll die.

'*Not letting us all die out,*' it protests. '*I could save you.*'

Don't. Despite my parasite's determination, its leaving will change little. But paired with that knowledge is a fiercer, truer reason I object—one I'm almost afraid to admit because it's too terrible and too beautiful. Instead, I repeat, *Don't you dare.*

Like a part of my subconscious, my parasite senses the things I can't yet say. It warms, all affection and wonder.

Above us, the scientists examine their backlit pictures: our body—our *bodies*—cut into slices and viewed straight through, as though my skin and organs have gone translucent around my bones. My parasite's black gashes curl across my ribs, filling the center of my chest. They work their way down through my stomach and into my gut. From the back of my neck, they weave through my brain, tendrils coiling into one of my eyes.

My chest tightens, but my parasite nudges it open again, flooding me with a rush of calming understanding. It fiddles through my memories, finally selecting Tavish's words, though it has to mangle them to get its point across: '*Have a bit of . . . life together.*'

I ignore the way it winds within me, clutching my organs, so close to full control, and focus instead on that final word. *Together.* We are doing this together. And that . . . that is amazing.

These last few days, I've dreaded Tavish's departure, mourned the betrayals in my past, grieved for the mother torn too soon from my young life, and all the while, my parasite has stayed with me, has moved me from one moment to the next when I couldn't move myself. Without it, perhaps my life would never have been at risk, would have been easier, simpler, just me and my front porch and a bottle of wine. Just me slowly sinking into myself. Just me dying alone, with no fight left.

The scientists point out parts of the diagram. Places to cut. My parasite bares its teeth at them, sending me another rush of affection. *'Together.'*

If one of us dies, we die together. And we die fighting, for us and for the auroras and, a little bit, for a damned drink. My only regret is that I won't be able to apologize to Tavish. That, and the auroras might all perish and the ignits fail and the mutation infection develop further with people like the Findlays exacerbating everything as they try to take advantage of it.

I curl my fists as the scientists prepare their blades. One of them leans over the table, replacing my full bag of blood with an empty one. It seems to fill slower. Perhaps a symptom of blood loss. Perhaps a sign that it's time to act.

Because there's something we've skipped over, a piece of knowledge that's been sitting at the back of my mind since they first bound us to this table. Something I fought so hard against but might be the only solution after all. The little bit of pure me left in my body still recoils from the knowing that there would be no going back from this. If we do it, there will be no scenario where my parasite dies and I do not. No scenario where I breathe, alone, in my own head, ever again. No scenario where the emotions I feel are really mine, where I can trust who I am to be fully and utterly me.

I want more time to think about it, to figure out how I, me, myself, truly feels. Time, the one thing we don't have.

But before I can pull on my parasite in one final

attempt—in the hopes that if we're stronger together now, that being even more together will make us stronger still—a fresh set of footsteps echoes down the stairs, interspersed by a softer rumble. All eyes turn to the entrance, and the lab goes still, until only my heartbeat remains. My heartbeat, entwined with the rapping of a cane.

CHAPTER TWENTY-EIGHT

with teeth and bureaucracy bared

But I am more than that sea, more than this situation,

more than the place between grief and desolation.

Not replaced, not consumed.

I control my own transformation.

Not past, not future, but the result of my actions.

I choose where to root and when to meander.

The world asks the questions.

I am the answer.

TAVISH ENTERS THE LAB, not as a princeling, but as a king, a god, an almighty. The cane I left in the guard's shoulder clicks in front of him, black as the night sky with shining silver accents. His cuticles are bloody, but a victor's smile lights his face, bold and brave and beautiful.

His name rises in my throat, but it sticks like cotton, like grief, as though the only way to burst through it is with an apology I don't know how to make. All my parasite and I can force out is a whisper. "I'm here."

Tavish's left cheek spasms, and an angry flush appears around his ears. When he speaks, though, his voice resounds in majesty. "Raghnaid, I've considered your offer from earlier, but I'm afraid I must decline. You see, there is a statute set by the assembly under the request of your father and the heads of the O'Cain Fishery, Druiminn Health, Callum and Callum, and the BA, which states that all research efforts should be conducted within regulated, assembly-approved laboratories. This converted ballroom is in direct defiance of that rule."

Raghnaid's lips curl ever so slightly, the hint of a snarl forming. "And you believe you can blackmail me with this, do you?"

"Indeed, I absolutely could. I nearly did, too. I was sure threatening you would come back to haunt me, but it would have been safe, for the moment. It would have been barely enough." He plants his cane between his feet. "But then I remembered why that knowledge would make such potent blackmail—who else would want it."

Pride and grief well in my chest. Pride, because Tavish is, and will always be, so much stronger than either of us imagined. And grief, because my misguided love thought to hold him back from this. Thought he couldn't manage it.

He takes a step to the side. "Greer, Dr. Druiminn, Callums, and Macindoe, if you would be so kind?"

Greer steps between the tarp screens. Their glasses sit on a wrinkled nose, their lips drawn taut, but their glance at Tavish holds the slightest of smiles. They're trailed by a middle-aged woman with a frizz of light-strawberry hair tied back from her face, and a pair of well-dressed, older men as different as two red-haired, freckle-faced people could possibly be. The selkie who emerges behind them wears a scowl and a pocket handkerchief embroidered with the initials *BA* on the corner.

"Oddly enough," Tavish continues, "neither the Gayles nor Morvan Ros have heard of this particular lab either."

At that, three more women enter, two wearing heavy boots and coats more suited to mountain excursions than upper-district life, and the final boasting enough jewelry to sink a city. The group stops behind Tavish. They gaze around the room, some with jaws dropped and others with lips curled.

Despite the distance of Tavish's gaze, he seems to stare his mother down. "In light of this violation, and considering the great lengths at which you went to hide potentially citywide threats such as the ignation mutants and the auroras' sickness, I, as heir to Findlay Incorporated, have conducted an emergency radio board meeting, which voted to suspend you, Raghnaid Findlay, from any influence on this city or its corporations, pending a further assembly summit to remove you officially from any states of power and allow for all big seven corporations to contribute to the research and salvation of the auroras."

Raghnaid's brow pulls tight, her eyes a little too wide. She struggles over her words. "This was hardly even my laboratory—Lachlan is responsible for it; its creation, its upkeep. I thought it merely his futile hobby."

"Futile hobby?" Lachlan's cheeks burn red.

The youngest Findlay, last of his line, interrupts them both. "Silence." When he speaks, he surpasses his parents: devours them. His upper lip twists. "I take it back. The bureaucracy of this situation can be damned! This is a take-over, a coup. A formalized rebellion. It doesn't matter what legal loopholes you find or how you attempt to worm yourself back into power. I am seizing control of Findlay Inc. and all your other assets. Because unlike you, I will distribute ignation fairly and open aurora research to anyone looking to make a brighter future. And it seems that is enough to make a lot of people you've kept under your boot very, very supportive of me." His snarled lip turns into a smile. "This is where the war ends, Mother."

My heart swells, the adoration pouring into my parasite.

Macindoe steps forward. "Raghnaid Findlay, you will be taken into BA custody until this uprising of the lower districts is dealt with. I would sincerely love to see you resist."

"You cannot—" Raghnaid objects, but her voice has lost its edge, her words sinking into the background as one of the guards disarms her of her pearl-studded pistol.

"Tavish!" I call. None of the company heads give me so much as a glance, but Tavish's attention snaps in my direction. I jiggle my cuffs. "I'm afraid we've—I've—the aurora and I have accidentally been fools of the highest order."

"Good fuck, Ruby." Tavish rushes across the room, his cane clicking before him. He bumps his way around the table and finds the cuffs. "Someone get me a key! Now!" He snaps his fingers, and a scientist immediately shoves one into his palm, looking abashed. As though the expression is contagious, Tavish's cheeks redden and his shoulders slump as he unlocks my bindings. "I'm sorry I left. I only fully realized what I had to do after my mother appeared, and if I had told you outright—"

"You did tell me." I yank my wrist free and try to sit up. A wave of darkness tunnels my vision, but I breathe through it, and the world returns in stars. I cup Tavish's face, running my thumb along his cheek. I savor the feel of him, his presence, his whole being—brilliant and powerful and compassionate. "You're forgiven, utterly and forever. And you convinced them all to stand behind you! You spectacular, almighty princeling, you did it. You won."

He leans into my touch, but a trickle of moisture appears in the edges of his eyes. "Aye. I knew I had to remove her, even if it meant risking everything. I just needed a way to do it that wouldn't require bloodshed. Perhaps I am strong enough for violence, but no one should want to carry it through, not if there's another way." His single tear glistens off the crisscrossed lines of rainbow-filled black that twist beneath my fraying fishnet.

I wipe it away. "You are stronger still, stronger and braver than anyone who wields a knife."

A small sob leaves him. He holds the key so tightly that I worry for his fingers. "But while I was doing so, my mother put you on a table. Trenches—I failed you."

I grab his hand, key and all, and kiss him. A heartbeat of shocked hesitation separates us; then he melts against my mouth. As we break apart, we also come together, our foreheads bumping and then resting presently, neither of us ready to be our own beings yet. "You could never truly fail me, not if you were doing what was best for us all," I whisper. "I'm not perfect either. I should have let you make your own damn choices, even when they took you away from me. I'm sorry, too."

"You're forgiven." No edge, no stipulations. The words slip from Tavish like they were born in the world's earliest days, just waiting for the right time to be uttered. "The moment I left, you were my only concern. If I had gained the whole city but you had died, it would have been for nothing." Now he's the one who kisses me, soft and passionate all at once.

My lips tingle by the time we part, warmth spreading through me despite the cold of the table. "Lucky me, I have a strong, scheming prince to come to my rescue. Though, I think his city might require a bit more of his help." Gently, I nudge Tavish toward the company heads who wouldn't raise a finger to help Maraheem as a whole, but all of whom I know Tavish can control with ease if he puts his mind to it. "So go do your thing, princeling."

"Still not a prince." Tavish chuckles, all wind chimes and starlight. He turns back to the chaos of aristocrats.

My parasite warms me in his place. I can't tell if it's hope that floods us or the lingering effect of Tavish's kiss, a kiss to savor, whether we both make time for another or not. He's done it: won over the company heads, dethroned his mother, become one with his own flesh. He won his war.

The effects of it spiral through the lab. Greer takes inventory, trailed by the head of Druiminn Health and one of the Callums as though none of them quite trust each other to create an impartial tally. Raghnaid watches with narrowed eyes, her usual authority replaced by a bitter vacuum. There will be some kind of inferno to put down in her eventually. But after what Tavish has done today, I know he will handle it.

The loss of Lachlan's minuscule power sets him aflame as well, but he clearly has not the insight to restrain it. He grabs Greer's arm. A shock transfers between them, as though this is the first touch the siblings have shared in a decade. "This is my research," he shouts. "I worked for this— I married that fiend for this! You cannot take it away from me."

"Let go, Lach," Greer hisses. They shake him off with a harsh twist.

He jerks back. "But this is mine; it should all be mine!"

Their argument continues, but my parasite pulls our attention to the tank. Our vision shimmers as our shared eye focuses past the bonds of my human vision, turning the world to a silvery veil. We see the auroras as they are— filaments of light and dark forming into the shape of a feather duster worm with iridescent strings which stretch between the fabric of reality, connecting them to some other place. Some other dimension.

But even with my parasite's view, they look wrong. Half of their filaments glow with a brilliant white twined with shimmering black, while the rest appear hollow, as though ravenous termites have swooped in and left them with only weak husks of their flesh. And this disease, this corruption, this death, is spreading. We can nearly feel it turning our bones brittle and slashing ribbons out of our muscles.

All the energy—hope and fear, relief and doubt—that had filled me just minutes before leaks out, leaving me with the kind of exhaustion that sticks inside the chest, clogging up and weighing down. Tavish has won his war, but my parasite and I still have to win ours.

Apprehension slams us in the gut, so strong we nearly gag. A flicker of confusion—my confusion—proves the feeling isn't mine. With a deep breath, I filter through it to find its source. Desire sits on one hand, affection and agony on the other. And I understand: we're asking for these auroras to die for us, to die so we—so my parasite—might find a way to live. It tears at my heart, too.

Who are we to make that choice for them, for anyone? Who are we at all, two minds strung into one mess of a body, half apart and half each other? We, to save an ecosystem, a world, a life?

We are nothing. We are a hangover, a hollow threat, the bark without the bite, empty and aching and useless.

'You are stronger still.' My parasite whispers the phrase, but as it does, it curls itself around the words I'd spoken next, like it's claiming them, branding them into itself: *'I'm not perfect either.'*

Maybe perfection is overrated. A hollow threat is a threat, and to ache means to live. We breathe in, and out, and in again. *It's their choice*, I think. *If the auroras want to give us their strength, then it's their choice. They can believe in us or not. We'll do what we can with what they decide.*

My parasite releases a sob that makes me think of flower petals soaking up my mother's blood, but a calm affirmation fills us. Together, we're strong. We'll be stronger still.

Before we can attempt to slide from the table, though, one of the Callums swears loudly and calls for the radio to be turned to the emergency broadcast channel. It emits a soft, static-garbled alarm. All commotion stumbles to a halt as the announcer's quavering voice comes on.

"The BA has cut off the primary rebel party at the main gate and is securing the premises as we speak, but the small faction who came through during the initial breach an hour ago seemed to be continuing their ascension when we lost track of them again beneath the Findlay Estates two minutes past. Reports state that this group carries an ignit device which incapacities by some kind of hypnosis. All citizens between the Bubble Communication Center and the Findlay Estates are to shelter inside with their doors locked until further notice."

I wish my own heart didn't mirror the dread that creeps from face to face. I wish I could cheer the rebellion on and hope for the selfish snobbery of the upper districts to finally feel the spines of those they've been stepping on. But if Lilias takes this city, then the city itself will be better off, while everyone Lilias was willing to step on to gain the upper will be crushed alongside it.

My stomach turns.

"An update will be released as soon as we have one," the announcer reports, and with a click, the static returns.

The head of Bubble Entertainment squeals into the stillness and rushes the hallway exit like a panicked parrot, her glam and wealth flashing in her wake.

A bodyguard steps in. She grabs the frantic woman by the arm, looking as though she's trying her upmost to be polite as she says, "Ma'am, they're likely already in the building."

That simple statement launches the room into a ruckus of shouts and overlapping conversations from scientists and company heads and bodyguards alike, most too difficult to track with so many unfamiliar voices speaking at once.

"Can we barricade ourselves behind the air lock?"

"We build these large, single-entrance buildings without manual triggers for safety purposes. To activate it, the entire outcropping would have to break off from the main—"

"I saw Raghnaid's personal underboat docked off the tower entrance on our way in! We could—"

"We shouldn't run, we should fight!" Lachlan is easy enough to identify, his face so red he looks like he might combust. "The ignation mutants are a viable weapon, and this—this rebellion is the experiment of a lifetime. We have everything we need right here!"

"She's the one they're coming for." Greer points at Raghnaid. "If they passed every other estate to get here, you know they want her head."

"Then we give her to them!" someone shouts,

accompanied by multiple agreements.

"What will that solve?" Tavish sounds like no less the leader now than upon his initial entry, but he worries his little finger against the side of his cane. "Will they not want my blood next? Or yours?"

But all four bodyguards are already pulling cuffs from their belts with expressions between indifference and outright joy at the idea of binding their old boss.

The argument bounces around in the back of my head, each high-and-mighty, panic-laced voice only vaguely registering as my parasite and I argue, not with each other, but with the world at large—with the wooziness still hiding behind the backs of my eyes and the now panicking part of me that, however irrationally, had thought the worst was already fought and won.

It leaves my gaze to wander from Tavish's wobbling pinkie to Lachlan's furious sputtering to the calculating determination that calcifies Raghnaid's jaw. She tries to escape her approaching guards only to back into the crowd of arguing corporation heads. When she bumps into an exasperated Macindoe, she slips her hand beneath his jacket.

We realize in horror: if we know the war isn't over yet, then so does she. And she'll doom us to reclaim her victory.

CHAPTER TWENTY-NINE

death do us

Our spirit is not our only commodity.
A candle burns just as well as a body.
I must be the one to light the fire in me,
match by match.
Spark by spark.
And grant myself, too, my own apology.

DISMAY CASCADES BETWEEN MY parasite and I, tightening our chest and clogging our throat.

"Stop her," we shout, but Raghnaid is already drawing the pistol from under Macindoe's jacket. She fires two bullets through the chest of each approaching guard.

Tavish barely scoots out of the way as their bodies fall, a few drops of their blood splattering across his cheek. He wipes at the liquid, leaving a red smudge behind. His voice sounds hollow, but it cuts straight through the room's silent shock like a knife. "Mother, what have you done?"

"What I had to. Your father wanted an experiment, after all." Raghnaid smiles at Lachlan, all teeth and lust and blazing fervor, but she looks away from him too quickly to see the twitch in her husband's cheek, the way his scowl only deepens.

Tavish scowls as well. "You cannot—"

"I have, therefore I can." She snatches his cane with her free hand and tosses it to the side.

Tavish looks as if she slapped him. His shock and misery transfer straight into my parasite and me in the form of fury. We slip off the table. Our knees give out beneath us, our head swimming. Clasping the tabletop with one hand, we try again, slower, breathing through the darkness until the world returns.

Greer clears their throat, and for a moment, I hope. But they only back toward the lab's exit, palms raised in a supplicating gesture.

"Cowering as always?" Raghnaid scoffs. "Run if you'd like. You'll be dealt with in good time."

They flee. The other company heads follow, attempting to cover their panic with disdainful chin lifts and spiteful huffs. As they do, I track Raghnaid's gaze to the security screens on the corner dais. One of their hazy, black-and-white displays shows a band of rebels charging down a lavish estate corridor. Raghnaid's mouth twitches.

Two very different cities, two very different unrests, one from the bottom and the other from the top.

Somehow my parasite and I have to get Tavish out of here, past the rebellion, and free of Maraheem. Quickly. But before we leave, we need the energy of the dying auroras, or we'll be right back to where we started.

I take a small step, not quite toward Tavish and not quite toward the tank, either, the two beings in my body warring. Between us both, I can't tell who wants what. Another step. As soon as we let go of the table, our vision tunnels. We grab for the metal again.

Raghnaid turns toward the counters. "Let's see to that army, shall we?"

But Lachlan already holds the rack of my distilled blood. His hands quake around it as he looks from the vials to Raghnaid, his ambition so wild and reckless that it vibrates out of him.

As she stares at him, her surprise settles into understanding. "It's always you, isn't it? Forever trying to pull down my spotlight."

He laughs. "And always you, forever standing in my way."

"Until death," she says, and lifts her stolen gun. Without a twitch or a flinch or even a tightening of the brow, like she has played this out in her dreams, she pulls the trigger.

It only clicks.

Raghnaid Findlay, owner of the auroras, the most powerful woman in the North, looks at her weapon with the stunned expression of someone who has never had to number their life in bullets before. I almost laugh, but the sudden inhale makes my head spin.

Raghnaid drops the gun and launches herself at Lachlan, the curls of her dress waving behind her. They tumble like a pair of jaguars, rolling and crashing, the vials of my silvery blood pinched between them. As they come to a stop beside the aurora tank, Raghnaid's hand slides beneath it. She draws out the scientist's fallen eruptstone-tipped knife and plunges it into Lachlan's chest.

A little shudder goes through them both. Lachlan gasps as his wife pulls the blade back out. Gurgles of dark crimson seep through his shirt. A maniacal sound bubbles from him as he touches it. Raghnaid's grip tightens around her knife, but when he reaches for her, she doesn't stab again. He cups the side of her face. She jerks back, leaving streaks of red running down her cheek, and as she does, her gaze catches on the vials of my distilled blood—on the cracks now running through them. Their iridescent light spills onto Lachlan's stomach.

Panic takes Raghnaid. She clutches at the fabric. "No. No, it can't—"

"Mother?" Tavish shouts, half a king and half a child. Or, perhaps, all a king, now that the old king is dying. Which he doesn't know. But the way his chest quivers, he must guess.

If he stays here, he'll share his father's fate, one way or another. On the black-and-white security screens, more blood spills in the form of a burst of dark grey out the back of Greer's head as a small rebel band rounds on the company heads. But the thought of getting past Raghnaid and the rebels both—of just crossing the room—makes my head spin.

"Tavish?" I whisper.

His head whips toward me. "I'm here," he says, so softly that it seems his diamond voice is only for me. Slowly, he moves in my direction.

As he does, my parasite drags our attention back to Lachlan so fiercely that it nearly drops us to our knees as it slams me with its view of the world, colors taking on a silvery haze. Lachlan's chest heaves. The distilled blood soaked across it glows, the shine burning to black behind my eyes. It twists around his gash like a curious dog. Then, it dives in.

It splits into a hundred threads as it winds through him beneath the veil of his skin, like the light and dark through the auroras or the backlit pictures of my parasite through me. His back arches in a soundless scream, and the cords within him thrum.

Raghnaid curses and scrambles away, still clutching the knife. Her back hits the stairs.

Pained wails rise from the ignation mutants. Through my parasite's vision, I see the iridescent-lined blackness that flows through them, turning into those ghastly splotches of color where it brushes against their skin. Each strand within the mutants vibrates like an instrument being plucked.

The threads of my distilled blood vibrate in Lachlan, too, with each silent chord mirrored by the mutants a moment later: his pain, his death, played right into their souls through some kind of other-dimensional resonance. Not-Jean catches the chords with the most precision, echoing his being like they're one and the same. She clutches at her chest just where Lachlan's wound sits, her eyes pinched shut and her body stiff.

There is something terribly and utterly wrong about all of this—wrong in a way my parasite cannot explain and I cannot understand but can still feel, aching, blistering, overwhelming.

Lachlan's shuddering chest heaves a final time, then releases. His threads fray at the edges, curling into nothingness within him, until he is a husk again. A corpse. The room goes silent, each earsplitting howl and tragic whimper cut out as the mutants cease echoing his emotions.

Tavish stalls, halfway between the center of the lab and where I stand at the table. "Rubem?" he whispers again.

But his soft words are cut into by another sound: the slice of Raghnaid's eruptstone-tipped knife and her sharp, breathless muttering like the chink of diamond on diamond.

"I will . . . not lose," she snarls.

She stands at the top of the aurora tank's stairs, tendrils of glittering black dripping from her mouth as dark, thick, rainbow-laced lines work their way down her chin and across her throat, diving beneath her strings of pearls. Her irises turn a haunting array of colors against her whites. Her lips turn black.

Suddenly, the aurora within Raghnaid goes taut, stopping its progression. Her muscles strain as though she's forcing her will upon the creature. It rattles with anger.

I don't know which of us breaks free of our horror first, my parasite or me, but we have to do something, anything. We step around the table, toward the tank, each stride tunneling our vision further. Through the part of us that isn't in this body, we reach. But we can't quite grasp the other aurora's hand any longer, too much of its consciousness sealed away within Raghnaid's as they battle.

Threads of their fury and pain resonate through the mutants. The wolves snarl and grate their claws down the glass as the walruses bash their tusks and the cats hiss and leap. Mutated dolphins and sharks pound themselves against the translucent lab floor.

The whole building trembles as something larger and stronger crashes into it. An alarm blares, a red light flashing above the ignation mutants' cages. One by one, their doors slide open.

The mutants burst out, some ramming into each other with tooth and claw as others smash through shelves and scratch at the glass floor tiles as though they might tear the eyes from the mutated dolphins that snap at them from below. Through the howls and crashes, Tavish doesn't notice the emaciated bear loping toward him, doesn't feel its presence in his chest the way my parasite and I do, its rage almost as sharp as its teeth.

We tuck our body into a protective nook between the table and one of the lab machines and focus our attention on the bear, calling to it the way we did the orca. The strain of it aches in our bones the moment we do so, feeding off our limited strength. But the rhythm of the bear's threads shifts to match our own. It shies away from Tavish, circling him and snarling at the other ignation mutants.

A hot, wet line drips from my nose. My parasite wipes it off. We call to Tavish, but he turns away from us. We try to step toward him. I stumble, and my parasite catches us on the table.

Our attention slips to the security screens where a figure appears in the largest of them: Lilias, ignit peeking through her satchel as she wavers alone in the tower hallway. I feel just a hint of its energy already. She must be right above us. Fear vibrates through me, reflected off the bear protecting Tavish. It cowers away from a rampaging wolf, and I force myself to refocus.

The mutants slam their ignation-strengthened bodies into the lab, and an ominous crunching resounds through the ceiling. The room jerks to one side, throwing me against the table. Supplies spill out of their containment, and the eruptstone-tipped knife clatters across the floor. The mutants slide and skid with a chorus of screeching as the ceiling grinds like metal coming apart. Raghnaid seems not to notice.

Water cascades through the entrance hallway, but it's cut off by what must be the automatic emergency air lock rising into place out of sight at the top of the twisting stairs. In a series of tremors so loud they seem to bend my spine, the lab detaches from the Findlay tower. It falls through the water, taking us with it as it descends toward the seafloor with the layered city of Maraheem in its way.

Raghnaid and her aurora's newfound fear only sharpen the mutants' aggression. A walrus plows toward me. Half supported by the table, my parasite and I take another step back. Not-Jean climbs over the table behind us, fists raised. I turn to keep her in my sights, my parasite lifting our hands defensively. Panic wells through our already pounding heart and rushes like the sea through our ears. There's not enough of us—not enough *in* us—to fight Not-Jean and the walruses, to dodge or reflect my emotion onto them and still control the bear protecting Tavish.

Through the fray, the lab's primary ignation supply gleams at me, its rainbow twinkle coming and going as though winking. But its glass casket sits on the far end of the lab counters, past the dying aurora's tank and leaping mutants, above a quickly approaching city. My parasite yanks my attention nearer to the stuff winding through the lab equipment. It all looks too hard to access but for one handheld device on a nearby counter: the ignation shining in a tube along the side.

A table blocks us from it. Our attention slides between it and the bear protecting Tavish, between the walrus and Not-Jean and the wolf pack surging around us. Between every piece of our end, closing in.

The lab shakes with such force that I collapse into Not-Jean as the room's glass bottom crashes into one of the upper's enormous, enclosed bridges. It twists once more before sliding over the side and falling into a channel between the buildings.

The mutants right themselves before I can, Not-Jean latching onto my neck from behind as the walrus swings its tusks toward my head. A fluffy, silver streak tears up its back, launching off its head and catapulting over my shoulder with a yowl. Our hearts skip, and my parasite and I understand in unison: Lavender. Blessed, beautiful Lavender. She crashes into Not-Jean's face, claws extended and teeth bared. The scream the mutated conspiracy theorist releases sounds more beast than selkie.

As Not-Jean's hands jerk, I duck out of her grasp, avoiding the walrus in the same motion. Lavender leaps from Not-Jean's face into my arms. I tuck her to my chest and dive us both across the table. As we roll, the blackness comes in, yanking at my grip on Tavish's bear protector. But I can't let go. I can't. We can't. We—

A mutated wolf crashes into the counter we need. The handheld device clatters across the floor. We snatch it up, but its back plate won't budge. Lavender cries, trying to bury herself beneath our chin, and we can feel the ignation mutants closing in even if we can't see more than mangled glimpses of the world.

I barely catch the flash of metal and glass through the clear tile beneath me as the lab crashes into the top of a silver building. It skids along the building's roof, grinding its way toward the city's great central waterway. One corner of the room bows. Water trickles from it.

My parasite and I tighten my grip on the lab device and think of home. Instead, I see a brilliant, strong selkie with a young jaguar in his lap, and Lavender in my own, and I don't know whether we're in the Manduka or in Maraheem, but I know that it's what I want, whatever the cost. Tavish and I are only liminal if we choose something else over each other.

With all the strength my parasite and I can muster, we slam its ignation-filled side into the floor. It shatters, silver liquid slipping out. We slap our palm into it. The glass cuts through our fraying fishnets and into our skin, the pain of it coming too fast and strong for my preoccupied parasite to stop. Something glorious seeps out of the wreckage, something that feels like light and tastes like wine and smells like honey. Like Tavish.

We embrace it. My parasite's tendrils shoot and slide, closing a bit more of the small gap between us, but I relish the sensation. The room keeps grinding around us, the warp in the far wall growing more prominent, and we fling the energy we've acquired outward, reverberating it through the mutants in a single desire: stop the lab.

The mutants within go perfectly still as the orca braces itself against the building's exterior. Dolphins and sharks join it, even a few larger fish press into the glass wall to slow the room's sliding. It grinds to a terrible halt at the edge of a roof. It quavers, the massive waterway looming just beyond with its drop straight to the main gate. The bowing wall rattles, still leaking. But it holds.

Raghnaid screams.

With the last of our new energy, we spear our emotions, not at the mutants, but at her, willing, wanting, needing her to stop this. We hit the same wall as before. With a final push, we shove through it, roaring our desire into the tangled being of Raghnaid and the aurora. They both scream this time, and a wave of blackness rolls over my parasite and me.

We drift, counting our breaths, lying on the floor. One. Two. Six. Nine. Ten.

As our consciousness steadies, I hear Lavender whimper. She shoves her face pleadingly against my shoulder, my neck, my head. I force my eyes open.

The mutants move almost listlessly around us now, their chaotic twitching and pacing coming in bursts. One of the cats with blue-grey tabby stripes gashed in vibrant green and red creeps across a bodyguard's corpse, leaving bloody paw prints behind. The sight of her tears into me.

Lavender's ears perk toward her old companion. Before I can stop her, she scampers forward, only to trail after Not-Blue in confusion, her shoulders hunched and tail low.

They pass Raghnaid, crumpled on the tank stairs. I can't tell whether she's alive. Her chest seems not to rise, and the threads woven through her look more ash than light. When my parasite and I try to resonate with the mutants in her place, though, a little more blood trickles from our nose, and something hot and hazy slips from our ear. We pull back, drawing all our remaining energy into ourself, harboring it like it's a boat in a hurricane, and turn our attention to Tavish.

As he turns toward the lab entrance, he wavers from one leg to another like a man half-drunk, half-enthralled. His voice sounds wrong in an eerily familiar way, a little tired and a lot intoxicated. "This place smells like a nosebleed."

Then he giggles. Hundreds of feet below the tower, below the rebels, below where Lilias should be standing with her stolen yellow ignit, Tavish giggles over the scent of corpses.

I feel not only drained, but dried and stretched. It's not enough to have stood against the grasping queen beside her dying throne. Win all the battles, and another war only forms from the wreckage.

Kill all the villains, and new ones will arise.

CHAPTER THIRTY

to care enough

Hollow but not vacant, alight, alive, and free,
I will reach for you, palm open and heart unhindered.
Be not the moon or the tide, nor the ship to my sea.
Be not fire or ember or near-destroyed cinder.
Be merely the one who walks beside me
as we create a new path, both of us builders.
Be, most of all: just be.

MY PARASITE AND I grasp at the energy buzzing from the nearby yellow ignit, refilling what we lost like pouring shot glasses into an empty lake. But it has to be enough. At least enough to get to Tavish, to protect him somehow.

We ignore every alarm our body blares and slowly, painfully, slide one arm under us. Our head swims and tosses, turning dark then light. With shaking arms, we use the table to pull ourself up.

Lilias knocks aside a fallen tarp screen and strolls into the lab. The yellow ignit pokes out of her satchel, her left hand still bandaged around her missing fingers. Even from this distance, I pick out the tiny yellow earpiece shining in her ear, the same ones her team wore in Glenrigg. Her team, stranded somewhere above us, and somewhere below as well, abandoned by her.

The cruelty of it all infuriates me. "Your allies are dying in the main square without that ignit."

Her shoulders bounce. "I never had enough earpieces for all of them." She bears the guilt of that like it's nothing, her chin tipped up and her shoulders relaxed. Her gaze sweeps over the laboratory wreckage, taking in the ignation mutants stepping aimlessly through spilled supplies and the water dripping from the corner of the far wall. Her brow lifts at the limp body of Raghnaid. "And here I was looking forward to killing her myself." She turns her attention my way. If the Findlay's voice cuts, hers stabs, volatile barbs spat like darts. "You'll have to do instead . . ."

"You can't cut the aurora out of me anymore. It'll die without a host."

"How convenient for you." She drops the satchel with the ignit for Tavish to fawn over and strides toward me. "*Too* convenient. I think I'll just have to test it."

I see her coming, but I can't stop our collision any more than I can stop the tide as it rushes in from the sea. She balls her unbandaged hand into a fist. The impulse to block and duck clashes between my parasite and me, and instead of doing either, we take her punch straight across the jaw. Our head snaps to the side. The pain rocks us. Lilias slams a knee into our side, and we stumble.

Trembling, we try to regain our footing. We have to hit back. But all we have right now is bark, no bite, and so little even of that.

Lilias laughs. "You could have pulled that aurora from its tree long before you ever shook my hand—you could have used it to fight me, to take power, to do anything."

As she speaks, we tighten our fingers and launch them at her throat in a cheap shot made for pain. She slips to one side so quickly it seems like she phases through another dimension, or perhaps that's just our vision spinning, waning, weaving in and out of itself.

Lilias sweeps in, her whole hand on our collar and the other grabbing our hair with its remaining thumb and finger stubs. "But you ken the difference between you and me? I will burn down everyone who stands between myself and justice. And maybe that damns me, but at least I win."

She brings up her knee again, slamming it into our gut as she yanks our body down to meet it. We stagger back. She kicks us in the stomach, sending us toppling into the lab table. We grab its edge, gasping, but the air feels stale, like nothingness tinged in blood. No amount is enough.

"I will bring justice, no matter what price it comes at." Lilias's words take on a growl. She grabs us again. "No trials, no loopholes, no mercy."

We feel the flecks of spit she scatters across our face—she, this woman who has come to end her war at any cost. A deep, oxygen-deprived part of me wants to cackle at her, to tell her that every war is just a battle in something even larger than itself. Instead, we bare our teeth. "That sounds an awful lot like Raghnaid." Now it's our face that's too close to hers, snarling at her, even if we have no energy to back our threat. "I thought you were killing the villains, not becoming them."

She scoffs. "At least I'll let an assembly have Maraheem when I'm done with it—a real one, not the puppet show the corps put on. But only after I've cleaned out this house, this city of every last one of these hollow, pompous nobs, clean it out so my son can live in it, safe and happy and wanting for nothing."

"My aurora and I aren't them. You're fight isn't with us." We know it won't change her mind even before we say it.

Her grip tightens around the back of our neck, her thumb pressing into our pulse, and her pinkie caressing the soft back of our skull with the stumps of her missing fingers tucked between, as though she might kiss us or kill us. "You, I'm going to kill just because you've been such a damn pain in the arse. I'd like that aurora first, but I can compromise."

Her favorite little knife flicks out from the cuff of her sleeve. We grab at her arm, but she only redirects her stab. The blade buries into our side, its edge grating against a rib.

The pain hits us, sharp and white-hot. We swarm it, strands of us—of my parasite—slipping around the wound as the weapon is withdrawn, knitting the flesh back together, just as those same strands knit deeper into the rest of our—my—being. The agony turns to a tingle, and everything else goes with it: distant, diluted, numb. We swim in our own head, watching the ground pulse, Lilias's hand pinning us against the dull pressure of the table.

River-born.

Murk blood.

I hear them both as her blade sinks in again.

The next breath we draw is agony. It's fire and metal, and something in our lungs, wet, red, rusting there. We try to mend it like we did the last, pressing one piece of ourself through the space after another. With every single suture, ten other strands tear into deeper spaces, into something that could be a life, a soul, a future. It eats us—it eats me. It eats me up.

Attempting to latch.

I can't quite wrap my mind around it, around me and I and myself. But I see glimpses of my old life—of quiet days and quieter nights, sitting on my porch with a case of wine, surrounded by my pets, the world sparkling and blissful. Of no-man's land. Of everything I want to return to.

Everything I thought I wanted.

But no longer. I pull my parasite deeper, feeding it myself as I strain, not against it, but beside it. Its work comes to a sudden halt when the last of our energy snaps out. Our eyes roll, our consciousness slipping for a moment. We have nothing left—not enough even to become one.

Lilias swarms us from every side, only pieces of her making it through our failing comprehension: her metallic smell, the heat of her presence, the fire in her voice.

"You're pathetic," she says. "I will see justice done. But you? You would have run, sooner or later, back to that little shack in the jungle, back to your apathy. You won't right any of the wrongs you made under my thumb. You won't help any of the people who've helped you." With each initial *you*, she twists the knife in, twice, thrice, a fourth time.

The pain should diminish. Everything else has. But the pain, the pain keeps coming.

"Maybe that's smart. Why risk your old life for anything more?"

Just good enough. Greer had accused Tavish of the same thing. And he had shattered that accusation, shamed it, shown the world there could be better. Now he sits at the laboratory's useless entrance, giggling as he drags a finger back and forth over the yellow ignit.

Lilias follows our gaze, our stupid, irresponsible gaze. And she grins, not a villain but a monster. "There's one *better thing* you do want, though, isn't there? One thing here you actually care about." She drops us.

We slump against the table. Each time our lungs expand, they gurgle. Our side has gone from fire to ice, but the cloth pressed against it is drenched. We can't look down. We can't look anywhere but Lilias.

She walks slow, sure strides toward Tavish. "But do you care *enough*?"

We try to let go of the table, try to reach out to the mutants still pacing listlessly, try to turn back time and do this all differently, but our head goes to darkness and knives. Blood drips from the corner of our mouth.

Each step seems to take longer the closer Lilias comes to Tavish. She nudges his cheek with her blade. He bats it away like it's a fly and returns to his intoxicated mutterings, a smear of red welling on his freckled skin.

She rears back and kicks him in the shoulder, knocking him to the ground. The wet thud of it echoes in our mind, playing over the memory of her boot crunching into my favorite caiman until its chest went slack and its eyes glazed over. With her heel, she presses Tavish down. "Give me the aurora, and maybe he can live."

"Please." It's all we can force through the lake of blood in our lungs. "Please."

She shrugs and slams her heel into Tavish's chest. He yelps, a breathless, terrible sound that chokes me. It draws pure joy across Lilias's features though; cruel, merciless joy.

"Stop!" It's a scream and a sob, and I think we're crawling, want to be crawling, but our body doesn't get any closer to Lilias. Any closer to Tavish.

What will you do when you reach her? It's my thought, but my parasite wraps around it, forcing me to feel it in my shaking bones. *I'll die with him. I won't let him be alone*, I reply.

"You prefer the aurora, then, do you? Really?" Lilias's bloody boot plows into Tavish's side, and he mumbles something small and heartbreaking, so much confusion in his voice that it fractures us. "Pathetic."

Our heart seizes as though it's curling in on itself, withering away. "What do you even need it for?" The words gurgle, and we cough blood between them, too weak to wipe it from our lips. "You already won. The ignation, the Trench, the city, it's all yours. What use will one more aurora be?"

"Use?" She scoffs. "You have it. I want it. What else is there?" It's not a question, but a way of being: all emotion and no rationale. She brings her heel down again, producing a sickening crack like the splintered sound of a rib breaking, or perhaps just my imagination hoping for nothing worse. "So, do you care enough to save him?"

Care enough.

In the midst of our anguish, her question knocks the last week into perfect clarity. I care a whole damn lot. And maybe half of that started as my parasite's fury and pain, but the other half of that is ours, our shared affection, our desire to make a change, one which goes beyond rage, beyond vengeance, beyond a return to life as we knew it. We do not feel as we once did, neither me nor my parasite. And thank the gods for that.

Because we're done not caring. This outskirts existence isn't just barely enough for us.

But caring or not, we can't give Lilias that half of ourself; we don't have the strength to peel ourself apart any more than we do to fully become one. And if we did, if we ripped in half and I handed my parasite over, and if by some miracle it survived, we have no assurances Lilias won't kill Tavish all the same. We would be bargaining with a bomb.

There has to be another option.

Something touches us, something so foreign yet so familiar: the dying second aurora still in its tank but clinging to our other body with a phantom hand. They weave their fingers through ours and squeeze.

Their emotions pour into us, yearning and peace and pain. We feel their name on the edges of our consciousness, not in words but in song, a lament so hopeful it brings us to tears. This dying aurora wants to give us its remaining energy, not to see into the other dimension, not to save its kind, but just for us. For us, for our life, for our future.

For my stupid, selfish, wonderful parasite and me, together. And I know letting my parasite latch to me won't be easy. It will mean being reminded of my past and urged toward my future. It will mean sharing myself and my flaws and my addictions and my lowest points. And it will mean having someone there to remind me that I am more than those.

Together? I ask.

Its answer comes like a flood, so full of warmth and affection that it nearly surpasses our grief for a split second. *'Life together,'* then, *'asshole.'*

Silt-breather.

I relax into my parasite, and as one, we squeeze the dying aurora's otherworldly hand with ours. Its energy rushes into us. We can't tear our gaze from Lilias, her cruel grin fixed to Tavish and her knee lifting for another stomp, but we can feel the motion of the energy twisting out of the aurora's body in the tank, up through the strands that connected it to the other dimension, and down through our own filaments, so bright and hot and wonderful. As it burns up, we resurrect from the ashes. All we know how to say is: *Thank you.*

We feel its acknowledgement as its consciousness fades.

With this fresh rush of energy, I pull my parasite—my aurora—deeper into myself. We wind together, one cell at a time, overlapping until there is no more *us*, no more *we*, because I am the aurora, and the aurora is me, a single person, perfectly united. My aurora's tendrils course through me, supporting every beat of my heart. They throw themselves into the lake of blood forming in my lungs, transporting and transforming and clearing. I take in one deep, fresh breath, then another.

Lilias's boot slams into Tavish, too heavy, too bloody. He yelps and curls, but the yellow ignit does its work, and he relaxes back into intoxicated mutterings and tiny sobs, so confused as to why he hurts that it breaks my heart anew.

As I pull my legs under me, my fishnet gloves catch on a fallen test tube rack. I tear them off, leaving only the ones woven through my skin in iridescent crisscrosses. I stand. My head goes light, and a gush of blood leaves my side, but I pull the wound closed with a fresh weave of my aurora flesh.

Lilias's gaze snaps to me. She stiffens.

I step toward her. "Maybe you were right, once." My voice sounds like the old human one and more, as though its deep pitch harbors something else within it. A threat, perhaps. Or a promise. "But I'm not that man. Not anymore." I smile. The black cords that wind erratic patterns up one side of my face tear beneath my gums and coil around my incisors, forming them into rainbow-flashing fangs. "It turns out I am still getting odder."

As I pass the cask of ignation, I slam my fist into the side.

The glass splinters. The silvery liquid gushes out through a hole in its center, spilling over my hand and along my arm. It keeps pouring out behind me.

Lilias could press her blade to Tavish's throat and stop me in my tracks, but she has always been more rage than reason. She launches herself at me.

The ignation's energy pounds through me as I duck her attack. I twist the knife from her grip and drive it into her shoulder so hard she slams to the floor. It pierces out the other side of her back as I pin her down. The tip of the blade scrapes against the glass tile. Her shriek reverberates through the room. She struggles, but I hold her down as her blood trickles across the transparent flooring.

The silver glow of the spilled ignation mixes with it. As it reaches the knife in Lilias's back, her lurking and seething turns to tension. Her back arches, and her mouth opens in a soundless scream that looks as though she might swallow the world.

In my aurora vision, the ignation touching Lilias's wound seems to tear open a doorway in her flesh. The same threads that wind through the ignation mutants rush into her. They hit her heart, then her brain.

On her skin, the gashes form. They cut up her neck, blue and orange, and tear along her cheeks, taking over one eye with scarlet so violent it could be blood. She draws in a breath like it's the first one she's ever taken. When she looks at me, I know—know—she's not Lilias anymore.

A rush of revulsion floods me, because I also know, even if I don't know why, that this is wrong in every way—wrong for the living, conscious thing that's threaded through her and wrong for the powerful, terrible woman it has overwhelmed. My chest catches it in something between a curse and a scream. I jerk back from her.

She cocks her head, staring blankly. Not-Blue walks by us, Lavender still trailing her in bewilderment. Not-Jean watches, her shoulders wavering, and to our left the orca curiously rubs its rainbow-marred back against the laboratory's glass viewing wall. Slowly, in twitches and lurches, Lilias stands, her rage gone. After all she spent to get here, everyone she stepped on and everything she kicked aside, she meanders with the rest of the ignation-mutated herd, a ghost awaiting orders.

Her yellow earpiece gleams on the floor. I snatch it, wiping it free of blood and ignation as I rush to Tavish. The rest of the world seems to turn a little slower than my pounding heart. With shaky hands, I press the little device into his ear.

A sob instantly wracks him. He huddles inward, his arms wrapped loosely around himself as though he's still fighting to understand what happened to him. So much blood coats him. It streaks across his face and stains his once-stunning blue outfit and clumps his fiery-red hair in scarlet. The shimmering silver glow of the spilled ignation mixes with it, giving a ghastly beauty to the terrible sight.

My chest aches. I drop to the ground at his side, touching him gently, like he might shatter under too much pressure. "It's over, she's gone."

Some of the tightness leaves his face. "Ruby?"

"I'm here." As tenderly as I can, I lift him into my arms, cupping his head with one hand. "Where does it hurt?"

"It—" The word seems to catch in his throat. He chokes on it.

And it comes again, the rushing of the ignation, the tearing open of space itself, this time through the tiny burst vessels in a boot-sized scrape along Tavish's side. The chaotic other-world threads twist into him, cutting the first small gashes through his insides. He screams.

CHAPTER THIRTY-ONE

edge of the knife

I will not ignite for you, but our flames we'll exchange.

I will not rise for you, but each other we'll raise.

Lifting together, we'll go higher than ever.

My hold, always a caress, not a cage.

Committing each day to knowing you better,

in mutual endeavor, and not a crusade.

Heart open, voice tender,

it's to you, I surrender.

"YOU CAN'T HAVE HIM." The demand comes from all parts of me, human and aurora equally, resounding inside and out. Though I am only a single me, I feel half of myself form into a separate physical presence: a person made from shards of glass, a hundred rainbows sparkling in its center.

'I won't let him die.' This time, the voice in my mind isn't built on memories but formed of darkness and warmth and velvet.

No, a gruffer, more human voice replies, *neither will I.*

With the aurora part of my mind, I reach for the threads crashing into Tavish. I grit my teeth and do my best to yank them out of him. It feels like guiding metal ropes with a pair of magnets, but the effects appear in the natural world almost instantly, silver liquid dripping in rivulets as the mutation strands revert their course. The gashes seal inside him, and the last of the ignation seeps from his wound.

He drags in a gasp, his eyelashes fluttering.

"Tavish?" I fight the urge to shake him or else to grip him tighter. "Tav!" What if I wasn't fast enough, what if the bestial presence brought by the threads harmed something internal—inside his body or inside his mind? I brush his blood-soaked curls out of his face, leaving a new red smear in their wake, and pray to any and every god in the entire sun-forsaken North that he'll be whole, be all right, be unharmed by the chaos that nearly took him over. "Please, please, Tav."

Tavish makes a sound, low and whimpered. "I am here."

I sob in relief and hold him. The ignation mutants pace, and the radio plays static; endless, haunting static. The white noise surrounds us, bearing down, almost suffocating. It's broken by a sound that shouldn't be—by the crack of the ignation cask.

Raghnaid stands before it, one hand plunged into the liquid at its base. She sways as the shimmering liquid seeps into her. Beneath her skin the glaring white and void-black of her aurora fights its last, but she controls it now the way mine had controlled me—the way I had controlled my human.

Fatigue turns my anger into a self-destructive dread. My strength feels flimsy, like the force of ten mugs of coffee after a week without sleep. More energy can only sustain my body as long as my mind can keep up. Mine is bruised, cracked, torn out, and sewn hastily back together.

But what I am—hungover or functional, bark or bite—it doesn't matter compared to this. This must be stopped. For Tavish, who won his war a hundred times over already. For Maraheem, which a perfectly human Raghnaid already managed to grind beneath her heel. For the aurora inside her. And for me.

Perhaps, for me most of all. Because I care.

I lay Tavish gently onto the floor. His mouth opens, but I press a finger to his lips. Letting go of him feels like twisting back my ribs to yank out my heart and set it in the path of a rampage. But the worst thing I could do for us right now is to hold to him too tightly.

Silent as a ghost, I slip behind the ignation-feasting Raghnaid, so near she should feel my presence, but it seems I'm still made of mist and the in-between things, perhaps now more than ever. I curl my fingers into the iridescent gashes in her neck and use the aurora part of my mind to yank. Raghnaid howls.

Her aurora writhes, trying to coil itself around me—into me, past me, through me—but even with my aid, it only manages to tremble free of Raghnaid's hold for heartbeats at a time, ripping chaotically in and out of place.

The same way I grabbed at her, Raghnaid grabs back. Her reverberating threads hit mine like a white-hot inferno. When our consciousnesses meet, hers blazes so fast and hard it feels like an explosion has gone off inside me. I curl into myself, forcing my lungs to open and close, but it's not enough. She flings me away with unnatural force. Her anger spills outward, thrusting them on the mutants around us. They turn toward me with snarls and howls, teeth bared.

Something crashes against the lab.

The building teeters, one side rising as the other lowers. With a terrible grinding, it skids over the edge of the roof it's perched upon. It catches. The cracked corner bows around its gilded wallpaper. As it comes loose, the trickling leak turns into a violent stream. The lab falls. It drops like a brick into the submersible channel, sinking steadily toward the main gate.

Seawater rushes through the room, carrying the eruptstone-tipped knife past my arm and plunging it toward the yellow ignit. My breath hitches, and panic rushes from me, resonating into the nearest ignation mutant—a small cat. It leaps in front of the weapon before it can collide with the ignit and detonate us all into nothingness. We both flinch as the blade sinks into its side, but it barely seems to notice, the wound turning a bright emerald against blue-grey tabby stripes.

I realize what I've done with a pang to the chest.

The lab jolts me out of my mourning when it hits the top of the gate, slotting into the submersible's water-removal chamber. Supplies bob in the rising flood as it pushes us toward the ceiling. Tavish treads water, one hand on the wall. I snatch his cane and attempt to swim to him.

A blast of radio static tears through the room so loud it seems to burn out the inside of my eardrums for a moment before it fades to a hum.

"People of the lower"—Ivor Reid's gruff voice crackles in and out, disrupted by shouts and explosions—"we can still win this. I beg every one of you who fought back when you were stepped on and survived through the pain when you couldn't: Don't give up. Make us a new Maraheem."

The air lock opens beneath the lab's glass floor. We drop into the main gate, skidding against one of the empty submersible platforms and hitting the ground with a deafening crash. The bowed wall tears away. Water shoots up my nose as it pushes us all out of the lab and across the floor of the main gate, through the open entrances to the upper's central square.

Still clinging to Tavish's cane, I roll across the square, wet and ragged, and come to a painful stop.

A barricade of tables and chairs and a lopsided cart has been erected in front of the central fountain. Most of its living occupants—and all the soldiers assaulting them—turn from fighters into inebriated fools as the giant ignit rolls to a stop near Tavish's feet, leaving Tavish and the pulsing yellow the only things between the overwhelmed rebels and Raghnaid. Even the upper-city civilians watching from balconies and street edges seem to relax, goofy grins appearing on the nearest. The few sober people in the room transition from surprise to fear. From the edge of the barricade, Ivor fumbles with a pistol.

Raghnaid is already on her feet. Her wet hair clings to her face, and her aurora-wrought skin glitters. Ignation mutants gather at her back—wolves, walruses, and bear. What was once Jean crouches on her right, and the knife-plunged Not-Blue hisses near her feet. Beyond the massive glass windows behind her, a crown forms of orca, dolphins, sharks, and fish. Raghnaid's desire vibrates within them all.

I grip Tavish's cane tighter. If I could get to her, I could end this. But it has to be now. I'm out of energy, and the rest of Maraheem is out of time.

Raghnaid's gaze moves over Tavish, over the barricade, and lands on me. Her eyes flash.

Not-Lilias streaks toward me. I barely stand in time for her to swing at my face with unnatural speed and a snarl that's bestial even for her. Fire rushes through my limbs. I thrust my own desires onto her, overwhelming Raghnaid's for an instant. My little remaining strength falters. Darkness swarms close, tunneling my vision. I swear I'm tearing back in two, but the halves I once was no longer have a neat seam, and each popped stitch takes part of myself with it.

Not-Lilias's full fist hits me, coating my world in a new set of sparks, but I dodge her next blow, attempting and failing to slip around her back, toward Raghnaid. Tavish struggles to his feet in front of her, dripping and pale. The control in each motion, the poise and determination despite his clear confusion, fills me with affection.

Raghnaid steps up to him, her mutants snarling behind her. Her voice seems to pierce a hole in their violent howls, a black diamond now, reverberating on a new level. "Stand aside, Son. I've no wish to kill you."

Tavish's fingers curl into fists. He does not move.

As I duck Not-Lilias's next assault, my heart pounds for

him, each beat screaming no. *No, I just saved you. No, you're finally mine. No, I can't lose you now.* But beneath that rhythm roars a pride so strong it makes my chest ache. This is my Tavish, beautiful and brave and good. I would not ask him to be anyone else.

I tighten my hold on his cane and crack my elbow into Lilias's jaw. She barely stumbles, her threads repairing what little damage I did. Her knee slams into my side.

"These people have been wounded by us long enough." Tavish's words come out strong and righteous. "I won't let you—"

Raghnaid lifts an aurora-gashed hand and knocks him to the ground. I cry out as he falls. She balls her sopping skirt in one hand and steps over him.

Her mutants burst forward. Sea life slams into the square's windows as the land beasts leap for the necks of intoxicated rebels.

I try to slip around Not-Lilias once more, but she grabs me, one hand around my neck and the other at my arm, nails digging in like claws. Through the crashing bodies and flying blood, I see Tavish rise again. He turns toward his mother's back, something in his gait, in his shoulders, in the tip of his chin. Something strong.

I roll the cane across the main square. As it clatters beneath the feet of the charging mutants, I tug at them, letting my will redirect theirs just enough to lift paws and tails, letting the cane's course stay true. It comes to rest against Tavish's boot.

He picks it up and stands. Its blade gleams as he unsheathes it. His grip tightens. He steps forward, once, twice, tracking a sound I can't hear above the howls of the mutants. He finds his mother's shoulder with the tips of his fingers. Face contorted, she swings back toward him.

He plunges the sword cane into her chest.

Raghnaid's aurora fibers twist to stop it, but the being they belong to fights back. It finds the rhythm of threads with my own, its hand with mine in the reality we both once came from, and with the last of my energy, I pour into it the way its kin poured into me. Be enough, please, please be enough.

Through the network of threads that weave from this world to the other, I feel the Trench auroras reaching too. They sing in a soundless string of vibrations, their language cascading through me like a kind of energy. Together, we give Tavish's blade space to rend. To end this.

Tavish must feel the lessened resistance, because his lips curl, not in joy or despair, but resolution. He leans forward, his mouth at her ear as she chokes. "I have no wish to kill you, either, Mother. I did this the right way. I gave you the choice, and you couldn't accept that." He pushes the blade farther, shoving until the tip pokes out from Raghnaid's back. He twists it. "I only said it had to end. You were the one who chose how."

Her mouth opens, but no words come out, no denial or apology, only a slim line of blood slipping down the corner of her lips. Tavish pulls out the blade, and that same scarlet drips along its hilt, covering his freckled hands. His mother stumbles. She reaches out, fingers extended as though to brush away Tavish's wet bangs or to smother him with an ashen palm. But as her hand creeps toward Tavish's stiff jaw, the skin of it sloughs off in a wave of ash. The disintegration spreads, chipping away at her, through flesh and bone and organ. As her face peels up, her eyes seem to widen.

Then, she's gone. Her empty dress collapses, gusting the last of her ashes around Tavish. After a moment, they, too, vanish.

Raghnaid's anger deserts the ignation mutants, replaced by twitches and confusion as they release their prey and cease their attacks. Slowly, Not-Lilias lets me go. Her red-gashed eye seems to bore through me, as if trying to remember the person she was. Or to break free.

I could kill her now. Even weaponless, it would be easy. I could tell her to grab the eruptstone-tipped knife from the mutated Not-Blue waddling among the intoxicated soldiers and shove it into the space between her spine and skull.

But even after everything she's done to me, I don't want to kill her. I don't want to kill her like this, with this otherness infecting her mind, making her no longer her. And I don't want to kill her as herself either. Even if I don't care about *her*, I still care. Perhaps Lilias deserves to die, but what becomes of her here will affect more than just herself. It will be the first act of murder in a reborn city, the death of a young boy's mother, a person executed not to protect anyone, but to enact justice. After all I've done, justice lies in someone else's hands.

I lift my palm to her cheek. My aurora's fishnetting gleams with a rainbow of colors, dazzling in the bright upper-city light. "She did not ask for you," I whisper. "It's time to let her go."

I reach the aurora half of my consciousness, out to the strands of the thing inside Lilias, strumming them gently. They recoil, the impression I get from them as bestial and chaotic as their physical manifestations, but their presence doesn't let go. The further I push, the more I feel it: the mix of their alarm and confinement. A beast, yes, but a beast with its legs trapped in tar.

"Poor things, you don't want to be here, either, do you?"

It shivers. I feel like a veil draped over a corpse, but I have to fix this atrocity all the same. With whatever I have left.

Like I had with the strands invading Tavish, I take hold of those inside Lilias and pull. My vision wavers. I tell myself this is the last thing I'm needed for right now. This is the end of the war. But every moment I've thought that so far, something worse has come. Every time I hit the bottom, I've been forced to dig deeper. And this time I have nothing left. I sway.

The song of the Trench auroras rises around me, lifting

me up, like a cloud, a breeze, a loving embrace. They twist their energy into mine, and together, we pull. With their boundless power rushing through me, I extend my reach to the other mutants, tugging at a hundred beings like the one within Lilias. Their bestial presences release, and the colorful gashes they caused close over. The ignation flows out, sweeping from them through wounds and mouths and eyes. It drips from Lilias's nose, and tears of it roll down her cheek.

As the last of the chaotic threads slip back to the place from where they'd come, a final burst of power from the Trench auroras flings me with them. I feel more than see my consciousness stretching out across a network of life as though it's a tapestry I can weave myself into.

I sense the way the auroras' threads are spread across the natural world, from Mara to the Murk to Alkelu and beyond, but in the place of their origin where I first grasped hands with them, they huddle together, locked tightly in one place. A dying place. Sickness creeps in, siphoning off the auroras' energy little by little. Some are more infected than others, but none are safe.

There, I have no lungs to sob, no heart to bleed, nothing but breath and light and a subtle weight across my phantom body, but I feel an ache all the same, so sharp it seems to pull me inward. I curl my fingers where they once grasped the dying auroras in the laboratory, but there's nothing there any longer. I feel as though a friend has died, even if I can't quite remember them—can't quite remember anything about this other world.

But from this new viewpoint, I can piece together what's happening a bit more clearly. I can feel beyond the auroras, to other little gashes in the fabric between these two realities, where I find the source of the sickness: round, bright, energy-devouring stones and shimmering veins of liquid. Ignits and ignation. They're pulling the energy out of the place where the auroras originated and giving it to the humans, to the selkies, to a dozen other species who have no idea where it's coming from. No idea that they've taken so much they're killing the auroras by accident.

I feel across the network for the extra-large gash of Glenrigg's yellow ignit and find the place where it pulls its energy. It presses against that of too many others, the stone itself being slowly suffocated until it can't drag in enough to continuously power itself. It's too much, all at once: the knowledge and the experience both. My mind feels overwhelmed and my body overworked. I realize with a curse that the final massive boost of energy from the Trench that let me slip into this state is snapping out. It feels like that soundless, star-filled moment before passing out.

Frantically, I yank myself back into my host body. The plaza returns in a swirl of colors. I sway but catch myself, blinking until my eyes readjust to the way this world looks.

I reach for the Trench auroras one last time, to thank them, but I find only ash, all of them burned up like the one who sacrificed for me in the lab and the one we helped blaze out of Raghnaid. I inhale too sharply, pressing my hand to my mouth. Slowly, I let it out. They chose this. They were at peace with it. I need to be too.

Jean crumples as a blood-covered bear snarls in pain and slumps onto its side. The other once-mutants only look dazed, except for Blue, who howls and staggers, the eruptstone blade still sticking from her side.

My heart aches for her. Somehow this feels like my fault. Maybe that's a good thing. Maybe the pain and joy that surround me can either be everyone's responsibility or no one's. And I don't want to believe in that second version any longer.

Lilias sucks in rapid, panicked breaths. She lifts a hand to her head, and her gaze darts, unfocused. Trembles start up and down her arms. Her shoulder bleeds slowly. She grabs onto my wrist to lower herself to the ground. I let her drop there.

She tries to grab for me again, but I step away. I left her

alive. Someone else can do the rest.

Across the square, Tavish stands alone, wet, and a little bloody, but he looks to be in one piece. I feel so light I could fly. Instead, I wobble.

As I watch him, the ignit a little way behind him flickers and fades to grey. Through the mess of waking bodies, Elspeth's wheelchair creaks from behind the far barricade. My relief hits so sharp and strong that I can only laugh at myself. Me, worried over a person I met ten hours ago. It feels nice for a change.

Elspeth takes one look at the scene and immediately plucks a glowing earpiece out of a dead rebel's ear, shoving it into their own before wheeling at breakneck speed toward Tavish. A young, acne-covered man from the lower follows their example, stealing his own earpiece not a moment before the ignit flares back to life.

Seeing Elspeth and Tavish meet, hands clasping, smiles beaming, I want nothing more than to run to them. But near the barricade, Ivor releases a hiss through his teeth, one hand clamped to his leg. And I care.

I rip a length of my tattered vest off and wrap it tightly around the gash. He clearly needs more than that, but he still manages to stand and move toward his people. One of the other rebels with earpieces scoots by him on a broken ankle, pushing a box of medical supplies along. Behind her looms the acne-covered young man, but he pays no attention to us, his gaze locked on Tavish.

"A fucking Findlay," he hisses.

His sentiment is repeated throughout the half dozen conscious rebels.

"That's the youngest."

"Still alive—"

"But didn't he just—"

"Who cares, he's one of them."

Tavish cringes. When he lifts his voice, the diamond edge sounds not like a knife, but a chandelier lighting the space with dazzling brilliance. "I ken that you are of no mind to like me much right now. My family let Maraheem suffer for their own gain, and I sacrificed little to stop them." The last word cracks.

I want to run to him, to stand by his side through this. But it's his family and his speech to give, his heritage to disavow. As he puts himself back together, piece by piece, not hiding the pain but breathing through it, I've never been more in love.

"But this rebellion," he continues, "what you've done here—"

"Death to the Findlays!" shouts the young man, cutting down Tavish's voice as though the shift in power has already changed them both on a physical level. And I see, far too late and not nearly close enough, the eruptstone-tipped knife he holds, Blue's corpse at his feet.

But Ivor sees it too. And Ivor is closer. The old rebel doesn't hesitate. He throws himself between the boy and his target, struggling to close the short distance between them despite his slashed leg, his expression unyielding and his hand outstretched for the weapon.

The boy's gaze flickers across the square to where Elspeth kneels with their wheelchair beside the yellow ignit, just enough to the right of Tavish that Ivor's body doesn't block it. He launches the knife. It flips, end over end. Its eruptstone-tipped edge hits the ignit with a ting, only accompanied by the sound of Tavish's final words fading through the room.

"What you've done here . . . was right."

Then, the ignit explodes.

CHAPTER THIRTY-TWO

the here and the gone

I accept the consequences of one final question:
Will you stay? Because I am here,
not just an imprint but a maturing inception.
The dawn of an era soon to appear.

I FEEL NOTHING WHEN the yellow ignit detonates. Not heat, though its light blinds me. Not grief, though it engulfs both Elspeth and Tavish, the devastating orb traveling so fast that they don't even have time to turn and look. Not fear, though it expands ever closer.

I reach into it, toward the imprint of Tavish on the inside of my eyelids, reaching for the space I know he must be. The orb of light grows over my fingertips, working along them, up part of my thumb, around my first two knuckles. The skin within tingles; a numb, meaningless sensation as if my overwhelmed mind is failing to make sense of the truth.

And a distant part of me thinks I should be able to change this—I should have the power to take in its deadly energy and turn it into something life-giving. But my human cells resist the urge, too grounded in this world, in a reality marred by strict rules. Rules like death.

In a flash, the light vanishes. It leaves nothing in its

place.

Gone are the archways of the gate's upper side, the floor, Tavish and Elspeth, most of my fingers, half my thumb, and two of my knuckles. People from the lower districts stare up at us in horror from the level beneath. A scream arises, then a series of shouts. All I want is to go to the empty space where Tavish had stood.

All I do is sink.

"I'm here," I whisper. *I'm here. I'm here. I'm here.*

But there's no Tavish to respond to me.

I draw in a sob and can't seem to let it out again. The world turns to a haze, dark and light blurring into one, the clatter of voices echoing uselessly against my pounding ears. Iridescent blood seeps from the places my fingers and knuckles should be. It should hurt, but I can feel nothing over the pain in my chest. My aurora tendrils shimmer along the wounds and wrap a thin membrane of darkness over them, leaving only the flickers of rainbows and the faint memory that something there is missing. The same way a part of my heart has vanished. A part of myself, gone in a flash of unnatural light.

The aurora half of me takes full control, not like a parasite or a monster, but like a friend, gently lifting me off the ground. In the wake of the ignit's destruction, the selkies come to their senses. The BA soldiers shout into their radios, their gazes leaping back and forth between the decimated laboratory and the pistols aimed at their heads while a fresh stream of rebels with makeshift weapons charges in from beyond the gate. No one calls to me, or perhaps the noise simply bounces off or blunders past. My shoulders shake, but no tears come.

I'm here . . .

The aurora half of me detaches just enough to wrap itself around my human half, disengaging from the rest of my consciousness to whisper, *'So am I.'*

On shaky feet, it walks me around the edge of the hole

the ignit's detonation left. I can't quite reach into the fabric that separates us from the other dimension, but somehow I know if I could, the gash the ignit once made would be closed over. Each step feels like a new death. I don't want to be in a world he's vanished out of. I need to leave, to transport myself into a cask of wine, to fling my threads into the sickness, to—

But I hold fast to the aurora part of myself, letting it reinforce me, stabilize me. As I come into the main gate, toward the ruins of the lab, something moves within their mess of sopping supplies. Tavish sits up. His wet hair sits askew, half plastered to his face and half sticking out, and his detached gaze looks unusually glassy. But there he sits. Alive.

I run to him and sweep him into my arms. My stub of a hand knocks against his side as I try to grab into his jacket, and the last of my energy abandons me so hard and fast that suddenly it's Tavish who's holding me. I laugh, then sob, digging my unaltered hand into his shirt and holding him close. "I thought you were gone."

Tavish clings to me in return, his face nestled in my hair. "For a moment, I felt the oddest sensation, but then Elspeth pushed me so hard I went flying. Elspeth—" He lifts his head, tipping his chin as though listening. "Where are they—are they hurt?"

The moment replays in my head: Elspeth six full strides behind Tavish, their eyes going wide as they watched the ignit-tipped blade. In the gap where they once stood, I see nothing, not with my human eye nor my aurora one, not their ashes, not even the imprint of their energy. Wherever their body is, it's not in this world. Considering the kind of ugly sickness that incapacitates the other dimension, I can't be sure they're even still alive.

That kind of optimism perished with my mother.

"Elspeth was taken by Glenrigg's ignit exploding. They're probably dead." The words stick in my throat, bringing with them a metallic taste.

There are too many dead already. Sheona, dead. Ailsa, dead. Blue, dead. Maybe Lavender, too. My grief bubbles back up, raging against the warmth Tavish has left in my soul. I can see the same emotion in the shinning edges of Tavish's eyes and the tremble in his lips. Elspeth deserved so much better. They deserved medals and laboratories and their name on a hundred more papers.

Not all the pieces fit together, though. "Elspeth was too far from you. Even with their wheelchair, they couldn't have reached you in time."

"I only ken what I felt," Tavish replies. "Something like two hands on my shoulders. They flung me back."

The aurora half of my mind buzzes with curiosity. But it withdraws back into my consciousness as an argument flares among the higher-ranking rebels, the names *Tavish* and *Findlay* bouncing between them increasingly louder. With the BA solders in disarray after the effects of Glenrigg's ignit, the small lower-district force has pushed them into the glass-topped hallways that lead out of the plaza. Fresh rebels clamber through the main chamber to reinforce them, clearly spurred on by Raghnaid Findlay's death.

I pull Tavish to his feet. "If we go now, we can still slip away quietly."

Tavish releases a heavy breath. "I won't run from the consequences of my actions. This city deserves better than that."

As much as it hurts, I can't disagree with him. Together, we work our way around the hole.

"But he's a Findlay, isn't he?" one of the older rebels snaps as we approach, their eyes boring into us.

The woman at their side looks less convinced. "He stood against his mother."

"Interfamily squabbling doesn't make a person good," barks a man wrapping his own leg into a splint.

The rebels continue to quarrel. Ivor lifts a hand to silence them. His freckles stand out against his ghostly cheeks, but a fresh bandage wraps his leg, and he barely leans against the barricade as he stands to face Tavish.

Tavish clears his throat. "I ken your misgivings, I do. Compared to the path of freedom and justice, what is the life of a rich man who celebrated himself for giving away what he never truly needed, who was too cowardly to instigate any real change?"

The crease between Ivor's heavy eyebrows tightens. "Laddie, you aren't making a great case for yourself here, you ken that, aye?"

"I don't think the case is mine to make," Tavish replies. "My actions should have spoken for themselves, yet the story they tell is one of arrogance and ignorance."

Ivor's gaze narrows. He turns to me. "Do *you* want to vouch for him?"

Every good and wonderful thing about Tavish comes to mind at once, but this crowd merits only a single defense. "This man gave his last drop of ignation to the finfolk, to help protect a suffering town that your actions have since destroyed. You've no right to judge him." I scowl at the other rebels. No matter how little a part they played in Lilias's stealing of the ignit, they did not stop her.

They have the decency not to protest. One by one, they look to Ivor.

He grimaces, putting more of his weight on the barricade. "After what you've done for us today, it isn't right to sentence you with anything. But there's more decisions we've gotta make beyond that, and this isn't the moment for debating." He hesitates, glancing at his fellow rebels before looking back to Tavish. "If you wish to leave the city now, I won't stop you. But if you wanna stay, we can't have you in the way, scaring people who don't know everything yet."

Tavish's brow lifts. "You'd like to lock me somewhere for a bit?"

Ivor looks relieved to not have to say it. "Aye."

Tavish wastes no time. "I will accept this, and whatever your leadership determines after it, under these conditions: The finfolk must be included in what you divide among the lower, and if your new assembly is to control all of Mara, the other species who live here deserve a say in it as much as any selkie. Also, I request some decent seating. I'm afraid my poor body is rather spent for the day. Or possibly the year. One of my ribs may be broken."

"I think those can all be happily arranged." Ivor nods. "Sweeny! Find this Findlay a comfortable room, out of the way."

One of the younger rebels snaps to attention, adjusting her glasses with a quick "Aye, 'course, right away."

I press my hand to Tavish's shoulder.

Before I can ask if he needs me, though, he says, "I'll be fine if you wish to stay to help them."

What I wish for right now is three bottles of merlot and about a hundred hours of uninterrupted sleep. But the sooner the fighting in Maraheem stops, the sooner Tavish's future can be decided. And, I care. Against all odds and all logic and all reason, I care. I squeeze Tavish's arm. "I'll be here when you need me."

He smiles, broad and bright and beautiful. I watch him as he leaves, his crystal voice echoing back, "Sweeny, if you could speak as we walk, it's far too loud to hear much else at the moment."

Ivor is quick to give me something to do—reacquired weapons need distributing, news spread of the company heads' deaths, and half a city left to clear of anyone foolish enough to still fight now that the tide is turning—but before he leaves, I ask, "What will you do with Lilias?"

He smiles faintly, grief where joy should be. "All I owe is to her son."

I let him go.

With so much ignation running through the upper city, I find no shortage of energy, and despite my bizarre appearance, the rebels are happy to have someone fighting with them who doesn't drop under bullets and electricity. Once the BA guards and grunts who live full-time in the lower realize what's happened, though, they turn on their superiors, taking large parts of the upper city by swarm. By the early morning hours, the group I'm working with returns to the main square, exhausted but in good spirits, except for me: I return merely exhausted, the shock still not quite worn off yet.

In the main square, notebooks and half-gnawed pens have become the rebel's new weapons. Far above us, bullets might still ring, but the war is clearly won now that the full populace of the lower are bending their backs to the work, and the sheer numbers of them will soon take the pathetically few wealthy.

Even Ivor seems to have shifted his efforts from conquest to stabilizing the newly upturned city. He meets me near the old barricade, his worn expression taking a soft, hopeful quality. "The New Mara interim assembly's chosen not to sentence your Findlay for anything, though his assets are forfeit outside a reward for his service to the city. He's arguing for what that reward should entail, but they're mostly wrapped up." Ivor glances around, and his voice lowers. "I got word the Trench's auroras all vanished."

"They died to help us kill Raghnaid." Their sacrifice wasn't for him, but it might as well have been, considering the salvation it brought his rebellion.

His expression falls. "I knew we'd lose something for this, but . . ." He presses his fingers to his eyes, releasing a long breath. "We've gotta figure out a whole city of change—a whole country—if we can make the rest of Mara accept the new assembly. Guess we'll add that to the list. Still, if you're in need of anything, we've got your back, laddie."

I don't reply. My gaze steals across the plaza to the gap where gateways and floor panels used to stand. Steam creeps up from the lower districts, following the path of its people.

They need Ivor to have their back, but I'm not sure I want him to have mine. This city is not my city. It's barely even Tavish's city anymore. And I have other things to tackle, problems that span further than a simple metropolis.

I pause at the hole's edge, and part of me, not aurora or human, just a strong mixture of both, wants to veer back toward the fallen lab, to search for Lavender's corpse among the wreckage and place her beside Blue, like this will all be all right if only they're together in death. As though their spirits won't find a way to each other again without the nearness. But I can't—I can't see her small body crushed or mangled, silver fur bloodied into mats. I can't even look back at Blue's lifeless form, can't bear to see whether someone has dumped her to the side or placed her gently out of the way with the rest of the day's dead. So, I do what I can. I utter them both death proclamations, short and sweet, my eyes closed, tears piling along the edges. There will be many more to come, I think.

After wiping my cheeks, I work my way through the growing crowd to a tucked-away pub where I can still make out most of the central area. I drop into one of the patio seats and lean across the blue-and-green glass of the tabletop, surveying the pitch-black tendrils that cap my hand. Phantom sensations creep along their velvety exterior, but I feel nothing from them, not heat or pain, not even the rough skin of my calloused human palm.

It's not alone in that. Everything, I think, must be numbed right now: the deaths I've watched, contributed to, felt with my own being; the revelation of a bigger, more dangerous world beyond my own; the changes in my body; the loss of the better half of my human hand—my hand, a hand that cuts and caresses and pulls me up from the dirt, that I'll never see or feel again, that will bonk bluntly as I reach for joy and comfort and protection. My gods-damned hand—

I close my eyes, and the human part of my mind pointedly

refuses to think about it. I let the shock linger. Shock is all I can bear right now.

My drive slips from me, as though I am ending alongside my world, until I can barely hold myself in one piece, can barely even think. It chokes me. This shouldn't happen anymore—not with the aurora—not to the human—not with us together. But the painful, jumbled impression of fear passes as soon as it comes.

Whomever I am now, I'm still me. I am still the man who craves the boost of a bottle of wine and the serenity of home. I am still the man who said *depression* out loud and lived. And I am also more. My world will keep turning. No matter how many villains there are, I will keep fighting. I just need a nap first.

Desperately, need a nap.

I lay my head into my hands and stare at the patterned glass of the tabletop. Despite my detachment, I feel the little bundle of energy that lives inside my threads. It pulses gently, like an ignit. Or a heartbeat. It can't fix the exhaustion I feel, or the pain and grief that will come after it, but it will keep me alive a little longer. Until the sickness comes for it.

This knowledge, like the deaths, is too much to handle right now.

My mind gropes for something more accessible. *Tavish thinks someone pushed him out of the ignit blast. But there was only Elspeth.*

The aurora half of me slips free, letting its own thoughts run in tandem to the human's without quite syncing. *'Only Elspeth in* this *world. If the pulse of energy opened a doorway between them, then what's to say this door only goes one way?'*

Something curls between us: hope maybe. *Then if Elspeth is alive still, they might find a way back.*

'I guess there are many things that get odder the more you know of them.'

I almost laugh, but I'm too tired to force the sound out of my lungs. It echoes eerily through my head instead. *All the ignits and ignation, all this technology we've fueled using them: it'll end, sooner or later. Sooner, if we want to not kill every aurora in the process.* I remember the power that burst through me from the ignit and ignation I consumed. *If we can convince people to break the ignits and feed them back to their auroras, we might be able to save them.*

'Few people will like that.'

I know. Just the thought of all the work it'll entail to convince an entire world to send their precious energy back to where it came from makes me tired.

'And if we can't get ahold of enough ignits in the meantime, we might still die before it's over.'

My insides prickle as though I can already feel where I will turn to ash first. *If we die, then we die together, remember?* I release a shaky breath and fight the urge to rub my face, because I know half the fingers I'd do it with won't be there anymore. *Why did you choose me? I was hardly the only one to hold you during that first day you were removed from your mangrove host.*

It thinks within the confines of its own half of me, curled loosely through my mind, and I feel it picking each word with waves of emotion. *'I chose you because I know the way you feel inside, how you can get lost in that empty, echoing space within your own head. I chose you because I saw my sorrow in you, and that made me feel less alone.'* It drenches me in the same sense of rejection and longing I had felt in my teenage years, things I'd bundled up and hidden, waiting for them to come true with each breath. Warm humor follows. *'And I appreciated your sense of fashion.'*

I return its joy with a small spark of my own, but the feeling cuts out when something plunks against my table. I look up to find a full beer in front of me. Without a word, the rebel who delivered it wanders with their tray to the group of lower-district citizens who've come to lean against the café wall a little way off, not giving me so much as a backward glance. I feel as though I stand with one foot in this world and one foot out, a ghost drifting through its edges.

'And that,' my aurora says.

I lift the beer to my lips, pausing to hum. *And what, my rootlessness?*

'*You're disconnected from this dimension already. You make no sound as you move through it, leave less impact than you should.*' It must sense my coming reply because it continues, '*Metaphorically, yes, but physically, too. You know this. Even for a child of the Murk, you're too silent.*'

I sip my beer. It goes down smooth, a deep amber that's not as filling as the dark stuff Ivor serves, but far better than the finfolk's light, crisp nothingness. I don't have to ask it whether it knows why. It has only vague imprints of its memories from before the Murk, its past life more a feeling than a reality, but those are now integrated into me as potently as my own history. The aurora past and the human past meld so easily together, both wrought in loss and desperation, in being something the world wants no part of.

I don't know how the human in me came to be not quite of the human world or why the aurora in me never felt quite fully aurora, either, but I think I prefer it like that. Together, we are simply a single vagabond from two different no-man's lands. Perhaps that's enough.

I lean back, a single-minded being again, and take another sip of my drink. From beneath the table, a small creature thunks into my lap. She curls herself in a circle and begins licking a matted spot of blood off her back. My shock holds me together for a moment. Then, it cracks.

I cry again, cry like I'm crying for the entire world, an impossible, incomprehensible, overwhelming sort of grief and joy all bundled together into sobs. My tears sink into her fur, making it easier to wipe away the gore. Beneath, Lavender is nearly unscathed, the small scrape already scabbed over.

I pet her gently, letting her rest her head in my halved

hand.

And quietly we both watch the flow of the new Maraheem. The lower districts' favorite cohosts crack jokes and banter flirtatiously between excited radio updates: the BA guards and grunts who turned on their superiors finished taking the BA's main station for the rebellion; a maid snuck open the back door to the Callums' estate; the O'Cain Fishery's ecology laboratory staff preemptively offered up their building so long as they could continue their research under the new management. Other updates come with less flare, documenting skirmishes gone bad and wealthy families more willing to blow themselves and their home off Maraheem's map than surrender. But as the city is proclaimed officially under the rebellion's control, the deaths are ridden out with tired but genuine celebration, beer flowing and songs rising.

We killed the villains, we did. Lilias had been taken somewhere a while ago, but I can still see her influence in the square before me. We killed the villains.

But there will always be more. From this entire city unwittingly killing the auroras with their ignation to the greedier citizens of both districts who will find a way to use the upheaval to vault themselves to the top, to every selkie who will take their newfound freedom and use it to step on the finfolk or the pixies or the ocean itself. The lower's songs of merriment sound like equal parts an exaltation and a dirge. Maybe all change is a type of death. Something always has to die for a new thing to live.

In a way, I'm proof.

I almost miss Tavish when he knocks his cane into my table and taps around for a chair. He slumps into it, but his face is alight, more so than I've seen it since we left Glenrigg. "If this is the wrong table, then I'm going to feel like quite the arse," he mutters.

"If you were aiming to sit with someone else, then you might just *be* quite the ass." I slide my unaltered hand over his, basking in the simple feel of his skin. "A gorgeous, brilliant, genius ass though."

"Ha." His unfocused eyes twinkle.

My halved hand still holding Lavender close, I take his fingers in my other hand and relay to him all that I learned through the Trench auroras' power, along with parts of what I've figured out since. Other parts are mine alone. My own pain, which I still need to process.

At the end, Tavish accepts my offer of beer, draining a third of it in one cringing go. "And you think we can stop this by ceasing the use of ignation and ignits and feeding their energy back to the auroras?"

"If we *could* manage that, yes." The answer springs lightly to my lips, but it drops like a weight in my heart. "But I think the best we can hope for at this point is to slow it. There is so much ignit power in use, and so much of the other dimension is already eaten away, it would take more than we can manage alone to permanently save all the auroras, maybe more than any number of people can." I grab back the beer in an attempt to ward off my nausea. It will be hard work, even here. Whatever Ivor might claim, I doubt his debt to me covers things like abandoning his new city's primary power source. "But no one else will tell people if we don't, so we have to try." I'll also have to get a letter to someone near the Murk—one of the teens Lilias terrorized, perhaps— begging them to check on my pets for me.

"It's lucky, then, that we're in a city with one of the highest usages of ignit power," Tavish says. "It's a good place to start."

"To start, yes. But there are so many other cities— countries—powered by ignits. Places like . . ." I pause, trying to turn the words into something that might convince Tavish better, that might make him come with me. But I stop myself. Tavish will do what he does because he chooses to. He's chosen me before. If we're to have any future together, I have to let him choose me again.

"Places like?" he asks, brow lifted.

I set out my heart for him, to take or to politely decline. "Places like the rivers and swamps of Manduka, and places that neither of us have ever been, that would be just as little a home to me as it would be to you. If you'd be willing to take the trip. It wouldn't be forever—I'd never ask that of you—but perhaps we could give ourselves the chance to both love something new, the way I think we might be able to grow to love each other. And maybe it won't work. Maybe you'll come back here and I'll go to the Murk, and this will become a bittersweet memory, or we'll move between, and we'll make that work instead, or the world will collapse into starlight and none of it will matter. But I'd like to try. If you'd like to." It's the end of my speech; anything more would be running over his decision, his desires, his well-deserved life.

Tavish chews on his tongue.

Every moment he doesn't answer, I have to fight away a hoard of suspicions, but I keep battling them. For him. For us.

"I've been thinking," he says, finally, looking pensive and a little wistful, "that perhaps home isn't a permanent thing, you ken? Whatever this place is becoming, it's not mine any longer. I will miss it, but it's time for Maraheem to move on without me. In its absence, perhaps I can do the same." He squeezes my hand. "What I'm saying is, I'd like to try too."

I don't know where he gets that kind of courage from. But also I do. I know because I watched a vibrant world that felt like home fall apart, and it forced me here, to this dimension, to a mangrove in a swamp. To a human who felt just as alone and unwanted as I was. And together we found Tavish.

He leans toward me, until our arms brush. His head drops onto my shoulder.

My heart fills, blooming like a fresh bud after the rain has finally cleared. And I think, maybe all of that loneliness, those decades of solitude, only a grave to watch over me, maybe I was not as alone as I assumed, because all that time was driving me toward this moment. And toward him. I catch his chin and kiss him, tender and devoted, connecting us. "My princeling," I mutter.

I can feel his smile against my lips.

Together, we sit, and we drink our shared beer and listen to the city being reborn. For all that we helped and all that we hurt, it will carry on. And so will we. Tavish and I, his fears and my sorrows, and the two halves of me that brought us together. A trio of vagrants. A family, despite all those we lost. A home.

That's the best word for us.

A home.

THE ADVENTURE CONTINUES IN SUMMER 2023 WITH...
BOOK TWO: STRONGER STILL
Pre-order today!

He's telling the truth.

It rocks me, just a bit—Rubem genuinely is this lowly. It's an odd fact to fit with what else I know of him: his intimidation and his gentleness, his foolishness and his thoughtfulness. I can't quite wrap my head around him yet. And I like that. "You're a wee bit odd, Rubem of No-Man's Land."

Read Rubem and Tavish's first meeting from Tavish's perspective, exclusively through D.N. Bryn's newsletter! Sign up via their website, dnbryn.com.

If you enjoyed this novel, please consider reviewing it!

A first look at *Stronger Still...*

Every time, this grows harder, not easier, because every time, the aurora I find are closer and closer to death. And every time, my heart breaks a little more. Again, I tell myself. Once more. And if we have to, once more after that, and after that too.

Rubem has become the voice of the auroras—or their rage, at least. Between his threats and Tavish's diplomacy, they've convinced most of the world that the auroras can be saved through the return of their ignits. But pockets of denial and refusal linger, including in the Findlay's old trading partner, a city who has completely ignored Tavish's attempts at contact. With a cat on their back and apprehension in their step, Rubem and Tavish set out to confront them directly.

They arrive to a metropolis of watery channels and balconies on the verge of collapse, the once glorious city now overwhelmed the sea monsters that snap at their front doors. Only their dying aurora's song keeps the dangerous creatures at bay, but with apocalyptic prophecies running wild and the government split into stubborn factions, Rubem quickly realizes that someone wants the city destroyed. Whoever they are, they're willing to destroy its aurora protector to do it. And Rubem is the only person standing in their way.

But amidst the chaos, the Findlay's past involvement with the city comes to light in ways Rubem never expected—and Tavish wants nothing to do with—adding grudges, broken hearts, and freckle-faced pre-teens on Rubem's list of problems. As those intent on destroying the city and its aurora grow more threatening, Rubem seems always one step behind and never quite strong enough.

ACKNOWLEDGMENTS

When I first decided to expand the These Treacherous Tides world beyond Our Bloody Pearl, I imagined this book as a simple, short standalone romance between a lonely human and a selkie he meets while wandering the beach, with no larger story and no real progression of the overarching world. Instead, I got something so much fuller and more complex, something that's become the start of a beautiful series all of its own. It will forever hold a special place in my heart.

Rubem has inherited many things from me—his love for animals, his snarky introversion, and his struggles with chronic depression and self-medication. Many addiction-related stories deal with the ultimate destruction endpoints of addiction, but with Rubem I wanted to tell a story that I related to more, one about a person whose self-medication isn't (yet) an active harm to them, but rather a passive one: the cause of stagnation for their mental and emotional healing. While that elusive "perfect" representation is a myth—we are all unique and flawed, and so will our characters be—I hope he resonates with some readers out there the way he has with me.

The fact that Rubem's story has come this far is due to a number of amazing people, all of whom I am incredibly grateful for. The little world building details of this book would not have come together without the long hours spent with my brother, Barik, and while the rest of my family may have vastly different reading preferences, I am honored that they continue to support me in writing these weird science-magic books. Without my wonderful team of beta readers and cheer leaders at the These Treacherous Tides discord server, you would surely be reading a complete mess of a book, or else none at all, and I owe my editor, Chih, an unending debt for gently correcting all my impossible wordages. And no acknowledgement would be complete without a thank you to the wonderful congregation of progressive Christians I had the blessing of stumbling into last fall and the amazing God we exalt.

And last but not least, I'm grateful for you, reader, for being a part of this! I do hope you've enjoyed what Rubem and Tavish's story has become as much as I have and will continue on their journey with me.

APPENDIX

THE FINDLAY FAMILY

Raghnaid Findlay: Head of Findlay Inc.
Lachlan Findlay: Married into the family. Originally an O'Cain.
Alasdair Findlay: The eldest Findlay sibling. Heir to Findlay Inc.
Ailsa Findlay: The middle Findlay sibling.
Tavish K. Findlay: The youngest Findlay sibling.

FINDLAY BODYGUARDS

Mx. Malloch: Bodyguard for Ailsa Findlay.
Sheona Aris: Bodyguard for Tavish Findlay.

LOWER DISTRICT RESIDENTS

Ivor Reid: Owner of Reid's Bar.
Jean: Conspiracy theorist.
Lilias Erskine: Selkie who kidnapped Rubem.
MacNair: A popular radio host in the lower.

RUBEM'S PETS

Blossom: One of Rubem's caiman triplets.
Blue and Lavender: Cats originally owned by Alasdair Findlay.
Diadem and Monsoon: Jaguar rescues.
Sheila: A crocodile raised by Rubem from birth.

FINFOLK

Beileag: The head of Glenrigg's governing committee.
Dr. Elspeth Coineagan: An ignit cycle physicist.

* For "big seven" company heads, see list of companies.

PLACES

Falcre: An abandoned port town near Maraheem.
Glenrigg: The last free finfolk city.
Manduka: The continent where Rubem is from.
Maraheem: The capital city of Mara, home of the selkies.
the Murk: The swamps from which Rubem's mother comes, which
    he grew up just beyond the edge of.
The Trench: The Findlay Inc. laboratory where they keep their
    auroras.

"BIG SEVEN" COMPANIES:

Battery Arms ("the BA"): A security and weapons company, run by
    Macindoe.
Bubble Entertainment: A media company, run by Morvan Ros.
Callum & Callum: A technology company, run by the Callums.
Druiminn Health: A medical company, run by Dr. Keavy Druiminn.
Findlay Inc.: An ignation and aurora research company, run by
    Raghnaid Findlay.
O'Cain Fishery: a food company, run by Greer O'Cain.
Sails and Co.: A transport company, run by the Gayles.

FULL CONTENT NOTES

Alcohol consumption, alcoholism, and drunkenness (without alcohol-related anger or violence.)

References to a past violent **pet death**, and multiple instances of animal death, including those of cats and dogs.

General fantasy **violence** with minor fantasy gore.

References to feeling a **parasite** move inside the body of the point of view character.

Near **drowning**.

Instances of severe **blood loss** due to scientific experimentation.

References to the **dissection** of a parasite from the main character's body.

Body horror of an aesthetically-pleasing, shimmering rainbow variety.

OTHER BOOKS BY D.N. BRYN

OUR BLOODY PEARL
Forty years ago...

After a year of voiceless captivity, a blood-thirsty siren fights to return home while avoiding the lure of a suspiciously friendly and eccentric pirate captain.

This adult fantasy novel is a voyage of laughter and danger where friendships and love abound and sirens are sure to steal—or eat—your heart.

ONCE STOLEN
The prequel to Odder Still...

An autistic, naga thief must guide a poisoned hero through his ex-homeland while fleeing cartel leaders, swamp monsters, and his own feelings in order to claim the hero's payment of precious stones.

This fun and fast-paced YA-style adventure comes complete with a hate-to-love romance and a boat-load of sass.

D.N. Bryn is part of The Kraken Collective—an indie author alliance of queer speculative fiction committed to building an inclusive publishing space. For more adult fantasy titles featuring the diverse rep you love, check out the ones below!

THE XANDRI CORELEL SERIES
by Kaia Sønderby

Fascinated by complex underwater societies and non-human races?

In the second Xandri Corelel book, *Tone of Voice*, an autistic, bisexual woman leads a first contact ship in a story full of intrigue, compassion, alien accommodations, and intricate alien cultures—including squid and whales symbiotic aliens.

CITY OF STRIFE
by Claudie Arseneault

Love Maraheem's ruling families and politics underpinned by deeply personal narratives?

City of Strife is a mosaical, epic novel with a large and majorly queer cast, a web of political intrigue, and a heart of gold, in which an elven noble's attempt to stop imperialist wizards from taking over his city will have repercussion from its richest towers to the homeless shelter at its very bottom.